ACCLAIM FOR JEREMY BATES

"Will remind readers what chattering teeth sound like."
—*Kirkus Reviews*

"Voracious readers of horror will delightfully consume the contents of Bates's World's Scariest Places books."
—*Publishers Weekly*

"Creatively creepy and sure to scare."—*The Japan Times*

"Jeremy Bates writes like a deviant angel I'm glad doesn't live on my shoulder."
—Christian Galacar, author of GILCHRIST

"Thriller fans and readers of Stephen King, Joe Lansdale, and other masters of the art will find much to love."
—Diane Donovan, *Midwest Book Review*

"An ice-cold thriller full of mystery, suspense, fear."
—David Moody, author of HATER and AUTUMN

"A page-turner in the true sense of the word."
—*HorrorAddicts*

"Will make your skin crawl."—*Scream Magazine*

"Told with an authoritative voice full of heart and insight."
—Richard Thomas, Bram Stoker nominated author

"Grabs and doesn't let go until the end."—*Writer's Digest*

BY JEREMY BATES

HOTEL CHELSEA

World's Scariest Places 6

Jeremy Bates

HOTEL CHELSEA

PROLOGUE

The young woman hurried along West 23rd Street, her hands gripping fistfuls of her dress so the hem didn't drag on the dirty sidewalk.

It was the spring of 1884, late evening, the air so muggy it felt like a physical force. Recently installed electric incandescent streetlights lit the New York City darkness with an artificial moonlight. Horse hooves and carriage wheels clacked against the granite-block street. Shouts and laughter floated down from the roofs of grimy tenements, competing with the boisterous sounds spilling out of gaslit saloons and restaurants. Factory workers, ditch diggers, stone cutters, and men and women from all walks of life bustled this way and that, going about their nightly business.

When the woman arrived at the newly built Chelsea Association Building between Seventh and Eighth Avenues, she released her grip on her skirt and brushed the pleats straight. Sweeping an errant lock of blonde hair away from her blue eyes, she tilted her head to look up at the mammoth Victorian Gothic building. The tallest structure in the city, its façade was an assortment of dormer windows, horizontal bands of white stone, and black iron balconies wrought into the shapes of flowers. Asymmetrical chimney stacks poked the starry sky.

Keeping her back straight and her chin lifted, the woman entered the building through the front glass doors. Well-dressed men mingled in the high-ceilinged lobby, which featured mahogany wainscoting and enormous Hudson River School landscape paintings. Through a set of arched doors to

1

the right, upper-class ladies socialized in a frescoed sitting room.

The woman spotted Arthur Schmid right away. He stood in front of a large carved fireplace conversing with a cranky-looking man with white hair and a thick mustache. His eyes met hers for the briefest of moments before breaking contact.

Lips tightening, the woman crossed the lobby to the elevators, pushed the bell for the one to the left of the reception desk, and waited for the terrifying machine to arrive.

◆ ◆ ◆

Arthur Schmid was a bon vivant and womanizer par excellence. He was also the most fashionable man in New York City. Just last month, after he'd entered the luxurious Hoffman House Bar on a Saturday night clad in a cashmere dinner jacket dripping with gold ornamental braiding, tight white trousers, and thigh-high black patent leather boots, the New York Times had crowned him "King of the Dudes" ("dude" having recently replaced "dandy" to describe an impeccably dressed male socialite). The title was no doubt pejorative, but Schmid embraced it proudly.

Tonight he was dressed no less fashionably in a crimson tailcoat, multi-colored waistcoat, stiff shirt with a spread-eagle Byron collar, and burgundy cravat. His ever-present monocle was propped between his left cheekbone and brow, and a gray silk top hat sat importantly atop his head. This was his third outfit of the day, as he'd already changed twice. He had no qualms changing as many as six or seven times a day, depending on his mood or the social occasion. Finding interesting and new outfits was not difficult, mind you, when one owned five hundred pairs of trousers, five thousand neckties, and more than three hundred tailcoats.

Born fifty-three years ago in 1831 into a de-facto aristocratic family, Schmid had inherited two million dollars on his twenty-first birthday. This fortune had allowed him to spend much of his adult life drinking champagne, shopping in the finest department stores, and mingling with old-money individuals, celebrities, and artists alike.

Now he was enjoying a glass of champagne—his drink of choice—in the magnificent lobby of the Chelsea Association Building with his old friend, Sam Clemens. Clemens, dressed unfortunately in a frumpy white suit and dubious bowtie, was currently on a worldwide lecture tour to pay back all the debts he had accrued by investing unwisely in unproven inventions. He'd moved into the Chelsea Association Building two days ago and had bumped into Schmid in the lobby earlier this morning. They had agreed to meet later for dinner in one of the Chelsea's dining rooms. During their meal beneath gilded fleurs-de-lis and lion-faced gargoyles, a photographer for the *Tribune* had taken a photograph of them together, which had delighted Schmid, who firmly believed one could never be a victim of too much exposure or fame.

"I wonder what page we will make in tomorrow's newspaper," Schmid remarked thoughtfully as he sipped his champagne.

"I wish you hadn't given that damn weasel permission to take our photograph," Clemens griped in his slow drawl.

"Do I look like someone who would pass up the opportunity to be seen with the most popular American writer and raconteur in the world?"

"Bah," Clemens said.

"Oh, come now," Schmid said. "You like the limelight as much as I do, my dear sir. I recommend you try smiling in your next photograph, however. It's all the rage now, and your teeth aren't that bad."

"A photograph is a most important document," Clemens said with his typical composure and gravity, "and there is nothing more damning to go down to posterity than a silly, foolish smile caught and fixed forever."

Schmid sipped champagne in acquiescence to the man's cantankerous nature. "Are you enjoying your life here at the

Chelsea so far?"

"It's an impressive building, I do say."

"Indeed! With every modern convenience available. There's even a long-distance telephone in the manager's office available to all residents."

"I particularly enjoy the elevators. I've been installed up on the sixth floor, and my knees are old and do not fare well with stairs."

"You don't find them too noisy, I hope?"

"Noisy? Hardly. You don't have to hear noise if you don't want to. The only time I hear the elevators is when they stop."

"They have certainly ushered in the era of the tall building. The Chelsea itself is an astonishing twelve stories. I wonder what this city will look like in, oh, another ten years from now?"

"I would temper your optimism about what the future holds, Mr. Schmid. There has already been talk of the city banning the construction of further large residential buildings due to fire and health concerns."

"Poppycock!" Schmid blurted. "Fire? The apartments are separated by cement-filled brick walls three feet thick, and the building's iron girders are sheathed with fireproof plaster. It is virtually impossible for a fire to spread from one residence to the next."

"Six hundred individuals living together under one roof does not concern you?"

"There are two million residents in this city, my dear man. If we're on the precipice of an American Black Death, it will originate in some unsanitary tenement slum, not the Chelsea. Indeed, I suspect the fear motivating our great city leaders is neither fire nor disease but that the intimacy of Parisian-style apartment living will lead the residents to looser moral standards—and you know what I think about that? What happens in the bedroom is none of their goddamned business!"

"You seem quite worked up about this, Mr. Schmid."

"Because ignorance bothers me greatly, Mr. Clemens, and

there seems to be more and more of it going around these days." Schmid sighed. "But yes, let's talk of something more agreeable, shall we? How fares your writing?"

"It's interesting that you ask," Clemens said. "For the last three months I haven't written anything. Not a single page. Authorship is always easy when one has something to say. When one doesn't, it can be as grueling a process as any. But then I had a dream the other night—"

"Here at the Chelsea?"

"My first night here, yes. I dreamed I was a medieval knight, severely inconvenienced by the weight and cumbersome nature of my armor. Upon waking I thought it would make for a delightful satire of feudalism and monarchy, and I've been writing prolifically since."

"I adore this march you writers are making toward socio-economic discourse! May I ask how many pages you have written?"

Clemens scratched his head. "Well, I...I can't seem to recall."

Schmid's eyebrows shot upward so far he almost lost his monocle. "You can't recall? That's the most extraordinary statement I've ever heard! How can you not recall how many pages you write if you are the man writing them?"

"It does seem rather curious, doesn't it? And what's more, I don't quite recall what exactly I have written."

"My friend, you are making no sense. Surely you have taken the time to read over what you have written?"

"Surely I have. But the details are foggy in my mind."

"This is quite remarkable!"

"It is indeed..." Clemens confessed into his mustache.

"Very well then. Can you tell me about this story in broad strokes?"

"I have tentatively titled it *A Yankee in King Arthur's Court*. You see, after receiving a severe blow to the head, a Yankee is mysteriously transported to England during the reign of King Arthur."

"An intriguing premise. I would like to—"

Just then Nicola Krieghoff strode through the front entrance of the Chelsea Association Building. She glanced at Arthur Schmid momentarily before continuing purposefully toward the elevators.

Schmid finished what was left of his champagne.

Clemens glanced at his own empty glass. "Where's that damn head waiter? He hasn't been by once to check on us."

"I do fear, my friend, that your residence abroad in Europe has cossetted you to the ministration of servants whose parents were servants and who will be servants themselves for the entirety of their lives. You are back in America now, you would do good to remember."

"Yes, yes, I remember," Clemens drawled. "I'm not senile yet. Will you join me in the basement parlor for a game of billiards?"

"As tempting as it would be to challenge and defeat the great Mark Twain in billiards, I admittedly must pass. Dinner, it seems, has reacted unfavorably with my gut, and I believe the best remedy would be to retire early this evening. But what say we meet for dinner again tomorrow? I'm positively enraptured to hear more of this book you are writing..."

◆ ◆ ◆

When the elevator car arrived, the uniformed operator pulled back the wrought iron door, and Nicola Krieghoff stepped inside the claustrophobic box.

The operator closed the door with a loud clank and asked, "What floor, ma'am?"

"Third, please," she said.

The young man pulled a large lever, and with a lurch and a clang the car began to rise. Nicola balled her hands into fists and held her breath. She had only experienced an elevator on three previous occasions—all here at the Chelsea Association Building—and the brief ride always scared the color out of her. She couldn't help but think of the great chasm growing below her feet as she ascended, and the deadly plummet if the rope supporting the car frayed and snapped.

When the elevator rudely stopped, the operator pulled open the birdcage door. Nicola gratefully and quickly stepped into the landing. It was empty. She went through a door into the west wing and stopped before a door numbered 328. She glanced the way she had come. The hallway remained empty. She turned the door's handle and stepped into the apartment.

Wrapping around the west end of the building, the suite boasted six bedrooms, two salons, a library, and a large kitchen with a pantry. The furniture was an eclectic mix of Victorian and Néo-Greco pieces, including a life-sized bronze statue of a half-naked Greek god. Electric lamps cast pools of light over the hand-molded William Morris tiles, while coals smoldered warmly in the marble baroque fireplace.

Nicola Krieghoff was not used to such luxury. She was from a small Prussian village in the heart of the German Rhineland, which had been surrounded by verdant forests, rolling hills, and meandering brooks. When she arrived in New York City on a combination steamer/sailing ship at the age of sixteen, she felt as though she had stepped into a different world. The city was enormous, frightening, confusing, dirty, and overwhelming all at the same time.

And life certainly was not easy there.

In Prussia, her father had been a successful baker. But in New York City, on the Lower East Side where they lived, German-American bakers were amongst some of the lowest paid workers, and her father toiled away for seven days a week, from sunrise until sunset, for ten cents an hour. This income was not enough to support Nicola and her two younger sisters, so to help, Nicola worked as an advertisement writer for a fashion company. The job bored her senseless, but the hours were acceptable and allowed her to pursue her true passion in the evenings: acting. At first she had performed in variety shows in Little Germany's concert saloons and *biergartens* for men of the working class, but recently she had secured minor roles and understudies in musical comedies and vaudevilles in some of the neighborhood's better music halls. It was a tough business. Stage fright caused her to sometimes rush her words, and audience members often criticized her thin figure. But she was ambitious and talented and persistent, and she knew someday she would become famous.

Last week, she was in a burlesque comedy at the newly renovated Star Theater on the northeast corner of Broadway and 13th Street. It had been one of her worst performances. She was wearing a dress with a long train and had to move about quite a bit on the crowded stage. During one scene her trailing skirts got so tangled up with a chair that upon exiting the stage, the chair went right along with her!

After the show, she had been brooding in her changing room when a man wearing the most ridiculous finery knocked on her door and praised her performance. When he introduced himself as Arthur Schmid, she could hardly believe her ears. Arthur Schmid was a source of constant gossip and scandal, and one of the city's best-known celebrities, even if his source of greatness was based on nothing at all.

They shared a bottle of wine an admirer had given Nicola after her last show, and Arthur Schmid asked her to join him for dinner the following night. He confessed he was a married man, but insisted he and his wife didn't live together and were divorced in all but name. Even so, it would not do his reputation well to be seen in public with a mistress, so if they were to meet, they would have to do it with the utmost secrecy.

Nicola didn't have any qualms with the arrangement. She was young and impressionable, but most of all, she knew an opportunity when she saw one. In the back of her mind, she was planning how a man like Arthur Schmid, with all his money and connections, could help her fledgling acting career.

Over the following two weeks they met secretly on three occasions. Tonight would mark their fourth rendezvous at his apartment, and she'd decided it was time to request a favor.

She was pacing nervously and thinking about all of this when the door opened and Arthur Schmid entered. After closing and locking the door, he grinned widely and threw open his arms.

"Come here, dearest," he said gaily.

Nicola ran to him and wrapped her arms around his neck and kissed him profusely over his freshly shaven cheeks.

"Did anybody on this floor see you?" he asked, stepping apart from her and hanging his top hat on a wall hook.

"Nobody at all. Oh! You got a haircut."

"There is a barbershop right in the basement of this building. Do you fancy it? It's in the Roman fashion. I call it 'à la Brutus.'"

"It complements you perfectly."

Arthur Schmid admired his reflection in a large gilded mirror and sighed. "To die and live before a mirror," he said, running a hand through his hair.

"You certainly do enjoy looking at yourself."

"To paraphrase Thomas Carlyle, my dear, a dandy is a clothes-wearing man, a man whose trade, office, and existence consists in the wearing of clothes. Every faculty of his soul, spirit, purse, and person is heroically devoted to the wearing of clothes wisely and well."

"I'm most impressed by how you take infinite pains about your appearance...only to appear so indifferent about it."

"It is hard work being me, dearest. Champagne?"

"Please."

They went to the kitchen where he poured two glasses.

"I adore what you've done with your hair," he told her. "It positively bounces. When I saw you on the stage at The Star, I thought to myself, *This is the most beautiful woman I have ever laid eyes upon.* And I haven't changed my mind."

Blushing, Nicola said, "I was hoping I could ask you something?"

"Of course, dearest."

"It seems from the stories in the newspapers that you know everybody in this city."

"Not true at all. I only know the *important* people."

"Well, I was wondering... The first-ever revue is opening on Broadway later this year at the Casino Theater. It's called *The Passing Show*. It's a vaudeville-like collection of songs, sketches, and specialty acts. I've heard they're looking for a lead actress, and I know I'd be perfect for the part. The problem is, they won't even consider someone like me, someone who's never had a lead role before." She gripped his forearm. "But if you mentioned me to the director or producer...?"

Arthur Schmid was nodding agreeably. "I would love to help you, my dear. And I do in fact know the producer. George is his name, and he's touting *The Passing Show* as a 'tropical extravaganza.' Spoofs of theatrical productions of the last season and all that. You would be dazzling in the lead role, simply dazzling." He turned grave. "The unfortunate problem is that, outside of this room, you and I do not know each other. How could I explain my relationship to you?"

"Couldn't you just say something like, 'I saw this understudy at The Star. I think she has remarkable talent. She would be perfect for this part...' Something like that?" She realized she was squeezing his forearm with tremendous force, and she made herself relax.

Arthur Schmid smiled kindly. "Well, yes, I suppose I *could* say something like that, couldn't I? After all, I *did* see you at The Star, and you really *do* have talent."

"Oh, Arthur!" Nicola set her champagne down on the table, wrapped her arms around his neck, and once again smothered him with kisses.

"Perhaps we should take this celebration into the bedroom —"

A loud banging at the door caused them to jump apart.

"Arthur?" came a shrill voice. "Arthur? Open up. I've come all this way to see you."

"Who's *that*?" Nicola demanded.

Arthur Schmid's face turned white. "My wife," he said.

◆ ◆ ◆

"You must hide," he told her.

"Where?" Nicola demanded.

"There," he said, pointing to what appeared to be a small rectangular cupboard built flush into the wall. He yanked open the door to reveal a small dark space half the size she was tall. There were vertical ropes on either side of the opening.

"What's *that*?"

"Never mind what it is! You must get in it! Now!"

"I'm not getting in there!"

"You must!" he insisted.

"I won't fit!" she said.

"You will!"

"Arthur?" came his wife's cold soprano voice. "Arthur, I know you're in there! Open the door!"

Knowing there was nowhere else to hide, Nicola gathered her dress above her knees and climbed headfirst into the cupboard.

She froze when it swayed slightly beneath her weight.

"It moves!" she cried, realizing at the same time what the ropes were for. "It's another one of those elevators, isn't it?"

"It's an elevator for food," Arthur Schmid said. "Now get in there!" He planted his hands on her behind and pushed firmly.

Squawking in indignation as much as surprise, she scrambled further into the space and pulled her knees up against her chest.

"There you go," Arthur Schmid said approvingly. "You fit."

Nicola felt extremely cramped and claustrophobic. "What if your wife looks in here?"

"She won't. She won't be here for long. Now you must remain absolutely silent."

Nicola nodded.

"Very good," he said. "I will be back soon to let you out."

11

He closed the door.

❖ ❖ ❖

It was perfectly dark in the little box with no hint of light from the kitchen's electric fixtures.

Nicola strained to hear the conversation coming from the front of the apartment, but what she could hear most was her breathing. It sounded inappropriately loud and somehow inside her head.

The air, she realized, was stale and stuffy and hot. Perspiration beaded her forehead and the back of her neck.

What am I doing? she wondered. *Having an affair with a man older than my father is disgraceful in itself. Now I'm hiding in some newfangled contraption meant to transport food like some unsightly tramp?*

Was getting a role in a Broadway revue worth all this—?

A whiplash snap.

The box lurched.

Nicola cried out a moment before slapping her hands over her mouth.

I'm too heavy! The rope can't support my weight! I'm going to—

Another snap.

And then she was plummeting down the shaft.

❖ ❖ ❖

Arthur Schmid and his cow-eyed wife (who had come by for a handout because she'd already exhausted her monthly allowance) both spun toward the kitchen.

"Who was that?" his wife demanded.

"Who was what?" Schmid asked innocently, despite having heard the brief shout. He kept a pleasant face but was inwardly fuming.

What is that damned girl up to? How hard is it to keep her mouth shut?

"Who's there?" his wife said, marching toward the kitchen on her short, sturdy legs. "I heard you! Come out now, you miserable little whore!"

"Dearest!" Schmid said, chasing after her. "Stop this! There's nobody here."

In the kitchen his wife peeked below the oak dining table. She planted her pudgy hands on her ample hips. "Where is she?" she demanded.

"There is nobody here, darling, I insist."

"I *heard* her, you silly fop! Don't take me for a vapid fool!"

"What you heard was likely a neighbor. Goodness knows, they're on every side of this apartment, above and below as well!"

His fuming wife stalked into the next room to continue her search.

Schmid hurried to the dumbwaiter and opened the door. He gasped. The small elevator car was gone. The two hand ropes used for raising or lowering the dumbwaiter remained intact, but the third one, which had connected to the top of the car and to the corresponding counterweights, was gone, the end that dangled before him frayed.

Schmid peered down the shaft but could see nothing but blackness.

"Oh my," he said.

◆ ◆ ◆

Nicola's fear was so great she was unable to scream as she dropped like a stone. The impact with the ground came fast. It shattered her pelvis and several other bones. Her left knee drove into the soft flesh of the underside of her jaw, causing her to bite off the tip of her tongue. Splintered wood lacerated her face and impaled parts of her body. The second or two of pain she experienced was so powerful and inclusive her consciousness fled from it and she passed out.

❖ ❖ ❖

When she opened her eyes, all was black, and she didn't hear anything. This confused her, because she almost always woke to dawn's anemic light coloring the sky and to the neighborhood crows cawing over their territories.

Then she recalled the food elevator, the fall.

No, God, no. It's a dream. This must be a dream. I'm still dreaming...

She coughed a frightening amount of blood from her mouth. She coughed again, this time more forcefully, causing her to tilt forward. Monstrous pain erupted inside of her. Out of panic, she tried standing but couldn't move her legs.

She lifted her hand, which caused tremendous pain to pulse through her arm, through her shoulder, all the way to her chest. This was immediately forgotten when she gripped her leg.

It wasn't hers.

She gasped, a wheezy, clogged sound, as her mouth was swollen, numb, and unresponsive. She touched the leg again. Her fingers followed the thigh up to the hip, where feeling returned.

The leg was hers, she realized. She simply didn't have any sensation in it.

The hope she was dreaming died then. It was real, all of it. Hiding in the food elevator. The rope snapping. The fall.

A terror the likes of which Nicola had never experienced crushed her soul, and she began to cry.

❖ ❖ ❖

Nicola continued to pass in and out of consciousness, finding it harder and harder to distinguish one nightmarish state from the other.

At some point she found herself wondering why nobody

had come to help her. Arthur Schmid would have realized what happened when he went to check on her. Why hadn't he come to the basement, if that was where she was, to help her? Did he believe she was dead? Was he going to continue with the pretense he did not know her?

Yet even if this was the case, shouldn't someone else have discovered her by now? She didn't know how long she had been crumpled up in the bottom of the shaft, but it felt like an awfully long time. Hours, certainly. Perhaps even days.

Nicola's thoughts were fading when she heard a noise. It sounded like footsteps, or something being dragged or moved, or perhaps something else entirely.

"I'm here," she said, though she was not certain she had spoken the words out loud or not.

She heard what might have been a handle turning, then the protest of wood on wood and the squawk of old hinges as the door to the elevator car opened.

Despite it being pitch black, Nicola could see her rescuer clear as day because he glowed with a translucent phosphorescence that seemed to emanate from within him.

Then she saw his eyes, and with the last of the strength in her broken body, she screamed.

PART 1

2013

"Eyeing the traffic circulating the lobby hung with bad art. Big invasive stuff unloaded on Stanley Bard in exchange for rent. The hotel is an energetic, desperate haven for scores of gifted hustling children from every rung of the ladder. Guitar bums and stoned-out beauties in Victorian dresses. Junkie poets, play-wrights, broke-down filmmakers, and French actors. Everybody passing through here is somebody, if not in the outside world."

-PATTI SMITH, *JUST KIDS*

CHAPTER 1

It's going to be one of those days...

Malcolm Clock was having a bad day.

He didn't get up on the wrong side of the bed. His sixth-floor studio apartment in the East Village was so small the only reasonable placement of his bed was stuffed into a corner beneath a window, which meant there was only one side—the left—to get up on.

But as Malcolm made his way to the bathroom to relieve his aching bladder (too much gin the night before), he stepped in a squishy pile of feces. It wasn't his, which meant it was courtesy of the three-month-old pug he was babysitting for his brother, George, while George and his fiancé were vacationing in Paris for two weeks.

If stepping in dog shit at six-thirty in the morning wasn't disgusting enough, he then stepped in a puddle of urine, also courtesy of the puppy. His feet shot out from beneath him and he came down flat on his back, cracking his head on the linoleum.

And so the rest of the morning went. No toothpaste left in the tube; spoiled milk in the refrigerator; green fuzzy mold creeping over his only loaf of bread; missing his train by seconds, causing him to be ten minutes late for work the second time this week (and it was only Wednesday); getting locked out of his computer for failing to update his password (even though a notification had warned him several times a day, every day, for the last seven days).

Now the final insult: a taxi nearly running him over as he crossed Eighth Avenue, causing him to jump backward in alarm and spill a dollop of Starbucks coffee on his white T-shirt.

He almost yelled after the cab but couldn't be bothered.

Half a block later, he arrived at the Hotel Chelsea.

◆ ◆ ◆

Malcolm had been born in Augusta, Maine, but had lived most of his life in New York City in three of the five boroughs —his childhood in Queens, his college days in Brooklyn, and the last three years in the East Village in Manhattan. The Hotel Chelsea was one of those landmarks like the Empire State Building or Madison Square Garden that had always been there and would likely always be there, monolithic wallflowers hidden in plain sight to those who lived in the city.

Malcolm didn't know everything about the Chelsea's storied history, but he knew enough. He knew, for instance, that a hell of a lot of people had died in the building over the years, lots of drug addicts, but some famous people too, most notably Sid Vicious' girlfriend, Nancy Spungen. Andy Warhol had shot parts of *Chelsea Girls* there. Janis Joplin and Leonard Cohen met in the elevator in 1968, kicking off a one-night tryst that Cohen recorded in his song "Chelsea Hotel #2." Arthur Miller moved in after separating from Marilyn Monroe. Tennessee Williams had a room there, as did Jackson Pollock, Jack Kerouac, Allen Ginsberg, Stanley Kubrick, Joni Mitchell, Jimi Hendrix, Bob Dylan, and a laundry list of other famous writers, filmmakers, and musicians.

In fact, if you chronicled all the art created at the Chelsea over the last century, you'd probably find yourself with a list of masterpieces to rival those created in any American artistic movement, ever.

So yeah, the hotel had a storied history, all right.

And now Malcolm had been tasked with writing

its obituary.

CHAPTER 2

Stanley who?

The stately redbrick Hotel Chelsea rose against the dark morning sky, imprisoned in a skin of steel scaffolding and construction netting. Built in an architectural style described variously as Queen Anne Revival and Victorian Gothic, it shared elements of both, and if you didn't know better, you could be forgiven for mistaking it for a gigantic old insane asylum. The hotel had been under construction for a couple of years now to keep it in lockstep with the rapid development of its namesake neighborhood. Once the glittering gem of what Mark Twain had coined the Gilded Age at the end of the 19th century, New York City had entered a socioeconomic spiral in the 1940s and 50s, reaching a low point in the 70s and 80s when it was plagued by poverty, urban blight, and soaring crime rates. This was the clichéd Manhattan you saw in the opening credits of that old sitcom, *Night Court*, a dog-eat-dog city characterized by drug addicts and alcoholics, hustlers and con artists, cops walking their beats on lonely nights, dingy subway cars rumbling through the graffitied underground, and steam rising from manhole covers on dangerous streets. However, since the dot-com bubble in the 1990s, and the corresponding influx of new money, the city had stepped back from the abyss. Trendy cafés and pubs and restaurants replaced the greasy mom-and-pop diners and dive bars, boutique shops and spas rented out the boarded-up storefronts, penthouses sprang up in abandoned lofts, the punks and degenerates went elsewhere (or perhaps simply traded in their spiked hair and leather jackets for alligator shirts and khakis), and gentrification invaded even the sketchiest neighborhoods.

To adapt to this changing reality, in 1995 the Hotel Chelsea adopted a "No Tolerance" policy to clean up its image. This was the beginning of the end of its illustrious 100-year-old tradition of supporting eccentric, counterculture creativity. The gritty, desperate, oftentimes crazy artists who had called the hotel home were kicked to the curb, while the ones who took their spots had already achieved success, or were born with silver spoons in their mouths.

As Malcolm approached the entrance to the hotel beneath the red-and-white awning, he glanced at the bronze plaques on the front of the building memorializing some of the celebrated former residents: Dylan Thomas, Virgil Thomson, Sir Arthur C. Clark, Thomas Wolfe, Shirley Clarke, Brendan Behan.

Malcolm's reflection in the glass doors was of a man in his early thirties in slim-fit jeans, a white tee, and navy blazer. He'd been likened to John Cusack and a young Alec Baldwin on enough occasions to take the comparisons seriously. The flatterers were being generous, of course, but he did acknowledge some similarities to the actors, such as his dark hair, brown eyes, and the tendency of his lips to pucker when at rest. The lips would have been more at home on an art critic, but they were his, and there wasn't much he could do about them.

He pressed a buzzer next to the entrance.

The man behind the front desk saw him and pushed his own button. The doors unlocked and Malcolm entered the hotel's empty lobby. The white marble floor tiles were dirty and scuffed from years of neglect. All the furniture had been removed, and the ornate fireplace sat cold and empty. Unsightly discolorations on the walls indicated where artwork had once hung. Incongruously, a ghoulish papier-mâché sculpture of a child on a swing, hanging from the ceiling, had been left behind to preside over the uninviting space.

The man behind the front desk stood. He eyed Malcolm's photography bag. "You the guy writing the story for that magazine?" he asked. His powder-blue dress shirt was unbuttoned at the throat. The rolled-up sleeves revealed muscled, hairless forearms.

"That's me," Malcolm said.

"Welcome to the majestic Chelsea." He smiled to reveal a gap between his front teeth and spread his arms in mock grandeur.

"Doesn't look too majestic to me."

"It's a shithole. Have some trouble with your coffee today?"

Malcolm glanced down at the brown stain on his shirt. "Taxi nearly ran me over."

"Taxi drivers in this city hate the world 'cause of Uber, you know?"

"I take the trains."

"Hear ya. I'm Darnell."

"Malcolm."

"Okay, Malcolm," Darnell said. "So I was told to expect you today. I was told you were writing a piece on the renovations. But that's all I know. Anything I can do to help?"

"Mostly I'm just going to wander around the hotel, take some photos, if that's okay? Renovations been going on for what...two years now?"

"About that. I've only been here since the new management took over a few months ago."

"The previous developer didn't have much luck with the place?"

"It's been headaches for everyone since Stanley Bard left."

"He was the old manager?" Malcolm had spent the first part of the morning browsing internet articles about the Hotel Chelsea.

"And part owner," Darnell said. "The Chelsea used to be owned by three families, the Bards and two others. Stanley Bard took over the day-to-day operations from his father in the 50s. In 2007 the heirs of the other two families wanted to start turning a profit—and can you blame 'em?—and ousted Bard as manager. They sold the place a couple of years later to a real estate bigwig for a cool eighty million. Plan was to turn it into an upmarket hotel, make it the crown jewel of New York again. But the guy didn't get too far with that. There've been issues with the long-term tenants. It's been a real shit-fest here."

Malcolm was surprised. "There are still tenants living here?"

"Most have been evicted, but some of 'em banded together, got lawyered up, and got to stay in their apartments. Something about the state's tenants' rights laws. So what did the real estate bigwig do? Started renovating the hotel around them. The tenants filed more lawsuits complaining 'bout the living conditions. This caused a shitload of work stoppages, delays, cost overruns, all that. Finally the bigwig had enough and palmed off the hotel to my bosses earlier this year. They convert residential hotels into high-priced boutique ones, and they're pouring some forty million into the renovations here. Is it gonna be enough?" He shrugged. "You tell me after you've had a looksee around."

Malcolm nodded and asked, "Where can I leave this?" He raised his empty paper coffee cup.

"Give it here." Darnell tossed the cup in a bin behind him, then produced a hard hat from beneath the counter. He gave it to Malcolm. "You'll need this. Compliance with building regulations and everything. Elevators are right behind you. Stairs are through the doors if you prefer to take them."

"I think I'll take the elevator to the top floor and work my way down the stairs."

"Whatever floats your boat."

Malcolm went to the elevator to the right of the reception desk and pressed the call button.

"Yo, Malcolm?" Darnell said.

He turned around. "Yeah?"

"You run into any of the residents, take what they tell you with a grain of salt, will ya?"

"What will they tell me?"

"There's no love lost between them and my bosses. They

do their best to demonize them any chance they get. That's their right. Just a heads-up not to believe everything they say. Also, a couple of them are nuttier than a Christmas fruitcake. They've got it in their heads the Chelsea is haunted. You don't believe in ghosts, do you, Malcolm?"

"No, I don't."

"Good man." Darnell's mobile phone began to ring. He checked the number. "Gotta get this. Nice talking to you, buddy."

He turned his back to Malcolm and answered the call.

CHAPTER 3

The woman on the roof

The rickety elevator groaned and creaked its way up to the tenth floor. When the car came to a stop, Malcolm stepped into a two-story atrium. The glass roof offered a view of the heavy storm clouds overhead. To his left, a door with sidelight windows led to the floor's west wing; an identical door on the right led to the east wing. In the center of the landing, an elaborate staircase with wrought-iron florid metalwork spiraled down to the lower floors. It also went up to the roof.

Malcolm decided to go up. A small alarm attached to the rooftop access door gave him pause. He pushed the door open anyway. The alarm made a faint sound like an asthmatic gasping for air. Unconcerned—nobody could hear it, and if it triggered another alarm at the front desk, Darnell would assume it was him—Malcolm stepped outside onto the roof. It was an expansive, open space littered with piles of demolished timber, upturned and broken bricks, and large garbage bags overflowing with vegetation. He withdrew his Nikon from his bag and picked his way through the debris, snapping photographs as he went.

While he was peering through the camera's viewfinder at a faded mural that had been painted on one section of brick wall, someone spoke from behind him.

Whirling around, Malcolm found a prim woman in her sixties or seventies scowling at him. She was dressed Jazz-Age chic in a cloche hat and a peacock-patterned velvet cape shoulder-draped over a royal-blue flapper dress. From beneath the hat fell coiffed blonde curls that had to be a wig. She'd used a boatload of eyeshadow to do her eyes up like a cat's, slanted upward at the ends. Her fake eyelashes were like batwings. Malcolm suspected she had been ravishing in her youth, though age had taken its toll on her, creasing her skin in all the usual places and hardening her features.

"Uh, hi," he said, confused as to where she'd come from. "Sorry, I didn't know anybody else was up here."

"Who are you?" she demanded in a robust voice. "One of ze developer's lackeys?"

Malcolm couldn't place her accent, but it sounded Romanian, like in those old vampire movies.

"No, ma'am. I'm a magazine reporter for *City Living*. We cover pop culture, fashion, current affairs—"

"I know the magazine," she quipped. "I'm not that out of touch with the world. Why are you writing about the Chelsea?"

"It's an iconic New York City landmark, and it's been closed to guests for a couple of years now. People are curious as to how the construction is progressing."

"It's progressing at a snail's pace, I can tell you that much. It was only supposed to take a year. That's what the previous owner told us two years ago. Construction will take a year." She huffed. "Two years later and what's been accomplished? Nothing! Nothing but a whole lot of destruction, that's what! They're destroying the soul of this hotel."

He extended his hand. "I'm Malcolm Clock."

After a moment, the woman shook, her hand little more than bones and skin, as fragile as a bird's wing. "I am Quinn. That is it. One name."

Malcolm surveyed the roof. "Are they building something up here, Quinn?"

"Building?" Quinn scoffed. "No, not building. What you see, all the debris, is the remains of the gardens. That's right, there used to be gardens up here, beautiful gardens. Honeysuckle and Virginia Creepers and lavender cascading over trellises. Cozy spaces where you could sit with a coffee and watch the sun rise over the city. Flowers and fruit trees and a communal herb garden. A pair of hammocks used to hang right over there, between those two chimneys. I would read there on pleasant days." Her hazel eyes darkened. "And those greedy bastards just took their chainsaws to it! Hauled it away in garbage bags! Over a century of cultivated beauty and life, gone. Not even a single planter box left behind."

Malcolm allowed a few moments of respectful silence to pass before asking, "Why did they tear it down if they're not building anything...?"

"Oh, they'll build—eventually. There's been talk of a bar. Maybe even a spa. A spa!" She pressed a trembling hand to her forehead. "Forgive me for getting so worked up. But the Chelsea isn't just any other building. Its legacy should have been protected."

"May I ask what you're doing up here?"

She looked at him quizzically. "Why, I live up here."

Malcolm wondered if she'd misunderstood his question. "Sorry?"

She pointed to a pyramidal turret jutting up from the building's rooftop.

"You live in *there*?"

"I most certainly do. Other residents used to live up here too. Not in anything as special, mind you. They had small sheds we called bungalows. But they've all been evicted and their bungalows torn down. I'm the last survivor."

"You're a modern-day Quasimodo."

"A deaf, hideous, deformed hunchback?"

"I didn't mean that..." He pushed on. "How long have you lived up here?"

"I moved in on February 11, 1961," she said without hesitation.

"You've been up here for over fifty years?"

"Thank you for making me feel so young." She waved a

hand dismissively. "I've lived a full life. I'm proud of my age. And I'll tell you this much: many former residents of this hotel can't claim the same longevity. But, yes, 1961. I was a young girl then, a ballerina. I was lucky enough to have danced in one of Virgil Thomson's operas. When I mentioned to Virgil I was looking for somewhere to live, he called up the old manager of the Chelsea—Virgil was living here then—and said, 'Stanley, I have a lovely young dancer without a home. Can you help her out?' I came to the hotel the next day. Stanley showed me these horrible rooms on the lower floors, though by the way he was praising them, you'd think he was showing you the Palace at Versailles! Finally we ended up here on the rooftop. A pianist had just moved out of the pyramid, and Stanley said I could have it. I was skeptical about living in a pyramid on the rooftop of a hotel...until he told me that the actress Sarah Bernhardt had had it built."

"Sarah Bernhardt had it built?" Malcolm said skeptically.

Quinn nodded. "She used to live in one of the two-story penthouse apartments that had access to the roof, and she wanted a pyramid on the roof. She was eccentric like that. She used to sleep in a rosewood coffin. Perhaps she slept in her coffin in my pyramid? In any event, I agreed to pay Stanley two months' rent, believing I would find more suitable accommodation in the meantime. He told me I'd likely never leave the hotel." She smiled wistfully. "Turns out he was right, wasn't he?"

"What was the Chelsea like in the 60s?"

"Certainly not the luxury residence it had once been. Arthur Miller probably described it best when he said, 'No vacuum cleaners, no rules, no shame.' After the Depression, the Chelsea went bankrupt, and throughout the 40s and 50s, the magnificent suites were chopped up into small individual rooms. The stained-glass windows, the floor-to-ceiling mirrors, and much of the intricate woodwork were torn out. The hotel became a flophouse—but also a bohemian refuge. The 60s were the Warhol years. Andy and many of his superstars lived in the hotel then. Nico, Viva, Brigid Berlin, Gerard Malanga. They all starred in his film, *Chelsea Girls*, the first stab at reality TV, I suppose you might say. Bob Dylan lived here for three years. Leonard Cohen and Janis Joplin, of course. You may not believe me, but I inspired Leonard to write that song about her."

"You were friends with Leonard Cohen?"

"Friends? I suppose you'd call our relationship that. He was having a rough time then. He'd been an accomplished poet and novelist in Canada and had come to New York to join the folk singer-songwriter scene. But he was already in his thirties. That was considered by many as too old to kick off a music career. His debut record sold terribly, and he had copyright issues with some of his songs. I'd go down to his room sometimes. It was this little shoebox with a single lightbulb dangling from the ceiling, a tiny black-and-white TV, and a hot plate. That was about it. He used to sit on his bed with his guitar, and I'd sit on the floor, with my back against the wall. We'd smoke cigarettes and just talk mostly. That's what we were doing on New Year's Day in 1971 when he told me about meeting Janis Joplin at three in the morning in the elevator."

"This was after she died?"

"Three months after, yes. It was the first time he'd ever spoken about her to me. He told me the full story, going back to her room, all that, and I told him he should write a song about it. A couple of weeks later he did just that, on a cocktail napkin in some restaurant, if my memory serves me right... Anyway, that was the 60s."

"And the 70s?"

"The 70s—oh my, the 70s! That's when the Chelsea cemented its tabloid character due to all the rock and roll people who stayed here—in large part, I should say, because no other hotels in the city would accept them. And the bands brought the roadies, who brought the drugs. Really, drug-use got out of control. People smoked weed like cigarettes. You could get high riding the elevator! I remember visiting a

Puerto Rican drug dealer on the third floor. He kept a five-foot-high pile of marijuana sitting in the middle of his living room, complete with roaches running in and out of it. That was his cheap stuff. He kept his better stuff in a back room. He had about twenty different kinds of marijuana in little file boxes in a cabinet, all the baggies labelled with colored stickers. He was quite the professional. And it wasn't only pot going around. Speed, LSD, cocaine, heroin. You could get whatever you desired here."

Malcolm had battled a soul-crushing heroin addiction for much of his adult life, and he recalled all too well the frustration and desperation of the daily hunts all over the city to find his next fix. The Hotel Chelsea that Quinn was describing—a one-stop pharmacy of illicit drugs—would have been an oasis for him and his deadbeat friends.

Ignoring a hunger in a corner in his mind to get high, a hunger he had fought every day of the last three years of his sobriety, he said, "You must have met a lot of the celebrities who'd stayed at the hotel over the years, Quinn?"

"I did indeed, Mr. Clock. But most of the famous people who stayed here didn't act like famous people, and you didn't really think of them as famous. We were all neighbors under the same roof, all part of the same coterie, which was based on talent and passion for our art rather than how much money you made, or how many fans you had. You'd walk down the hallways, and everyone would have their doors open, they'd invite you in for a drink and a smoke. Of course, you could just as easily find yourself in a pimp's room, or a prostitute's, as you could an established or up-and-coming artist's."

"Sounds like a wild time."

"Wild, seedy, scary, insane. A man on the ninth floor kept an alligator, two monkeys, and a snake in his room, and sometimes his monkeys would get out and run free rein around the hotel. I think it was Patti—that's Patti Smith, the singer-songwriter—who used to joke that the Chelsea was like a doll's house in the *Twilight Zone*. Not only because very strange things happened here, but because every room was different than the next, each its own little world in a larger universe."

A strong gust of wind soughed past them, sweeping Quinn's coiffed blonde curls in front of her eyes. She glanced up at the dark sky, frowning at the storm clouds gathered there. Malcolm glanced at them as well, noting they were darker than they'd been earlier.

"It was a pleasure meeting you, Mr. Clock," she said, tugging her cape snugly at the throat. "But I catch a chill very easily these days and must return inside to warm up. If you'd like, you're more than welcome to join me. I can put on a pot of tea?"

"I'd like that very much. Thank you."

She cast another weary glance at the sky. "I don't like the look of those clouds at all. It's going to be a big storm, isn't it?"

"It's forecast to hit the entire northeast of the country."

She sighed. "I used to enjoy the rain when there were gardens up here. Now...what's the point in rain if there's nothing for it to nourish? Come, Mr. Clock, let's get inside."

CHAPTER 4

Wally & Iggy

Stepping into the fairytale spire on the roof of the Hotel Chelsea was like stepping into a carnival funhouse: you didn't know where to look first. The conical walls were splattered with paint—red, green, yellow—and covered with all sorts of Voodoo-inspired paintings in elaborate frames. Two towers composed of small square cages (like those you might find in a pet store to hold birds) were stacked almost to the tip of the spire, and from these hung an impressive collection of dresses and gowns and furs. A half-dozen eerie mannequins were dressed up in more glamorous clothing. Complimenting all this was eccentric furniture, such as a chandelier that resembled a glob of dripping honey, a sofa designed to resemble a bird nest, and a zebra-striped chair with four ruby-red high heels for legs.

Malcolm asked, "Where did you get all of this…stuff?"

"Oh, here and there," Quinn said. "Odd things have always had a way of showing up in this hotel. That armchair with the heels used to belong to Andy Warhol. Those mannequins I found in the sixth-floor hallway. One of the former residents was a fashion designer. She left them in the hall when she moved out."

"Would you mind if I took some photos?"

"Please do."

Malcolm treaded carefully around the room, snapping photographs of the old woman's furniture and knickknacks, which included stacks of cassette tapes and old records, Ukrainian Easter eggs, fine china, tarot cards, cheap plastic toys, and all sorts of pop ephemera.

"I've never seen a bed like this before," he said, referring to an intricately carved red lacquered bed that had a back and arms like a sofa.

"It's a mid-19th century opium bed from China. I purchased it at an auction a number of years back."

He snapped a photo of a vintage baby grand piano.

"How did you ever get a *piano* up here?"

"I found that in the hotel's basement. It's a graveyard for all sorts of old tables and dressers and chairs, items abandoned by previous tenants. I got lucky finding that piano. I paid the maintenance man and two bellmen to carry it up here for me."

Malcolm did a double take. In a jar on a small side table was a cockroach the size of a rhinoceros beetle. "Is that bug real?"

"That is Wally. He's my pet."

"You have a cockroach for a pet?"

"It can get lonely up here all by myself."

"Why did you name him Wally?"

"It is short for Wallflower. About a month ago I spotted him for the first time over there by the bookshelf. I let him be. There are roaches throughout this building. It's infested. You get inured to them. But he was in the same spot the next day. I thought he was dead, but he was most certainly alive. You can tell if you get up close to him. When he was still on the bookshelf later in the day, I decided he might have gotten too fat to move. His legs are quite tiny in comparison to his body, as you can see. So I decided to give him a home."

"What do you feed him?"

"He has a voracious appetite for sweets."

"Spoiled bug."

"He's good company, but I do miss my previous pet, Iggy. Let me put on the tea." Quinn went to a cluttered kitchenette and took two mugs from a cupboard painted a kaleidoscope of trippy colors.

"Was Iggy another cockroach?"

"What kind of name would Iggy be for a cockroach?" she

said, taking two tea bags from a box. "No, Iggy was an iguana. I found him standing right outside my door one day."

"What was an iguana doing on the roof of the Hotel Chelsea?"

"I suspect he escaped out a lower-floor window and climbed up the hotel. Iguanas are magnificent climbers. I never heard anybody mention they were missing an iguana, however, so I kept him. I had him for three years or so before he did something very stupid." Quinn filled a kettle with water from a small sink. "He snuck outside on a warm winter day," she continued. "I'm not sure how he got out, but iguanas can be very patient...and sneaky. I never noticed he was gone until the next morning when I opened the door and found him on my doorstep, exactly where I'd found him three years earlier. Only this time he was frozen stiff—oh, dammit! No gas!" She tried the stove's electric ignition again, which made a loud *click-click-click*. When the sparks failed to ignite the burner, she threw her hands up in the air. "That damn developer! He's doing this on purpose!"

"Shutting off your gas?"

"He does it all the time. And it's not just the gas. He cuts off the heating and the water as well. Laws protect rent-stabilized tenants like me and the others still living here, he can't evict us, so he's trying to make our lives so unbearable we get fed up and move out on our own. That's why he's been dragging on the construction."

"You think the developer is deliberately dragging on the construction?"

"Yes, I do, and it amounts to harassment, if not psychological warfare. Do you know what he calls us behind our backs and to our faces? Leftovers. That's right. Leftovers, like we're a moldy old meatloaf that should be tossed in the bin."

"How many tenants remain in the building?"

"I'd say there's about eighty of us still here...but for how much longer, I don't know."

"But if you're protected under the law—"

"Don't be naïve, Mr. Clock," Quinn chided. "When you have expensive lawyers, there are ways of getting around the law. And even if the bastard can't strongarm every one of us out, he'll simply bring more and more cases against us and let them drag on in the courts until we can't afford to fight him any longer."

"Have you considered simply moving out and finding somewhere else to live?"

"And let the greedy bloodsucker win? Never! He'll get his comeuppance in the end. Besides, where else am I going to find another place like this for a thousand dollars a month?" She shook her head. "No, Mr. Clock, I'm going to remain here fighting until my death. And I'll tell you this. While I am happy to die in the Hotel Chelsea, what I have always wanted was to *live* in the Hotel Chelsea—and when you see the sad state of the rest of the hotel, you won't call this living."

CHAPTER 5

Shane's music & the friendly neighborhood cat

S hane McSorley was sitting on the faux leather sofa in his two-room apartment in the Hotel Chelsea, his feet up on the glass coffee table, watching an old *Married with Children* rerun. He took a last drag of his Pall Mall, stubbed it out on the overflowing ashtray next to his feet, and shot another from the pack. He lit it with a silver Zippo, the dry tobacco crackling, the blue-white smoke wafting up his face. His long exhale ended in a series of singeing coughs.

"Bloody hell," he mumbled, drawing his hand across his mouth and knocking back a mouthful of whiskey from a nearby glass.

Shane had smoked ever since he was a teenager in Cork, Ireland. He'd rarely bought a pack, since he only smoked when he boozed. On nights when he knew he'd be on a tear, he went to the corner store, where Mr. Wilkinson kept an open pack of Camels behind his counter and sold cigarettes for ten pence a pop. Shane usually bought five or six, which would usually suffice.

Social smoking was something he'd continued throughout his adult life. Recently, though, he wasn't smoking a few cigarettes on a Friday or Saturday night; he was chain-smoking about two king packs a day. He hadn't reneged on his only-smoke-when-lit philosophy; he was now lit all the time.

Eight days ago, after the first of the two Incidents on the eighth floor, Shane returned to his apartment on the first floor, cracked open a bottle of Jameson, and spent the morning drinking until he passed out. When he woke in the late afternoon, he hit the bottle again until he blacked out around midnight—and this became his waking routine. Drink, pass out, drink, pass out. The one positive during the downward spiral —and it was a big positive—was that he was making the best music of his life.

Shane had grown up listening mostly to blues, folk, soul, R&B, and reggae. He started playing guitar at six years of age, after he found his father's acoustic guitar collecting dust in the furnace room of the family house. During his teen years he became interested in the slide guitar, mimicking the styles of Robert Johnson and George Harrison. He'd never been a fan of school, but at his father's urging he attended Trinity College in Dublin and studied business management. Once he was degreed, his parents (who owned several successful restaurants in Cork, two in Belfast, and one in Derry) wanted Shane to work for the family business, with the end goal that he would one day take full control of the operation.

Managing restaurants, however, was not something he wanted to do, and he spent the next several years writing music and playing gigs around Ireland. On his twenty-eighth birthday, he told his parents he was moving to New York to pursue a career in music. They were furious. They'd supported him over the years with a generous allowance, and they always told him they were happy he enjoyed singing and playing the guitar, but it became clear to him that day that they'd never believed in his talent. They thought his interest in music was a fad, and they had been biding their time until he grew out of it. The revelation that he wanted to fly to America to make a name for himself left them gobsmacked. His father made the argument that most musicians failed. His mother acted the victim, telling him that New York was dangerous and that she would worry about him every day.

Nevertheless, Shane would not be dissuaded and bought a plane ticket from Dublin to New York City the following week.

The day before his flight, his father courted him with a deal. He would pay for Shane's lodgings for two years, he'd said. If Shane became successful in that time, then all the power to him. But if he didn't, then he would return to Ireland and manage one of the restaurants.

And if he didn't take the deal, he was on his own.

Shane took it. He had little choice. Without his father's money, he'd have to wait tables or work in a kitchen to pay his rent, which would detract from the time he could devote to his music. Moreover, he thought his father's terms were fair. If he couldn't make something out of himself in New York in two years, then perhaps he didn't have what it took to be a professional musician.

Shane had been living in the Hotel Chelsea in Manhattan for numerous months now. He'd made some good progress finding his feet. He knew the music scene in the city. He was booked for gigs every weekend. And he'd created some catchy songs. The problem was that the gigs, mostly at Irish and British pubs, paid next to nothing (and sometimes nothing at all, his compensation instead being a meal and a few pints of the black stuff), and his music, while good, wasn't great, as evidenced by all the big record labels showing zero interest in the demos he sent them.

Then one week ago—a day after the First Incident—he was boozing and playing a circusy warmup riff on his guitar...and ended up creating some of his most sophisticated and imaginative melodies ever. He didn't remember any of it until the next day when he found his song notebook on the floor, filled with pages of scribbled lyrics and notes and chords—

A crash made Shane sit up straight, instantly alert, his eyes scanning the room.

Just the cat, he thought with relief as he spotted the white Siamese standing on his kitchen counter, looking imperiously at the empty whiskey bottle it'd knocked over, as if wondering who'd put it in its way.

Shane didn't know for certain to whom the cat belonged. There were three other residents on the Chelsea's first floor. Only one of them had an apartment that, like Shane's, faced West 23rd Street, and the owner, Barry Church, told Shane the cat wasn't his.

Shane suspected it had been part of Roger James' brood. Until very recently, James had lived up on the tenth floor with about fourteen cats. Shane had never been to the old man's apartment, but his ex, Jolene, had often played bridge up there with James and the crazy woman who lived on the roof. Jo was the one who'd told him about all the cats.

Roger James had killed himself nine days ago, and somebody had taken the cats. The white Siamese standing on his counter, he guessed, had avoided this fate by slipping out James' window, because it had started showing up at Shane's place immediately after the suicide. The best he could figure, it had made its way down the front of the building balcony by balcony until it reached the first-floor balcony where it found itself stranded.

Shane got up and went to the part of the room that served as his kitchen. The cat meowed at him. He scratched its head between its ears.

"Scared the bejaysus out of me, ye little shite," he mumbled.

He opened the refrigerator door and took out the container of chopped chicken liver he'd bought specifically for the cat. It was nearly empty, so he tossed it in the microwave and punched in thirty seconds. He'd learned early on the cat wouldn't eat any meat cold. It wanted it warm, approximating a fresh kill.

When the timer beeped, he retrieved the container, set it on the counter, and let the feline go nuts. He opened the fridge again. He wasn't lacking in food; he'd done a decent shop the other day when he'd bought the chopped liver. But he had no appetite. Instead of making something for breakfast, he decided on the unopened bottle of Jameson on the bottom shelf.

He returned to the sofa and picked up his Fender Stratocaster, the same model Harrison used on the *Magical Mystery Tour*. He plucked a few melancholy notes, then strummed a series of moving chords, building to the coda of the latest song he'd written.

It wasn't long before his fears and anxieties had receded and he was lost in his music.

CHAPTER 6

Checking out

Quinn and Malcolm talked for another half hour about the plight of the Hotel Chelsea's current tenants before she said, "Would you like me to accompany you on your tour of the building?"

"Absolutely. If that's not too much trouble?"

"No trouble at all. I enjoy your company, Mr. Clock. You seem genuinely interested in the fate of the hotel. I just hope you don't turn around and write a hit piece on us tenants."

"I'm on your side," he assured her.

"Let me throw on something warm then. By the way, would I be correct in assuming you hail from a distant family of clockmakers?"

"That's what most people think. But Clock is from the Old English word *cloke*. I come from a distant family of cloak makers. You sound Eastern European?"

"Yes, that's right." From one of the mannequins, she retrieved a wrap coat with a shawl-style collar trimmed in fur that she fastened with a large silver button. She exchanged the T-strap heels she was wearing for a pair of Oxford-like shoes more suitable for climbing stairs. "I was born in Romania, in a small medieval town in southern Transylvania. I studied dance in Bucharest and moved to New York City when I was twenty-two."

"May I ask you something...?"

"As long as it's not to hear me say 'I vant to suck your blood.'"

"I'm curious about your surname. There are only so many mononymous people around."

"Mononymous? Is that what I am? I suppose I should trust a writer to know such a word. The reason I dropped my surname is quite simple really. I despised it."

"What was—"

"Patapievici," she said, anticipating the question. "Everyone around here called me Patty Pie, and somehow that became Patty Cakes. I was Patty Cakes the Ballerina. That's what people would say. 'Where's Patty Cakes the Ballerina?' I hated being referred to like that. It made me feel like both a child and a stripper, and I don't know which was worse. So I dropped the surname after about six months of living at the Chelsea. I introduced myself only as Quinn and, over time, that is who I became."

◆ ◆ ◆

Outside on the roof, the wind had picked up, snapping at their clothing. The sky was a uniform battleship gray, scuffed charcoal in places, though it had yet to release its payload of rain.

As they passed through the roof's access door, Quinn punched a code into the alarm unit to turn it off, explaining to Malcolm that Stanley Bard had had the alarm installed because of one particularly out-of-control roof party. After that, access was only permitted for the residents on the tenth floor and, of course, those living on the rooftop itself.

As they descended the staircase, Malcolm asked, "Where did all the paintings go? In some pictures I've seen they used to cover nearly every wall in the hotel."

"The previous developer stole them."

"He *stole* them?"

"Well, they weren't his to take, were they?" she stated matter-of-factly. "I removed the ones my late husband painted the day Stanley Bard was fired as manager. Other tenants weren't so lucky."

"Your husband was a painter?" he asked, thinking about all the Voodoo art in her pyramid.

"Painting was a hobby for him, that's all," she said simply before changing the topic. "Now as you'll see, the hotel's demolition has been a top-down affair. First to go were the roof gardens and bungalows. Then the tenth floor was gutted, then the ninth, and so forth. They've made it all the way to the second floor. The first is the only one remaining in its original condition."

"What are the plans for the façade?"

"The Chelsea was deemed a national landmark in 1968, so the developer can't touch the exterior. His permit only extends to the interior demolition."

"Then why's the building covered in scaffolding?"

"Oh, they're doing minor touchups. Stripping and painting the window trim, cleaning the tar from the gutters. But so help me God if they touch a single brick or balcony..."

When they reached the elevator landing, Quinn ran a hand over the grand stairwell's brass handrail. "A few days after I moved into the Chelsea, I found a shoe right there." She pointed to a spot on the floor nearby. "I couldn't understand how someone could lose a shoe without noticing—until I reached the lobby. There was a man sprawled out on the white marble floor, a large puddle of blood around him, a horrible sight. He'd jumped down the stairwell."

Malcolm peered over the bannister. At the nadir of the rectangular shaft was a hardwood floor surrounded by a brass railing.

"That's not the lobby," he said, confused.

"It's the first floor. Stanley had that flooring put in because so many people were jumping he feared someone was going to land on him or one of the other desk clerks."

"How many people have jumped from here?"

"I wouldn't want to count. But it wasn't just here. One morning I was in the courtyard behind the hotel when a man leapt from his window and landed on his head on the aluminum chaise lounge next to me. The very next day another man jumped from his window on the west side of the building. His suicide was foiled because he jumped a little too enthusiastically, and instead of landing in the alley, he landed on the roof of the synagogue next door. When someone asked him why he'd jumped, he replied, 'Because John Lennon was just shot.'"

"You didn't witness that one?"

"Thankfully, no. But everybody used to know everybody else here. Everybody gossiped. And then there was poor Dee Dee..."

"From The Ramones?" Malcolm asked. He was quite sure the bassist for the punk band had died from a heroin overdose, not a suicide.

Quinn nodded. "Dee Dee lived in the Chelsea in a number of different rooms over the years. In the late 80s he sequestered himself in one of these rooms to kick his drug habit. One morning I was in the lobby and Dee Dee came through the front door, his face white as a ghost. It turned out this was the first time he'd left his room in about two weeks. And what happened the moment he stepped outside on his way to get a coffee and a donut? A woman threw herself from her window and landed right in front of him. Her head struck a manhole cover that used to be out there in the pavement in front of the awning. I heard the impact inside the lobby. It sounded like somebody striking a large gong. Poor Dee Dee... I think he was back on the drugs later that day." Quinn's eyes had taken on a distant look. "Those who wanted to kill themselves didn't always jump, and they weren't always the long-term residents. We had a saying. People check in to check out. These people seemed to think the Chelsea was a suitable place to kill themselves, and they'd come here and rent a room to do it in. There was this one woman who rented a room for two weeks and refused maid service. When her time was up, and she failed to check out, Stanley opened her apartment. It turned out she had overdosed on pills in her bathtub. The tub had been full of water, and she had been decomposing in it for a long time. It took the coroner all day to remove what remained of her. She had stage-four cancer, we later learned."

Trying not to visualize that death, Malcolm asked, "Why do you think so many people commit suicide here?"

Quinn shrugged. "The Chelsea has a dark side. It seems to bring out the best in artists, but it brings out the worst in them too. After all, not everyone who comes here becomes a success. Those who don't feel frustration and bitterness toward those who do, and that can lead to a lot of anger and despair. The existentialist writer Albert Camus once wrote that the only truly serious philosophical problem is suicide. The option to kill yourself, you see, is with you every day. Anyone can do it, any time they wish. But judging whether to live or not requires a degree of introspection. In other words, you must be rather philosophical to kill yourself. Many artists and writers fit that bill. So what you have here at the Chelsea with some of its residents and transients is a perfect storm of desperation, insecurity, emotional instability, and self-introspection that can lead one to believe, unfortunately, that life is no longer worth living."

Quinn started down the stairs to the ninth floor. Malcolm didn't follow.

"If it's all right," he said, "I'd like to have a look at every floor."

She glanced back at him. "The ninth floor is just like the tenth. So why don't we start there?" She took another step, but Malcolm still didn't follow.

"What aren't you telling me about the tenth floor?" he asked.

"If you must know, someone killed themselves in the west wing the other day."

Malcolm raised his eyebrows, wondering if this was what had started Quinn on the suicide tangent in the first place.

"The man's death was quite messy," she added, "and I don't think anybody's cleaned up any of the blood yet."

He thought that over, and morbid as it may be, he wanted to see the room.

"I'm going to have a quick peek," he told her. "You can wait here. I won't be long."

CHAPTER 7

My way

Malcolm pushed through the door to the floor's west wing and stepped into a jerry-rigged construction site. Spools of wiring and copper pipes and silver air ducts clogged the exposed ceiling. Many of the doors to the apartments were boarded up with plywood, while others were covered with plastic sheathing. Metal framing crawled along the walls and ceiling. Stepladders and mop buckets and brooms cluttered the walkway. The temporary lighting left much to be desired in terms of brightness and ambiance, making Malcolm feel as though he had been transported to a dingy wing of some early 19th century hospital.

The suicide room wasn't hard to find. Yellow police tape crisscrossed the door.

Crouching, Malcolm gripped the red zip at the bottom of the plastic sheathing and unzipped it. The door was a big, solid thing, probably oak, and whitewashed like all the others that remained. Pushing it open, he ducked under the police tape.

The small apartment featured hardwood floors, peach-colored walls, and limp, matching drapes in the single bay window.

And blood, everywhere.

It splattered the dated furniture and the threadbare oriental carpet in anarchic patterns. It even reached the moody oil paintings hanging high on the walls, and the bronze-framed mirror suspended over the mantel of the ornate marble fireplace.

Malcolm didn't know what to make of the scene. When Quinn had told him the man's death was messy, he'd assumed the blood would have been localized to one spot, wherever the man had chosen to do the deed. But this... It was as though someone had cut off the heads of a half-dozen chickens and let them run loose.

Breathing shallowly—the smell of the blood was pungent and sweet and nauseating—Malcolm withdrew his Nikon from his bag and snapped several photographs of the room. In a sleeping alcove was a neatly made bed and night table.

Both stained with blood.

On a nightstand stood a wood-framed photograph of a sour-looking old man next to an equally old yet smiling woman.

Malcolm studied the couple for a long moment, then left the alcove. On his way out of what was feeling more and more like a slaughterhouse, he stuck his head into a small bathroom. More blood on the tiles and the sink and the mirror—

He jumped in fright.

◆ ◆ ◆

Back in the hallway Malcolm slammed the door to the suicide room closed, unable to comprehend what he'd seen in the mirror.

It had been a face—only not his face.

He couldn't recall clearly what it had looked like—the light from the living room's bay window had barely reached the bathroom—but he was sure he wasn't mistaken.

A face, not his.

How was that possible?

It wasn't, of course. He'd imagined it. He'd been thinking of the dead tenant, and he'd projected the man's face on the mirror in place of his own.

If he went back to look, he'd see only his reflection, he was sure of that.

So go look, he told himself.

Malcolm took a step toward the door. Adrenaline had kicked in. His heart was pounding, and as he reached toward the doorknob, he saw that his hand was trembling.

He pushed open the door, ducked beneath the police tape, and entered the room. He hesitated at the bathroom door before sticking his head inside it once again.

The face in the mirror staring back at him was ghostly white and terrified.

But at least it was his own.

Quinn was waiting patiently at the stairwell.

"Did you find what you were looking for?" she asked him.

"What happened in there?" he demanded.

"He killed himself."

"There was blood everywhere."

"He cut his wrists."

"And wandered around his apartment with blood gushing out of him? If you're going to slit your wrists, don't you usually do it one spot, like the bathtub?"

"I wouldn't know, Mr. Clock. I've never attempted to slit my wrists."

Malcolm ground his teeth, frustrated by her obtuseness. He asked, "Why'd he do it?"

"Nobody knows. He was a stubborn, angry old man. Some say he was a genius. But always angry. He didn't leave a note." Quinn began descending the steps. "Let me show you the ninth floor."

CHAPTER 8

Who killed Jimi?

T he ninth floor proved to be a near replica of the tenth.

"I find it hard to believe people are actually living in these conditions," Malcolm said as they moved through the unfinished wing.

"It's horrendous," Quinn agreed. She pointed to a plastic garbage bin filled with water. "Ever since they destroyed the garden on the roof, the ceiling on the tenth floor is always leaking. When they don't change the garbage bins, they overflow, and the water leaks down here and to the floors below."

"What's with the plastic over some of the doors?"

"Those are the occupied units. The plastic is supposed to protect the tenants from the asbestos in the walls and the lead in the dust—which is more than twenty times the federal limit, mind you. There's nothing anyone can do about the constant noise though. Five days a week you have an army of construction workers sawing and hammering and drilling. Vibrations shake the entire building. A debris truck crunches rubble down on the street. On the weekends you'd think we'd have some peace and quiet, but that's when they jackhammer the street for only God knows why."

It struck Malcolm that it was Friday. "Where are all the workers today?" he asked.

"Strange thing, that," Quinn said. "They haven't shown up for over a week now. As far as I know, it has nothing to do with any of our lawsuits. But I'm certainly not complaining."

They walked past several smelly garbage bags heaped atop one another. "There used to be trash bins in the hallways," she told him, "and a trashman would take the garbage away several times a day. But the developer fired all the staff except the front desk clerks and nightguards, so there's nobody to take the garbage out for us anymore. And Mr. Roxborough here"—she pointed to a plastic-sheathed door—is a lazy old man who lets his garbage pile up in the hallway. As if the hotel doesn't have enough problems without him contributing to them." She raised her voice. "Do you hear me, Mr. Roxborough?"

If he did hear her, he didn't answer.

Quinn stopped a little farther down the hallway before a rubble-filled cavity in the wall. "This used to be my bathroom. My pyramid is an SRO—single room occupancy. No bathroom. I used to share this one with four other tenants. As well as junkies and prostitutes, I might add."

"Junkies and prostitutes?"

"The junkies would break the lock and shoot up in there. The prostitutes, on the other hand, would have a key. Three or four of them would rent a room on the floor and take turns using it with their john. The ones who weren't in the room were in the bathroom washing their bras or underwear or just sitting around smoking. And worse than the discarded needles on the floor and undergarments hanging everywhere—there was never any toilet paper! They always stole it!"

"How'd you ever live like that?"

"It's the way it was," she said simply. "Yes, you bumped into a lot of undesirable people here, but you had your friends too. We looked out for each other and supported each other through thick and thin." She indicated a door across from the bathroom that was neither boarded up nor covered in plastic. "A well-to-do writer and his wife used to live there. They were dear friends of mine. Evicted last year. They've visited me once since, but they said they wouldn't be back. They couldn't stand the condition the hotel was in."

Malcolm tried the doorknob and found it unlocked. A

short hallway opened to a series of north-facing rooms with arched-brick ceilings. The walls between the rooms had been gutted. Splintered timber, chunks of plaster, broken ornate moldings, and shards of stained-glass littered the floor. Metal framing indicated the intention of the developers to divide the cavernous space into smaller units.

"This was one of the few remaining apartments not chopped up in the 40s and 50s." Quinn scowled. "And do you see what the developer's doing to it?"

"Chopping it up."

"That's right. Chopping it up. He's turning every apartment, no matter how magnificent, into cookie-cutter rooms. I don't care how much he fancies them up, do you think Jimi Hendrix would have ever stayed in a cookie-cutter room?"

"Did Jimi Hendrix stay in this room?"

"Whenever he came to the Chelsea, yes. Devon Wilson was thrown from one of those windows there."

"Devon Wilson...?" Malcolm said, the name sounding vaguely familiar.

"Jimi Hendrix's girlfriend. And the woman who killed him."

"I thought he overdosed on barbiturates?"

Quinn shook her head, as if Malcolm had just said something terribly ill-informed. "Devon Wilson was a kind of super groupie in the 60s. She'd had flings with Eric Clapton, Mick Jagger, Miles Davis. But she always came back to Jimi Hendrix. The night before Jimi died, Devon was at a party with him that was being hosted by Kit Lambert, the manager of The Who. Their relationship was coming to an end by then. Jimi was getting fed up with all Devon's sleeping around, and there just wasn't room for her in his circle anymore. So in a desperate attempt to win his affection, she made him a cup of coffee and dumped a tablespoon of heroin into it."

"How would that win his affection?"

"Because heroin made Jimi very affectionate, and that was the only time she'd get him away from the other groupies and to herself. The thing was, Jimi had already been doing heroin all day, and the tablespoon she put in his coffee put him over the edge. He went back to his hotel and died in his sleep. And *that's* why he didn't wake in the morning. Not because he took too many sleeping pills—though I imagine those didn't help either."

"Huh," Malcolm said. "That's news to me." *And when you've been a junkie yourself*, he thought, *you usually pick up on lore like this, at some point or another.* "Do you really think Jimi Hendrix would have been drinking coffee at some big rock and roll party?"

"He might have been trying to get sober after all the heroin he'd already done. Besides, if Devon made this story up, why wouldn't she say she spiked his whiskey? Why his coffee? The truth is often in the details, Mr. Clock."

"Why would she incriminate herself in his death?"

"Because she was heartbroken she'd killed him. She was filled with guilt. At his funeral, she tried to throw herself into his open grave. When she returned to America, she lapsed into drug addiction—she'd always been an addict, but her grief pushed her over the edge. Eventually she ended up at the Hotel Chelsea—where someone threw her out one of those windows."

"Who?"

Quinn shrugged her frail shoulders. "Friends of Jimi's, more than likely. She probably should have kept her mouth shut about spiking his coffee. She was blabbing about it to everyone she knew."

"Maybe she jumped? If she was so filled with guilt...?"

"The Chelsea's walls have eyes and ears, Mr. Clock."

"And nobody spoke up to the police, or even the media?"

"And risk getting thrown out a window themselves?" She shook her head. "No, dear. People here might have loved to gossip, but they knew how to keep a secret. And believe you me, the Chelsea has more than her fair share of dark and dirty secrets."

CHAPTER 9

*In good company * The man
in the porkpie hat*

As they continued the tour, Quinn showed Malcolm many of the Hotel Chelsea's historic apartments, such as 822, where Madonna shot photographs for her raunchy black-and-white photo book *Sex*; 712, where the actor Ethan Hawke spent some time after breaking up with Uma Thurman; 614, where Arthur Miller lived along with his daughter for several years to get over Marilyn Monroe; 415, where Janis Joplin fellated Leonard Cohen (and where someone painted on her door, "Janis, you are the best fuck I ever had!"); 211, where Bob Dylan went days without sleep while writing "Sad Eyed Lady of the Lowlands" (about the woman he'd married only three months earlier); and just down the hall, 205, where Dylan Thomas fell into a coma from which he never recovered after downing eighteen straight whiskies at a nearby bar.

Quinn showed him where Arthur C. Clarke wrote the short story that would become *2001: A Space Odyssey* (and where he trained his telescope into the apartment windows across the street); where William Burroughs wrote *The Third Mind*; where the Beat poet Jack Kerouac wrote *On the Road* in one Dexedrine-fueled, three-week marathon (as well as where he had a one-night stand with Gore Vidal); and where George Kleinsinger composed the music for "Tubby the Tuba" (while keeping a tank of piranhas by his piano, which he dipped his fingers into whenever he felt drowsy).

Indeed, by the time Quinn and Malcolm reached the first

floor, Malcolm felt as though he knew the Hotel Chelsea personally.

As they entered the floor's west wing, he said, "So this is what the hotel looked like before the demolition." With run-of-the-mill fluorescent lighting, goopy-painted walls, and worn floors, it resembled any other past-its-prime hotel. However, there was also a cold, ominous feel to it, although Malcolm couldn't place his finger on why.

Quinn said, "This was what it looked like, yes, but not what it *felt* like. The Chelsea always had so much life. You felt it as soon as you entered the lobby. It permeated the hallways, and the tenants themselves. Everyone was always doing something, creating something. Now...well, now the hotel feels like a tomb, doesn't it?"

Malcolm agreed with that analogy and said, "Wrapped up in a construction site."

"Stanley put certain types of people on certain floors. Musicians on the second, tourists on the third, ordinary people on the fifth and sixth and seventh, rich and famous people in the suites on the eighth and ninth...and those he needed to keep an eye on—the waifs, strays, drag queens, and pariahs of society—closest to the reception here on the first."

"So this floor was Skid Row?"

"That's one way to put it."

They continued to chat while Malcolm photographed the unrenovated wing. On the way back to the stairwell, a man around Malcolm's age wearing a leather jacket festooned with patches, pins, and badges stumbled out of a door ahead of them. He had black spiky hair and hollowed-out eyes and cheeks. Despite being less than ten feet away, he hadn't seen them until Quinn spoke.

"Good morning, Mr. McSorley."

The man squinted at them. Initial surprise hardened to irritation. "Howsa goin', Quinn?" he said in an Irish brogue. He frowned at Malcolm. "What's the craic?"

"Hi," Malcolm said simply, as he wasn't sure what he'd just

been asked. "I'm a magazine reporter. Do you live here?"

"I do. You be writin' a story about the dump?"

"About the renovations."

He pointed across the hall. "Did you tell him who used to live there, Quinn?"

"That's Sid Vicious' old room," she said. "Or a variation of it. To discourage the punks who made pilgrimages to it from all over the world, you see, Stanley walled up the original door and merged the room with those on either side, effectively erasing it from the hotel."

The man poked a cigarette between his lips and pushed through the door to the stairwell. "Grand meetin', lad," he called over his shoulder without much sincerity.

The door swung closed.

"Who was that?" Malcolm asked.

"That was Shane McSorley," Quinn said with little fanfare. "He's lived here for about a year and fancies himself a rock star."

"Have you heard him play?"

"Goodness, no! Why would I ever want to listen to that sort of racket?"

Malcolm held out his hand. "Well, thank you so much for the tour, Quinn. You've been a wealth of information."

She shook in that dry, fragile grasp of hers. "It's been my pleasure, Mr. Clock. I would like to read your story about the hotel when it comes out."

"I'll drop off a copy of the magazine when it's printed."

"Don't leave it with Darnell," she cautioned. "He'll just toss it out. Horrible, horrible man."

"He seemed okay to me."

"He's on the developer's side. He hates the remaining tenants. He won't even say hello to me when I enter the building. He just gives me the evil eye, like *I'm* doing something wrong living where I've lived for the last fifty years."

"I'll deliver the magazine to you personally then," Malcolm assured her. As an afterthought, he added, "Darnell mentioned to me that some of the residents believe the hotel is haunted. What do you think about that?"

Quinn didn't bat an eyelid. "I think, Mr. Clock," she said curtly, "that if the Hotel Chelsea has any ghosts, they would be turning over in their graves at what's being done to their former home."

◆ ◆ ◆

As he stepped into the lobby, Malcolm discovered the reception desk unmanned. While setting the hard hat he'd borrowed on the counter for Darnell to retrieve (whenever he returned), it struck him that the abandoned desk was a powerful symbol of the hotel in its current state. He took out the Nikon and clicked a photograph of it.

Turning toward the front doors, tucking the camera back into his bag, he jumped in fright for the second time that morning.

A man in a beige trench coat and a porkpie hat stood off to his right, facing a blank section of wall, his face nearly touching it.

"Uh, hello?" Malcolm said, unnerved.

The man didn't move or reply.

Malcolm took a single step toward him, but that was all, for an inexplicable wrongness had encased him like a cold second skin.

"You all right?" he asked.

The man ignored him.

And that was fine with Malcolm, he realized. The uncanny scene was becoming quietly threatening, and he wanted nothing to do with the guy or his problems.

He left the hotel without looking back.

CHAPTER 10

The basement

The basement of the Hotel Chelsea was a dark, dungeon-like warren of hallways and rooms with dirty brick walls and ancient, exposed piping overhead. Jolene Hathcock had been down there twice in the past to loot from the graveyard of discarded junk that had accumulated in a storage room over the years. Most of the stuff was either broken and rotting furniture from the 60s and 70s that belonged to the hotel, or whatever former tenants couldn't be bothered taking with them when they checked out.

On Jolene's first visit, she scored a chipped yet perfectly functioning chest of drawers. She also discovered an old pirate trunk made of solid oak with bronze lion head rings. She and a friend lugged the trunk up to her room on the first floor, where she used it as a coffee table. But given that the room was a tiny 220-square-foot space without a kitchen or bathroom, the chest soon became more of a hindrance rather than the vintage centerpiece she'd anticipated. Reluctantly, she dragged it down the hallway to the elevators, where she left it with a note that read FREE!, and that was the last she ever saw of it.

On her second visit, which was more than five years ago now, she'd hoped to acquire a decent-sized mirror, as the one she'd owned had been little larger than a hardback novel. She had no luck, and finding nothing else worth taking, she decided to explore the rest of the basement. The rooms closest to the stairs included one stocked with hundreds of cans of paint that had been used to refurbish the hotel over the years;

another stocked with bedding and towels, soaps, toilet paper, and shelf upon shelf of cleaning supplies; and a third cluttered with a small hardware store of tools, plumbing and electrical supplies, and tins brimming with nails, screws, and bolts.

The farther along the main hallway she went, the more decrepit the basement became, with sections of the walls crumbling and cobwebs dusting the low ceilings. The boiler room was a huge jigsaw of pipes and valves and gauges that looked as though they'd been excised from the pages of a Dickens novel. The insulation covering the steel pipes was frayed, the tanks were rusted, and much of the machinery appeared inoperable.

Beyond this point, the overhead fluorescents ceased to function. To navigate the witch-hat blackness, Jolene used her phone as a flashlight. The remaining rooms contained miscellaneous items such as moldy mattresses, numerous ladders, a variety of building materials, garbage bins, rolls of carpet and foam underlay, and stacks upon stacks of cardboard boxes containing who knew what.

To her surprise, however, after passing through a couple of doorways into the farthermost room, she discovered a bookcase crammed with books and magazines. Yet unlike everything else she'd come across, it was dust- and grime-free. In fact, the books and magazines were arranged with some aesthetic consideration.

A light much brighter than the glow from her phone washed over the bookshelf. At the same time, a gruff voice demanded, "What are you doing in my bedroom?"

Jolene whirled around, her heart lodged in her throat. A disheveled, scarecrow-thin man with tangled gray hair that fell to his shoulders and a suspicious, pale face stood not ten feet away, a heavy-duty yellow flashlight gripped in one hand.

"I'm—I'm sorry," she stammered, squinting at the light stinging her eyes. "I didn't know this was...your bedroom."

The man lowered the flashlight beam to the floor. In the backsplash, Jolene saw she was indeed in an improvised bedroom, as there was a mattress with pillows and bedding in a corner, a little rug, two chairs, and a few other pieces of furniture.

"You were going to steal my books!" the man said.

"No, I wasn't. I swear. I was just looking around."

"You better leave right now," the man growled, "or I'm going to tell Stanley on you."

Under different circumstances, Jolene would have found the threat amusing because Stanley Bard likely didn't know he had a hobo living in his basement, and if he did, he would have immediately evicted the freeloader. But even though her initial fright had dispersed, she promptly took her leave, returning through the zigzag of doors and halls until she was back at the stairs, bathed in the safety of the overhead fluorescents.

She never told Stanley about the hobo. To her, he was just some homeless man who had snuck into the hotel to get off the streets, or a tenant who had been evicted but had nowhere else to go. She believed he was harmless. She was not going to be the one to ruin his secret life.

◆ ◆ ◆

Today marked Jolene's third trip to the basement. She had not come for more furniture; she had come for doors.

Over the last two years, many of the original doors to the rooms in the Hotel Chelsea had been removed, as they didn't meet modern fire safety codes. She had not given them any real thought until yesterday morning when she woke with the inspired idea to do rubbings of them.

Frottage—the technique of rubbing charcoal or another medium over paper laid on a relief-like surface—was her art and her profession, what paid the bills (though just barely). For years, she had been doing rubbings of the gravestones of famous people. She wouldn't simply make a replica of the names and dates and epitaphs, but rather she'd arrange the lettering and textures and inscribed patterns and images into a collage that told a story. Sometimes she'd use colors to emphasize a theme, such as the blue wax she'd used for the legendary blues guitarist Muddy Waters' rubbing, or the crimson wax she'd used for "Son of Sam" David Berkowitz's. Other times she'd combine the rubbings of two gravestones into a single collage if the celebrities had something in common...or sometimes to juxtapose their differences in acting or politics or whatever. Really, there were no rules.

This past week or two, Jolene's art had been more inspired than ever. Instead of visiting cemeteries once or twice a week, she'd been sneaking into them every single night. The problem was, she was running out of famous gravestones in New York City, and she didn't have money to travel until she received her next paycheck.

Which was why she was so excited about the historic doors. She didn't have to travel anywhere. They were right here in the hotel's basement.

She hoped.

It had been over a year now since she'd learned that the doors were being stored down here, and for all she knew, they might have been tossed out a long time ago.

At the bottom of the stairs, Jolene flicked the light switch. The overhead fluorescents didn't turn on. She flicked the nub repeatedly before giving up.

Damn construction, she thought angrily, digging her phone from her pocket and using the flashlight app to light her way. With a sense of déjà vu—and trying not to think too much about the homeless man who may or may not still be creeping around—she began her search.

◆ ◆ ◆

Jolene found the doors in the hotel's former trash room. There must have been more than a hundred of them leaning against the walls, stacked seven or eight deep. They weren't anything special to look at. Most of them were chipped and scuffed, the white paint peeling. Many didn't have hinges or doorknobs, and some had big Xs spray-painted across their faces. Yet none of this concerned her. What mattered was their connection to the past and the famous people who had walked through them. This would be possible to chronicle because each door still featured its little bronze plaque at the top and corresponding room number. Here was 126, the door to the room that both Bette Davis and Iggy Pop had stayed in, albeit decades apart. And here was the fifth-floor door to the room where Tennessee Williams had lived, as well as Jon Bon Jovi. And here, 211, the door to the room that Bob Marley, Bob Dylan, and Lee Jaffee had all called their own.

Jolene had uncovered many of these connections yesterday at the New York Public Library, where she had spent hours researching which celebrities had lived where in the Hotel Chelsea. Yet her friend Quinn, who had lived at the hotel since time out of mind, had proved to be an invaluable help as well.

After a preliminary examination of the stacks, Jolene began moving the doors she wanted to do rubbings into the center of the room. The process was rather like playing Solitaire. To work her way through the first stack she had to transfer the unwanted doors to other stacks and then back to where the first stack had once been.

Throughout the labor-intensive work, she kept an eye out for the most infamous door of all, 100, behind which Sid Vicious had murdered his beloved Nancy. Quinn had told Jolene she likely wouldn't find it, as it had been removed decades ago, but she was—

A loud noise reverberated from somewhere within the basement. It had sounded like...she didn't know exactly. She strained her ears to hear it again even as her muscles tensed.

She heard nothing more.

She eased the door she was holding back against its stack as quietly as possible. Retrieving her phone off the floor, she went to the hallway and listened.

A vague feeling of unease had gripped her, akin to what a child might feel while wandering into an unknown section of forest. It was telling her she was in danger, telling her to flee back upstairs where she would find light and familiarity.

She didn't run, because she wasn't certain what exactly she'd heard. For all she knew, the source of the noise might have been one of those stacks of boxes falling to the floor.

All on its own?

"Hello?" she called in the strongest voice she could muster, as she thought about the hobo whose bedroom she had stumbled into. He must have made the noise. The question was why? Had he heard her rummaging through the doors and decided to try to scare her off? As much as she'd like to believe this, she couldn't, not really, because if the man still lived down here, he had not lasted so long by trying to scare off anyone who ventured to the basement; he had lasted by remaining silent and hidden.

Maybe it's Edie Sedgwick? she thought, knowing she was needlessly freaking herself out, but unable to stop herself. *Edie Sedgwick, or more precisely, the ghost of Edie Sedgwick, coming to finish what she'd started...*

Earlier in the week Jolene had woken in the middle of the night to find herself standing in a T-shirt and underwear inside Room 105, where Edie Sedgwick had once lived in the 1960s. She had been bewildered. She had never sleepwalked before in her life. She had also been afraid because the dream she'd woken from was still crystal clear. In it, Edie was gluing on her thick eyelashes by candlelight when she accidentally knocked the candle over and set fire to the drapes, just as Jolene had heard the woman had done in real life. As the flames spread, Edie scrambled to the closet, where she screamed for help. Jolene, however, had been unable to help. She'd been rooted to the floor and could do nothing but watch in horror as the flames whooshed around her.

Yet what had frightened Jolene even more than the dream itself was that...it hadn't *felt* like a dream. It had felt as real as a recent memory.

Even so, she'd told herself it was a dream because for it to have been anything other than that would have been impossible. She told this to herself over and over as she lay in bed that night, tossing and turning, until she eventually fell back to sleep.

Sure enough, upon waking in the reassuring morning light, the dream felt exactly like a dream and nothing else.

Yet that was then and this was now.

Jolene was no longer in the safety of her bedroom; there was no rosy light to soothe her mind. She was in the bowels of the Hotel Chelsea—a hotel that had had more than its share of haunted tales told about it over the years—and her midnight fears had come back with a vengeance.

Managing one last hello—weaker than the others, barely more than a hoarse whisper—Jolene dashed to the stairs, ascending them two at a time, all the while waiting—expecting—some cold hand to drag her back down into the darkness.

CHAPTER 11

*The curious neighbor & the
equally curious bard*

Malcolm spent the rest of the morning and afternoon at his desk at the *City Living* office on Sixth Avenue, researching the Hotel Chelsea and drafting a rough outline for his article. The storm clouds that had been gathering all day finally burst while he was walking home. The rain came as though a faucet in the sky had been turned on: hard, cold, incessant. He was soaked to the skin within seconds, and soon rainwater was gushing along the curbs to the gutters. The first burst of thunder followed shortly: a pent-up explosion that seemed to shake the city.

By the time Malcolm reached his pre-war, six-floor walkup, he was as wet as if he'd just jumped into the Hudson River. He usually didn't mind climbing the stairs to his studio on the building's top floor, but right then was an exception, as doing so with his clothes and shoes saturated with water seemed like twice the usual effort.

He was rummaging through his photography bag for his keys when the door next to his opened and his neighbor, Nikki, emerged. She was girl-next-door cute with dark brown eyes, crimped blonde hair that fell halfway down her back, and pretty features she covered with too much makeup, including a garish amount of lipstick and blush. Today she had an all-green look going on, from blouse to pants and even her socks.

The thing with Nikki, he had learned, was that he never

knew if what she was telling him was the truth or not. On one occasion, for instance, she told him she was from a happy home in Florida. Another time, she told him she was from an affluent suburb in Boston.

He didn't know what to make of the inconsistencies, and he'd never asked.

"Hi, Mac!" she said, eyeing his wet clothes. "Fall in a puddle?"

"It's raining outside if you haven't noticed."

"The National Weather Service is saying Brooklyn and Manhattan are going to flood."

"I don't doubt it—and you're going outside without an umbrella?"

"No, I'm just going down to check my mail. You know what I'm waiting for?"

"No idea."

"Underwear."

"You order your underwear online?"

"I've joined a club. You pay a reoccurring subscription fee, and they send you a new pair of underwear each month."

"You must have a lot of underwear."

"I've only been a member for a few months now. What do you say? Want to join the club with me?"

"I'm pretty happy with my current selection."

"Your loss. Hey, do you want to come by for dinner later?"

The invitation surprised Malcolm. Nikki had lived in the co-op for two years. She'd spent the first year on the second floor and the last year as his neighbor on the sixth. During that time they'd bumped into each other often, but she'd never invited him to her place before.

He wondered if she was asking him on a date, but he quickly dismissed that idea. She had a boyfriend. At least, Malcolm had seen the same guy leaving her apartment on a handful of different mornings.

He said, "Thanks for the offer, but I have a lot of work to do tonight."

"You don't cook," she said.

"How do you know that?"

"I've never seen you with groceries, and I always see you with takeout."

She was right. His cupboards were all but bare. He said, "Manhattan has great takeout. Cooking's redundant."

"You really want to go hunting for food in this rain?"

"You're persistent."

"I'm making lasagna, Caesar salad, and garlic bread. A home-cooked Italian dinner is perfect for a stormy night like this. What do you say?"

A home-cooked meal did sound good. "What time?"

"Seven?"

"Okay—should I bring anything?"

"I have wine, but if you prefer something else, bring that. This is going to be fun!" She continued down the hallway to the stairs, green hips swaying and green arms swinging.

Malcolm watched her go, wondering if he'd agreed to a date after all.

◆ ◆ ◆

As soon as he opened the door to his apartment, the tiny pug attacked him with unbound energy, his short-muzzled face grinning and his curled tail wagging.

"Okay! Okay!" Malcolm said, trying to shake the puppy off his legs. "Give it a rest, will you?"

He went to the small kitchen, grabbed the bag of dog food off the counter, and filled one of his cereal bowls with kibble. He set the bowl on the floor and said, "Enjoy."

The pug dug in.

Malcolm went searching for any messes the little imp may have made, and he was pleasantly surprised when he saw a turd in the litter box in the bathroom, even though there was a puddle of urine next to it on the floor.

"At least you're improving," he said.

After cleaning up the pee with toilet paper and washing his hands, Malcolm returned to the kitchen and poured a gin on the rocks. Drink in hand, he went to the studio's balcony doors and watched the storm rage outside. There were three advantages to being on the top floor of a walk-up. One, he got daily exercise. Two, the rent was cheaper than on the lower floors. And three, his view peeked out above the surrounding neighborhood, offering an open view of the city.

Tonight, however, he could see little more than slashing rain and the twinkling lights and silhouettes of the downtown skyscrapers in the distance.

Sitting at his desk, Malcolm flipped open his laptop and accessed the draft of the Hotel Chelsea article on which he'd been working. He didn't know how other magazine reporters or journalists went about their writing, but his involved sketching out a basic structure for his article, then dumping everything in his head onto the page in a stream-of-consciousness manner. Once the bones were down, he would slow up and flesh it out, draft by draft, until he had created a compelling story.

He had already sketched out the structure of the Hotel Chelsea article at work, so now he went into stream-of-consciousness mode. His fingers flew over the keyboard as he wove together what he'd gathered from his visit to the hotel this morning with everything else he'd learned online.

He was so immersed in his work he barely heard the knocking at the door. His fingers paused over the keyboard. Another knock. The pug was yapping excitedly.

Reluctantly, Malcolm got up and opened the door a wedge, keeping his leg in front of the gap so the puppy didn't escape into the hallway.

It was Nikki, still dressed all in green, and holding a plateful of food.

"Oh, hey," he said. "I—uh—thought I was coming to your place. What time is it?"

"Eight o'clock," she said.

Malcolm blinked. "Eight!" He'd arrived home at about 5:30 p.m., which meant he'd been writing nonstop for more than two hours. He usually didn't get through one hour without taking several breaks.

"You must have really been into your work," she said, holding out the plate. "I'm sure all that thinking works up an appetite. It's cold, but you can heat it up in the microwave. You *do* have a microwave, don't you?"

In fact, he didn't. "I feel terrible," he said. "The time just got away from me. Look, give me a few minutes to clean up, and I can come over—"

"It's okay. I've already eaten. Take this."

He opened the door farther and accepted the plate. The pug squeezed past his calf and gamboled around his neighbor's legs.

"Oh, you're so cute!" Nikki said, picking up the dog and nose-kissing him. "You're so cute, aren't you?" she went on in a singsong way. "What an adorable little thing you are!" To Malcolm, "I didn't know you had a dog. Is it a boy or girl?"

"I'm babysitting it for my brother for a couple of weeks—"

"*Dog*sitting."

"Dogsitting," he said. "And I'm pretty sure it's a boy."

"Pretty sure? How can you not know?" She lifted the squirming puppy above her head. "Yup, a boy, all right."

"Why don't you come in for a bit?"

"You're persistent," she said, parroting what he'd told her earlier.

"Guess it runs in the building."

"Let me go get my wine. I've been drinking alone. Can I take the puppy with me?"

"Please. And don't bring him back."

"You're so mean!"

Malcolm left the food on the kitchen counter and changed into a fresh shirt. He'd just finished gargling mouthwash when Nikki knocked on the door again. She'd changed into a boxy blazer over a white blouse and high-waisted jeans. She held a bottle of red wine in one hand and the pug in the other.

"You're a fast changer," he observed.

"I had this outfit on earlier when I thought you were coming over. You changed too."

"Just my shirt. The other one I'd been wearing all day…"

"It's always nice to put on a clean shirt."

"I got this one in Chinatown."

"I like Chinese food. Sweet and sour pork—yum."

"Chow mein if it's prepared in light oil."

"Kung Pao chicken."

"Egg Foo Young—"

"Let's just stop this right now," Nikki interrupted him. "Are we going to spend the evening talking about Chinese food in the hallway, or are you going to invite me inside?"

Malcolm stepped back to let Nikki in and closed the door behind her. She set the puppy down on the ground, and he immediately began nipping at her ankles.

"Nice place," she said. "Looks just like mine but with different furniture."

"You should see the apartment I was in today. It's inside a Mayan-like spire on top of the Hotel Chelsea. An old lady lives in it."

"Why were you on top of the Hotel Chelsea?"

"I'm writing a story about the place."

"Is that what you were working on so hard that you forgot all about our dinner?" she asked as they moved into the kitchen. She saw the plate of food on the counter. "Are you going to eat now?"

"I'll have a drink first."

Malcolm built another gin, while Nikki poured herself a glass of wine. In the living area, he gestured for her to take a seat on the red leather sofa, and he sat across from her in a gray armchair.

"So what's this story about?" she asked him.

"Mostly the ongoing renovations at the hotel. The place is a mess. Aside from the woman on the roof, there are about eighty other tenants still living there. They're not happy, and I don't blame them. There're holes in the walls and wires and pipes sticking out all over the place. Someone committed suicide in their room recently."

Nikki's heavily mascaraed eyes widened. "What! Because of the construction?"

"I don't know the reason. But I saw the man's apartment. Apparently he slit his wrists—but it was like he just kept going about whatever he'd been doing because there was blood everywhere."

"Maybe he was making a point. If he killed himself in protest of the construction, he might have wanted his death to be as dramatic as possible."

Malcolm nodded. "You could be right. I didn't think of that." He fell silent as he recalled the face in the bathroom mirror. "Do you believe in ghosts?"

"Ooh," Nikki said, sipping her wine. "You think a ghost got him?" The pug had joined them in the living room and was snuffling Nikki's feet. She set her wine aside and picked him up. "I love dogs. I've always wanted one. But I start sneezing if I'm around them for too long."

"Didn't you tell me you used to have a dog?"

"Did I?" she asked, nonplussed.

She did. It was during the same conversation she told him she was from Boston. According to her, it was a black-and-white Border Collie that would always escape her yard and chase cars down the street until one day it was run over.

"You said you had a Border Collie."

"No, I don't think I would have said that. You're probably confusing me with someone else."

"You're probably right," he said, though he knew he wasn't mistaken.

"Anyway, back to the Chelsea…?"

"A lot of people have died there over the years. Doesn't that give it ghost cred?"

Nikki laughed. "Have you ever been to prison, Mac?"

He frowned. "No."

"Had a teen baby mamma?"

He shook his head, confused.

"Been shot and survived?"

"What are you talking about, Nikki?"

"*Cred*?" she said. "White guys from Maine aren't allowed to say cred."

Malcolm rolled his eyes. "How do you know I'm from Maine?"

"You told me you were from Augusta when we first met."

"Did I?"

"Glad I left such an impression on you."

"I do remember..." he said. "I was carrying a vacuum cleaner I'd just bought. We met in the lobby. You were going out."

"Where was *I* born?"

"Boston?"

"Nope."

"Florida?"

"Nope."

"I think you told me you were from one of those two places."

"I don't think so. You're probably confusing me for someone else."

Malcolm stared at her. He couldn't decide if she was pulling his leg or batshit crazy.

"So come on," she said. "Where was I born?"

She had a neutral accent, so Malcolm guessed, "Nebraska?"

"Cold."

"Kansas?"

"Cold."

"Vermont?"

"Col*der*."

"I have no idea, Nikki. Do you want me to run off the other forty-seven states?"

"California," she said with a sigh. "I told you that that day you were carrying the vacuum. I said, 'I'm from L.A.,' and you said, 'You don't look like a L.A. girl. What's my last name?"

"I don't know."

"De Santis! It's right there on my mailbox. How have you never noticed?"

"I don't look at other people's mailboxes."

"My parents emigrated from Italy when I was two. My name is actually Noémie, but I changed it to Nikki. I like Nikki much better."

"It suits you." He was one hundred percent sure she'd never told him she was from California, and her mind games were really starting to trip him out, so he said, "We're getting off topic. We were talking about ghosts..."

"That's right," Nikki said. "And I don't think the Hotel Chelsea has ghost *cred* because ghosts don't haunt hotels. They're too noisy, too many people coming and going. That's like a ghost haunting a train station. It doesn't happen. Ghosts prefer quiet places. Abandoned old houses and graveyards and that kind of stuff."

"Ghosts haunted the hotel in *The Shining*," Malcolm pointed out.

"That was a movie, or a book. Anyway, it was a mostly *deserted* hotel. That's a bit different."

"The Chelsea isn't exactly Grand Central. It felt dead inside."

Nikki studied him curiously. "I think *you* believe in ghosts, Mac."

"I don't believe in ghosts," he said simply. "But when I was in the room of the man who committed suicide—"

"Why were you in his room?"

"I wanted to see it."

"That's a little morbid, isn't it? I'm not going to go missing tonight, am I, Mac?"

"I'm writing a story about the hotel," he said, crunching a small ice cube between his teeth. "Anything that can add color to it is relevant. As I was saying—when I was in the man's room, I stuck my head into the bathroom and saw a face in the mirror."

Nikki seemed unimpressed. "When I look in the mirror," she said, "I see a face of a woman. She's really beautiful."

"It wasn't *my* face," Malcolm clarified.

"You're saying you saw a ghost?"

"No, I think I was spooked by all the blood in the room and my imagination went overboard."

"Hmmm...."

"What?"

"I don't believe you."

"Why not?"

"If you think you simply spooked yourself with your own reflection," she said, "then why are you asking me if I believe in ghosts? The fact you *are* asking means that you, or maybe just a part of you that you're not acknowledging, believes what you saw might be a ghost."

Malcolm shook his head. "You're overthinking it, Nikki. I don't think what I saw was a ghost."

"Why not?"

"I told you. I don't believe ghosts exist."

"Why not?"

"Oh, I don't know," he said flippantly, "maybe because I value science and secularism over myth and superstition." He crunched another ice cube. "Look, what do ghosts do? They scare us. They go 'boo.' That's about it. They don't do anything other than that. They have no purpose other than that. The only reason they exist is to scare human beings. That's because we've made them up to scare us."

"Well, I happen to believe in ghosts. And I don't think they just want to scare us. I think they live on a different plane or dimension or whatever you want to call it. We're energy, they're energy, and sometimes our energies cross paths. Maybe your face scared the guy in the mirror as much as his did you?"

"Have you ever seen a ghost?"

"Yes, I have," she said confidently. "When I was younger, I

woke in the middle of the night and couldn't move. I could barely breathe. There was this heavy weight on my chest. When I looked...I don't know how to describe what I saw. But it terrified me."

"You experienced sleep paralysis," he told her.

Nikki frowned. "What are you talking about?"

"I did a story on sleep a while back. Sleep paralysis occurs when a person wakes up while they're still in the dream-inducing REM stage of sleep, in which their body is paralyzed. A lot of people experience it at least once in their lives. Some also report difficulty breathing and hallucinations."

Nikki huffed. "It wasn't sleep paralysis, Mac, thank you very much. I know what I saw."

"What do you think it was?" he asked. "The spirit of a dead person? Why would he or she want to sit on your chest in the middle of the night?"

"I don't know what it was. Ghosts don't have to be spirits. They could be anything. I'm just saying, you have to be pretty naïve to believe there are only the three dimensions you live in."

"What are the other dimensions like?"

"How am I supposed to know? I'm not a scientist. But there's a lot of science out there on other dimensions. Maybe you should read up on it for your story?"

"I'm not writing a ghost story. I'm writing a..." He frowned.

"What?" Nikki asked.

Malcolm's lips tightened. He could recall the outline of the article he'd whipped together at work earlier, but he couldn't remember a single word he'd written after arriving home.

For a terrible moment he wondered if he'd written anything at all.

"Mac?" Nikki said.

Malcolm blinked. "Forgot what I was going to say, that's all." He cleared his throat. "Another drink?"

After Nikki left an hour later, Malcolm sat down at his laptop and opened the Hotel Chelsea document. At worst, he expected to find the pages filled with something crazy like, "All work and no play makes Jack a dull boy"; at best, a rote chronology of the hotel's past, present, and uncertain future. But what he spent the next ten minutes reading was a sweeping, romantic narrative of the soul of a hotel that had served a vital role for some of the greatest artists of the last century, in a city where art and capitalism were in constant competition.

By the time he had read the last (and unfinished) sentence, his pulse was racing almost as fast as his thoughts.

He got up and went to the balcony doors. The rain fell in slanting arrows, pelting the glass and boiling through the street. He ran a hand through his hair and exhaled loudly, not sure if he was excited or frightened by his inexplicable burst of productivity.

In the kitchen, he poured another gin over ice and returned to his laptop to see if he could finish what he'd started.

CHAPTER 12

*Midnight miracle * Past
mistakes * An invitation*

Malcolm woke at an unknown hour to find himself sprawled out on the floor of his apartment, fully clothed and the light on. His mouth was cotton dry, and something rough and wet was licking his face. He pushed away the happy-go-lucky pug and sat up, groaning as a headache buzz-sawed through his head.

He noticed the bottle of Tanqueray gin on the floor nearby. It was empty.

Surely he hadn't drunk a fifth of booze last night?

He did the math. He'd had a drink when he came home, two with Nikki, another after she left...so four, about a quarter of the bottle.

Nevertheless, he certainly *felt* as though he'd polished off the entire thing. And that might explain why he'd blacked out on the floor—and blacked out he had, for he couldn't remember a thing about last night after Nikki had left...

No, not true. He'd worked on the Hotel Chelsea article.

A shot of dopamine raced through him as he recalled just how good the article was.

No, not simply good, he thought. *It's one of the best pieces I've ever written.*

Getting carefully to his feet so as not to antagonize the Freddy Krueger inside his head, Malcolm looked at his laptop. The screen was black. He tapped the keyboard. It didn't wake. Then he noticed the battery indicator was red.

He glanced at the balcony doors. It was dark outside and still raining.

He went to the kitchen. The clock on the wall told him it was almost 7:30 a.m. If not for the storm, it would have been bright outside already. He filled a glass with water and gulped it down, spilling a good amount on his shirt. When the glass was empty, he refilled it and drank more slowly.

The ugly-cute pug was looking up expectantly at him and wagging his tail.

Malcolm filled the bowl on the floor with kibble, then went searching for the laptop's power adapter. He found it on the floor by the sofa, retrieved his laptop, and plugged in the cord. Then he went to the bathroom to take a shower.

By the time he had dried off, he felt marginally better. He sat on the sofa, opened the computer on his lap, and powered it on. Once it booted up, he clicked on the Hotel Chelsea article.

Filled with anticipation, he scrolled to the end of the document and discovered it was twelve pages long—twice as many as he'd completed before Nikki had knocked on his door.

If they're all as good as the first six had been...

He started reading the article from the beginning.

❖ ❖ ❖

Standing beneath a black umbrella, Malcolm watched as a man across the street hurried through the downpour to the front doors of a colorfully painted former synagogue.

Someone had once told Malcolm that the chains of addiction were too weak to feel until they were too strong to break —and this analogy described his battle with drugs intimately.

His addictions began while he was a freshman in Brooklyn College. Pretty much out of the gate, he began drinking booze and smoking pot on a regular basis. He didn't think there was anything wrong with it; after all, everybody else was doing the same. The difference, which he didn't identify at the time, was that while his friends would make their way back to their dorm rooms and wake for class the next morning, he would keep partying until he passed out wherever the night had taken him. Halfway through his sophomore year, he'd gotten to the point where he would experiment with whatever someone put in front of his face. By his senior year, he'd developed a serious addiction to benzodiazepines, opiates, and cocaine. When Xanax and heroin became his daily go-to substances of choice, he fell hopelessly behind in all his classes and dropped out of college six months before graduation.

That summer Malcolm got a job in a Blockbuster Video rental store, and his life outside of work revolved around finding drugs, abusing them, and finding more. Deep down, he wanted to stop using. Every morning he woke and told himself he wouldn't get high that day. However, his addiction always prevailed over his willpower, and after work he would find himself with a needle in his arm.

This self-destructive lifestyle continued for another year before he sought treatment. Over a six-month period he tried everything from a detox center, to a mental and behavioral health hospital, to a wilderness program. And while each attempt helped him squeeze out a week of sobriety, the problem was that it was easier to not be sober, and he always resumed using immediately upon returning home.

He remained stuck in the vicious cycle for the next several years. He'd use to the point where his life would become unmanageable, he'd get sober for a week, things would start to look up...then he would leave the program and use again.

Malcolm's low point came at the beginning of 2010. His girlfriend died of an overdose, and he knew if he didn't make a drastic lifestyle change, he was going to end up dead himself, either by an overdose or by his own hand.

So he went cold turkey—and stuck with it. That first month was the most difficult of his life, not only because of the withdrawal symptoms, but also because of how lonely he felt being sober. He had lost the ability to connect emotionally with other people, which prevented him from repairing his old friendships or making new ones. Moreover, deep down in the back of his mind, he still didn't really want to succeed. If he began to enjoy sobriety, he would never do drugs again—and that possibility depressed him almost as much as the sad state of his life.

At his first 12-step meeting, an avuncular, reassuring man named Buck approached him and offered to be his sponsor. Malcolm didn't know how the whole sponsorship thing worked, but he said yes anyway. The following morning they met for coffee, and Buck told him, "If you could get sober yourself, don't you think you would have done it already? Listen to the guys who've made it through what you're going through." Buck handed him a list of phone numbers of the recovering addicts in his support group and told him to call one person each night to begin building healthy relationships. Malcolm followed the advice, slowly forging his own support group, and his sobriety took on a new meaning. It no longer meant isolation, misery, and boredom. The other recovering addicts taught him how to cope with his emotions, begin repairing relationships, rediscover old hobbies, and start enjoying a life that didn't obsess over where the next fix would come from.

Malcolm went back to college and finished his undergraduate degree in journalism. At the age of twenty-eight, he got an internship with City Living, which ultimately led to a full-time position as a staff writer. Admittedly he still boozed too much, but he hadn't touched any drug stronger than aspirin in over three years.

With the rain hammering the ground around him, Malcolm crossed the road to the 6th Street Community Center, hoping the bad weather hadn't deterred many of his fellow Narcotics Anonymous regulars from attending the meeting.

◆ ◆ ◆

Back in his apartment two hours later, Malcolm was reading over the Hotel Chelsea article for the fifth time (not to proofread it but because he was still so damned impressed by the quality of the writing and the narrative) when his cell phone rang.

The number was private.

He hesitated a moment before answering.

"Malcolm speaking," he said.

"Hello, Mr. Clock, it's Quinn, from the Hotel Chelsea."

"Hi, Quinn," he said, surprised to hear her voice. "What can I do for you?"

"First, let me tell you again how much I enjoyed your company yesterday. It's so nice to speak to someone open-minded about what's been going on at the Chelsea. Have you started writing your article?"

"As a matter of fact, I have."

"That's good to hear. And that's the reason I'm calling. Some of the other tenants and I get together every now and then in one of our apartments for dinner. When I mentioned to them that you're doing a story on the hotel, they practically pleaded with me to invite you to dinner. They're a very colorful bunch, and I'm sure you would find their company quite enjoyable."

Malcolm was flattered by the offer. "When were they thinking?"

"Have you eaten already?"

"Tonight?" he said, glancing through the balcony doors at the rain-thrashed night. "I haven't," he added. "But I've already been out in this weather today, and I'm not too eager to do so again."

"I understand," she said. "I wouldn't want to venture out in this weather either. It's just that everybody was so excited to meet you. They have so many of their own stories to tell you about the Chelsea. I thought the earlier you heard them —if you wanted to hear them at all—the more convenient it would be for your article…"

Malcolm thought that over. If Quinn's neighbors had even

half the number of stories that she'd had about the hotel, he could hardly pass up the chance to hear them.

The clock at the bottom corner of his laptop screen indicated it was a quarter to seven. "What time were they thinking of having dinner?" he asked.

"We usually get together about eight o'clock. I apologize for getting in touch last minute, but Darnell has been away from the reception desk all afternoon, so I wasn't able to get your number. We could make it later if that's better suited to you?"

"The Chelsea is only a ten-minute cab ride from my place. Eight would be fine."

"Oh, how wonderful! I really think you will enjoy yourself."

"Is there anything I should bring?"

"No, no. We usually just order something in. Our host's name is Harvey Collings. His apartment is on the eighth floor. Number 829. Tell Darnell if he's still on his shift, or the night-guard, though I don't know why it would be any business of theirs. So see you at eight?"

"Harvey Collings. 829," he said. "I'll see you there shortly."

◆ ◆ ◆

The yellow taxicab pulled up in front of the Hotel Chelsea at five to eight. Some of the hotel's neon letters had burned out, and they now spelled:

HOTEL HEL

Fitting, Malcolm thought as he paid the driver and ducked through the rain to the hotel's awning.

Darnell, ensconced behind the reception desk, buzzed him into the lobby.

"Forget something here, did you?" he asked.

"Quinn invited me to dinner," Malcolm said. "She wants me to meet some of her neighbors."

"So that's why she wanted your number?" Darnell's eyes

narrowed suspiciously. "Why does she want you to meet her neighbors?"

"Said they'd have a lot of stories about the Chelsea that might be helpful for my article."

"I told you that you gotta take what these crazies say with a grain of salt. I bet all they want to do is badmouth me and my boss."

"The article is all but finished, Darnell. I don't know how much more I can add to it."

"Already finished? You must be one hell of a writer. Used to take me a week or two in high school to write a paper. And that was only a thousand words."

"It practically wrote itself," Malcolm said, punching the button to call the elevator.

"How many people are going to be at this dinner?"

"I don't know. Quinn didn't tell me. She just said it was in 829."

"Ah shit…"

The elevator arrived with a bright *ding!* Malcolm stepped into the car and held the door open with his outstretched arm. "What's the problem?"

Darnell shook his head. "No problem—it's just that 829 is Harvey Collings' apartment. He's one of those fruitcakes I told you about who thinks the hotel is haunted. If he unloads that bullshit on you, just smile and nod, you hear me?"

"I hear you," Malcolm said, removing his arm and letting the door slide closed.

CHAPTER 13

The dinner party

The plastic sheathing covering the door to Room 829 was unzipped and hanging open. Malcolm could hear conversation coming from the other side of it. He knocked.

The door opened a moment later and Quinn appeared, her hazel eyes shining welcomingly. She was once again dressed Jazz Age-chic in another flapper dress, this one black and gold, as well as a lace shawl, black fishnet stockings, and gold heels. A rhinestone headpiece spruced up her blonde wig, and beaded jewelry wreathed her neck and black-gloved wrists. All she needed to finish off the Daisy Buchanan look, Malcolm thought, was a slender cigarette holder pinched between her fingers.

"Welcome back to ze Hotel Chelsea, Mr. Clock!" she said in her Romanian accent, smiling at him. "Thank you so much for joining us this evening. Please come in."

Malcolm followed her down a hallway papered with magenta and indigo stripes and into a spacious room featuring polished parquet floors, a high ceiling, and three large windows. The room was painted completely red: walls, ceiling, moldings, fireplace, mantel, all red. The furniture was a mishmash of expensive-looking antiques and garage-sale bargains, including a trashy chandelier. About a dozen Greek- and Roman-inspired busts occupied the nooks and crannies (though Malcolm also spotted one of Batman and one of Einstein). All were accessorized with colorful wigs, crowns or tiaras, feathered boas, sequined hats, and masquerade eye masks.

Standing in the middle of the burlesque-inspired room was a pair of well-presented men holding amber-filled, cut-crystal tumblers.

"Our acclaimed writer has arrived!" the older man said as they approached Malcolm. He spoke with a buttery inflection reminiscent of Michael Redgrave in *The Importance of Being Earnest.* "I'm Harvey. Wonderful to meet you." Harvey was in his sixties with slicked-back black hair and a Gomez Addams mustache. He wore a knife-sharp navy suit and a raspberry-red cravat. He hooked his arm around the other man's shoulder. "This is my partner, Jeffrey."

"A pleasure," Jeffrey said. He was younger than Harvey by a decade, taller, thinner, his face drawn and gaunt with a narrow nose, watery gray eyes, and a graying Van Dyke goatee. He wore a light blue suit with windowpane patterns, a white French cuff shirt, and a black tie with silver polka dots woven into the fabric.

Malcolm shook hands with both men and said, "I'm Malcolm Clock. I thought Quinn's place was something else..."

"Location, location, location," Quinn chirruped. "I would never in a million years trade my pyramid for a pedestrian cube."

"It's much bigger than I expected," Malcolm said, peering into the adjoining rooms, which were painted in less offending earthy tones.

"Jeffrey and I find it quite comfortable," Harvey said. "On a pleasant day, we have views of Uptown and the Empire State Building. Tonight, unfortunately, you get what you get. Care for a drink, Mr. Clock?"

"Gin would be great."

"Follow me."

Harvey led the way with an ethereal bounce to his step, as though he were walking on clouds. "The apartment originally featured eleven rooms," he explained when they reached a small kitchen. "It was carved in half after the Great Depression. Unfortunately for Jeffrey and I, this was the half without the kitchen. What we're standing in used to be a linen closet."

"It's still nearly as large as my entire studio," Malcolm remarked.

"Space in Manhattan is tough to come by these days. I'm afraid I don't have any gin chilled…"

"I prefer it over ice."

Harvey opened a cupboard chock-full of booze. He filled a glass with ice and a generous pour of Grey Goose, then topped up his own glass with cognac.

"To meeting new people!" he said.

Malcolm clinked, and they returned to the living room, where Quinn and Jeffrey were chatting in front of a portrait of Jesus wearing green eyeshadow, blush, and red lipstick.

Quinn waved him over and said, "We were deciding what to eat. Is there any particular cuisine you fancy?"

Malcolm shook his head. "I'm fine with anything except Filipino food."

"That shouldn't be a problem, as I don't think anybody had Filipino food in mind! May I ask why you take exception to it?"

"I had a bad experience at a buffet once. My egg had a half-developed bird fetus inside the shell."

"*Balut,*" Harvey said from where he stood, placing a record onto the mahogany spin table of an antique gramophone with a huge golden horn. "It's a popular Southeast Asian street food."

"Have you tried it?" Malcolm asked him.

"Not yet," he said, joining them as the marching band opening of a Bob Dylan song began to play. "But perhaps one day, variety being the spice of life and all."

"How long have you lived here?"

"I'm from England, and Jeffrey's from Spain. We met while I was vacationing in Barcelona in the mid-80s, or thereabouts. A few years later my business took us here." He looked at Jeffrey. "Eighty-eight?"

"Eighty-nine," Jeffrey corrected.

Harvey nodded. "A friend was living at the Chelsea. She told us that one of the larger apartments was going up for sale because the previous owner had died. We had a look and fell in love with it. As a bonus, about a week after we moved in, we learned that one of the Beat poet greats, Herbert Huncke, lived down the hall."

"I don't think I've heard of him."

"Herb didn't achieve the success of some of the others, but he was an extremely talented writer. In fact, it was Herb who coined the term 'Beat' in a conversation with Jack Kerouac. Jack had asked him how he thought their generation would be remembered. Herb's response was 'I'm beat,' as in, you know, beat down, bottomed out. And there you go, a term to describe an entire generation!"

"Huncke the Junkie," Jeffrey said. "I've never known a man to abuse so many drugs, which he did right up to his death."

"Amazing he made it to eighty-one," Harvey agreed. "I'd be heading off to work, and I'd see Herb in his room smoking joints and shooting up with gangsters, hustlers, celebrities, and sometimes ordinary tourists. I don't think Herb ever went to bed until after the sun rose."

"He was definitely a cult hero," Jeffrey said. "Jerry Garcia of the Grateful Dead must have thought so too because he paid Herbert's rent here at the Chelsea for the last few years of Herbert's life. And they'd never even met!"

Wanting to move on from the topic of drugs, Malcolm said, "Why do you think so many creative types have been attracted to the hotel over the years?"

Harvey said, "Because the Chelsea has always been accepting of them."

Quinn nodded. "The hotel was conceived as a kind of socialist experiment to bring together the rich and the poor. Laborers lived in modest two-room apartments down the hall from twelve-room suites occupied by some of the city's wealthiest families. But it was also an attempt to connect artists with patrons. The studios on the tenth floor all have high ceilings and large windows for a reason. They were built for painters and sculptors, who would need the ample space and light. Over the years, the artists drew luminaries to the hotel, who in turn drew more artists. By the time Stanley Bard took over as manager, the hotel's reputation as a haven for artists was well established, and he continued to nurture that reputation."

"Stanley was an artist himself at heart," Harvey said. "He wanted nothing more than to surround himself with artists, so he ran the Chelsea like an artists' colony. If he thought you had some talent and liked your paintings or novels or plays, he'd give you a good deal on a room. If times were tough and you couldn't pay your rent, he would let it slide, or take some of your artwork in lieu—most of which used to cover every inch of the hotel's walls."

Malcolm said, "Not exactly a profitable business model."

Quinn shrugged. "Perhaps not, but Stanley was not a sentimental fool. He was in fact quite shrewd when it came to who owed him money and how much. Yes, he might let your rent slide for a while, but if you got too far behind, he would hound you mercilessly, calling your room at all hours of the day and slipping threatening notes under your door. He'd scold you in the elevators where you couldn't escape, or shout after you as you crossed the lobby. Everybody here seemed to have owed him rent at one point or another. I had friends who would peek through the front windows to see if Stanley was behind the reception desk. If he was, they would enter the hotel through the restaurant on the ground floor, where they could take the stairs up to their floor without Stanley seeing them. Some of them were too scared to even leave their room until nighttime after Stanley had gone home."

"Viva was the absolute worst rent dodger," Harvey said, "though she never tried to hide from Stanley."

"Andy Warhol's Viva?" Malcolm asked.

"The very one, Mr. Clock. You should have heard some of

their shouting matches! They were apoplectic. Stanley would shout, 'Two years, Viva! Your rent's two years overdue! I don't know who you think you are!' And Viva would scream back something along the lines of, 'This place is a hellhole! I'm not paying you another dime!' Or 'Fuck you, Stanley, and your rent! I made this hotel famous!' In the early 90s Stanley finally took her to housing court and was able to evict her."

"I'm surprised he let her stay as long as he did."

"If you were an artist, or you were famous," Jeffrey said, "Stanley would turn a blind eye to almost anything you did. There was one young lady who used to live right across the hall from Harvey and me about twenty years ago. She was a poet laureate of New York in the 80s and 90s. She was also a schizophrenic and a masochist. When she was in one of her moods, she would go out and get drunk and bring home the worst lowlife she could find. There would be screaming and cursing and scary loud noises coming from her apartment for hours. When it was over, she would often come by our place for a cigarette. She'd be bruised and bleeding, her clothes ripped and sometimes falling off her, but she'd be happy as a clown."

"Perhaps Stanley Bard simply didn't know everything that went on here?"

"Oh, no, he knew, all right!" Quinn said. "There was a reason we called him The Watchman. He was always watching what was going on. He had all these spies gathering intelligence for him. The front desk clerks, the bellmen, the switchboard operators, the nightguards and maintenance people and room maids, they were all in on the gossip. They had to be because Stanley just knew *everything.* He knew if your art was selling or not, if you were using drugs or not, if you had kids or pets, who was sleeping with whom. And of course who was behind on their rent, and by how much. So, yes, he knew all the shady stuff that went on here, and all the shady people. He would, as Jeffrey mentioned, simply look the other way—although he did draw the line at Grateful Dead roadies, mind you."

"In any event," Harvey said, "he's the reason the Chelsea is what it is, or what it was—"

A loud knock at the door interrupted him.

Quinn said, "It's about time those two got here! I'll go let them in."

CHAPTER 14

Southern charm

A man and a woman, both in their late twenties or early thirties, followed Quinn into the burlesque room. The woman, a lithe brunette sporting a pageboy with short bangs, wore what looked like a large brown towel that had been stitched into a sweatshirt and pants. The man was the hollow-cheeked Irishman that Malcolm had briefly met on the first floor yesterday. Quinn had mentioned that Shane considered himself a rock star, and the guy was going all in tonight with his hairsprayed do, hard-worn suede boots, tattered jeans, big-buckled belt, leather vest over a bare and tattooed torso, chains and rings, and black shimmer scarf.

Malcolm wondered if maybe he was a rock god after all.

"So sorry we're late y'all!" the woman said in a pleasing Southern drawl. Her green eyes flashed over Malcolm before acknowledging the others. They came back to him, along with a French-tipped, outstretched hand. "I'm Jolene, hon. This here is Shane."

Shane gave Malcolm a nod in recognition but no hand.

"We're from the first floor," Jolene said. "Oh! *Blonde on Blonde.* One of my favorite albums! Can we turn it up?"

"You two certainly took your time getting up here," Harvey said, going to the gramophone and inching up the volume. "It's already half-past eight."

"Shane takes a *long* time to do his hair."

Shane scowled at her. "Don't be goin' on about my hair, Jo."

"Well, it *is* why we're late."

Fisting a bottle of vodka by the neck, he sauntered off, presumably to the kitchen.

"Is he soused already?" Harvey asked in a hushed voice.

"I reckon," Jolene said. "He's been drinking nearabout every day recently, it seems."

"How is his music going? Is he still playing in the pubs?"

"He says it's going really well. In fact, he's written a number of new songs just this last week."

"He should have brought up his guitar so we could hear them."

"He wouldn't play them for you. He's a bit shy like that."

"But he plays in front of people at the pub," Jeffrey pointed out.

"He doesn't know *them*. He knows all y'all though, and the only person he'll play in front of that he knows is little old me."

"I can't say I'm terribly disappointed," Quinn said. "I grew out of rock music decades ago. It's just noise to my ears now—"

Shane returned holding two vodka and tonics in highballs.

"What?" he demanded. "It was me youse were talkin' about, wasn't it?"

"Just your music," Harvey insisted. "Jolene says you've written some new songs?"

"I have," he said, handing Jolene one of the drinks. "Not that that's any of yer business."

"Oh, lighten up, young man!" Quinn chided.

"Don't be lecturin' me, oul woman."

He stalked into another room by himself.

Jolene rested her hand on Malcolm's forearm, and the touch sent an unanticipated tingle through him. "He's not always like this, hon," she said. "Something's been eating at him lately. I just don't know what."

"Speaking of eating," Harvey said, "have we decided what we want to order yet?"

"I think Mr. Clock should decide," Quinn said.

"Like I mentioned, I'm fine with anything but Filipino."

"Why's that?" Jolene asked.

"Post-traumatic stress," Harvey answered.

"How about Japanese?" Quinn said.

"Shane doesn't like seafood," Jolene said.

"Dim sum? There's a place on Third Avenue."

"Actually, Shane doesn't really like *any* Asian food. He's more of a chicken and steak guy."

Harvey huffed. "We're certainly not ordering Popeyes, thank you very much."

"There's the Texas BBQ down the street," Jolene suggested. "They're always open."

When nobody protested, four sets of eyes turned to Malcolm for his verdict.

"Fine by me," he said.

"Great!" Quinn said. "I'll order a little of everything. The only problem is that I don't think they deliver, so one of us will have to go pick it up."

Malcolm said, "I don't mind going—"

"Nonsense! You're the guest of honor. Shane can go."

A deafening clap of thunder caused everyone to glance apprehensively at the windows and the stormy night beyond.

"Right then," Harvey said. "Who wants to go tell the chap?"

CHAPTER 15

*Forty hits of acid * The man
in the porkpie hat (2)*

I n the end, Jeffrey offered to get the food. When he returned, the six of them sat down at a large oak table in the dining room (which was ordinary enough except for a pink fireplace with colorfully painted plates glued to its face). Jeffrey sat at one head of the table, Harvey at the other. Malcolm was beside Quinn, and Shane next to Jolene. The food—a cornucopia of jumbo shrimp, chicken wings, fried chicken tenders, baby back ribs, and a rotisserie chicken—was tasty and messy. In fact, it felt as though they were having a picnic in the park, with all the leaning and reaching to share from the plates in the center of the table.

The conversation focused mostly on the Hotel Chelsea, with everyone (except Shane, who Malcolm could now tell was definitely smashed), pitching in with a wild story from their time living there.

Jolene shared a tale of a volatile young couple who'd lived across the hall from her and were always hurling invectives at each other, breaking dishes, slamming doors. One day Jolene arrived home to find the husband standing outside his room with a bottle of whiskey and a cigarette. His face appeared flushed, and she couldn't be certain whether he was especially happy or sad. While she was asking him if everything was all right, a dozen policemen, pistols drawn, clambered up the stairwell and ordered him to the floor, handcuffing him and lugging him away. She later learned he had strangled his wife to death, called 911 to confess, and was waiting for the cops to come arrest him.

Not one to be outdone, Quinn offered a glimpse into the life of a perky, pretty five-foot-two blonde woman who ran a gambling parlor and drug ring out of her room on the second floor. On the walls of the room hung photographs of William Burroughs and Allen Ginsberg and others who'd gambled there over the years. Ziploc bags filled with drugs, envelopes stuffed with cash, and an assortment of weapons littered the poker tables. Residents used to call the woman a gangsterette, and if they ever smelled her fragrant perfume lingering in the hallways, they'd often make a break for their room as quickly as possible to avoid running into her. Bad things tended to happen to anybody who slighted her, regardless of it being intentional or not.

Most of the stories told during the meal, however, were on the lighter side, such as the one about a painter/poet who found his fifteen minutes of fame, though it was more like fifteen minutes of infamy. The man, according to Harvey, was a haughty twenty-something who always wore three-piece suits despite not having a nine-to-five job. He only occasionally used drugs, but one day he decided to buy forty hits of acid with the plan to take one every now and then to serve as inspiration for his art. As he walked home that day, it started to rain. The LSD blotter paper in his trouser pocket became soaked, and the acid—all forty hits—was absorbed into his thigh. While on a psychedelic trip to end all trips, he ended up hanging out with two of Harvey's gay friends who had a closetful of S&M gear in their room. The painter/poet dressed up in bug-like goggles, spiked shoulder pads, spiked gauntlets, leather boots with shin plates, and a leather skirt. Wielding a samurai sword, he descended upon the lobby, where he terrified residents and tourists alike. Then he made his way to the front of the hotel, where he continued to terrify passersby when David Letterman—who was shooting one of his skits in which he cruised Manhattan on the lookout for some of the city's more colorful characters—pulled to the curb in his lim-ousine and called out, "Oh, look at that weirdo over there!" The skit was live, and the poet/painter was broadcast across the nation as a raving sadomasochist. Allegedly the man was so embarrassed when he came to his senses the next day, he checked out of the hotel and nobody ever heard from him again.

During dessert—homemade butterscotch pie from Harvey and Jeffrey's fridge—Malcolm finally asked what had been on his mind for much of the evening. "Why did the man on the tenth floor kill himself?"

Jeffrey turned serious and said, "Roger James was a dear friend of mine. I spent a lot of time up in his room. He was a brilliant man, intellectually as well as artistically. He was a fashion designer, a visionary far ahead of his time. Ironically he dressed like a bum, always in rumpled clothing. And he had about a dozen cats up there."

"Those damn cats," Harvey said. "Whenever I visited R.J., they'd be crawling all over me. I'm allergic to the bloody things, so I started wearing a knee-length rain jacket when I visited to keep them from shedding over my clothes."

Quinn said, "I don't know what you two saw in that man. He was the grumpiest person I've ever had the misfortune of meeting."

"Most genii are to some extent unpleasant to be around," Jeffrey told her. "Regular people find it hard to understand them or relate to their way of thinking, but they're drawn to their intellect. I imagine that having people clamoring for your attention every day, people who don't understand you, would become rather frustrating and tiresome over time, enough to turn anyone into a grump."

"Grump is too kind a word," Harvey said. "R.J. was a com-plete arsehole! But, yes, that was his way of keeping pests at a distance."

"I'm glad to know I was a pest in his eyes," Quinn remarked.

"Don't take it personally," Jeffrey said. "Roger was simply

happiest when he was by himself. Now to answer your question, Mr. Clock—why did Roger take his own life? That, I don't know. He was an old man, an angry man, at eighty-six. He had stopped working years ago. Perhaps he figured he had done everything with his life that needed to be done, and it was simply time to move on. He had bad arthritis in his hips, which affected his mobility. I have no idea whether this contributed to his death, but you never know, do you? And nobody *will* ever know because he didn't leave a note. Roger never thought he needed to explain anything to anyone."

"He made sure to make a dramatic exit," Malcolm said. "I had a look in his room. There was blood everywhere." He offered Nikki's theory. "Was it possible he was upset with the construction in the hotel, and this was some sort of protest against the developers?"

"Now *that's* an interesting premise," Quinn said.

"No, no, no," Jeffrey said, stroking his Van Dyke. "Interesting, perhaps, but accurate, no. Roger was never especially fond of the Chelsea. He was always complaining about the riffraff that Stanley Bard was letting stay here and lamenting the hotel's long, slow decline. He often called it an aging whore in need of a facelift. If you want my honest opinion, I believe he viewed the construction indifferently, if not as a positive development."

"How anyone could ever think that is beyond me," Quinn griped.

"Perhaps he was about to be evicted then?" Malcolm suggested. "He had nowhere else to go and was angry at the developers for kicking him to the curb. You mentioned he was an angry sort of man."

"Angry but not vengeful," Jeffrey said. "And I'm afraid what you've suggested couldn't be further from the truth. Despite living in relative squalor, Roger was worth many millions of dollars. He lived here simply because he had always lived here and couldn't be bothered to relocate. If he had been evicted, he had the wealth to move somewhere much nicer. It would have been nothing but an inconvenience to him."

"If you ask me," Harvey said, "I think the old badger died how he died simply because he was never one to do things by the books. He once confessed to me that when his time came, he would like to die singing. Perhaps he had been singing while he was painting his apartment red?"

Shane belched loudly. "I got one o' his cats," he slurred.

"Glad you're finally joining the conversation, my boy," Harvey said.

"Are you married, lad?" Shane asked, apropos of nothing, as he glared blurry eyed at Malcolm.

"No, I'm not."

"Ever been?"

"No, I haven't."

"Are you thinking of proposing, doll?" Jolene said, causing ripples of laughter around the table.

Shane ignored her. He was still glaring at Malcolm. "Have you written somethin' grand before? No five-page magazine article. Somethin' like a novel?"

"Don't be rude, Shane," Jolene said tightly.

"It's all right," Malcolm said. To Shane, "As a matter of fact, I have started a novel."

"Started, have ye? G'wan then. When did you start it?"

"A little while back," he said, despite the fact it had been more than two years ago. "I haven't gotten into it because I've been busy lately with my day job."

"I do wonder you have it in ye? Maybe it be best you stick to five-page magazine articles?"

"Shane is an aspiring musician," Jolene said, stressing *aspiring* in what sounded like a kind of backhanded insult.

Shane clearly took it that way. "Aspiring!" he spat. "I've written more than two records worth of songs, Jo. That's no *aspiring* musician. That's an *accomplished* one!"

With this off his chest, Shane shoved back his chair, stood unsteadily, then staggered away from the table.

Harvey called, "Bathroom is through the—"

"Fack aff ye!"

"Please ignore him, darlin," Jolene told Malcolm. "He had no right speaking to you like that. He can be a real jerk sometimes, God love him."

"Why did you even invite that man?" Quinn asked. "You know he gets like this."

"He's not usually *this* bad."

"Did I do something to insult him?" Malcolm asked.

"Of course not. He either takes to folks or he doesn't. There's no real middle ground with Shane McSorley."

"Well, enough about him," Harvey said. He raised his glass of brandy in the air. "To Roger James! May the old bastard be watching down over us from that fluffy place in the sky."

"In his rumpled trench coat and porkpie hat," Jeffrey added.

A chorus of "hear-hears" followed.

Malcolm had gone cold. "Trench coat and porkpie hat?" he said.

Jeffrey nodded. "It was Roger's go-to get up. He didn't go anywhere without his shabby old trench coat and porkpie hat."

"Is something wrong, Mr. Clock?" Quinn asked him, a note of concern in her voice.

Malcolm swallowed tightly. "Yesterday when I was leaving the hotel there was a man in the lobby," he said. "He was staring at one of the walls. His nose was almost touching it. I asked him if he was okay. He didn't respond to me. And...he was wearing a beige trench coat and a porkpie hat."

Everyone gasped.

"Well, there you have it!" Harvey spoke up above the others and slapping the table with his palms. "It's not just Jeffrey and I who've seen a ghost!"

"Whoa, whoa," Malcolm said. "I didn't say the man was a ghost—"

"Of course it wasn't a ghost!" Quinn snapped. "Really, Harvey, you must stop with all this hocus-pocus nonsense."

"It is not nonsense," he said, speaking to Malcolm. "Jeffrey and I experienced the most extraordinary case of paranormal activity just this week. I won't go into any details now for fear of frightening our dear Quinn, but believe me when I say it happened."

"I am not frightened," Quinn said. "I'm embarrassed. For *you*. Ghosts!"

Harvey and Jeffrey wore grave expressions, while Quinn appeared exasperated. Malcolm glanced at Jolene, who smiled sweetly and shrugged.

"It was Mel," Quinn declared. "Mel Peat." To Malcolm she clarified: "Mel lives down on the fifth floor. He's a little mad and likes to dress up and wander the halls. He has all these costumes he wears. Sometimes he's an angel, sometimes a devil. Sometimes he dresses like Bert or Ernie from *Sesame Street*."

"But never like Roger James," Harvey said.

"Call him up," she said. "He's in room 510, I believe. Ask him if that was him in the lobby yesterday."

"All right, I will." Harvey got up and went to an old rotary telephone on a sideboard buffet cabinet. He punched in four numbers to make a room-to-room call and tapped his right foot impatiently. A moment later he said, "Mel! It's Harvey from up on the eighth. How are you doing, my good man? Oh, that's too bad. Perhaps you should pay your doctor a visit...? In any event, I'm sure you've heard about old Roger James' passing...? Well, yes, but that's not a very nice thing to say, Mel. Now I heard... What's that? No, no. No, Mel. Now, I've heard that somebody saw him standing in the lobby yesterday in a trench coat and a porkpie hat. Would you happen to know anything about that...? Well, yes, I understand if he's dead that would be impossible. But I have Quinn over, Quinn from the roof...? Now, now, Mel, that's not a very nice thing to say either."

Harvey smiled apologetically at Quinn. Her eyes flashed daggers.

"Now stop that, Mel!" Harvey said firmly. "Thank you, and

please listen up. Quinn believes that the person in the lobby yesterday might have been you... No, not *with* Roger James. *Dressed* as Roger James. You do enjoy having a good dress up every now and then—"

Harvey held the receiver away from his ear, and Malcolm could hear a high-pitched tinny voice shouting very loudly.

Harvey put his ear back to the receiver but proved unsuccessful at getting a word in edgewise. After about ten seconds he shouted, "Well, fuck you too, Mel!" and hung up.

"What a vile, belligerent man," Jeffrey said, tsk-tsking.

"A vile, belligerent man," Harvey concurred, "but a man who is quite adamant it wasn't him in the lobby yesterday."

CHAPTER 16

Did he just do that?

"There are a few rather questionable people Shane knows in the building," Jolene said. "Perhaps I could get him to ask around?"

"Ask around what?" Shane said, appearing from a connecting room.

Jolene said, "Malcolm was just saying that he saw someone dressed like Roger James in the lobby yesterday..." She frowned. Shane had started swaying on the spot. "Hon, maybe you should sit—"

He lurched forward and vomited all over the table. Most of it landed right in front of Malcolm, spraying him in the chest like buckshot.

"Ugh!" Malcolm said, leaping to his feet. He looked down at his chest. The sight and smell of the vomit was making him queasy. He held his hands shoulder-high, as if about to brush the gunk from his shirt, then realized as repulsive as it was to have it on him, it would be worse to have it on his bare hands as well.

The others were already scrambling into action. Jolene was leading Shane away from the table in case he wasn't done sharing his dinner. Quinn was plucking all the clean napkins she could find, while Harvey and Jeffrey were hurrying to the kitchen, telling him they would be right back with some water and dishtowels.

"I'm so, so sorry, Mr. Clock!" Quinn said, rushing over to him. "I can't believe that man! Here, let me—"

"No, let me," Malcolm said, taking the napkins from her. He leaned his chest over his dessert plate and brushed the largest undigested chunks of vomit onto it.

Jeffrey returned with a large glass bowl filled with soapy water and a couple of dishtowels.

"Thank you," Malcolm said, wetting one dishtowel and blotting his shirt.

"Disgusting," Jeffrey said as he did his best with the other dishtowel to clean up the mess on the table.

Quinn scrunched her face and said, "Ooh, you got a little bit along your neck right there." She pointed.

He wiped his neck clean. "Anywhere else?"

"Right there." She pressed a finger to her chin.

He wiped his chin too.

Harvey returned holding a pink button-up shirt on a hanger. "Put this on, my friend. You can change in the bathroom if you wish. There's another one this way..."

"It's okay, thanks," Malcolm said. "I've got most of it cleaned up."

"Nonsense! You can't wear a shirt that's been so hideously fouled!"

"It's okay, really," he insisted. "In fact, it's about time I head home anyway."

"Oh, no, no, no," Quinn said. "You can't leave on a note like this."

"I've had a great time. Thank you for inviting me, Quinn. And thank you both very much," he said to Harvey and Jeffrey, "for having me in your home."

Quinn was looking grim. "I suppose it is getting late..."

"Are you leaving?" Jolene asked, emerging from one of the connecting rooms. "I apologize terribly for Shane. He's..." She shook her head. "Let me walk you out."

"I'm okay—"

"I'd like to." She turned to Harvey. "Shane's praying to his porcelain god. I'll be back up to get him in a jiff." She took Malcolm's hand in hers and said, "Shall we?"

❖ ❖ ❖

Jolene pushed the button to call the elevator . "I can't believe he puked on you, darlin."

"I have a suspicion he might have done it on purpose."

"I wouldn't be surprised, given the way he was acting."

The elevator arrived and they stepped into the dingy car. Jolene pressed the button for the lobby.

As they descended, Malcolm said, "I like Harvey and Jeffrey."

"Ain't they just dolls? Really snazzy dressers too."

"Do they always wear suits like those?"

"I don't reckon I've ever seen them in anything more casual than a cravat."

"Have you been to their place many times before?"

"Oh, I couldn't count! They enjoy hosting dinner. And theirs is one of the few apartments big enough to hold more than two people comfortably."

A few seconds of silence passed.

Malcolm said, "This might be the slowest elevator I've ever ridden."

Jolene nodded. "A lot of folks would say it's the slowest in the city."

More silence.

Finally the elevator stopped with a rattle, and they stepped into the lobby. Nobody was behind the reception desk.

"Is that not manned during the night?" Malcolm asked.

"It's always manned. The nightguard is probably doing his rounds or having a cigarette out back."

He nodded, having run out of anything else to say. "Well, thanks for escorting me down. You really didn't have to."

"It was either this or watching Shane puke into a toilet."

"And I thought you just enjoyed my company."

"I *do* enjoy your company, hon. As a matter of fact, if it's not too late, would you like to come over to my place for a drink?"

Malcolm was at a loss for words. "I, um, don't think that would go over too well with Shane, would it?"

Jolene frowned. "What in heaven's name does Shane have to do with anything? I'm certainly not inviting *him*."

"You don't live with him?"

"Well, I declare!" She laughed. "You thought we *lived* together."

That's exactly what he'd thought. "You came to the dinner party together. You said you were both from the first floor..."

"We're friends. That's it. We used to date casually, yes, but that was a few months ago. I called it off, and we've been just friends ever since. Oh my, ain't that embarrassing! Well, now that that's been cleared up...would you like to come by?"

Malcolm would have said yes under different circumstances, but he didn't feel very dapper having just been on the receiving end of a drunk's vomit. Maybe it was in his head, but he thought he could still smell the sour-milk stench on him. "Thanks for the offer, Jolene," he said. "But it's been a long evening. I'm almost ready for bed."

"Of course," she said easily. "I better get back upstairs to check on Shane then. It was nice meeting you, Malcolm."

She stepped into the elevator and waved as the door slid closed.

As Malcolm crossed the lobby to the front doors, he glanced at the spot where he'd seen the man in the trench coat and porkpie hat the day before. Although nobody stood there now, an icy chill prickled the nape of his neck.

"Just one of the hotel's crazies," he said to himself as he ventured into the storm.

CHAPTER 17

The (not so) friendly
neighborhood cat

Shane could barely think on the way down to his apartment. He only knew that Jolene was with him, steering him in the right direction. She was bitching at him for drinking so much. He tuned her out. He didn't need her telling him what a piece of shite he was. He needed all his concentration to stop from falling over.

As soon as he stumbled into his apartment, he swung the door closed in her face.

A few unsteady steps later he slumped down on the sofa with an aggrieved sigh. His head lolled backward, and his eyes slid closed. He told himself he should get some water, but he was too knackered to move. His body and mind were both too heavy. He couldn't get up. He couldn't think. He was comfortable right where he was.

Snippets of the evening darted in and out of his thoughts in a blur of memories. Jo telling everyone about how long it had taken him to do his hair. Wandering around the suite of rooms by himself. He couldn't recall much of dinner except for puking in the jacks. He knew he had already polished off most of the bottle of vodka by then, on top of all the whiskey he'd guzzled during the day. But he also knew he had made a right bags of everything.

He probably never should have gone to the dinner party in the first place. Jeffrey was an all right fella, but he didn't particularly like Harvey or Quinn. He definitely didn't like that dryshite, Malcolm.

The reason Shane went was Jolene. He wanted to spend time with her, even if he had to share her with everyone else. And time with her was rare these days. She would no longer hang out if it were just the two of them. She always wanted others around. Why? Hell if he knew. They'd been friends for months before they started dating. She always came over to his apartment by herself. She loved the space. They'd drink and smoke joints and he'd play the guitar for her and sometimes she'd sing along. If it was okay to hang out one-on-one with him then, why couldn't she do that now?

Anyway, whatever. She'd dumped him. She didn't want to get back together. She'd made that clear, so it would be best for him to forget about her. Look for someone else. He was attractive. He had fine things eyeing him whenever he played a gig. Sometimes they gave him their phone numbers. He never called them because he'd never gotten over Jolene. He didn't want her to see him parading around the hotel with different floozies. He might hate the bitch sometimes, but he still loved her. He didn't want to hurt her.

But that's the thing. Seeing you with some bird won't hurt Jo. It won't bother her in the least. She'd be over the moon for you, happy 'cause you're moving on...

Yeah, maybe, he thought, pushing the voice aside.

Speaking of gigs, Shane remembered he had one tomorrow afternoon at the Stag 'n' Boar up in Hell's Kitchen. That was something he was looking forward to. He needed to get out of the hotel. Also, the Stag would be a good place to give one of his new songs a test run—

Meeeooooow.

Shane opened his eyes.

The white Siamese cat was sitting on the coffee table, staring at him with its glassy blue eyes and slit pupils.

For whatever reason—the animal's stillness or its stare (or perhaps because it had been watching him so coolly, predatorily, while he'd been passed out and vulnerable)—Shane became immediately uneasy.

"What?" he grunted, getting ready to kick it off the table so it would stop creeping him out.

The cat smiled—a big, Cheshire cat smile, far too broad for its narrow muzzle, revealing a series of pointed, menacing teeth.

"Jaysus!" Shane exclaimed, kicking wildly, his foot missing the cat, at the same time as he scrambled up and over the back of the sofa, landing hard on the floor.

Breathless, he raised his head to peek over the sofa.

The coffee table was empty.

The cat was gone.

Had he imagined it?

Pushing himself to his feet, Shane didn't see the devilish thing anywhere.

Must have imagined it, he thought—a moment before spotting the cat, crouched up where the wall met the ceiling, defying gravity, grinning hideously.

It sprang toward him, claws and fangs bared.

◆ ◆ ◆

Shane jerked awake in a cold sweat, raising his forearms to deflect the cat's flying attack until he realized he'd been dreaming.

"Jaysus Mary," he croaked, dragging a hand over his damp face and looking around the apartment.

The Siamese cat was sitting on the kitchen counter.

Shane stiffened, but there was nothing ominous about it now. As if to reinforce its innocuous nature, it began grooming itself by lifting a leg and licking.

Shane got up and swayed—he was still drunk, he realized—and made his way to the kitchen.

"Want somethin' to eat, do ye?" he said, feeling a need to appease the animal.

From the fridge he produced an unopened pack of chopped

liver, dumped some in a dish, and heated it in the microwave. He mushed the meat up with a fork and placed it on the counter.

The cat lowered its chocolate face, sniffed the dish, and then began to eat.

Shane watched it for a little longer, half expecting it to look up at him and flash that godawful, impossible grimace. It did not, and after drinking about a liter of water, he shuffled to the bedroom. He never closed the door when he slept, but he did so now. Then, fully clothed, he dropped onto the bed.

Within seconds he was asleep.

CHAPTER 18

The woman in the mist

Jolene stripped out of her clothes, wrapped an Egyptian-cotton bath towel around her torso, and went down the hallway to the bathroom. She transferred her bottles of shampoo, conditioner, and bodywash from the little shelf along the wall to the edge of the bathtub. When there were more tenants living on the floor, she would take whatever belonged to her back to her room after each shower. But now there were only four people left on the first floor, and just Shane on this wing with whom she shared the bathroom. He didn't seem to mind her stuff being here, and sometimes he left a can of shaving cream or hair gel or whatnot behind (though she drew the line at old toothbrushes or gunky tubes of toothpaste, which she would toss in the bin without a second thought).

She ran the shower. While she waited for the water to heat up, she went to the mirror, where she feathered her hair with her fingertips and examined her reflection from varying angles.

Was she getting old?

She still looked good, and she didn't feel old. But she was thirty now. Her age no longer started with a 2. Before long, it would start with a 4. Then she would be fifty, and where did time go?

She recalled Malcolm's rejection earlier: *It's been a long evening. I'm getting ready for bed.*

She rolled her eyes. Really?

He seemed to be about her age. Could he be one of those

men who didn't date women in their age bracket, preferring them to be five or ten years younger?

Then again, Shane *had* puked all over him. He wouldn't have felt great about that, or very romantic either.

The more Jolene considered this line of reasoning, the more she agreed with the conclusion. After all, they seemed to be on the same page intellectually, their humor meshed, and there had been some subtle eye flirting.

I'll call him in a couple of days, she decided, feeling better about herself already. Ask him out for coffee or something like that. She'd been single for nearly two months now. It was time to start enjoying herself.

She wasn't getting any younger.

Slipping off the towel and draping it over the shower curtain rod, Jolene stepped into the tub.

◆ ◆ ◆

Washed and refreshed, Jolene turned off the taps and patted her face dry with the towel. She slid the shower curtain aside, the metal rings whining along the rod. She shivered as the cooler ambient air touched her warmed skin.

She was about to step out of the tub when she cried out, slipped, and crashed to her side.

She immediately looked to where she'd seen the person standing amidst the clouds of steam.

Nobody was there.

"Hell's bells, girl!" she exclaimed, getting carefully to her feet so she didn't slip again. "You trying to get yourself killed?"

She wrapped the cotton towel around her body and stepped out of the tub. Her right elbow, which had taken the brunt of the fall, smarted, but other than that she was uninjured. She opened the door to clear the steam from the bathroom. As an afterthought, she poked her head into the hallway.

Nobody fleeing the scene. Of course not. She'd imagined

what she saw.

And what do you think you saw?

She didn't know. Probably nothing but a trick of the mind. Like when you wake in the middle of the night and see someone standing in the corner of your bedroom, only to realize it was nothing but a pedestal fan or some other inanimate object.

There's no pedestal fan in the bathroom, and it's bright as day with the light on.

"Well, there ain't nobody here, is there?" she told the empty bathroom in a stern tone. "Get a hold of yourself, Jo."

She withdrew her hairbrush from a drawer under the sink, but instead of brushing her hair in the large bathroom mirror as she usually did, she returned to her room—closing and locking the door behind her. She exchanged the towel for a warm pair of pajamas, then went to the small mirror on the wall and began brushing the tangles from her hair.

While her reflection grimaced each time she pulled at a knot, her mind was not on her hair but back in the bathroom, playing over what she'd imagined she saw in the steam.

And the more she thought about it, the more she thought what she'd seen might have been a lithe woman with short blonde hair and dramatic eye makeup.

A woman who might have borne a strong resemblance to Edie Sedgwick.

CHAPTER 19

The next Great American Novel—not

O nce home Malcolm tossed his vomit-soiled clothes into the hamper, showered, then climbed into bed. After about ten minutes of lying there with the lights off, he realized he wasn't tired and got back up. He poured himself a glass of water and went to the balcony doors, where he watched the storm. Mostly he thought about the dinner party at the Hotel Chelsea, playing over all the stories he had been told and wondering which ones he could incorporate into his article. He also spent a fair bit of time thinking about Jolene. She was attractive, friendly, and a pleasure to talk to— so why had he refused her invitation back to her apartment?

Because you smelled like the bathroom of a dive bar, that's why.

Maybe she would have offered to let me take a shower?

And what would you do after the shower with no clean shirt to change into? Hang out with her bare-chested? You're not exactly Sylvester Stallone.

Maybe she would have stepped in the shower with me?

Now you'll never know, will you?

"I'm an idiot," Malcolm mumbled to himself.

Looking for someone else to blame for his poor decision-making, he chose Shane. If the guy hadn't vomited all over him, he would likely be hanging out with Jolene right now, sharing a bottle of wine, perhaps cuddling on her sofa, perhaps doing more than cuddling...

Malcolm forced these thoughts aside. He didn't want to get hung up on what-could-have-beens. But he remained pissed off at Shane, and not only for puking on him. What was all that shit about writing five-page articles for a magazine? Fuck him. The guy might fancy himself a musician, but it sounded as though success had been eluding him.

It's been eluding you too, Mac.

He would finish his book sooner or later. He would get it published. He would—

The book's a piece of shit.

The bluntness of this thought surprised him, but it was true. In fact, on some level, he had known the book was a piece of shit for some time now. It was the reason he had never made it past one hundred pages, and why he hadn't looked at the manuscript in nearly two years.

It was shit.

Subconsciously he had known this. Consciously he had denied it.

He hated to admit that Shane might be right, but writing magazine articles and writing a novel were indeed very different animals, and it seemed he just didn't have it in him to write a novel.

At least not a literary novel.

Malcolm considered that. He had always believed the only kind of novel to write was a literary one, because they had merit, themes, meaning. They commented on social inequality, politics, the human condition. The novel he'd been working on, for instance, had delved deeply into the contrasts of materialism and spirituality. His characters were Jungian and Freudian archetypes with religious and psychosocial conflicts. They were introspective, complex, tormented—

Boring.

Were they?

You know they were, Mac. Fleshed out? Sure. But nobody would have given a damn about them. You yourself didn't even want anything more to do with them. Which is why you stopped writing.

I stopped because—

Because you set the bar too high. You were trying to write the next Great American Novel. And what do you even know about

Great American Novels? You read Catcher in the Rye *in high school. You read* Ulysses *and* The Grapes of Wrath *in college. That makes you qualified to write the next* Brave New World? *Shit, Mac, you never even liked any of those novels. You liked...*

Malcolm glanced at the bookshelves screwed into the wall above the headboard of his bed. They were crammed with stacks of beat-up paperback novels ranging from Tom Clancy and Vince Flynn, to John Sandford and Jonathan Kellerman.

That's *what you like reading, Mac. Genre fiction. That's what you've always liked reading. And if you're being honest with your-self,* that's *what you should be writing.*

Spy novels? Police procedurals? What did he know about international espionage or detective work? He was an expert on neither. He would be in the same boat he'd been in when he was trying to write literary fiction...

What about horror?

What about it?

You don't need any special knowledge to write horror, do you? It's domestic stuff. A broken-down RV in cannibal country. Inbred hillbillies terrifying a family on a camping trip. You just have to scare people.

Malcolm chewed on that. Did he have it in him to write a horror novel? Did he *want* to write a horror novel? Horror was the black sheep of publishing. Nobody took those kinds of writers seriously.

Are you sure about that? his devil's advocate shot back, and Malcolm's eyes went again to the bookshelves, picking out titles by Stephen King and James Herbert and Dean Koontz. *Pretty darn good company, wouldn't you agree?*

Malcolm would—but what would he write about?

You know the old maxim: write what you know.

What did he know?

Where did you just spend the evening?

"The Hotel Chelsea," he said, trying to keep up with his thoughts.

The hotel is reportedly haunted. Scratch that—it's reportedly one of the most haunted places in the country. You don't have to be-lieve in ghosts to write about them. And you have first-hand access to people who live at the hotel...some who have confessed to believ-ing in ghosts themselves.

"The Hotel Chelsea," he said again, realizing he might be onto something.

He set aside the glass of water, sat down at his desk, and powered on his laptop.

CHAPTER 20

The blackout

Malcolm awoke in the middle of the night, or at least he thought it was the middle of the night, because an inky blackness filled his studio apartment.

Someone was knocking on his door.

He rolled out of bed and shuffled across the room. The pug, always alert to his movement, followed at his heels, the bell on his collar jangling.

Malcolm hit the light switch but nothing happened. He flicked it up and down several times to no avail.

"Great," he said. Then, louder, in response to another impatient knock at the door: "Coming."

He scooped the puppy into his arms so he didn't make a break for freedom. The little ghoul began licking his cheek, spraying his saliva everywhere.

Grimacing, Malcolm opened the door and found Nikki standing in the hallway in a pair of black silk pajamas. She was holding a scented candle that smelled like a Christmas tree.

The pug yapped happily.

"Shush!" Malcolm said.

"I didn't say anything," Nikki said.

"I was talking to the dog."

"Power's out."

"I noticed."

"What are you two cuties up to?" she asked, scratching the pug's scalp.

"We were sleeping."

"It's so *boring* without power," she said, indifferent that she'd woken them. "It's been out for half an hour already. The internet on my phone doesn't work."

"What time is it?"

"Six thirty. Can I come in?"

Malcolm blinked. "Um...why?"

"Because I'm so *bored*, Mac! Just for a bit. It will be light in half an hour. Then I'll go outside and see what's going on."

"Well...I guess," he said, deciding he wasn't going back to sleep. He stepped aside to let her in, closed the door, and set the pug on the floor. The puppy began jumping against Nikki's shins.

"You're lucky you have company," she said, crouching to pet the dog. "Maybe I should get a pet? I never asked you his name?"

"Bitcoin," he told her.

"Like the cyber currency?"

Malcolm nodded.

"That's so silly!"

"I wasn't the one who named him. My brother works on Wall Street. Guess he thought it was cute."

Nikki stood. "Have you eaten breakfast?"

"I've only been awake since you knocked," he reminded her.

"Shoot me for jumpstarting your day, Mac! You should be thanking me. Sleep is such a waste of time. Do you know that if you slept an hour less each night, and used that hour to work out each morning, you'd be super fit?"

"I do know that. Do you work out every day?"

"I don't need to. I have a fast metabolism." She went to the kitchen and set the candle, which was housed inside a blue pottery jar, on the Formica countertop. The small flame did little to alleviate the darkness. "What do you usually have for breakfast? I'm guessing not much since you don't buy groceries."

"Toast," he said, following her.

"Where's the bread?"

"In the fridge."

"Right," she said, facing him. "I'll make you some toast while you go have a shower. The building still has hot water, but who knows for how long. Better take advantage of it while you can."

◆ ◆ ◆

Navigating the studio apartment with the glow from his mobile phone, Malcolm grabbed some clothes out of his wardrobe, then showered in the small bathroom. He toweled dry, brushed his hair and teeth, then dressed in jeans and a long-sleeved shirt.

As he exited the bathroom, he discovered the darkness in the studio had lightened a few shades of gray. He peered through the balcony doors at the sky. The sun remained hidden behind the raft of storm clouds, and the rain fell hard and fast, though no longer as torrentially as the night before.

In the kitchen, the pug was slobbering down kibbles from the bowl on the floor that Malcolm would likely throw out when he gave the puppy back to his brother next week. Nikki was spreading peanut butter over two pieces of toast.

"I had to trim moldy bits off the crust," she told him. "How do you live like this?"

"One day at a time," Malcolm said as she offered him the plate. "How did you toast the bread without power?"

"There's still gas in the lines so I put them in the oven. I also boiled water for coffee. But you don't have any milk."

"It went off. I threw it out."

"Why am I not surprised? You really need to go grocery shopping, Mac. Do you know what's in your fridge?"

"The Zuul demon?" he said jokingly.

Nikki yanked open the fridge door—no light came on—to reveal the bare interior. "Half a loaf of moldy bread," she inventoried. "A jar of pickles—I don't even want to know how long they've been in there for. A six-pack of Coke—two opened for God only knows what reason. Three bottles of Busch. And whatever the leftovers are in those plastic containers."

"Indian curry," he told her. "One's beef vindaloo, the other's butter chicken. You can help yourself."

She swung the door closed. "It's pathetic, Mac! You're going to have to take your coffee black."

"That's how I like it."

Malcolm's peach-colored kettle whistled. Nikki lifted it off the red-hot burner and poured the steaming water into two mugs she'd already set out on the counter.

"I couldn't find the sugar," she said.

"I don't think I have any." Malcolm bit a piece of toast, chewed, and frowned.

"What's wrong?"

"I don't know... The peanut butter tastes odd."

"Don't tell me it's gone off too..."

He examined the piece of toast more closely. "Did you butter this?"

"So?"

"Don't you think that's going overboard? Peanut butter is called peanut *butter* for a reason."

Nikki shrugged. "That's how my mother always made my peanut butter sandwiches. Butter and peanut butter." She took her coffee to the living room and opened the balcony doors, letting inside a gust of wet, cool air. "Smells so fresh! New York needs a bath every now and then."

"Shower," he said, correcting her metaphor. He left the toast on the counter and joined her with his coffee. "Can't see lights on in any other building. Power must be out all over the neighborhood."

"How's that article going?"

"It's just about finished," he told her. With a burst of satisfaction, he added, "I've decided to write a novel about the Hotel Chelsea too."

Nikki raised her eyebrows. "A history of it?"

"No, a fiction novel. Commercial fiction. A...uh...horror story actually."

"Are there going to be ghosts in it?"

"I imagine so. I've just started writing it."

"You can use my experience about the ghost sitting on my chest, I don't mind."

"I'll think about that."

She sipped her coffee. "Do you want to come on a walk with me to see how far the power is out?"

He hedged. "I was planning on getting into the novel..."

"Come on, Mac! This is exciting stuff! A once-in-a-generation storm. A power outage. Also, don't you have to take the puppy out for a walk?"

"He has a litter box in the bathroom he's starting to use."

"But he's a *dog*. He's not a cat that can hang around inside all day. He needs to be walked. Have you *never* walked him? How long have you had him for?"

"He's not very big..."

"Talk about animal cruelty! If you're not going to take him out, then I'll—"

"No, you're right," he said. "I guess he does need to be walked. Give me a sec to find his leash."

CHAPTER 21

*CBGB * Free ice cream*
* A tragic death

After pouring their coffees into matching red thermoses that Malcolm found at the back of one of his cupboards, they strolled south on Third Avenue to the Bowery. They both carried umbrellas (Nikki's was watermelon green on the top, fleshy pink on the underside) and remained relatively dry. The pug, on the other hand, was as wet as a drowned rat. It was his fault too, as he refused to stay close to Malcolm's legs, instead running as far ahead as the leash would allow, sniffing everything he came across, curly tail wagging, oblivious to the rain. You would think the wrinkly little rat had never been outside in his short life.

While the Bowery had once been known for its gritty homeless shelters, drug rehabilitation centers, and flophouses, it was now an upscale boulevard lined with condominiums and doormen, trendy restaurants, and upscale shops. The best example of the gentrification of the neighborhood was the black-fronted menswear boutique coming up on their left.

Malcolm pointed it out. "Do you know what that clothes shop used to be?"

Nikki shook her head. "No idea."

"CBGB. New York's Whisky a Go Go."

"Never heard of it."

"It was a club. The birthplace of punk rock in the US. The Ramones played their first gig there."

"Who are The Ramones?"

"Seriously?" He sang: "*Hey! Ho! Let's go!*"

"Oh, yeah, I know them."

"The bass player used to live in the Hotel Chelsea."

"Did you ever go there...what was it called again?"

"CBGB." He nodded. "I went to a few shows when I was in high school. I got in with my brother's ID. He's three years older than me."

"Did you used to be a punk?"

"I never had a mohawk or anything."

"When did the place close?"

"A while ago now. 2006, I think. Patti Smith played the last show. By the way, she also lived in the Hotel Chelsea for a while."

"You should start running your own city tours, Mac. Give those Haunted Manhattan guys a run for their money."

When they came to Houston Street, they went east for four blocks before turning north on Avenue B. Malcolm often ordered takeout from the restaurants in Alphabet City because they offered some of the best Mediterranean food around, and for a single guy who didn't eat too healthily, Mediterranean food was about as nutritious as his diet got.

While rocking on a swing in Tompkins Square Park, Nikki said, "It would suck to be trapped on a subway train right now."

Malcolm, standing close by and watching the pug sniff the trunk of a tree, looked at her. "You think there are people stuck in the subway?"

"The trains run 24/7. They run on electricity. If there's no power, they stop moving."

"Shit, I guess you're right."

"There are probably people trapped in elevators all over the city right now too."

"This is the kind of stuff you think about?"

"We're walking around like nothing's wrong, but for some people, they're in hell right now."

"At least there's been no mass looting or arson like in '77."

"How old are you?"

"Thirty-one. How old are you?"

"Thirty-three."

"You look younger."

"Thanks, Mac."

The pug spotted a squirrel scampering across the grass and went nuts, yapping and throwing himself against the end of the leash.

"He's soaking wet," Malcolm said. "Can dogs get pneumonia?"

"Of course they can. They have lungs, don't they?" Nikki jumped off the swing and landed in a shallow puddle. She splashed through it, unconcerned. "Better head home."

On East 12th Street, between First and Second Avenues, they came across a deli that was open for business even though no lights were on. Malcolm purchased a two-liter bottle of water, a loaf of bread, a large tin of tuna fish, some milk, and a jar of mayonnaise. Nikki grabbed two containers of rocky road ice cream (a piece of paper stuck to the non-functioning freezer at the back of the store read FREE ICE CREAM – LIMIT 2 PP).

Outside, she said, "You could have gotten ice cream also."

"I don't like ice cream."

"You could have given it to me."

"You can't store it. Are you planning on eating a gallon of ice cream this morning?"

"I told you I have a fast metabolism. I would have been okay."

Back on the sixth floor of the walkup, spinning her watermelon umbrella and shedding water all over the hallway, Nikki said, "How fun was that?" She folded the canopy against the metal pole.

"We didn't learn much about the blackout."

"We know the entire East Village is affected. And it wasn't just about that. It was about getting outside. You need to get more fresh air, Mac. You're going to turn into a zombie if you're always cooped up inside in front of your computer. Do you want to come by for dinner again later?"

Malcolm had been half-expecting the invitation and had an answer at the ready. "You can't cook without power."

"There's still gas in the lines."

"That might run out by dinner time."

"What are you going to eat? Bread and leftover curry?"

"You read my mind."

"Stop being so difficult!" she said. "Why is asking you to dinner always like pulling teeth? I have a fridge full of food I need to get rid of. I can't eat it all myself."

"You have a fast metabolism," he pointed out.

"I'm going to spend the afternoon cooking up a feast. It will be ready by five o'clock. You can come by then or not. Your choice. Okay?"

"Okay."

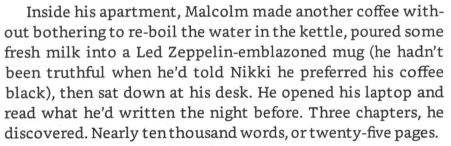

Inside his apartment, Malcolm made another coffee without bothering to re-boil the water in the kettle, poured some fresh milk into a Led Zeppelin-emblazoned mug (he hadn't been truthful when he'd told Nikki he preferred his coffee black), then sat down at his desk. He opened his laptop and read what he'd written the night before. Three chapters, he discovered. Nearly ten thousand words, or twenty-five pages.

And it was good. Really good.

Nevertheless, Malcolm's excitement was overshadowed by a growing concern that blurred the line with fear. Because once again he couldn't remember writing a single word.

He had been able to ignore, or at least brush aside, the hole in his memory regarding the magazine article because he'd drained a bottle of gin while composing it. Last night, on the other hand, he hadn't been drunk.

So what the hell was going on?

His first and most worrisome thought was that he had some form of dementia. Early onset Alzheimer's that affected people in their thirties, or another similarly frightening disease. His second thought—only slightly less worrisome—was that the fugue state was a delayed aftereffect of all the drugs he'd abused over the years. It was no secret that cocaine and heroin could mess up your brain chemistry and lead to severe depression and anxiety. But could they also cause cognitive impairment?

What about schizophrenia, Mac? You've taken your fair share of LSD too. Maybe you're a bit psychotic and you don't even know it?

"I'm not a schizo," he said to himself, and then dismissed the ruminations as alarmist thinking.

He was fine, healthy, and at his mental peak.

As he sometimes did, Malcolm opened the folder on his computer that held his digital photographs. He had taken only a handful during the hazy years of his heroin addiction, and he always went back to the same one, as he did now.

The photo was of him and a pretty girl with silver-and-green hair, both young and smiling, like they didn't have a care in the world. You'd never guess they were strung-out users. The girl's name was Lisa Brooks. She'd worked with Malcolm at Blockbuster Video. They started hanging out with each other soon after he was hired. At first they only smoked pot and drank beers together, but then he turned her onto heroin. After that, she became his partner in crime, always accompanying him on the city-wide hunts for the next fix. She was his best friend for a while, and then his girlfriend. She moved into the room he was renting in the basement of a house in Mill Basin, a residential neighborhood in southeastern Brooklyn, so they'd have more money for their habits. It was far from an ideal relationship. They stole from one another, fought, sometimes disappeared for days at a time. But they needed each other. They had alienated their families and friends; they didn't have anybody else; and had they not been slaves to the drug that ruled their lives, they might have loved each other.

On a cold night in 2010, they did business with a sketchy Jamaican dealer from whom they'd never bought before. They didn't know the heroin was cut with benzos and other dangerous agents and took their usual doses in the basement room. When Malcolm woke at some point during the early morning, Lisa lay next to him on the bed, making a gurgling sound from the back of her throat. Her lips and fingernail beds appeared blue, almost black.

Malcolm immediately called 911. While waiting for the ambulance to arrive, he turned Lisa on her side so she didn't choke on her vomit. She stopped making the terrible gurgling sound. This was a fleeting relief, however, because he could no longer find her pulse. He was searching desperately for it when the paramedics banged on the door. They administered Narcan, an overdose reversal drug. When Lisa didn't start breathing again, they performed CPR. It was to no avail. She was pronounced dead upon arrival to Mount Sinai Brooklyn.

No legal action was taken against Malcolm because under the umbrella of Good Samaritan laws, if a person committing a drug offence seeks help in the event of a medical emergency, and remains at the scene until that help arrives, he or she is immune to arrest and prosecution.

If there was any silver lining to Lisa's death, it was that it had saved Malcolm's life, inciting him to kick the habit for good and begin the 12-Step meetings.

A life lost, a life gained.

Not much comfort, but comfort nonetheless.

◆ ◆ ◆

Malcolm picked up writing where he'd left off at the start of chapter four. As soon as he typed the first sentence, he could feel his creative juices flowing and his energy spiking. By the time he finished the first paragraph in the gloomy apartment, he already had the next one composed in his mind, and the one after that. By the time he reached the end of the page, his fingers flying mechanically over the keyboard, he was so focused on the story he was no longer aware of anything else in the room.

◆ ◆ ◆

He stopped writing two hours later, not for a lack of inspiration.

The laptop battery had gone flat.

CHAPTER 22

Shane's gig

Shane rapped on Jolene's door with one of his heavy silver skull rings: tat, tat, tat.

"Come in!" she called.

He pushed the door open. Jolene was sitting on her bed, her back to the wall, a sketchpad and pencil in her hands. She wore beige sweatpants and a white crochet-knit tank top, through which he could see her flower-patterned bra.

"Howdy, sugar," she said, glancing up from the pad.

"What's the story?"

"Just doing some drawing." She flipped the sketchpad around, revealing a unicorn in gallop, its regal head cocked toward the viewer, its mane flowing.

"Brilliant, Jo!"

"I'm rather impressed myself."

"I didn't know you drew."

"I don't. Not often. But lately..."

Shane scratched his ear. "Sure look... I came by to apologize. I made a right holy show at dinner."

Jolene set aside the pad and pencil and looked seriously at him. "What's been going on with you? Every time I've seen you recently, you're drunk as a skunk."

Shane frowned, wondering if he should tell her about the Incidents on the eighth floor. He almost did—but chickened out. Now wasn't the time. After last night, she already thought he wasn't the full shilling. He wasn't going to fuel that impression with crazy talk. "Don't you be worryin' about me, Jo," he said. "I'm off the hard stuff startin' today. Also, I have a gig in Hell's Kitchen in an hour where I'll be tryin' out some new songs."

"But the power's out everywhere!"

"It's an acoustic gig. Kitchen's closed, but they still have beer to serve. Will you come by? Pints of Gat are on me."

"Thanks for the invite...but I'm feeling like a do-nothing day. I'll probably mosey arournd here and head down to the basement to do some more rubbings."

"The basement?"

"I'm rubbing the old doors stored there. They capture the history of this hotel like nothing else. But do let me know how the gig goes, you hear?"

Nodding, Shane left Jolene's room before she could read the disappointment on his face.

CHAPTER 23

Food, wine & Ritalin

With a gin on the rocks in hand, Malcolm knocked on Nikki's door at exactly five o'clock. He wasn't looking forward to spending the evening with her, but he wasn't dreading it either. He was mostly indifferent. It was something to do, and admittedly he was bored senseless. You didn't realize how much you took electricity for granted until it wasn't there anymore.

Nikki opened the door dressed in a long azure dress covering everything but her hands. A paisley scarf, folded into a band and tied in a bow, adorned her head.

"I didn't know this was a costume party," Malcolm said.

"Excuse me?" she said, her tone sharp.

"You look great."

She glanced past him down the hallway. "You didn't bring Bitcoin?"

"I figured my company would suffice. Something smells good."

Malcolm had never been inside Nikki's apartment before, and his first thought was that it would have been right at home in the Hotel Chelsea. The walls were draped with richly colorful fabrics, while the furniture was all low to the floor and surrounded by poufs and cushions. Velvet and chiffon pillows smothered the bed and sofa. About a dozen candles lit the room in a warm orange glow, and he couldn't be sure whether they were a regular fixture of the Middle Eastern décor or a temporary necessity of the blackout.

"What do you think?" Nikki asked him, waving her arm like a game show model revealing a prize.

"Cozy," he said.

"Just cozy?"

"I don't know—sensual?" Beneath the spicy aromas coming from the kitchen, he thought he could smell sandalwood incense.

"I'm not running a brothel here, Mac! How about luxurious?"

"It's definitely that. I thought you were Italian?"

"I am."

He wondered if he was going to have to ask the next logical question.

"I'm half-Italian," she clarified. "My father is Italian. My mother is Lebanese. I was born in Lebanon."

"Can you speak Arabic?"

"A little bit," she said, and then changed the topic. "Good, you have a drink. Let me get my wine."

She went to the kitchen and returned with a full glass of red.

"What are you cooking?" he asked.

"It's a surprise. Do you really want to know?"

"Not if it's a surprise, I don't."

"I can tell you."

"I can wait."

"Let's sit down."

Nikki plopped down easily on a vermilion cushion, and Malcolm sat more stiffly on a turquoise one. A decorative wicker table with almost non-existent legs separated them.

As Malcolm sipped his drink, his eyes roamed the room, picking out silver and gold trinkets, small stone and bronze sculptures, painted clay figurines, and a few religious-themed paintings leaning against the walls.

He said, "Didn't you tell me you work at a chocolate shop?"

Nikki's eyes narrowed. "Yeah...?"

"I just mean your apartment is really nice. How did you

afford to decorate it…so luxuriously?"

She smiled. "Most of what you see belonged to my parents. They have a huge house, and with that comes a lot of furniture and stuff they don't need."

"Where do they live?"

"Upstate."

"That's where you grew up?"

"Yup."

Malcolm smiled, but he was thinking, *First she grew up in Florida, then Boston, then LA, and now upstate New York? Which is the truth? And why isn't she being straight with me? What's the big secret?*

"Albany…?" he said. "Utica…?"

"Why are you so curious, Mac?"

"I'm not curious. Just making conversation, I guess."

"Buffalo," she said.

Malcolm sipped more gin. "How's that thing glowing?" he asked, tapping a replica of the moon that was cradled in a stand on the table.

"You charge it with a USB cable. It holds a long charge. Why are you acting so weird, Mac? You're asking a lot of questions."

"I get nervous when I'm in other people's houses."

She smiled again. "Am *I* making you nervous? Maybe you have a crush on me?"

He laughed. "Maybe."

"I've made some hors d'oeuvres. Let me get them."

She set her wine on the table, jumped to her feet, and went to the kitchen. Malcolm exhaled a pent-up breath. Suddenly he was feeling very iffy. Having Nikki lie to him while they chatted in the hallway was one thing, but having it happen while he was in her apartment was somehow more sinister. Maybe the lies were innocent. Maybe she had abusive parents, or had been raised by foster parents only in it for the money, and she'd invented happier childhood memories she couldn't always keep straight.

Maybe, Mac. Then again, maybe she's a serial killer wanted by the police for luring hapless neighbors into her lair, where she sneaks up on them with a hammer and feeds their bodies down her garbage disposal.

When Nikki emerged from the kitchen in a flourish of azure, he started.

"You okay over there, Mac?"

"Fine."

She set a filigreed silver tray on the table. It contained numerous small plates, dips, salads, and pita bread.

Malcolm broke off the corner of a pita and dipped it in baba ghanouj. "Mmm." The pita was spiced with thyme, sumac, and toasted sesame seeds.

Nikki seemed pleased. "You like?"

"Great." He tried some tabbouleh next.

As they picked from the plates, Malcolm relaxed his imagination and stopped thinking of Nikki as a serial killer. Eventually he found himself telling her some of the more amusing stories he'd heard at Harvey's and Jeffrey's dinner party. He even told her how the night had ended with Shane throwing up on him.

She laughed. "That's why you kept looking for an open coin laundry this morning! You said he didn't like you. Did he throw up on you on purpose?"

Malcolm scooped up some hummus with the last of his pita. "I don't think so, but who knows?"

"Sounds like a real jerk to me. And casting aspersions on you for writing magazine articles? What does he know? Oh!" She sat straighter. "Speaking about writing, I have an idea for the book you're starting."

"Shoot," he said, clearing his palate with a cold mouthful of gin. The drink was nearly finished, and he was thinking he should have brought the bottle over. The evening was turning out to be better than he'd anticipated.

"The Hotel Chelsea is where Leonard Cohen slept with Janis Joplin, right?"

"I'm not sure if they slept together. In his song he only recounts getting a blowjob."

"Okay, whatever. A blowjob's good enough. And it was a one-night fling, right?"

"To the best of my knowledge."

"So how about this," she said, leaning forward excitedly. "Leonard Cohen brings a woman back to the Hotel Chelsea a year or two after Janis Joplin's death. They do some drugs in his room, and he gets so messed up he thinks the woman is Janis Joplin, after all. While they're making out, the woman starts convulsing, going through what Janis Joplin went through while ODing in the final minutes of her life. Cohen freaks out and tries to leave the room, but the door is mysteriously locked, and he can't get out. Then everything gets trippy. The walls convulse and the lights flash on and off and all that kind of spooky stuff. Then Cohen starts experiencing all the painful memories Janis Joplin experienced in her life—and she had a lot, right? Insecurities with acne and her weight, getting nominated Ugliest Man on Campus by a fraternity in college, her addiction to alcohol and drugs. This is too much for Cohen, and he goes mad, jumping out the window and killing himself."

Malcolm stared at Nikki, once again having a hard time determining whether she was being serious with him or not. He said, "That's pretty wild, Nikki, but how would it fit into the larger story?"

She frowned. "What do you mean, larger story? That would be *the* story."

He raised his eyebrows. "The entire novel?"

"You'd need to build around it obviously. Maybe in the beginning you could show Cohen walking around town, meeting the woman, having coffee with her, all those things. Then there would be all the conversations between them, which would take up a bunch of chapters. You know, like that movie *Before Sunrise*. But sure, you could easily make a book out of it… What? You look skeptical?"

"It's just that I had something else in mind."

A timer dinged in the kitchen. "Hold that thought!" she said, getting up. "Your drink's empty. Do you want some wine?"

"Okay."

She disappeared into the kitchen. He heard the gurgle of wine being poured, then the clatter of something heavy being taken off the stove. She returned, handing him a full glass of wine and setting a cast iron skillet on the table. It contained eggs poached in a tomato and green pepper stew, sprinkled with onions and herbs.

He inhaled the spicy aromas. "The food gets better and better."

"It's called shakshuka. We need plates."

She ducked back into the kitchen for plates and silverware. She set them on the table and said, "Well, don't just look at it."

Malcolm served himself, making sure he got one of the poached eggs. He tasted a spoonful.

"What do you think?" Nikki asked.

He made an A-okay sign with his hand since his mouth was full.

"I'm glad you like it. My mother taught me how to cook. She was always saying the way to a man's heart is through his stomach."

Malcolm coughed, then swallowed hard.

"I'm not trying to get to *your* heart, Mac! I'm just telling you what my mother told me."

"It was a bit spicy, that's all."

"So what did you have in mind?"

He was dabbing his mouth with a napkin. "Sorry?"

"For your story?"

"Right." He took a sip of wine. It was rich and full-bodied, and he guessed it came from high-quality grapes. "There are three characters so far," he said. "An investigator of the paranormal. A man who lives in a room in the hotel where he cares for his autistic son. And another resident, a young woman, who's a bohemian artist and a source of comic relief.

The story's set in the hotel's heyday in the early 80s. It starts with the investigator checking into a room for a week, in the hope of finding scientific evidence to prove the existence of the supernatural. He forms friendships with the man and bohemian artist, and they share the hotel's dark history of suicides and violent deaths. Over the course of the week, the three characters begin to experience strange events during the nights...and, well, that's as far as I've gotten..." He glanced tentatively at Nikki, waiting for her to tell him that he should stick to magazine articles, after all.

Instead she clapped her hands, once and loudly. "That sounds great! Definitely better than my idea. Is one of them going to become possessed by a demonic spirit?"

Malcolm shrugged. "I don't know. I don't have an outline or anything. I'm just writing one chapter at a time."

"What about all the famous people who've lived at the hotel? You can't have a story about the Hotel Chelsea without incorporating them."

"I'm fairly sure I will. I simply haven't gotten to that point yet."

"How about a scene with the ghost of... Who's a famous writer who's lived there?"

"Thomas Wolfe?"

"A scene with the ghost of Thomas Wolfe hunched over his typewriter in the corner of some forgotten room. Or even better—a scene in which the investigator gets hot and steamy with the bohemian artist, and while they're going at it, she opens her eyes and see's it's not the investigator on top of her but Thomas Wolfe! Grinning ghoulishly, he plunges his thumbs into her eyes and laughs like an evil maniac with her blood going everywhere."

"That would be something. However, the tone I'm going for is more...terror...rather than horror. More the relationship between the unexplained events and the character's psyche's rather than blood and gore."

Nikki nodded. "Sure, I get that. In the meantime, I'll keep

thinking up plot twists that you could use. We can have a weekly brain-storming session or something."

Malcolm drank more wine. His stomach and fingers and even his testicles felt tingly, and he had the bizarre urge to get up and dance. "I feel really wired," he said, and realized he was grinning.

Nikki grinned back at him. "You're definitely talking a lot more than you usually do. You can be standoffish sometimes. Can I give you one last suggestion for your book? Add another female character. That way, you can get a love-triangle going with the investigator and the two women. That would really ratchet up the tension. You could make her...oh, blonde, dark eyed, a good cook..."

"Born in Lebanon, by any chance?"

"I'd make a great character, Mac! You know I would. And the best thing about writing me into the story, whenever you get writer's block, and need inspiration, you'd just have to come on over and ask me what I'd do in that situation."

"Let me sleep on it."

"How's that buzz going?"

"How do you know I have a buzz?"

"You said you're wired. Can I make a confession?"

"You're full of suggestions and confessions."

"I have attention deficit hyperactivity disorder."

Malcolm almost told her he wasn't surprised—Nikki was probably the most hyperactive and impulsive person he knew —before realizing how rude that would sound.

"That's hereditary, isn't it?"

"It's not caused by watching too much TV, Mac. It can be hereditary, yes. Or maybe your mom drank and smoked during her pregnancy. Or maybe your parents gave you a chunk of lead to play with as a baby. There are a lot of causes. I don't know why I have it."

"You don't appear to have any symptoms," he lied.

"I take Ritalin," she said. "Have you ever tried it?"

"Ritalin? No, why would I? I don't have ADHD..." A small

thought sprang to life in the back of his mind, and he didn't like what it was suggesting.

"It's weird," Nikki said, "it's a stimulant, but it makes me *less* hyper. But if you took it, it would be like taking speed..."

The small thought exploded into a giant one. "Did you give me Ritalin, Nikki?" he demanded. He didn't need her to answer to know that she had. He'd known his buzz wasn't from the gin or the wine, but he'd been having too much of a good time to care where it'd come from. He shot to his feet. "Fuck, Nikki!"

"What?" she said, getting up. "I always crush my pills in my food."

"Even when you have a guest over for dinner?"

"I thought it would loosen you up. You're having a good time. Are you mad?"

Yeah, I'm mad! he thought. *I'm a recovering drug addict, and you've just sabotaged three years of sobriety!* "That wasn't cool, Nikki."

"I guess I should have told you first. Do you want another one?"

"What?" he said, feigning repugnance. Malcolm did want another pill, and he found himself wondering how many pills she had, and how fun it might be to pop them all night long. "No," he told her, looking at the food on the table, his half-full glass of wine. There was no way he could sit back down and continue the evening. "I should go."

"What? Seriously, Mac—"

"Thanks for dinner," he said, and started toward the door.

"Mac!"

He opened the door and stepped into the hallway.

"Mac!"

He looked back. Nikki's arms were folded defensively across her chest. Her expression was a combination of animus, guilt, and incredulity.

"I'll see you around," he said.

CHAPTER 24

I'm not going to tell you again...

Malcolm lit a few candles in his apartment to see in the dark and paced from kitchen to living room, trying to burn off excess energy. He was still buzzing and—

—and it sure does feel good, doesn't it?

He ignored this thought and contemplated Nikki's chicanery. He couldn't believe she had slipped him Ritalin. Yeah, it wasn't going to kill him. And yeah, she didn't know he was a recovering drug addict. But shit, she could have simply asked him if he wanted a pill. What she did, mashing it up in his food, was plain creepy.

Malcolm eyed his laptop on his desk each time he passed it and wished there were power so he could sit down and get into his writing. It would have given him an outlet to vent his energy.

Grab a pad of paper and a pen. Write the old-fashioned way.

He stopped pacing. He hadn't handwritten anything much longer than a to-do list since high school. It wasn't how he worked. Nevertheless, right then it seemed like an ideal solution.

He found a pad of yellow paper in one of the kitchen drawers, grabbed a pen he kept on top of the refrigerator, and went to the sofa.

He'd written an additional two chapters of the horror novel earlier in the afternoon before the laptop battery died. The writing had come naturally and easy. However, as he sat there now, pen poised over paper, he couldn't muster up a single sentence.

"Come on, Mac," he said to himself. "Just jot something down, and it will start flowing."

Nothing came to him, not a single word.

"It's nighttime," he mumbled. "Dr. Ollstein wakes up. He heard something. Something that disturbed him. What? Footsteps on the floor above? Someone slamming a door? No, something scarier than that. What's scary, what's scary…?"

Malcolm finally began to write in his looping script, but by the time he'd filled two pages he cursed in frustration. It was all dribble.

He tossed the pen and pad aside. The pug, curled up at his feet, barked.

It's that damn Ritalin. I can't fucking concentrate.

He got up, blew out the candles, and went to bed.

◆ ◆ ◆

He couldn't sleep. His thoughts and pulse were racing. He got back up, went to the bathroom, and was washing his hands when there was a knock at the door.

He went to it and said, "Yeah?"

"It's me," came Nikki's voice.

Malcolm opened the door two inches.

"Hey!" she said brightly. She was holding a nearly full glass of wine and another scented candle, this one smelling of cinnamon and nutmeg. "What are you doing?"

"Trying to sleep."

"You're always sleeping, Mac! You're wasting your life away."

"I'm going to go back to bed now—"

"I'm sorry about the Ritalin. It was a stupid thing to do."

The apology sounded genuine, and Malcolm's anger faltered.

"Apology accepted," he said.

"Can we still hang out?"

"Now? There's nothing to do without electricity."

She peered past him. "It's pitch black in there. Want me to bring over some candles?"

"I have candles. I blew them out." He became decisive. "Look, I'm going back to bed—"

"We'll play cards!"

"I'm going to bed."

"Spoons? Hearts—?

"No, Nikki," he said, and began closing the door.

She jammed her foot between the door and frame.

"Stop it," he said. "I'm tired."

"War? It's super easy. I can teach you."

"I don't want to play cards, Nikki."

"What do you want to do then?"

"Please move your foot."

"Come on, Mac!"

"Nikki…" he said, exasperated.

Her disposition changed in a heartbeat. Her smile flipped to a scowl. "What's your problem, Mac? Why don't you want to hang out?"

"Because I'm going to bed! Because I'm tired!" *And because you spiked my food, you crazy bitch!* "Now please move your foot."

The scowl hardened. Beads of sweat appeared on her forehead. Malcolm tensed, half expecting her to toss her glass of wine on him, or try to shoulder open the door.

But then she removed her foot.

"Goodnight, Nikki," he said evenly. "Hopefully, the power will be back on in the morning."

He closed the door and shot the bolt.

CHAPTER 25

Edie Sedgwick

Holding a flickering candle, Jolene padded barefoot down the Hotel Chelsea's first-floor hallway in her pajamas. The small orange flame burned a pocket in the inky gloom, yet it also seemed to illuminate an ephemeral path through time itself, stripping away the linoleum flooring and the layers of white paint covering the walls to reveal the elaborate woodwork beneath, filling the empty transoms with the original stained-glass, and replacing the fluorescent tubes with elegant chandeliers.

When Jolene stopped, she stood before Room 105. To her alarm, tendrils of smoke were puffing out from the crack at the bottom of the door.

"Hello?" she called, slapping the door with her palm. "Edie? Are you in there? Are you okay? I think your room is on fire again!"

"Help me!" a frightened woman's voice called back.

Jolene shoved open the door. Clouds of gray smoke filled the room and stung her eyes. She fanned her hands in front of her face, but this did little to help her see.

"Where are you?"

"Help me!"

Jolene couldn't tell where the voice was coming from; it seemed to be emanating from every direction at once. At the same time she thought, *At least you can move now, Jo. You're not paralyzed like you were in the previous dream. You can move and you're not going to let Edie Sedgwick burn to a crisp.*

Jolene dropped to her hands and knees and found the smoke above the floor to be only slightly less suffocating. Regardless, she crawled forward, bumping into furniture she couldn't see and coughing compulsively and calling Edie's name.

"I'm here!"

"Where?"

"In the closet!"

Jolene couldn't find the closet. She felt as though she were crawling around in circles. Why was this so difficult? The room wasn't that big.

In frustration, she cried, "I can't find you!"

"I'm here!"

"Where?"

"*Here!*"

Finally Jolene banged up against a door.

"Edie?"

"I'm in here!"

Jolene gripped the doorknob. "Ouch!" she exclaimed, immediately letting go. It was blisteringly hot.

Coughing into her elbow, tears streaming from her eyes, she tugged the sleeve of her pajama top down over her hand to act like an oven mitt and yanked open the door.

A woman in leotards and an oversized fur jacket sat with her knees pulled to her chest, her arms wrapped around them, though her shoulders and head were hidden behind the curtain of clothing dangling from hangers above her.

"Is that you, Edie? We need to leave this room. It's on fire."

"I fell asleep without putting out my candles. One of them must have caught something on fire."

"That's okay. But we need to leave. If we stay here, we're going to suffocate."

"I'm scared."

"Follow me."

"I don't want people to see me."

"What do you mean?" Jolene asked, and all of a sudden the

clothes masking the woman's face assumed a sinister significance. "Why don't you want people to see you?"

"I'm no longer beautiful."

"Please, Edie, we have to go."

The woman raised her hands and parted the clothing hanging before her.

In the 1960s Edie Sedgwick had been a gorgeous, anorexic blonde femme fatale with a tormented, innocent beauty that had made her a fashion icon and had won her the affection of Andy Warhol, Bob Dylan, and many other celebrities of the time.

Now the face that stared back at Jolene from the bottom of the closet belonged to a corpse. Parchment skin clung precariously to bone, cataracted eyes in sunken sockets stared blankly, a crusty triangular cavity served in place of a nose, and rotten lips showcased a hideous, toothy rictus.

Then the corpse spoke, but the voice Jolene heard came from inside her head.

I told you I'm no longer beautiful.

"What happened to you?"

I killed myself.

"But why?"

I was pregnant.

"You killed yourself because you were pregnant?"

I shouldn't have done it. I don't like being dead. You won't like it either. And you're going to find out soon. You're going to die in this hotel, and you're going to be just like me.

Edie Sedgwick began to laugh.

Jolene lay curled in a tight, protective ball on the floor, and it took her nearly half a minute to realize she was in fact awake. She was overwhelmed with relief that she wasn't dead as she'd feared. Confusion followed as she pushed herself to her knees and found herself draped in near blackness. Though she could see little, she sensed she was not in her room.

Disorientated and frightened, she got to her feet, already suspecting she had been sleepwalking again. When her eyes adjusted to the silver moonglow coming through a distant window, she realized she was in one of the hotel's hallways. She felt for the door next to her and made out the room number: 105.

The dream about Edie Sedgwick returned with the force of a tsunami.

You're going to die in this hotel, and you're going to be just like me.

Clamping a cold hand over her mouth, Jolene fled silently back to her room.

CHAPTER 26

It's a date

T he power was not back on in the morning, and it continued to rain for the third consecutive day, a constant, heavy drizzle. Malcolm threw on a jacket and left his apartment to get breakfast. He half expected Nikki to be lurking in the hallway, waiting in ambuscade, but it was empty.

While wandering around the East Village—umbrella above his head, pug tugging at the leash—his mind remained fixed on Nikki. He'd always known she wasn't firing on all cylinders, but he'd never realized how messed up she was. Spiking his food with Ritalin was crazy in itself. But then coming to his apartment and demanding to hang out? They barely knew each other, and she was acting like a psychotic spurned girlfriend.

It was inevitable they were going to bump into each other around the building again, and he supposed he was going to have to remain friendly, given she was his neighbor. Friendly but not *too* friendly. Hellos and some small talk, but no more dinners together, or drinks.

And if she didn't get the hint and kept hounding him to hang out?

Then you're probably going to have to start looking for a new building, my friend. And that'll be your fault. They don't say 'don't shit where you eat' for no reason.

Eventually Malcolm came across a donut shop running off a generator. He bought two glazed buttermilk donuts and a large coffee. The woman behind the counter told him she'd heard the power outage was much more widespread than just New York, and that the subways were anticipated to resume limited service later in the day, but full power wasn't likely to be restored to the city until after midnight.

Walking home, Malcolm resigned himself to another day of boredom. What bothered him most about the continued power outage was not the inconvenience of having no lights or TV to watch. It was that he wouldn't be able to get back into his writing. He wasn't going to try working by hand again. That had been an epic failure last night, and he now blamed his lack of productivity on the change to his routine. Years of typing on a keyboard had trained his thoughts to travel from his mind, through his fingers, and onto a computer screen. It involved a kind of muscle memory that might better be described as mental memory. There was a rhythm to it, a flow, that shouldn't be tampered with.

Besides, he could manage another twelve hours or so without writing. The story wasn't going anywhere.

At home he chowed down the donuts, then picked out Stephen King's *The Tommyknockers* from one of the bookshelves above his bed. He'd read the novel when he was in his twenties but couldn't remember much about the characters or the plot. Stretching out on the sofa with the lukewarm dregs of the coffee, the pug sitting contently on his lap, he spent the next several hours reading. Around noon he made himself a tuna fish sandwich for lunch. After eating and rinsing the dishes, he picked up his mobile phone. The battery's charge was at thirteen percent.

Are you going to call?

It was too soon.

You're never going to call.

Malcolm navigated to the call log and dialed the most recent incoming number.

Quinn answered on the second ring. "Hello, Mr. Clock!" she said. "Zees is a pleasant surprise."

"Hi, Quinn," he said. "I wanted to thank you again for inviting me to dinner the other night. I had a good time."

"I'm glad you enjoyed yourself. Did you get more fodder for your article?"

"I did indeed. Enough to write a book, you might say. How are you holding up on the roof in this weather?"

"I survived the snowstorm of '82 and the nor'easter of '96 and many other acts of God. A bit of rain is nothing. It would be nice if I could walk around my gardens though…"

"I heard the power should be back on after midnight."

"Where did you hear that?"

"At a donut store."

"A donut store, did you say? Humph. I prefer to get my news from more credible sources than that." A pause. "Are you going to get to the point and ask me what you want to ask me?"

"Sorry?"

"You didn't call me, Mr. Clock, to chat about the weather, did you?"

He felt himself blushing. Quinn was sharp as a tack, all right. "No, I didn't. I was wondering—"

"Give me a moment, please."

Malcolm waited, perplexed.

When Quinn came back on the line, she said, "Do you have a pen?"

"I do," he said, picking up a pen from the coffee table.

Quinn read off a telephone number. He jotted it down on the palm of his hand.

"Is there anything else I can help you with?"

"That's Jolene's number, right?" he asked, to be sure.

"Jolene's? Why, no! It's Shane's. I figured you might want to send him the bill for your dry cleaning."

Now Malcolm's cheeks were really burning. "If it's not too much trouble, I was wondering if you had—"

Quinn chuckled. "Of course it's Jolene's number! Can't an old woman have some fun? I saw how you two were looking at each other all night."

"How was that?"

151

"Please, Mr. Clock. It was obvious to everyone. Why do you think Shane acted so unpleasant toward you? Did Jolene tell you that she and Shane used to date?"

"She mentioned something along those lines. She called it off."

"That's right. She called it off, and Shane didn't take it very well."

"She didn't tell me that he didn't take it well."

"He's never gotten over her. Now, out of the blue, a handsome and talented writer hits it off with her over dinner right in front of his very eyes."

"I really don't think I was flirting, Quinn. Shit, I thought Shane and Jolene were a couple!"

"You weren't flirting. Charming, but not flirting. The same can't be said of Jolene."

Malcolm recalled some of the looks Jolene had cast him during the evening.

"Don't fret over Shane's feelings, Mr. Clock. Attraction has to be a two-way street. Jolene's made it clear to Shane that she has moved on. He needs to do the same."

"Thanks, Quinn. And...thanks for the number."

"I'm sure Jolene will be happy to hear from you. In fact, I know she'll be."

"How do you know that?"

"Because she asked me for *your* number just this morning."

Malcolm dialed Jolene's number after he hung up with Quinn.

"Hello?" she said brightly.

"Hi, Jolene," he said, his throat a little tight. "It's Malcolm from the other night."

"Malcolm! How are you, hon?"

"Good, thanks. Granted, I'm going a little stir crazy."

"Ain't writers used to staying cooped up inside all day in

front of their computer?"

"My laptop is out of batteries, and I can't charge it."

"I wonder what Charles Dickens must have done when his laptop's battery died."

"I tried writing with a pen and paper. It didn't feel right. I couldn't get a flow going."

"I hear tell writers are notorious for their daily routines."

"James Joyce always wrote lying on his stomach in bed."

"Have you tried that?"

"Can't say I have."

"How is the Hotel Chelsea article coming along?"

"Almost finished."

"Maybe you could drop off a copy for me to read?"

"Actually, I was calling to see if...if you're not doing anything...if you'd like to get lunch later?"

"Aw, drat. I've already made plans with my sister for lunch."

"Oh. Your sister lives in New York?"

"We moved here together after college. She lives in a house in Brooklyn with her husband and two girls."

"She's older?"

"Younger. Her girls are two and four."

"Right, well... I guess I should let you go..."

"Hold your horse. I'll be free later. If you don't have any dinner plans...?"

Malcolm perked up. "No, no dinner plans. Anywhere in particular you had in mind?"

"It's going to be slim pickings with the city in the Dark Ages. Why don't we meet out front the Hotel Chelsea at seven? We'll have a wander and see where the night takes us."

CHAPTER 27

Shaking off the rust

Malcolm spent the next couple of hours tidying up his apartment in case Jolene ended up back there with him later in the evening. He was a neat person but not immaculate. He would leave all his shoes in a straight line at the door; he would wash up his dishes after he used them; and he would throw his dirty clothes in a hamper rather than on the floor. On the other hand, he couldn't remember the last time he had dusted anything in the studio apartment, mopped the floors, or scrubbed down the kitchen and bathroom—all of which he did now. When he finished the housework, he threw on some gym clothes and a pair of Asics and went for a run around the neighborhood in the rain. He was drenched when he got back, but exercised and feeling good. He took a shower, grateful the water was still running, dressed in some green Dickies and a black turtleneck, then poured himself a gin on the rocks. According to his phone—the battery now at six percent—it was five o'clock. He fed Bitcoin, then sat down on the sofa with *The Tommyknockers*. He was rather enjoying the story thus far. He could relate to the main character, James Gardner, poet and alcoholic. During the peak of Malcolm's drug haze, he was drinking about a fifth of whiskey a day. Drugs and booze and cigarettes—the unholy trinity.

He recalled what a bummer it had always been when he and Lisa, high as kites, realized they had no cigarettes left and had to leave the pleasant cocoon that was his basement to trek three blocks to the nearest gas station to buy a new pack.

In a strange way, though, he'd also enjoyed those treks. They had always turned into adventures. Just him and Lisa on a quest in a big, scary world.

Malcolm swallowed, wondering if he was ready to try dating again. To say he was out of practice was the understatement of the century.

His first girlfriend had been in high school, but that ended when she moved with her parents and brother to Arizona. In his freshman and sophomore years at Brooklyn College, he had his fair share of flings. In his junior year he became serious with a redhead named Susan Parker. During their second month of dating they were at a fraternity party together with about three hundred other people. At midnight he left with some of his friends to score coke, and he never made it back to the party, eventually crashing in his bed just before the sun rose. He woke a short time later to find Susan, who lived in the same apartment building, jumping up and down on his bed on her knees. She had a huge smile on her face and a large sign strung around her neck that read MEXICO. She was really coked up and told him how the fraternity had raffled off an all-inclusive trip for two to Cancún—and she'd won it. They booked their tickets later that afternoon and flew to Cancún the following week. The room was in a budget resort, but the weather in Mexico had been beautiful, and their first couple of days had been great. The tables turned on the third day when Malcolm went into the city to find drugs. The next four days he did little more than nod off around the pool in a heroin-induced state of drowsiness, while Susan snorkeled in the ocean and did all the other activities they had planned to do together on her own. She was not happy with him at all, and their relationship ended while on the airplane back to the US.

Malcolm didn't mind. His heroin addiction was already annexing his priorities, and there was no room in his life for someone who was going to nag him about how he spent his time and money.

Next came Lisa Brooks, but she was different. Having become an addict herself, there was no nagging. Not about how he spent his time and money, at any rate. More about who was injecting more heroin in a session, and how they were going to pay for the next fix.

Since finding sobriety three years ago, returning to college, and reintegrating into society, Malcolm had little interest getting back into the dating game. He'd felt emotionally distant from people, and socializing without drugs seemed like the antithesis of fun. His shell began to crack while he was interning at City Living. His colleagues were a close-knit, friendly bunch, and they always went out for drinks after work on Friday afternoon—and always invited him to come along. Eventually he began accompanying a single colleague named Brad to bars and clubs late in the evening. But when Brad met a cute Asian at one of these outings, he stopped going out, and Malcolm, lacking other friends, stopped going out too.

The closest he had come to a relationship since Lisa's death was back in April. He had been shopping in a Zara clothing store, and a brunette had asked him if he would try on a shirt for her. She claimed it was for her boyfriend, who was apparently Malcolm's same size. Later, while they were both lined up at the cashier, he asked her out for a drink. Her name was Sarah, and she worked at a woman's boutique in the same mall. They went out on several dates, and he was beginning to fall for her when she confessed that the request for him to try on the shirt for her boyfriend wasn't a cheesy pick-up line; she really did have a boyfriend.

Malcolm stopped taking her calls after that and went back into self-imposed monkhood. The last six months had been lonely, but he didn't mind so much. His job kept him busy, and for the most part he was happy.

In any event, he didn't exactly have a great track record with dating over the years.

So was he ready to try it again? Did he even really *want* to try it again?

The answer came quick and clear: he did. He barely knew Jolene, but ever since she'd told him she was single, he found himself unable to stop thinking about her. He was attracted to her in a way he hadn't been attracted to anybody else in his checkered past, and that had to count for something.

"Don't screw tonight up, Mac," he said to himself.

CHAPTER 28

Where I'm from, sushi is called bait

By late afternoon it had stopped raining, and Malcolm decided to walk the two miles or so to the Hotel Chelsea. He arrived at the hotel at 6:50, with ten minutes to spare. He sent Jolene a text message, telling her he was at the front of the building, while noting grimly that his battery was down to three percent.

The streets were busy with people who seemed to have no real purpose and were likely only out because they were sick of sheltering inside from the storm for the last three days. Cars zipped back and forth on the rain-slicked roads, drivers successfully navigating intersections with non-functioning traffic lights. The air was warm, sodden, and autumn-clean. Usually after a rainstorm, Manhattan dazzled all the brighter. Now, however, in the absence of the bright lights and neon, the buildings and highrises loomed dark and oppressive; the city felt like a hibernating giant.

Malcolm was marveling at the Milky Way—he couldn't remember the last time he'd been able to see it—when Jolene exited the Hotel Chelsea dressed in an Argyle sweater and tight jeans. She spotted him and waved.

"Hi," he said as they pecked cheeks. Her perfume was light and woodsy. "You look terrific."

"Thanks," she said. "So do you."

"How was your sister?"

"Good. We went to a café in Greenwich Village."

"Power's supposed to be back on later tonight."

"Thank the Lord. Which way do you want to go? North or south?"

"I came from the south, so let's go north."

They walked up Seventh Avenue to Times Square, which was unplugged and surreal. It felt as though they were characters in a post-apocalyptic film in which most of the population had been wiped out and the world had gone dark. The only places open were candlelit bars serving warm drinks and pizzerias that used wood-fired ovens. They meandered east through Bryant Park, where they nearly bumped into other strolling couples and dogwalkers since you couldn't see anybody until they were right in front of you. They returned down Fifth Avenue, passed the Empire State Building, and ended up in Koreatown, where several barbecue-style restaurants were open. They both agreed they liked Korean food, so they chose a place with some empty seats. Each table featured a lit candle, though they seemed unnecessary as the flames from the gas grills cast more than enough light to see by.

An old Korean woman with a brusque attitude gave them a menu and took their drinks order. When she returned with two bottles of Hite beer, Malcolm ordered what he and Jolene had agreed on, and Jolene added some deep-fried spring rolls at the last second.

"I know they're bad for you," she said when they were alone again. "But I can't help myself when I see them on a menu."

"They only seem bad for you when all the other food is healthy. If they were on a McDonald's menu, you probably wouldn't think twice about ordering them."

"Imagine ordering a Big Mac and spring rolls! Sounds like an alternate reality where McDonald's was founded in Asia."

"And called McWang's."

She raised her beer. "To having nothing to do."

Malcolm raised his beer and repeated the toast.

Jolene glanced around the restaurant. "This place sort of reminds me of where I used to work."

"You used to work in a Korean restaurant?"

"No, a Chinese restaurant," she said. "When my sister and I moved to Manhattan, we had nearabout five hundred dollars between us. We found a dingy little apartment to rent. My sister—her name's Grace—got a job in a shoe store. I got a job waitressing in a Chinese restaurant—and it was absolutely hell."

The Korean woman returned with a large tray. She transferred an array of small dishes—pickled vegetables, assorted kimchi, seasoned sprouts, different salads—to the table, filling up most of the free space.

"Is it rude to nibble at these before the meat comes?"

"They're not appetizers, if that's what you mean," Malcolm told her. "But nobody's going to throw you in jail."

Using a pair of silver chopsticks, she popped a piece of kimchi in her mouth.

"Why was the Chinese restaurant hell?"

"Because of the owner's wife. Her name was Ophelia. Imagine the strictest, bitchiest woman you can. That was Ophelia, all right. She used to carry around a ruler, like schoolteachers did in the old days. If I rolled a wonton wrong, or folded a napkin with an imperfect crease, she'd whack my knuckles with the ruler. Even worse, she made all the waitstaff put their tips in a jar, and at the end of the night she divvied the money out. It was supposed to be democratic— only she kept fifty percent of everything for herself, for doing nothing!"

"You should have pocketed half your tips instead of putting them in the jar."

"And rip off the other waiters and waitresses? Besides, Ophelia had eyes like a hawk. That's all she did all night, walk around the restaurant and try to catch you doing something wrong."

"I would have quit."

"I did, eventually. But I got her back first."

The Korean woman returned once more with a plate of beef and two bowls of rice. Using a large pair of scissors, she snipped the beef into bite-sized pieces, set them on the grill, and turned on the burner's flame.

"How did you get Ophelia back?" Malcolm asked.

"The restaurant moved to a new location," Jolene said, eating another piece of kimchi. "It was nicer than the last place, but it didn't have a liquor license yet, so Ophelia kept all the unused bottles of liquor in the basement, which was only used when bus tours came by. The last duty of my shift was to go around the restaurant and empty the bins into a garbage bag, then toss the bag into the dumpster out back. Well, when I emptied the bins in the basement, I added a bottle of booze to my bag and put it behind the dumpster. When I finished my shift, I went back there and retrieved my loot!"

"And I thought country girls had morals..."

"Oh, I've got morals, darlin. I've just got a whole bunch of gumption too. Besides, my sister and I drank a lot back then. We put the free alcohol to good use."

"Where are you guys from?"

"Where do I sound like I'm from?"

"Where in the South, I mean?"

"Deep enough that most folks there call sushi 'bait.' My brother, Donny, even used his *hand* as bait. You ever hear of hoggin'?"

"I don't think so."

"Donny and his pal would go down to the river and feel around with their feet for a hole on the riverbed, because that's where catfish like to hang out. Once they found one, they'd hold their breath and dive down. The water's too muddy to see anything, so they'd stick an arm into the hole, hoping a catfish would bite. If it did, they'd grab onto its mouth and yank it out. Some of those fish were real monsters."

"Don't catfish have teeth?"

"Sure do. They're nothing to mess with. Also, you never know what might be hiding out in one of those holes. Snakes, muskrats. Donny lost two fingers to a snapping turtle a few days before his eighteenth birthday."

"I don't think you'd ever catch me hoggin'."

"Because you have a good head on your shoulders. Donny, on the other hand, has the sense God gave a goose. But he fishes with integrity, you must give him that. He's very eco-friendly."

CHAPTER 29

You rub what?

Malcolm was in high spirts as he and Jolene made their way back to the Hotel Chelsea. Jolene was in even higher spirits. They'd ended up ordering two bottles of soju on top of the beers, and the alcohol had hit her harder than it had him.

Stopping beneath the hotel's candy-striped awning, he said, "Thanks for tonight."

"Thank *you*," she said. "I'm full as a tick!"

"I'll call you later?"

Jolene looked aghast. "Is the night over? Do I have a curfew?" She tugged up the sleeve of her sweater. "It's only 9:30! You ain't even seen my apartment yet."

Jolene went to the hotel's entrance and jabbed the call button. The door buzzed, and they entered the stark lobby.

Darnell, seated behind the reception desk, broke into a wide, gap-toothed smile. "Well, well, well. What do we got here? When did you kids start getting jiggy?"

"How are you, Darnell?" Malcolm said.

"Not as good as you two apparently. At least, not as good as *her*. Have a bit too much to drink?"

"*Her?*" Jolene said. "What am I? A pronoun? I have a name, thank you very much." She took Malcolm's hand, leading him past the desk. "The staff here are so *rude*."

"Yo, Malcolm," Darnell said.

Malcolm stopped inside the door that led to the stairwell. "Yeah?"

"If there's something strange...in the neighborhood..."

"Yeah?"

"If there's something weird...and it don't look good..."

Grunting in what seemed like exasperation, Jolene yanked Malcolm's hand, pulling him after her.

"*Who you gonna call?*" Darnell sang in a deep baritone, his voice following them up the shadowed stairwell. "*Who you gonna call?*"

Tiptoeing with exaggerated movements, Jolene gestured for Malcolm to do the same as he followed her along the first floor's west wing. At the end of the hallway they turned down a narrow corridor and stopped before room 218. She dug a key from her clutch, opened the door, and ushered him inside.

"What was that about?" Malcolm asked when she'd closed the door again.

"Shane lives on the main hallway. I didn't want him to hear us. We ain't together anymore, like I told you, he's just...not good with the whole post-dating thing."

"Quinn told me he made a scene when you broke up with him."

"Did she now? That woman will gossip till the cows come home!"

Jolene lit several candles, revealing a space even smaller than Malcolm's studio apartment, perhaps twelve by twelve feet. The floor was carpet rather than hardwood. A stash of jewelry, watches, and sunglasses covered the top of a chipped set of drawers. Flush against it was a giant antique wardrobe. There was no kitchen or bathroom, but a sink and a red mini-fridge occupied one corner. Atop the fridge were two over-flowing makeup bags. In another corner was a single bed with a mauve duvet and white pillows.

Large sheets of paper displaying grungy gothic-like tex-tures and patterns covered most of the white stucco walls.

"Are these the frottages you told me about?" Malcolm asked, going to the nearest one. He picked out snippets of lettering such as DIED NOV 12 and IN LOVING MEMORY and RIP. He looked at Jolene in surprise. "You didn't tell me you made rubbings of *gravestones*."

"What did you reckon I rubbed?"

"I guess I figured…" He shrugged. He didn't know; she hadn't gone into much detail during dinner. "So you spend a lot of time in graveyards?"

"Technically speaking, no," she told him. "Christians used to be buried in land near a church. That land had a name— the churchyard—and the part in the churchyard where folks were buried was called the graveyard. When these spots became overcrowded, folks were buried in land not related to churches called…"

"Graveyards?" he guessed.

"Cemeteries!"

"Right," he said. "So you spend a lot of time in *cemeteries*?"

"When I was homeless, darlin, I used to *live* in cemeteries."

Malcolm stared at her.

"I'll explain outside," she said, taking two Budweisers from the minifridge, handing him one, then climbing through the room's only window onto a fire escape.

"Is that safe?" he asked.

"Ain't as uppity as Harvey's balcony," she said, leaning against the railing, "but it does the job."

Malcolm climbed out and held onto the railing of the stairs leading up to the second floor. "You were saying you used to live in cemeteries…?"

Jolene sipped her beer. "That was Ophelia's fault, albeit indirectly. If she had been a good employer, I wouldn't have quit without having another job lined up. But I couldn't stand it there, and that's what I did, quit, and it happened to be right in the middle of the SARS outbreak. You know, right when cafés, pubs, and restaurants were cutting back on their staff, not hiring. My sister had moved in with her boyfriend. I was on my own and couldn't make rent. So I shuffled from one friend's couch to another, spending more and more nights on the streets. Now, I was twenty then, pretty as a peach, so sleeping on park benches was asking for trouble. Cemeteries, on the other hand, were private and safe. I never saw anyone in them at night—apart from teenagers on a few occasions. But they never saw me...if I didn't want them to."

"Why would you want them to?"

"Because teenagers can be obnoxious little brats, shouting the most awful things about the names they read on the tombstones, about dead people in general. If the mood took me, I would pull my shirt up over my head and burst out of the bushes, making animal noises. You've never seen kids run so fast!"

"My life seems so bland compared to yours."

"Those were some awfully tough times, I admit. But I wouldn't trade them for anything. It's how I discovered my art, after all. Spending time among tombstones gets you thinking about a lot of stuff. One of the things I thought about was how sad and neglected all the graves were. The living like to forget about the dead. I thought it would be nice to celebrate them instead. I didn't know anything about rubbings then. I was thinking more along the lines of putting together a photography book, or doing some drawings. Anyway, I was in the New York Library one day—I spent a lot of time there that summer—and I was looking for a Halloween book I'd read when I was seven or eight, and I came across a book on brass rubbings. That's how they usually reproduce the reliefs in Europe, on engraved memorial brass. That book led me to others on gravestone rubbings, and I knew right away that's what I wanted to do. I used the money I busked the next day to buy paper and crayons and started spending my nights making gravestone rubbings. After a while, I had so many I was giving them away to my friends, though many insisted on paying me. Then one of my friends living in the Chelsea told Stanley Bard about my rubbings and that I needed a place to stay. He agreed to see me."

"I was wondering how you found your way into the hotel."

"When I learned Stanley was a big fan of Andy Warhol, I took a bus to Pittsburgh and did a rubbing of Warhol's grave. Did you know folks leave cans of Campbell's soup around it? Anyway, when I met Stanley for the first time, there was no talk of background checks or any of that usual landlord stuff, bless the man. He just said, 'I heard what you do, and you're exactly the kind of person who should be living here!' He gave me this room and waived the first month's rent in exchange for the Warhol rubbing."

"And here you are now," he said.

"Here I am now, sugar," she said. "And the only way I'll ever leave, I reckon, will be feet first on a stretcher."

CHAPTER 30

Problem child

When Malcolm mentioned he needed to use the bathroom, they climbed back inside through the window, and Jolene gave him a key and a candle. She pointed out the bathroom down the corridor and told him that he had to jiggle the key in the lock.

The bathroom was a small box with a black-and-white checkerboard floor. Setting the candle on the lip of the sink, Malcolm urinated in the toilet. As he flushed, he noticed a syringe and hypodermic needle in the bathtub, next to what appeared to be several dried bloodstains.

"Aw, shit," he said, washing his hands and retrieving the candle.

When he returned to Jolene's room, she was standing by the open window, smoking a cigarette.

"Didn't know you smoked."

"I don't usually. But I keep a pack around for whenever I'm walking on a slant."

"Someone was shooting up in your bathroom."

"*What?*"

"There was a needle and blood in the tub."

"Shut my mouth!" she said, crushing out the cigarette in an ashtray. "Who would be shooting up in my bathroom?"

"How many people do you share it with?"

"Only Shane. There are four tenants on this floor, and the other two are in the east wing. And before you ask, no, Shane doesn't use needles. I'm positive of that. It must be someone from one of the upper floors. They must have a copy of the key. Was the door locked?"

He nodded.

"I'll tell Darnell about this tomorrow. And you know what? I reckon he won't lift a finger to help. The comfort and safety of the tenants doesn't amount to a hill of beans to that man. Lord, it will be nice when the renovations are over with and this hotel can get back on its feet."

"You sound upbeat about the renovations," he said, surprised.

"Wouldn't you be if you lived here? Look at this place! My, where are my manners? Would you like another beer?"

"Are you having one?"

"I think I should have water."

"Water's good."

She withdrew two bottles of Evian from the minifridge and handed him one. Since there were no chairs in the room, they settled down on the floor, their backs to the bed.

"By the way Quinn was talking," Malcolm said, "I figured everyone in the building was against the renovations."

"Quinn!" Jolene rolled her eyes. "Never say anything about the renovations in front of that woman unless you want to put her in a horn-tossing mood. She's lived here for a coon's age. She's lived through all the storied history you hear about. Her nostalgia and prejudice can't stand the idea of anything changing, ever, even if it's for the better. But you'll never hear her say that. Forget the cockroaches and the varmints, the peeling paint and the funky smells, the broken heating and plumbing. The renovations, according to her, will bring no good. They will only destroy the hotel's spirit."

"The Chelsea's not any ordinary hotel. It does—or did—have a special kind of spirit."

"Sure, it *did*. Once. But that spirit's been gone for a long time already, long before the renovations started. Even when I moved in nearabout ten years ago, the hotel was a shadow of its former state. It didn't have the grandeur of its early years, and it didn't have the celebrities and personalities of its heyday years. It was…mundane…by all standards, the worst type of fate for a hotel like this one. The renovations Stanley started were superficial. The place needed a complete overhaul, and that's what the new developer is doing. Will it be the Hotel Chelsea of the past? No. Will it be something special in its own new way? Hopefully so."

"Do you believe the renovations are being purposefully protracted?"

"Why would they be?"

"Quinn says the developers want to make life as difficult as possible for the remaining tenants in the hope they'll get fed up and move out."

Jolene shook her head. "She's just upset. And I understand that, I do. The renovations can drive you up the wall. But they ain't being purposefully drawn out, no. This is a large hotel. They're stripping it back to its bones. They're putting in all new plumbing, air conditioning, electrical systems. I reckon they're doing a good job with that. And I hear tell from other tenants that the developers are doing their best to minimize the intrusion. If a pipe breaks and leaks into someone's apartment, they clean up the water and stains lickety-split. If they're renovating right next door to your room, and the noise is too much, they'll put you up in a nice hotel, if that's what you want. Some of the tenants who've already had their apartments renovated say they got nice extras, like a bathroom if they didn't have one before, or crown molding where they wanted it. Pretty accommodating if you ask me."

"Doesn't sound too bad," Malcolm agreed. "So what's your beef with Darnell? I get why Quinn doesn't like him. But if you're on the side of the developer…?"

"He's just always making snide, smart-alecky comments. You heard him with the *Ghostbusters* song. He doesn't make a distinction between Quinn or me. We're all no-good bohemians in his eyes."

"You didn't say much at Harvey's when he was talking about ghosts. What's your opinion on the Chelsea being haunted?"

"What's *your* opinion?" she countered. "You're the one who saw the ghost of Roger James."

"I didn't say I saw a ghost. I said I saw a man in a porkpie hat and trench coat."

"Which was what Roger James wore every day—Roger James who died of a dramatic suicide only a few days earlier."

"Do you think I saw this man's ghost?"

"I don't know what you saw. I wasn't there. But you want my opinion on whether the Chelsea is haunted?" She paused for a beat. "A few years ago I used to babysit a boy up on the tenth floor. His parents were living in high cotton. The husband was a banker, the wife a well-known concert pianist. One night when they returned home, they were both drunk, louder than usual, and woke Christopher, who came out into the hallway in his pajamas. They didn't pay him any attention because his daddy was in the middle of telling me about the glamorous party they'd been at. I noticed him though. He just stood there, staring up at the skylight for the longest time. I remember the poor thing's face. It was pale and tight, his eyes glassy. When his daddy finally told him to go to bed, he wouldn't go, asking again and again who the man was up on the roof." She shook her head. "The whole episode wouldn't have been any big deal, all kids have active imaginations, except that Christopher...changed. The next time I babysat him, he wasn't the same. He wouldn't get out of bed, and he was so angry. The couple told me to keep any sharp objects locked up and to never take my eyes off him."

"Sounds like you were babysitting Chucky. Did he ever make a play for a butcher's knife?"

"I didn't let him in the kitchen. I sat in a rocking chair in his room with a book, watching him. I felt like a prison guard. At some point, though, I nodded off. When I woke, I found him out in the hallway, staring up at the skylight. I had to drag him kicking and screaming back inside. The hate in his eyes...

I remember thinking, *This boy would kill me if he could.* I was so unnerved I called the couple and told them to come home early. I never babysat Christopher again, and I didn't see the couple for about a year, until I ended up in the elevator with them one day. I asked how Christopher was doing, and they told me they'd had him institutionalized. They both looked like they'd aged about ten years."

"And all this because the kid thought he saw a man, or the ghost of a man, on the roof?"

"Thought he did, or did?"

"And it possessed him?"

"I have no idea, darlin. I just know that he was not the same after that night. And I've experienced other strange things at the Chelsea over the years. I ain't the only one either. Everyone who's lived here for long enough has a ghost story or two to tell. And recently..." She paused and shrugged aside whatever she was going to say.

"What's happened recently?"

"Nothing..."

In the silence that followed, Malcolm thought about the problem child, the mysterious reflection he saw in Roger James' mirror the other day, and the man in the lobby in the porkpie hat. Several minutes had passed before he realized he might be overstaying his welcome, and he said, "I should probably get going..."

Jolene didn't answer.

He leaned forward to see her face. Her eyes were closed.

"Jolene?"

No answer.

She had fallen asleep.

CHAPTER 31

Sid Vicious

Malcolm was contemplating whether he should stay or go when he nodded off himself. When he woke, only a single candle remained lit in the room, the small orange flame sputtering in the wet breeze blowing through the open window. Jolene's head was slumped forward, her chin resting on her chest, her hands at her sides.

Malcolm got to his feet and carefully lifted her onto the bed, pulling the mauve duvet up to her shoulders. The alcohol must have really knocked her out because she didn't bat an eyelid.

He opened the door slowly and quietly and shut it again equally so. He didn't like sneaking out in the middle of the night, but he knew he would not get back to sleep in the upright position he'd been in, and stretching out on the floor was questionable behavior for a grown man.

He made his way down the corridor to the main hallway. It was as dark as it had been earlier—only now, halfway down the hall, light seeped through the crack at the bottom of a door.

Power's back on, he thought gratefully a moment before wondering if that was the case, why were the hallway lights still out?

Malcolm stopped in front of the door. He heard a rustling sound from inside the room. He pressed his ear to the door, wondering what the hell he was doing.

"Waddya want?" a voice asked.

Malcolm jerked away in a panic. Resisting the urge to dash to the stairs, and knowing an explanation was needed, he said, "Is...uh...the power back on? I saw your light..."

"It's working in here, mate. You coming in?"

You'd think if you're standing in a near-black hallway in a hotel in the middle of the night, and a stranger invites you into his room, you're not going to take up the offer.

But logic and reason were in short supply right then, and he opened the door.

◆ ◆ ◆

A gooseneck lamp with an emerald shade stood on a chest of drawers. It illuminated a thin man lying on a threadbare mattress, propped into a semi-upright position by lumpy pillows. He wore a leather jacket rolled up at the sleeves, a leopard-print pirate shirt, a black studded belt, black drainpipes, and scuffed motorcycle boots. A padlock on a chain encircled his neck like a choker. His black hair was fluffy and spiky at the same time, in stark contrast to his pale, almost translucent skin. Dark circles beneath his eyes suggested he hadn't slept in a long time. He was scavenging through an old-fashioned medicine bag on his lap.

"Can't seem to find my rig," he mumbled in a London accent. "You haven't seen—? Ah, here it is!" he added, producing a stiletto-sized glass syringe attached to a hypodermic needle.

Malcolm's lungs felt like over-inflated basketballs, and he clutched his chest in fear of having a heart attack.

The man was a spitting image of the ex-Sex Pistol performer Sid Vicious.

"Wanna do some Chinese rocks with me, mate? I got us some good shit here." He stuffed a hand into the pocket of his tight jeans and pulled out a bag of heroin.

Malcolm breathed again, and the pain receded a little from his chest. He tried to speak, but the only word he uttered was,

"...Vicious?"

"Vicious? Me? I ain't vicious. I consider myself to be kind-hearted. I love my mum. Now waddya reckon? I already got some dope cooked up." A Sterno stove sat on the chest of drawers next to the gooseneck lamp. Sid Vicious stuck the hollow hypodermic needle into a tin coffee cup on the burner, loaded the glass syringe with liquified heroin, and shot up into a vein in his left forearm. He grunted, as if he'd been waiting for the fix all day. "You going to get stoned with me or not? These rocks are the real thing, and there's plenty in the cooker. Take the hypo."

Malcolm decided he was dreaming. It was unlike any dream he'd had before—everything was too vivid, too real—but it was also too surreal to be reality.

Too surreal? Try impossible, Mac! Sid Vicious has been dead for more than thirty years!

Yet still... Malcolm eyed the dope hungrily.

He took a step forward. Sid gave him a grin that was also a snarl—encouraging, menacing.

He took another step—and noticed the blood in the bathroom. The door was open a few inches. The white tiles inside were smeared bright red.

"Don't mind her," the lookalike said. "She's only trying to get attention again. Cunt's always trying to get attention." He held the hypodermic needle out.

Nevertheless, the spell over Malcolm had faltered, and on legs barely able to support his weight, he back-pedaled out of the room.

"Come back, mate, don't—"

He slammed the door shut, whirled about—and yelped in fear.

"Calm down, son," a shadowy shape said.

The shadowy shape was a man, just a man, an old man, dressed in loose-fitting blue pajamas. Small and frail, he was hardly threatening.

Malcolm glanced at the door he'd just exited. It remained

closed. No light seeped from beneath it. He turned back to the man.

"Who are you?" Malcolm asked, his voice shallow and shaky. He ran a hand over his jaw and breathed deeply. He'd been sleepwalking, that was all.

The slow, underwater-like sense of unreality began to fade.

"Who am I?" the old man said. "I live here. The question is, who are *you*?"

Malcolm wanted to touch him, to make sure he was solid, but he kept his hands at his sides. "I'm sorry. I was just leaving —"

"Malcolm?" Jolene said in a loud whisper. She was standing at the end of the hallway, holding a candle. "What are you doing? Who are you with?"

"It's Doug Switzer, Miss Hathcock."

"Oh hi, Doug. What are ya'll doing?"

Another door opened, this one from the other direction.

"What the bleedin' hell is goin' on?"

Malcolm couldn't make out the person in the dark, but he recognized the Irish accent.

"Jo? That you? Who are you two gobshites? It's the middle of the night!"

"I'm on my way home," Malcolm said.

Apparently Shane recognized his voice too. *"You,"* he spat.

Malcolm started toward the stairwell.

"Where are you going, Malcolm?" Jolene said.

"Home," he said. "I'll—I'll call you."

"Don't be silly! Come back here—"

"Are youse *sleepin'* together?" Shane shouted.

"I'll call you," Malcolm told Jolene again, pushing through the door to the elevator landing.

"Did you face him, Jo?" Shane bellowed. *"That* eejit? Blast you to hell, ye rotten bitch!"

His door slammed shut with a resounding echo.

CHAPTER 32

Room 826

G oro Yazawa was a chubby, manic fella who was easy to hang out with and who always tried to make you feel at home in his swanky two-bedroom apartment on the eighth floor of the Hotel Chelsea. He hailed from a wealthy Japanese family, and like Shane, he came to New York City to pursue his musical interests in defiance of his parents' wishes.

Shane liked him a lot. He always listened whenever Shane needed to unload his grievances about his music career, such as venues that refused to book him, or industry people who refused to listen to his demos. He kept his fridge stocked with Guinness, even though he didn't drink alcohol himself. And whenever they smoked a joint together, he was more than happy to listen to CDs of Freddie White or Tom Waits or other such singers, insisting in his stilted English, "They my favorite," even though this was anything but the truth.

Musically, Shane and Goro were at opposite ends of the spectrum. While Shane was a bluesy, folk rock singer-songwriter most often found strumming his moody songs on a small stage in the back corner of some little-known pub, Goro was an electro house DJ into heavy bass and 130-beats-per-minute tempos, performing at trendy clubs around the city, sometimes to the adoration of thousands of fans.

Kicking back in a white leather armchair, a glass of cold Guinness in hand, Shane said, "I had a gig yesterday in Hell's Kitchen."

Seated cross-legged on a matching sofa across from him,

Goro said, "You bring down house?" Black was the only color he wore, and today he was decked out in black shorts, a black jumper with a white logo, a black skull-and-crossbones bandanna, and black Adidas runners.

"Bring down the house?" Shane chuffed. "All twelve people. I played some new songs."

"Have I heard?" Goro asked.

Shane shook his head. "I only wrote them this week. But you'd like them. I should have brought up the guitar."

"You next superstar, man. Next big thing."

"Tis grand you think that, lad. How is the DJing?"

Goro, always filled with febrile energy, seemed to deflate. He stared at the floor.

Shane frowned. "What's the matter?"

Goro looked up, his eyes tormented. "I must go home. My father says time up. He give me no more money."

"G'way outta that! Yer doin' brilliant!"

Goro shook his head. "My father don't care, don't listen. He want me home, get wife, work in company like him." His eyes teared up. "I like Hotel Chelsea. I like New York City. I like you, Shane. You my friend. Now all gone."

"Yer making coin. Tell the oul fella to piss off! You don't need his money."

Goro shook his head again. "You want more beer?" He got up and went to the kitchen in the next room.

Shane was trying to come to terms with the fact that Goro, his only real friend at the hotel, might soon be leaving...when he had the uncanny feeling that he already knew this information, that they'd already had this conversation. This feeling continued to intensify, big and black and just out of sight, until it could no longer remain unseen, and Shane remembered sitting here in Goro's apartment previously, talking not about Shane's gig in Hell's Kitchen (it had not happened yet), but about other matters, when Goro dropped the news that his father was cutting off his finances, and Goro would be returning to Japan...and Goro going to the kitchen to get Shane another beer and—

"No!" Shane shouted, leaping to his feet and running to the next room. The large window next to the kitchen area was open, the lower sash shoved up all the way to the head, the sheer curtains fluttering in a breeze.

Shane scrambled through the window onto the iron balcony and leaned over the railing.

Far down on the sidewalk, small and unmoving, he saw Goro's broken, chubby body, surrounded by a dark corona of spreading blood.

◆ ◆ ◆

Pain lanced through Shane, jarring him awake. He found himself on the floor in a dark room with someone hovering over him.

"Fack aff away!" he cried, scuttling backward.

"Whoa there. Take it easy, Mr. McSorley, take it easy. It's Doug Switzer."

It *was* Doug Switzer, Shane realized, relaxing slightly. He could see the old man in the moonlight slanting through the open window behind him. He wore a pair of baggy blue pajamas and a concerned expression.

"What's happenin'? Where am I?"

But Shane knew without even looking around. He was in Room 826. Goro Yazawa's old room. The dream he'd been having was right there behind his eyes, clear as if it had really happened.

And it had really happened, he thought with a lump of despair, *four months earlier*.

"You were on the balcony, son," Doug Switzer said gently. "Standing on the railing. You don't recall that?"

Shane didn't say anything.

"You lifted your foot. You were about to... Well, I pulled you back."

"I was sleepwalkin'," he mumbled.

179

"Sleepwalking!" Doug Switzer said, relief in his voice, though the concern—and skepticism—remained on his face. "Hell, you're lucky I came in to have a look when I did. The door was open and it's never open. I pass it almost every night." He exhaled loudly, his breath whistling between his lips. "How about you come on down to my place? We can... talk, if that's what you want. I don't sleep much anymore."

Shaking his head, not trusting himself to speak—he felt like a man held together by fraying thread right then—Shane shoved himself to his feet and quickly left the apartment.

◆ ◆ ◆

Although Shane had managed to get through all yesterday and today without soaking his brain in booze, he now knocked back a long, stinging mouthful of whiskey and immediately took another.

Going sober had been a mistake that had almost cost him his life.

Twelve days ago, the Monday morning after the First Incident in Goro's old room (where Shane had woken to find himself standing on the balcony railing), he hit the bottle solely out of fear. He'd been scared senseless by the fact he'd been inches from his death—a death he likely wouldn't have known was coming until a second before splattering against the ground like a bug on a car windshield. This same motivation and desire to drink informed the entirety of the next day as well.

Upon waking on Wednesday, however, with the worst hangover he'd ever experienced in his twenty-nine years (and he'd had his fair share), he didn't go near the green bottle all day.

That night the Second Incident occurred, in which, once again, he'd woken to find himself standing on Goro's balcony.

Shane couldn't fathom why he was sleepwalking, and he certainly couldn't fathom why he was trying to kill himself, but he had a nagging suspicion about one very important thing: the booze was keeping the demon puppeteer pulling the strings at bay. He tested this theory by hitting the bottle all that day so that by the time he passed out around midnight he was in a comatose-like state. Lo and behold, he didn't wake that night standing on an eighth-floor balcony, staring death in its face; he woke the following morning in his bed, hungover but alive.

And so every day since had followed the same booze-until-he-passed-out trajectory.

Until yesterday.

Shane had planned to remain sober only until he'd finished his gig in Hell's Kitchen, but by the time that rolled around, and he was feeling half human for the first time all week, he decided to hell with it, he would remain sober, sleepwalking be damned. Was he frightened? He was. But he also knew he couldn't get battered every waking hour for the rest of his life.

Clearly he had been prematurely optimistic in his reasoning. His devious mind, as it turned out, had been lying in wait, for there Shane was again tonight, standing on Goro's balcony railing, the same railing the poor fella had climbed himself in the early summer, inches and perhaps moments away from following his pal to the grave.

Shane took another swill from the bottle that burned him to the gut.

PART 2

"I remember you well in the Chelsea Hotel / You were talking so brave and so sweet / Giving me head on the unmade bed / While the limousines wait in the street."

—LEONARD COHEN, "CHELSEA HOTEL NO. 2"

Some of the celebrated former residents of the Hotel Chelsea
(Danny Bright and Steven Miller/Elle Decoration)

The hotel facing West 23rd Street in 2012 (Wikipedia)

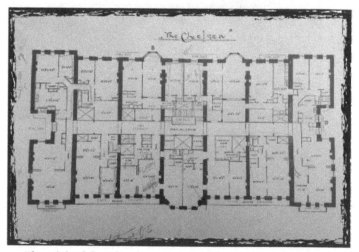

The original floorplan (New York Historical Society Library)

The lobby in 2010 before the artwork was taken down (Wikipedia)

The famed wrought-iron staircase in 2005 (Wikipedia)

Long-time manager Stanley Bard in 2011 (Emmanuel Dunand/AFP/Getty Images)

A bohemian apartment (Danny Bright and Steven Miller/Elle Decoration)

Janis Joplin shortly before her death in 1970 (David Gahr/Getty Images)

The Ramones with Iggy Pop (also a one-time resident of the Hotel Chelsea) at CBGB in 1976. Dee Dee Ramone is second from the right (Roberta Bayley/Getty Images)

Entrance to the 4th floor wing in 2011 (Marja M./Yelp)

A 4th floor corridor in 2011 (Marja M./Yelp)

Front of the hotel covered in scaffolding in 2018 (Travis T./Yelp)

The hotel's old doors, which sold at auction for over $400,000 in 2018 (NYCityLens)

A hallway under renovation in 2019 (Tod Seelie/Gothamist)

A renovated model room in 2017 (Kara Mann Designs)

The body of 20-year-old Nancy Spungen being carried from the hotel on October 12, 1978, after allegedly being stabbed by boyfriend, Sid Vicious. (Hal Goldenberg/AP)

CHAPTER 33

Let there be light (and power)

Malcolm woke groggy and unrested when the alarm clock radio on the bedside table switched on, playing the The Beach Boys' "Good Vibrations." The red digital numbers were flashing 12:00.

He climbed out of bed and hit the light switch. The overhead bulb blasted light. He powered on the TV and switched channels until he found a local morning news program that had the time—5:51 a.m.—displayed on a chyron in the bottom corner. He turned up the volume to hear what the hosts were saying while he made coffee in the kitchen. Over the next half hour he surfed from channel to channel, piecing together what had been going on in the world the last three days. Most of the news reports evinced the usual mixture of tragedy and death. Ten people killed in a hospital fire in Japan. Twenty-seven killed after a migrant boat sank in the Channel of Sicily. Fifty killed after a truck veered off a cliff in Peru. Fifteen killed by explosions in a fireworks factory in Vietnam. Over a hundred killed in a stampede on a bridge in India.

On a local note, there was a lot of information about the blackout. It was similar in scope to the Northeast blackout of 2003, affecting over fifty-million people. Power companies had resumed services in Michigan, Ohio, and Southern Ontario within hours. It was only portions of southern New York State, including much of New York City, that had remained dark for a record-breaking three days. He watched reporters interviewing hospital patients who'd had their operations postponed; passengers stuck at JFK Airport, as well as others who'd been on incoming flights diverted to airports with power; and small business owners who'd lost expensive refrigerated stock. There were videos of people being evacuated from trapped subway trains, shoppers hoarding groceries at supermarkets, police officers patrolling the rainy streets, and a barrage of negative-growth economic graphs since several US financial markets had shut down.

Initially the cause of the blackout was unknown, and news pundits floated the possibility of a terrorist attack. Americans blamed Canadians, Canadians blamed Americans, while politicians fulminated against the region's outdated power grid. Eventually a joint US-Canada taskforce traced the problem back to a privately owned natural gas power plant on the Rockaway Peninsula in Queens. A software malfunction in the computer system caused the plant to shut down unexpectedly, triggering cascading outages across the state and beyond. Investigations were ongoing, but reports were pointing to poor equipment maintenance at the plant, as well as a stalled alarm that impeded system operators from identifying the malfunction for over an hour.

Early estimates were putting the financial impact to New York City alone at north of one billion dollars.

As Malcolm sat on the sofa listening to all this, he was only half paying attention. His mind kept going to the bizarre sleepwalking episode he'd experienced the night before. It had seemed frighteningly real at the time—the details in the crummy room, the conversation with Sid Vicious himself—but the more he thought about it, and the more he replayed it over and over again in his head, the more it began to take on the foggy, disjointed air of a dream.

He made another coffee and sat down at his desk. He plugged in his laptop and turned it on, happy to find the internet was working.

He spent the next two hours reading articles and watching videos featuring Sid Vicious.

Born John Ritchie, he got the moniker "Sid Vicious" while at college. He'd been in the room of future bandmate John Lydon, aka Johnny Rotten, when Rotten's pet hamster, Sid, bit Ritchie, who exclaimed, "That Sid is really vicious!" After that, Rotten began calling Ritchie "Sid Vicious," and Ritchie's punk alter-ego was born.

Eventually Johnny Rotten formed the Sex Pistols. When the band's bassist couldn't make a gig, Sid Vicious filled in for him. Despite the fact Sid could barely play the bass, he had an anarchistic look about him and had invented the Pogo—the dance in which you jump up and down on the spot—and so Rotten made him a permanent member of the lineup.

The arrangement didn't last long. During the Sex Pistols' first and only US tour in 1978, Sid Vicious' heroin habit spiraled out of control, and he became unhinged on and off the stage. Rotten kicked him out of the band as promptly as he'd recruited him.

Sid reunited with his old girlfriend, the crass and combative Nancy Spungen, who had been banned from the tour since none of the other bandmembers liked her. She and Sid ended up moving into a room in the Hotel Chelsea together, where Sid decided to embark on a solo career with Nancy acting as his manager.

On the morning of October 12, 1978, Sid woke from a drug-induced stupor to find Nancy dead on the bathroom floor with a hunting knife that belonged to Sid protruding from her lower abdomen. Freaking out, Sid called the hotel's front desk clerk, who called the police. Sid was wandering the first-floor hallway in a confused state when the cops arrived. He confessed that he'd stabbed Nancy because he was a "dirty dog." He was arrested and charged with murder. In the following days, however, Sid reversed course, claiming he didn't kill Nancy because he had been passed out all night.

With no clear evidence of guilt, the judge in the case released Sid on $25,000 bail—paid for by his record label, Virgin Records—and Sid dove right back into his self-destructive ways. Ten days after Nancy's death, he attempted suicide by slicing his wrists with shards of a broken light bulb. He was committed to Bellevue Hospital, where he attempted to jump out of a window, shouting at the top of his lungs that he wanted to be with Nancy, only to be foiled by the hospital staff.

Not long after his discharge from Bellevue, he was charged with assault, his bail was revoked, and he spent nearly two months in Riker's Prison. On February 1, 1979, he made bail again and went to a party hosted by his mother. Early the next morning he died of a heroin overdose, leaving behind a suicide note that requested he be buried next to Nancy in his leather jacket and motorcycle boots.

Consequently, there was never a trial for the murder of Nancy Spungen. Her stabbing was never thoroughly investigated, and the truth of what happened to her never came to light.

The police continued to believe Sid had killed her. In their eyes he was a degenerate punk who was known to beat her with some regularity over petty disagreements. During one such fight, they held, he went too far.

Others, however, speculated that a drug dealer who had visited Sid and Nancy on the night of October 11 killed her, perhaps in an argument over money, while Sid was passed out. Witnesses, after all, claimed that Sid had ingested almost thirty tablets of Tuinal that night, which, if true, would have put him in a near comatose state.

Most fans of Sid Vicious favored a third and more romanticized version of events in which Nancy took her own life in some sort of botched double-suicide pact with the punk rocker.

Whatever really happened, Sid and Nancy became a modern-day Romeo and Juliet, despite the fact they were not only miserable apart like the original star-crossed lovers, but often miserable together too. Their legends peaked when the movie *Sid and Nancy* came out in 1986, portraying the couple as two young rebels struggling to break free from the conformity shackled upon them by society.

Throughout the 1980s and early 90s, idolizing punks hung Union Jacks on the door of Sid and Nancy's infamous room. They carved slogans into it such as "Don't Let Them Take You Alive" and "Love Kills." They left offerings of roses in empty liquor and beer bottles, as well as cigarettes, joints, used needles, and farewell letters.

For a long moment, Malcolm stared at a Google image of the young hellraiser Sid Vicious in his leather jacket and chain choker, his face screwed into his lopsided, trademark snarl.

"Fucking nut," he mumbled, snapping the laptop lid closed.

CHAPTER 34

The man in the porkpie hat (3)

At eight o'clock that morning, Malcolm called Steven Perry, the editor-in-chief at *City Living*, to ask if the office would be open later.

"I'm already here," Perry said. "How's the Chelsea copy coming?"

"I think I'll have it finished today."

"Today? When's the deadline?"

"You told me this Friday."

"You must have been busy these last few days."

"There wasn't much else to do. And I had some great sources at the hotel."

"If that's the case, then stay home. Finish it up there. You can bring it in tomorrow."

After hanging up with his boss, Malcolm made his third coffee of the morning and sat down again at his laptop. Instead of finishing up the Hotel Chelsea article, however, he decided to continue with the horror novel. He had little trouble finding inspiration, and before he knew it, four hours had passed. Riding a creative high, he whistled while he made a tuna fish sandwich. He ate his lunch looking out the balcony doors at the park across the street. He'd just finished washing up when his phone beeped. The message was from Jolene:

Welcome back to modernity! Sorry about falling asleep. I must have been worn slap out. And sorry once again about Shane...

Malcolm typed back:

I'm the one who should apologize for leaving like that, but I didn't want to wake you. Any idea what that old guy was doing wandering the hallway?

Her reply:

His wife passed away this year. He says he can't sleep at night anymore. Just wanders around the hotel to pass the time. By the way, you're sure you saw a needle and blood in the bathroom?

Frowning, he typed:

I'm sure about the needle. Pretty sure about the blood. Why?

Her reply:

Because there was nothing in the bathtub this morning. I guess someone came back to clean up.

After a little more back and forth, Jolene told him she was going to go make some lunch, and he told her he was going to get back into his work.

Malcolm didn't continue working on the novel. He was more than happy with how much he'd gotten down that morning, and he didn't want to risk exhausting his muse. Besides, he had to finish up the Hotel Chelsea story.

Over the next two hours he went over the body copy line by line, mostly proofreading to catch typos or rework a sentence here or there. Then he transferred the SD card from his Nikon to the card reader in his laptop. He'd taken sixty-one photographs at the hotel, and he selected those he believed best complemented the article.

He was clicking through the final few when his finger froze above the mouse button. The blood in his veins went icy cold as he stared at the photo he'd snapped of the Hotel Chelsea's deserted reception desk—only the desk was no longer un-occupied.

A man wearing a porkpie hat and a beige trench coat stood behind the counter.

CHAPTER 35

*Something strange is definitely
in the neighborhood*

With a sweaty, nauseous feeling washing through him
that he realized was a paroxysm of intense fear,
Malcolm clicked back through all the other photographs he'd viewed, looking for any other…discrepancies. He
found none, a small relief, and returned to the photo of the reception desk.

The man—Roger James—was looking at the ground, his
downcast face obscured by the curled-up brim of his hat. He
was out of focus, blurry in contrast to the clarity of everything else captured in the frame, but there was no mistaking it
was Roger James.

Or the man dressing up as Roger James.

Impossible! he thought. *I would have seen him when I took the
shot!*

Moreover, even if Malcolm had somehow missed seeing a
man standing smack-dab in front of his camera lens, there was
no way that man could have dashed past him to take up the
position facing the lobby wall mere seconds later.

The only way he could have accomplished this was if he'd
teleported from one spot to the other, or moved with Super-
man-like speed, or—

Or was a ghost.

Could ghosts exist in two places at the same time?

*Who the fuck knows, Mac! But look at your computer screen!
There's a blurry, transparent man right there! This shit is straight*

out of a haunted house movie!

Taking a final, incredulous look at the ghost, Malcolm got to his feet and moved away from the laptop as if it were cursed. He went back to it and slapped the lid closed. Then he began to pace. Bitcoin seemed attuned to his agitation, because he leapt off the sofa where he'd been snoozing and came over to him, yapping.

Malcolm lifted the dog into his arms and scratched his head, saying, "It's okay, bud. I'm okay. Everything's okay."

The puppy licked his face.

Malcolm carried Bitcoin to the kitchen, set him on the floor, and filled his bowl with kibbles. Then he poured himself a shot of gin. After draining it, he poured himself another.

"What the fuck?" he said to himself. "What the *fuck*?"

◆ ◆ ◆

He called Jolene a short time later.

"Well, howdy, darlin," she said in her syrupy drawl. "Isn't there an unspoken rule about not calling the day after a date?"

"You texted me earlier," he reminded her.

"That's a text. That doesn't count." He could hear the smile in her voice. "No, I'm only teasing. I'm happy you called. How are you?"

"That's sort of why I'm calling. Something happened today."

"You ain't pregnant, I hope."

He chuckled, a momentary reprieve from the stark terror beneath the calm façade he was putting on. "No, not pregnant," he said. "Are you?"

"I'd have to be the Virgin Mary herself for that to be the case, because, you know, we didn't..."

"Yes, I know," he said. "Um, listen... What happened, I don't really want to talk about over the phone. Are you free to meet later?"

"The intrigue. How can I decline?"

"I can meet you out front the Hotel Chelsea again?"

"Why don't I come by your neck of the woods for a change of scenery?"

"There's a little bar on the corner of First Avenue and East 7th Street I like. Is six too early for you?"

"Six is perfect. See you then."

◆ ◆ ◆

Malcolm had been going stir-crazy in his studio apartment, just him and the pug and tangential thoughts of the supernatural, so he walked to the bar an hour early. It was small and homey with stone accents, an abundance of plants, and warm lighting. The owners were a friendly Venezuelan couple, and aside from alcohol, they served small Venezuelan dishes.

By the time Jolene arrived at six, Malcolm had already finished two pints of lager and was well on the way to finishing a third.

"Cute place," she said, taking off a long-sleeved knitted cardigan and slipping into the booth across from him. Her pageboy cut was tousled from the wind, the ruler-straight bangs from the previous evening now feathered. She wore a light dusting of makeup and looked great.

The waitress, the owners' teenage daughter, came by, and Jolene ordered a glass of white wine.

"Another pint for me," Malcolm said. "Thanks, Jacky."

When the girl left, Jolene said, "I saw the smile she gave you. Either you two have a history, or you come here a lot."

"She's barely seventeen. And, yes, I come here a lot."

"You live nearby?"

"A couple of blocks away."

"I like the East Village. It has a good vibe to it. How long have you lived here?"

"Ever since I finished college—about three years now."

Jolene's eyes widened. "Am I robbing the cradle?"

"I dropped out when I was a junior," he explained. "I went

back when I was twenty-nine to complete my degree."

"What did you do in between? Travel the world?"

"I wasn't sleeping in cemeteries, unfortunately."

"Ha, ha," she said dryly, and it appeared she was still awaiting an answer.

Malcolm shrugged. "Nothing very productive. I had a shitty job and concluded I was wasting my life, which is why I went back to school."

"Have you always liked writing?"

"I guess so. I was rather good at writing essays in high school. And my major in college was English literature. I chose that before I'd ever considered working for a magazine. So, yes, I guess I've always had writing in the back of my mind."

The waitress returned with Jolene's glass of wine and asked, "Are you two having anything to eat?"

Malcolm had zero appetite. He looked at Jolene to decide. "Can you give us a few minutes, hon?"

"Take your time."

Opening the menu, Jolene said, "I'm so hungry I could eat the north end of a south-bound polecat." A few moments later, she added, "What *is* this stuff?"

"Arepas," Malcolm said.

"What are arepas?"

"Venezuelan food."

"That's all they serve here? I ain't eaten since breakfast."

"Arepas are versatile. You can have them for breakfast, lunch, or dinner. You can also have them as snacks, appetizers, side dishes, or as a full meal."

"How about in a box with a fox? In a house with a mouse?"

"I thought you're hungry enough to eat…whatever you said. But if arepas aren't your thing, there's some comfort food on the last page. No spring rolls though."

Jolene flipped. "Much better! I have a hankering for some potato wedges. That okay with you?"

"Sure."

"Anything else?"

"Not for me."

Jolene waved Jacky over and ordered a bowl of wedges with sour cream and sweet chili sauce. "I loved potato wedges growing up," she told Malcolm. "Sometimes when my family went out for dinner, it's all I'd order, a big old bowl of wedges and nothing else."

"Your parents let you do that?"

"My mama was about the least health-conscious person in all of Cave Springs—that's my hometown. Seems like all we ever ate was fried chicken, fried catfish, and apple and rhubarb pies."

"Don't know how you managed to stay so thin."

"I was like Forrest Gump, running everywhere. Up the street to knock on my friend's door. Across town to buy candy from the corner store. I never bothered with a bike. I'd just run." She exaggerated her southern twang. "Run, JoJo, Run!"

"Is JoJo your nickname?"

"It's one of them. Jo, Joly, Lenie. Take your pick. You've managed to remain fit as a fiddle. What's your secret?"

"Mediterranean food."

"I should look into that. And speaking of secrets...what's this one you wanted to see me about?"

Malcolm swallowed a mouthful of beer. He had been waiting for Jolene to ask him this. Yet now that the subject was broached, he didn't know if he *wanted* to talk about it. He wasn't afraid she would laugh at him, or call him a kook. He had his laptop right next to him, and the proof it held. He simply knew once he showed her the ghost photograph, the cat would be out of the bag. He would no longer have the option of willful ignorance, of deleting the photo and convincing himself it had never existed in the first place. He'd have to come to terms with the fact that ghosts existed, and all the spiritual and existential—and quite frankly, life-altering —implications such a conclusion carried.

He took his laptop from the bag. "It's probably best if I just show you," he said.

CHAPTER 36

Ghosts & potato wedges

Malcolm moved to Jolene's side of the booth and set the laptop before them on the table. He accessed the SD drive, then the folder containing the photographs from the Hotel Chelsea. He scrolled down until the cursor hovered over the thumbnail of the ghost photo.

"I took this shot at the Chelsea the other day," he said, his heart already racing. "It's the reception desk. It was unmanned."

"Okay..." Jolene said.

He clicked open the file. The ghost photograph filled the screen—only there was no longer a ghost in it.

Just the front desk, empty, unmanned.

"What the hell!" he blurted. "There used to be..." He slumped back in the seat. "Holy shit..."

"There used to be what?" Jolene asked, her brow knitted.

"I didn't make the fucking thing up." Malcolm sat forward decisively, closed the photograph, and scrolled through all the others in the folder.

There was only the single photo of the reception desk. He hadn't mistakenly opened the wrong one.

He ran a hand through his hair and said: "There was a blurry shape in that photograph earlier this afternoon. Of a man."

"You mean like a ghost?"

"It was Roger James. He was wearing the porkpie hat, the beige trench coat. He was *in* that picture. I didn't imagine it."

"What you saw wasn't a double exposure or anything like

that?"

"My camera is digital," he replied tightly. "And where is the ghost now? It was *right there.*"

"This was the same man you saw staring at the lobby wall?"

Malcolm simply shook his head. Jolene was indulging him, asking something banal because there was nothing to say in the situation.

Jacky arrived with the bowl of potato wedges. She frowned when she saw their expressions. "Um…did you guys want forks?"

❖ ❖ ❖

Jolene ate the wedges and scrolled through the other photographs Malcolm had taken at the Hotel Chelsea, commenting glibly on most, pretending everything was hunky dory. But the energy at the table had become forced and uncomfortable, and he said, "I need to get going. Sorry for asking you to come all the way over here."

"You can't go, darlin!" Jolene said. "I still have half my wine and all these wedges…"

"Jolene…" he said, his tone telling her to drop the act.

Her eyes hardened. "Would it make you feel better if I told you I believe you saw what you said you saw in the photograph?"

"No, it wouldn't."

"Why not?"

"Because I wouldn't believe you."

"Why not? The other night I told you I believed in ghosts."

"No, you told me a story about a kid who likely had schizophrenia."

Jolene pushed the bowl of wedges away from her and stared at her glass of wine. Without looking at him, she said, "I didn't tell you what's been happening at the Hotel Chelsea recently… because I didn't know if I was making too much out of it."

"What's been happening recently?"

"A few days ago I was in the hotel's basement. I wanted to do some rubbings of the old doors being stored down there. And, well...I heard a noise. I don't know what could have made it. Now I know that doesn't sound like anything too out of the ordinary, but that's because you weren't there. I'll tell you, I was utterly terrified. And then just yesterday I was about to step out of the bathtub after a shower—when I saw a woman in the steam."

Malcolm frowned at this revelation, thinking about the face he'd seen in Roger James' bathroom mirror.

"Also," Jolene said, "I've been sleepwalking."

Now he sat up straight.

"The first time was last week," she continued. "I woke to find myself in Room 105. The second time, only two nights ago, I was in front of the same room."

"Do you remember dreaming while sleepwalking?"

Jolene nodded. "Both times. But they didn't feel like dreams. They felt like...like this." She flagged her fingers back and forth. "Like how you and I are talking. Real."

"What did you dream about?"

"You mean, *who*. Edie Sedgwick. She used to live in 105."

"The 60s It girl?"

Jolene nodded again. "Both times the room was on fire. I wanted to help her but..." She shook her head. "In the first dream I couldn't move. In the second one I dropped to the floor to get under the smoke—that's the kind of thing that made the dreams seem so real. That I was in control. That I was making lucid choices. That's never the case in dreams. Usually you float along with wherever they take you. I ended up finding Edie Sedgwick in the closet. It was really...awful." She finished her wine and attempted a smile. "So what's your verdict, hon? Do you think I have a head full of stump water or what?"

Malcolm told her about his late-night chat with Sid Vicious.

◆ ◆ ◆

"What in tarnation is going on?" Jolene asked gravely when he finished. "Why are we both sleepwalking and dreaming about former tenants—former *dead* tenants?"

"Isn't it obvious?" Malcolm said, not sure whether he was being sarcastic or glib or what. "The Hotel Chelsea is haunted."

"Is that what you believe?"

"I can't make up my mind on what I believe."

"Before speaking to you just now, I didn't know what to believe either, even after what I've experienced this last week or so, because the rational part of me was insisting I was over-reacting or having some sort of mental breakdown. But here you are, telling me that on your first night in the hotel you had a sleepwalking episode in which you had a dream that wasn't a dream. And not only that, you saw the spitting image of a man who recently died in the hotel, and you captured that same man on film—only for him to disappear from the photo. Now, I can question my sanity. But I have good old-fashioned horse sense. You do too. So what I'm saying is, I can't see us *both* questioning our sanities. And it's either that—we're both crazy and feeding off each other's craziness—or the hotel is haunted."

Malcolm nodded, feeling bewildered and detached from the moment.

"Let's get out of here," Jolene suggested. "Some fresh air might do us good."

CHAPTER 37

Stomping grounds

While walking along Second Avenue, they didn't speak any more of ghosts. They didn't speak much at all, each distracted by their private thoughts. Then Jolene took her phone from her pocket and began tapping the screen.

"I'll wave down a taxi for you," Malcolm told her.

"Why are you always so eager to end our time together?"

He looked at her phone. "I thought you were ordering an Uber?"

She continued tapping. "Oh, there's *two* of them! Which way are we heading?"

"South," he said. Then, "Two of what?"

"I'll show you. They're only a couple of blocks away."

They continued south on Second Avenue to East 2nd Street.

Jolene checked her phone once more and pointed west. "One's right there across the street. The other one is on the next block over."

Malcolm realized what she was talking about. "You mean the cemeteries?" His eyes went to the large messenger bag hanging off her shoulder. "You want to do one of those rubbings?"

"Got everything we need right here." She patted the bag. "You never asked me about this. I thought you would."

"I thought it was a fashion accident."

"Aren't you precious? But no, darlin, it's my art bag. I

thought it would be fun to make a rubbing for you. I didn't reckon our conversation was going to take the direction it did. Are you keen?"

Malcolm wasn't sure if he was. "We've just spent the last half hour convincing ourselves that ghosts exist, and you want to go stomping around on their home turf?"

"I ain't ever seen a ghost in a cemetery. It seems they like places with more action."

Malcolm recalled Nikki's comment that the dead preferred quiet places to haunt such as cemeteries and old houses.

Jolene said, "If you don't feel comfortable..."

Malcolm shrugged. "I'm fine with it. I guess."

"Great! Which cemetery?"

"The farther one doesn't have any headstones."

"It's a cemetery, ain't it?"

He'd been curious about this too, as he regularly walked past both cemeteries, and he'd previously looked up the reason online. "Both have large underground vaults instead or traditional burial plots," he told her. "The one without head-stones has marble plaques along the stone walls to indicate which tombs are where. They wanted to keep it looking like a park. There are a few trees in it, and some benches. You can see in through an iron gate."

"And the closer cemetery?"

"All sorts of tombstones. Some pretty impressive ones too."

"Then it's decided for us."

They crossed Second Avenue and went west on East 2nd Street. The apartment buildings and tenements soon gave way to the black iron fence that bordered the cemetery. A little way on they stopped before a large gate.

"New York City Marble Cemetery," Jolene said, reading the sign to the left of the gate. She went to a plaque attached to the fence. "1832. Old place."

"Second oldest non-sectarian cemetery in the city. The one a block over is older by a year."

"Says some of the folks buried here include the founder of the New York Public Library, the founder of Roosevelt Hospital, and the Kip family of Kip's Bay. I didn't know that neighborhood was named after a family."

"Guess we won't be paying them a visit," Malcolm said, lifting a padlock chaining the gate closed. "Place is locked."

Jolene tugged the padlock to be sure. "Hmmm…" she said, looking up and down the street. She pointed. "That tree over yonder will do the trick." The street was lined with elms. The one she was pointing to featured a large branch extending over the cemetery fence.

"I don't know…" he said. The fence must have been at least twelve feet tall, the iron bars topped with pointed spades.

"It'll be easy," she said, and started toward the tree.

Malcolm jogged to catch up. "Those points can impale you."

"Don't fall on them then." She stopped before the trunk of the elm she'd selected and said, "You're going to have to give me a boost so I can reach that branch. Quick, hon, when no one's around."

Grunting his disapproval, Malcolm locked his fingers together to form a saddle. He cupped Jolene's left foot, and on the count of three, heaved her upward. She grabbed the branch above her head, taking some of her weight. He shoved her foot higher, up past his chest, and then she was straddling the branch, her feet dangling above his head. In the next instant she was in a crouch, moving around the trunk, and climbing to the higher branch that extended over the fence. She squat-walked along it, holding onto other limbs with her hands for balance. Then she hung from the branch by her arms and dropped a good seven feet to the ground, falling onto her side.

"Your turn!" she said, grinning through the bars at him. "Can you reach the branch?"

"People are coming. Go hide. I'll be over in a minute."

Jolene hurried deeper into the cemetery. Malcolm pulled out his mobile phone and tried not to act suspicious. When three men passed—joking loudly about a girl they apparently knew—he tucked his phone away, jumped to reach the branch, and ran his feet vertically up the trunk. On the second attempt he was able to hook a leg over the branch and swing his body up onto it. The acrobatics proved harder than he'd anticipated, and he was already panting. He crept through the tangle of limbs, feeling as though he were fourteen years old, which was probably the last time he'd climbed a tree. When he was halfway along the limb that cantilevered over the cemetery, he dropped to the ground and looked around.

"Jolene?"

She stepped out from behind a large monument. "Over here. All clear?"

"For now," he said. "But people can see us through the fence."

"They'll probably think the cemetery's open, or we're allowed to be here."

Malcolm surveyed the tall residential buildings surrounding the burial ground, all the windows looking down on them. "Someone might call the cops."

"We ain't vandals. In fact, we're here to *preserve* history. Now enough yackety-yak. I want to make you a collage, so pick out three graves you want me to rub."

The cemetery was quite large. Flat marble vault markers were laid out in narrow strips along the grass, punctuated by monuments of varying sizes and designs. Some were in better shape than others, and a few were in near-perfect condition, but most were weathered, cracked, or broken and crumbling.

Malcolm's first selection was a well-preserved, chest-high monument with a bas-relief of a hooded woman, perhaps a saint, standing beside a large cross.

"Perfect," Jolene said, taking a rag and spray bottle from her art bag. With a few spritzes of water, she wiped down the face of the gravestone, cleaning it of dirt and bird droppings and a patch of moss.

She produced a large piece of paper and said, "Can you hold this over the front?"

"It's pretty crumpled," he said, doing what she'd asked.

"I like my rubbings to look grungy," she told him, taping the paper in place.

Gripping a large clump of charcoal, she rubbed different bits of lettering and textures, varying her pressure to create degrees of shading. When she finished, she sprayed the charcoal with hairspray, telling him it prevented the charcoal from smearing.

She repeated the entire process with the next gravestone he chose, only this time substituting the charcoal for blocks of red and yellow wax.

"How about that one?" Malcolm said, choosing the tallest monument in the cemetery for the last rubbing. It was a thirty-foot obelisk topped by the bust of a monocled man, presumably the occupant of the vault below.

"Now we're talking!" Jolene said, and they hurried over to it.

"Arthur Schmid," Malcolm said, reading the name engraved into the marble. "Ever heard of him?"

"Never. But by the looks of his tombstone, he had enough money to burn a wet mule."

Malcolm read the brief epigraph: "'I do hope I have been buried in an extraordinary costume, as one's appointment with eternity is a most serious affair.'"

"Bless his highfalutin heart."

"1831 to 1921. Lived to the ripe old age of ninety."

After completing the rubbing collage, Jolene scrunched the paper away in her messenger bag, and she and Malcolm went searching for a tree by which to leave the cemetery.

"Holy shit," Malcolm said, pointing to a nearby hole in the ground. "An open grave."

"That's no grave!" Jolene corrected him, as they ventured closer. "It's the entrance to a vault!"

Indeed, the large slab of granite that had previously

covered the underground antechamber rested to the left of it.

Jolene started down the aluminum ladder poking out of the ground.

"Whoa!" Malcolm said, incredulous. "What are you doing?"

"This is a once-in-a-lifetime opportunity!"

"I'm not going into a crypt!"

"Just a quick peek."

"We should get going. It's getting dark."

"Wait for me here then. I won't be long."

At the bottom of the antechamber, she hopped off the ladder and pulled open an ancient stone door by a metal ring. It opened easily on massive, cross-shaped hinges, revealing a perfectly black room. Jolene took her phone out and stepped inside the tomb.

"Oh hell," Malcolm said, starting down the ladder.

◆ ◆ ◆

He joined Jolene on the other side of the stone door in the sunless black. Rather than being cool as he'd expected, the air in the crypt was hot and stuffy.

"Smells old," he said, wrinkling his nose.

"Old? That's it?" She sounded unimpressed with his description. "And you're a writer?"

"Dank."

They stepped forward on the earthen ground, the flashlight on Jolene's phone revealing a small room, rectangular in shape. The arched marble ceiling was sparkling white, protected and preserved down here from the elements. Three of the four walls were punctured with slate niches, each occupied by either a casket or urn, or sometimes both.

"This is incredible," Jolene said, moving along the wall to their left. "Look how small that coffin is," she added. "What do you reckon the poor thing died from?"

Malcolm shrugged. "Factory accident? Malnutrition? Disease? There were a lot of yellow fever and cholera outbreaks in the nineteenth century."

"I'm so thankful I was born when I was born."

"I'm glad I was born at all. Have you ever considered the odds?"

"Imagine *not* being born."

"Life's a fleeting gift. Appreciate it while you can."

Jolene made a bemused sound. "I bet you write really good Christmas cards, sugar."

When they reached the far wall, they discovered a casket that, at some point during its entombment, had fallen apart. Laying amid the wood planks was a skeleton dressed in its burial shroud.

"Goodness gracious me!" Jolene exclaimed. "I didn't expect to actually *see* a corpse."

"You know we're in a crypt, right?"

"You know what I mean... I wonder what happened to the coffin."

"Shitty carpenter."

"Maybe the person was buried alive? When he came out of his Lazarus-like sleep, he found himself trapped in the coffin and tried to break out and croaked for good in the process."

"You're freaking me out."

"Premature burials used to happen all the time. In one case I heard told, a man's family exhumed his body a month after burial to move it to a different cemetery. When they opened the coffin, they found him lying facedown. There were finger-nail scratches all over the wood, and he'd yanked out half the hair in his head."

"Okay, now you're *really* freaking me out," he said, glancing back to the stone door, which was obscured in darkness.

"You could have waited outside."

"I didn't know you'd turn into HBO's The Cryptkeeper. Have you seen enough yet?"

"All right, scaredy-pants," she said. "We can leave." Then, coyly: "Just hope whoever moved that stone slab didn't slide it back in place while we've been down here."

CHAPTER 38

The curious neighbor
turns...curiouser

When they climbed the ladder out of the below-ground antechamber, they found twilight had descended over the city, painting everything in otherworldly hues. They monkeyed up a tree bordering the iron fence near the western end of the cemetery and fell out of it onto the sidewalk, startling a woman walking a poodle. They went west to First Avenue, where Malcolm said, "I live six blocks that way." He pointed north.

"Sure, I'd love to come over," Jolene said.

Malcolm raised his eyebrows.

"I know it wasn't an invitation," she said, "but I fear you're going to try to stuff me in a taxi again."

"I'd enjoy it if you came over," he clarified.

They walked the six blocks north on First Avenue and turned onto Malcolm's street. Outside the walkup, he said, "Can you do me a favor? Don't make any noise when we get to my floor. I have a neighbor... She's a bit..."

"Malcolm, I do declare—you have a spited lover too!"

"Hardly," he said. "We've had a few drinks together. That's all. I think she's bipolar."

"Is she pretty?"

"You're prettier."

"Bless your pea-picking little heart, sugar. But don't you worry about me. I won't make a peep."

When they reached the sixth floor, and were halfway down

the hallway, Malcolm took his keys from a pocket, making sure they didn't jangle. He froze mid-step.

A large hunting knife with a polished black handle protruded from the middle of his door by the serrated blade.

Malcolm yanked it free and held it before him in utter shock.

Jolene mouthed the words, *Oh my God!*

He silently unlocked the door and waved Jolene inside the apartment. When he closed it, he engaged both the lock and deadbolt.

"Who did that?" Jolene asked, looking as startled as he felt.

"My neighbor. Had to have been." He set the knife on the kitchen table.

"What did you do to the poor thing?"

"I didn't do anything," he insisted. "I went over to her place during the blackout for dinner. She spiked the food with Ritalin, so I left."

"She *what*?"

"Exactly what I said."

"Whyever would she spike the food with Ritalin?"

He shrugged. "To get me in a good mood?"

"A good mood for *what*?"

"I have no idea, Jo. She's crazy. She knocked on my door a couple of hours later, but I wouldn't let her in. She got really pissed off."

"Reckon you should call the police?"

"And set her off more?"

"You can't have your neighbor lodging hunting knives in your door."

"I'm going to have to move."

"Call the police," she insisted. "I'll call them for you."

He shook his head. "What are they going to do? There are no CCTV cameras in the hall. She'll tell them she didn't do it."

"Let's give her a taste of her own medicine then. We'll stick the knife back in *her* door."

"No way. I don't want to start messing around with her.

Who knows how far she might take things? Let's just try to forget about her—"

A knock at the door. They both spun toward it.

"Mac?" Nikki called. "It's me. Can we talk?"

◆ ◆ ◆

Malcolm held a finger to his lips. Jolene nodded.

"Mac!" Nikki called, the pleasantness leaving her voice. "I know you're in there, Mac. I heard your door shut. And the knife's gone."

Malcolm spoke up: "I don't want to talk right now, Nikki."

"Why not?"

"You stuck a hunting knife in my door!"

"It was a joke. Can't you take a joke? Open up so we can talk."

"I told you, Nikki. I don't want to talk."

"Open the fucking door, Mac!"

"Malcolm has company right now, ma'am," Jolene said loudly.

Malcolm slapped a hand to his face.

"Who are *you*?" Nikki demanded.

"My name's Jolene Hathcock, ma'am. Malcolm and I are on a date. So please go away."

Silence—prolonged, threatening.

Then Nikki's door slammed shut with a resounding bang.

◆ ◆ ◆

"Can I get you a drink?" Malcolm said.

"I could sure use one," Jolene said.

"I only have gin or beer."

"Beer, please."

Malcolm grabbed the last two bottles of Busch from the fridge, twisted off the caps, and gave Jolene one. "Let's just forget about her."

"She's forgotten." Jolene surveyed the apartment. "I like your place."

"Would be nice if it were bigger."

She took the collage of the three graves out of her art bag and spread it out on the floor. Then she proceeded to walk all over it.

"What are you doing?"

"I always do this. I told you, I like them grungy." She picked it up and set it on the sofa. "There. Now all you need is a frame. When's your birthday?"

"February."

"Long way off. I'll get you an early present." She went to the balcony doors. The lights from the downtown skyscrapers twinkled in the early evening dark. "What a gorgeous view. Do you want to sit outside?"

"Sure—"

WHUMP!

Malcolm started so badly at the noise he spilled beer all over his shirt.

"Good Lord!" Jolene said, a hand pressed to her chest. "I nearly had a heart attack."

Furious, Malcolm stalked to the door, unlocked it, and threw it open, fully intent on confronting Nikki.

The hallway was empty. Laying before the door was the source of the noise: a fire extinguisher. The glass door of the white metal box down the hall that usually held it now hung open.

He picked up the extinguisher, closed the door, and set it on the kitchen table, next to the knife.

Jolene said, "You're acquiring quite the collection—"

Thump-thump-thump...

They both looked at the wall.

Thump-thump-thump-thump-thump...

"What the hell's she doing now?" he demanded.

"Sounds like she's playing Whack-A-Mole with a broom."

"I'll go over and talk to her."

"No, don't. That's what she wants."

"You can put up with that racket?"

"She'll get bored soon."

Malcolm didn't say anything. Just listened to the *thump-thump-thump*, growing more and more fed up with each passing second.

Finally he said, "Let's go out somewhere."

Jolene nodded. "My place?"

CHAPTER 39

"Everybody funny, now you funny too." —George Thorogood

They left Malcolm's apartment quietly, not in fear of Nikki accosting them in the hallway—Malcolm would have liked the opportunity to tell the Janus-faced bitch off—but so Nikki would continue her wall-banging to a vacated audience, hopefully to the point of futile exhaustion.

On First Avenue, they caught a taxi to the Hotel Chelsea. They walked down the block to a deli, purchased a bottle of wine and a heel of cheese, then returned to the hotel. They took the stairs to the first floor, where Malcolm was certain Shane was going to be loitering in the hallway, perhaps to grill Jolene on where she'd been, but the irascible Irishman was nowhere to be seen. They were in Jolene's room for only as long as it took her to drop off the art bag and get two glasses and a knife she kept in a box beneath her bed. They returned to the elevator landing and rode a car up to the tenth floor. Jolene punched the code into the alarm attached to the roof access door, and they stepped outside.

"How do you know the code?" Malcolm asked her. "Quinn told me the roof was only accessible to residents on the tenth floor."

"Quinn gave it to me years ago. We're bridge partners. We often play up here."

"Is Quinn good?"

"Devilishly so."

They went to the southeast corner of the roof, using the

ledge that overlooked West 23rd Street as a makeshift table. Jolene poured the wine while Malcolm sliced the cheese.

"Did you know the developer wants to put a bar up here?" she said.

"Quinn told me. She's horrified by the prospect."

"Horrified? I can't hardly wait!"

"You and Quinn...have drastically different viewpoints when it comes to the future of this hotel."

"You don't reckon a bar up here would be perfect? We would be sitting in chairs right now."

"It would be convenient, I'll say that."

She swished her wine around in her glass. "So...how are you doing with what we talked about earlier?"

Malcolm swished his wine too. "To be honest, I'm trying not to think about it."

"It's all I've been thinking about. Well, that, and the fact we were able to escape your crazy neighbor unscathed."

"I really think I'm going to have to move out of my building."

"If Stanley Bard was still around, I'd ask him to rent you a room here."

"Thanks for the thought. But I think I'd rather live next to a crazy neighbor than in a haunted hotel."

"In all the years I've lived here, I've witnessed some strange things like that poor boy Christopher turning crazier than an outhouse fly, but nothing like...well, I reckon I've seen a ghost, Malcolm. Twice, or maybe even three times. The ghost of Edie Sedgwick. I believe that now. And whatever ghosts may be—spirits of the deceased, recordings of the past—they're *something*. But what I don't understand is... Let me use a *Ghostbusters* analogy..."

"Go for it, Darnell."

"At the beginning of the movie, Ray and the others can't find a ghost for the life of them. Then they catch one in that hotel and business booms as ghosts start showing up all over New York City. Well, the same thing's happening here. For years, nothing but little blips on the P.K.E. Meter. Then in the last week or two…"

"What does P.K.E. stand for anyway?"

"PsychoKinetic Energy," she said. "You know why I know that? I had a crush on Egon."

"I thought all the girls like Dr. Venkman?"

"Venkman? God no, he was a sleaze. Egon was tall, kind, and intelligent. Sort of like someone else I know…"

Their eyes met. Seizing the moment, Malcolm leaned in for a kiss. Jolene's lips were soft, warm, and fruity from the wine. He set aside his glass to make better use of his hands when the kiss finished.

Jolene said, "Back to what we were talking about…?"

He said, "The P.K.E. Meter."

"Any guess as to why the ghosts here are suddenly letting us see them now?"

"Maybe they work on a cyclical timer? Every twenty-five years or fifty years or one hundred years the boundary between their world and ours is at its thinnest and they can slip through."

"I'm being serious now, darlin. I know what we're talking about sounds silly, but I don't want silly answers. I want to know why we're walking around the hotel at night and seeing the spirits of dead celebrities."

"I thought I heard people out here."

Malcolm and Jolene turned to find Quinn approaching them through the dark, her golden locks bouncing in the moonlight. Her eye makeup and lipstick were applied as lovingly as if she had been booked to appear on a late-night talk show. A brown fur cape draped a black dress with a short hemline. On her feet she wore a pair of fluffy pink slippers.

"Hi, Quinn," Malcolm said. "Have we been too noisy?"

"No, of course not. But it's quiet up here these days. Sound travels." She eyed the wine and cheese.

"The roof is more atmospheric than the fire escape outside my window," Jolene explained.

"Atmospheric? It's a barren wasteland! If only my gardens were still here..." Quinn didn't miss Jolene pressing her lips together to stifle a smile. "Yes, I'm a nostalgic, rambling old woman, aren't I? Well, don't mind me, please. I didn't mean to intrude. I'll let you two lovebirds finish your picnic." She breathed deeply. "The air *is* nice up here, isn't it?"

"Err, Quinn," Malcolm said. "A quick question. Have you noticed anything odd this last week?"

"Odd? Whatever do you mean? No, I think I understand. Don't tell me Harvey's nonsense about ghosts and the such has filled your brains too! But it has, hasn't it? Yes, I can see that on both your faces."

"Several nights ago, I had a sleepwalking episode," Jolene said. "I had another one even more recently. Both times I woke in or outside Room 105, where Edie Sedgwick had lived. And...I saw her. I had a conversation with her."

"You mean you dreamed of her?"

"That's what I originally believed, but then Malcolm stayed over at my place last night, and he had an experience similar to my own."

Quinn looked at Malcolm. "You dreamed of Edie Sedgwick?"

"No," he said. "I dreamed...or saw...Sid Vicious."

"You *saw* Sid Vicious?" Quinn's hazel eyes flitted between Malcolm and Jolene, her brow wrinkling beneath her golden bangs. "And you, dear, *saw* Edie Sedgwick?" She huffed. "I don't know if you two genuinely believe this balderdash, or if you're simply jesting at my expense. But I don't find it amusing at all. Now, I'm catching a chill and must return inside. Good night to you both."

She left without another word.

CHAPTER 40

Harvey's place

"Balderdash?" Jolene said. "Do folks still use that word?"

Malcolm shrugged. "Quinn has lived more years than both of us combined. She can use whatever words she wants."

"I know she can be brusque—but rarely to me. And I got a sense..."

"That she didn't think what we told her was balderdash at all..."

Jolene nodded. "Reckon she's seen something too?"

"Why wouldn't she tell us?"

"Because if you ain't a religious person, the existence of ghosts ain't something you can accept lightly. You're hard-wired to dismiss the possibility out of hand. Look how hard it was for you to change your thinking, and you'd taken a picture of a ghost. You had physical evidence right in front of your nose. Maybe it was a little bit easier for me to believe. I'm Baptist through and through. I went to church right up until Grace and I left for New York. My mama and daddy believed fervently in a Lord above, and many of their beliefs rubbed off on me. But even that being the case, there's still a little voice inside me right now, telling me I'm wrong about this hotel, spirits don't exist, there's another explanation for the woman I've seen."

"So Quinn's in denial?" Malcolm said.

"My, aren't I a bag of wind! Yes, Quinn's in denial."

He glanced at Quinn's pyramid, a black silhouette jutting against the night sky, the windows glowing yellow. He didn't think she could hear them talking, as they were speaking more quietly than before.

"Should we go talk to her?" he said. "Maybe she just needs to talk through whatever she's experienced, like we did."

"I don't know how much good that would do. She's stubborn as an ox in her views. It's unlikely we'd change them."

"I wonder if there's anyone else here who's experienced what we have?"

Jolene cocked an eyebrow at him. "You can't say it, can you?"

"Say what?"

"Ghost. I don't reckon you've used that word yet. You can't say, 'I wonder if there's anyone else here who's seen a ghost?'"

"Of course I can."

"Then let's start calling a spade a spade. We *are* on the same page, aren't we?"

"Do you think anyone else in the hotel has seen a *ghost*?" he said emphatically. "What was it that Harvey told us he and Jeffrey had experienced?"

"'Paranormal activity,' I do believe."

"It would be nice to know exactly what he meant by that."

"Well, handsome," Jolene said, "let's go pay him a little visit."

◆ ◆ ◆

They took the stairs to the eighth floor and knocked on Room 823. There was no answer. They knocked a second time to be sure no one was home, and just as they were leaving, the door opened, revealing Harvey, naked except for a red Ralph Lauren towel wrapped around his waist. His hair was wet, his skin shiny with water.

"I thought I heard knocking!" he said. "Excuse my appearance. I was in the bath."

"We should have called," Jolene said. "We can come back later…"

"Nonsense! Come in, come in."

They followed him down the wallpapered hallway to the red burlesque room.

"Make yourself at home while I throw on something more appropriate," he told them. "JoJo, you have a bottle of wine, I see. I like your style! Mr. Clock, you know where the gin is. Help yourself." He disappeared into another room.

Jolene set the two glasses on a table and filled one with wine. "How about you? Or do you have a hankering for gin?"

"I'd prefer gin," Malcolm admitted. "But I think I'd feel rude helping myself."

"Don't be silly. Harvey would be offended if you *didn't* help yourself."

Harvey did seem like that kind of guy, so he showed himself to the kitchen and fixed a gin on the rocks. He returned to the burlesque room and joined Jolene near a window overlooking West 23rd Street. A short time later Harvey arrived, now clad in a red silk robe with the initials HC embroidered in gold thread above the right breast pocket. It seemed he had stopped by the kitchen on his way, as he held a crystal glass filled with amber liquid in one hand and a fat cigar in the other.

"It's lovely to see you both again so soon," he said. "I heard through the grapevine—and that grapevine is Quinn—that you two might be something of an item now. Seeing you together, am I correct in presuming this to be true?"

Jolene laughed. "My, Harv, ain't you the forward one."

"I don't mean to be nosy. It's just that I never know when to believe Quinn or not. But I'll take your reply as an affirmation. How's old Shane handling this news?"

"He called me a rotten bitch when he saw Malcolm leaving my room last night."

"That's it? By all measures, he seems to be handling it quite well then!" Harvey said to Malcolm, "Have you heard about Shane's post-breakup antics?"

"Not exactly. I heard he didn't take the breakup well."

"That's the understatement of the century, my friend. You don't mind if I enlighten our dear writer by recounting the details of Shane's meltdown, do you, JoJo?"

"Let me preface by saying I botched the breakup part. My girlfriend, Rachael, organized a night out at a strip club for her thirtieth birthday. A men's strip club. She's bi. I went because I'd never been to one before."

Malcolm said, "I imagine the female strippers weren't thrilled to find a group of women infiltrating their domain."

"To the contrary! They were just as nice as could be. At the end of the night Shane sent me a message, saying he was out and would come by to walk me home. When I was in the bathroom with Rach, I mentioned Shane was coming...and then I started running my mouth about how Shane wasn't my type, how I was thinking of breaking up with him but didn't know how to do it tactfully. Little did I know, Shane had just arrived, and he was in one of the toilet stalls behind us. The strip club only had one bathroom for the customers—the men's."

"Yikes," Malcolm said, feeling a little sorry for the guy.

"Well, Shane burst out of the stall and pitched a hissy fit with a tail on it. Rach ran off to get help, and these two gorillas carried Shane out of the club, thrashing and yelling. I was too scared to go home that night, so I stayed at one of my friend's."

Malcolm frowned. "Why were you scared? Has he hit you —?"

"No, no, he's not like that. He can cuss like a sailor, God bless him, but he would never hit me. I was just worried if I went home, he'd be banging at my door all night, making a scene."

"Which," Harvey said, "is exactly what he did."

"Feel free to take over, Harv," Jolene said.

"The inconsolable devil returned to the Chelsea at around two in the morning, completely off his face. This was about two hours after he was thrown out of the strip club, so he'd more than likely parked himself on a bar stool during that time and fueled up on whiskey. He banged on JoJo's door for about ten minutes, ignoring the nightguard telling him to go to bed. Presumably, he thought she was in there, hiding out, so he climbed onto the fire escape from the hallway window."

"I leave my window unlocked," Jolene said. "He would have been able to poke his head in my room and see for himself I wasn't home."

"And for whatever reason," Harvey said, "instead of returning inside through the hall window, he released the ladder to the alley below. We have no idea why. Perhaps he was planning on camping out down there until he saw Jolene's window light up. But he must have slipped because he was lying on the ground, concussed, in the morning."

"I saw him down there from my window," Jolene said. "I thought he was dead!"

"Alas, he was not," Harvey said. "The paramedics roused him, but he refused to go to the hospital. Instead, he went to his room and shouted at anyone who came to check on him to fuck off."

"Two days later," Jolene said, "he knocked on my door and told me he'd made dinner reservations at one of the more romantic restaurants we'd gone to while dating. He was acting like the strip club night never happened. I figured this was because I'd never officially broken up with him; he simply overheard me talking *about* breaking up with him. So I made it official right then. He took it… I don't know, but he took it, at any rate. Or I thought he did. Because I didn't see him for the rest of the week. Then on a Saturday morning, I bumped into him outside the hotel. He was just sort of loitering there."

"Waiting for you?" Malcolm asked.

"I suppose so. Because he had printouts of two tickets to Paris on him. He told me he bought them for us."

"Paris, *France?*"

"The one and only. And the tickets were non-refundable."

"Did you go?"

"Of course not! We were definitely, officially, broken up by then."

"Doesn't seem like he thought that."

"I spelled it out for him yet again. Bluntly. We were over, and he had to move on. Well, he just went off, madder than a box full of frogs. Darnell came out to try to calm him down. You've seen Darnell. The man can handle himself. But Shane ended up giving him a bloody lip and nose before running away down the street."

"Did he end up going to Paris by himself?"

"He ended up going," Harvey said, toasting the foot of the cigar. "But not by himself, no. He invited a Vietnamese ex-ballerina named Mimi, who lives in the hotel. Mimi's a sweetheart. She's also ten years older than Shane and lives with her sixteen-year-old son."

Malcolm looked at Jolene. "He took her to make you jealous?"

"I can't read his mind, hon," she said. "He posted an awful lot of pictures of them cozying up together on his Facebook page though."

"Are they still together?"

"I don't reckon he's spoken to her since they returned."

"But you and Shane are friends now?"

Jolene nodded. "A little while after Shane got back from Paris, a friend of ours here at the hotel had a party. Shane was there, and we chatted for a while. He seemed back to his old, lowkey self. After that, we started hanging out again—platonically, usually with other friends around. He really is a sweet guy. He has a big heart. Maybe too big for his own good."

CHAPTER 41

Is Dylan Thomas in the house?

"**N**ow that you're all caught up with JoJo's love life, Mr. Clock," Harvey said, puffing on the pungent-smelling cigar, "shall we move on to more current matters? Jeffrey is out this evening at an industry event. The apartment is lonely without him around, so I'm exulted to have company. But I must confess, I'm curious as to the reason for the visit. You have never come by unannounced before, JoJo, although I wouldn't mind in the least if you did."

"Be careful with your generosity, Harv. I might just start coming around at all hours of the day and night. A girl can go a little stir crazy in a room the size of a human hamster cage."

"We'll set aside a room for you up here. We'll call it The Southern Suite."

"You're an absolute doll," Jolene said, smiling. "As to why Malcolm and I are here...we wanted to ask you what you meant by the 'paranormal activity' you mentioned the other night."

"Not to ridicule me, I hope?"

Jolene looked at Malcolm. "Should I just...?"

He nodded.

She told Harvey everything. Her encounters with the ghost of Edie Sedgwick, Malcolm's encounter with the ghost of Sid Vicious, and Malcolm capturing the ghost of Roger James on film, only for it to later disappear from the photograph.

Harvey listened with rapt attention, clearly growing more and more excited the more she spoke. When Jolene wrapped up, he said, "By Jove, I knew it! I knew Jeffrey hadn't imagined it!"

Malcolm asked, "What is *it*?"

Harvey set the cigar in an ashtray to let its flame extinguish on its own. He finished his drink and seemed to contemplate the empty glass. Then he looked at Malcolm and said in a somber tone, "I've believed this hotel is haunted for as long as I've lived here, Mr. Clock. What I've witnessed over the years would never convince a skeptic, but it's been enough to make me keep my eyes and ears open, keep me wondering. Then eight days ago, what Jeffrey told me he saw—good God, *that* would have convinced the Apostle Thomas himself! And here you are, telling me you both have had a similar experience?"

"What happened eight days ago?"

"Jeffrey and I were sleeping. At a little past midnight, Jeffrey got out of bed, waking me in the process. I assumed he was going to the bathroom. He is cursed with a small bladder. I was already drifting back to sleep when I heard the front door close. It's heavier than all the interior doors and makes a very distinct sound. I hopped out of bed to find out where he was going. Jeffrey was in the hallway, walking slowly toward the stairwell. I asked him what the devil he was doing, but he ignored me. I hurried after him. His eyes were open, unfocused, staring distantly."

Jolene said, "Sleepwalking."

"He wasn't playing chess."

Malcolm said, "You didn't try waking him?"

"It crossed my mind, but I feared that shaking him awake might give him a right start. Also, I was admittedly curious to see where his nocturnal adventure took him. If he made it down to the lobby and looked about to stroll out onto West 23rd in his pajamas, then of course I would have woken him. Yet it turned out this wasn't on the agenda. He went only as far as the second floor and stopped in front of Room 205. The apartment was unoccupied, no plastic covering the door, so when Jeffrey turned the handle, I didn't stop him. We entered a large, empty room—and something came over me then. It's hard to describe. It was like, well...I suppose it was like I had been...vacuum packed. I couldn't move, I couldn't work my mouth, I couldn't even blink. Worst was an overwhelming sensation that something was terribly, terribly wrong, though I had no idea what." He frowned, rubbing his jaw. "No, I've chosen the wrong word. I suppose I should have said... evil. Something about that room was evil."

"What was it?" Jolene asked softly. Her hand found Malcolm's and squeezed it tightly. He squeezed back.

"I don't know," Harvey said. "I don't remember much after. Just shaking Jeffrey awake and fleeing back to our apartment. When we got here, we were both out of breath. Jeffrey was so confused. He remembered entering the room, and he told me there had been a pudgy man in an old-fashioned suit lying in the middle of the floor, surrounded by several papers that might have been manuscript pages. He believed this man to be the Welsh poet Dylan Thomas. I've never seen Jeffrey so terrified in his life."

"But you didn't see Dylan Thomas?" Malcolm said. "You and Jeffrey had *different* experiences in that room?"

"Jeffrey was sleepwalking. I was not. And while I did not encounter Dylan Thomas, or the ghost of Dylan Thomas, I did experience something frightful in that room."

"And like Edie Sedgwick and Sid Vicious," Jolene said, "Dylan Thomas used to reside in this hotel."

"He did indeed, love," Harvey replied. "He spent the final few weeks of his life in Room 205."

◆ ◆ ◆

Back in Jolene's room, Malcolm said, "This has been one hell of a day. I woke this morning believing all was right in the world."

"All still is right, darlin," she said. "There's just *more* to the world than we thought."

"I think I liked the world better without ghosts in it."

"You and me both. But we've spoken enough about them today." She stepped closer to him and rested her forearms on his shoulders. "In fact, I don't want to talk about anything at all."

They kissed, and this time, kept kissing.

CHAPTER 42

Mind yer own business

Shane had gone to The Home Depot earlier that day, which was located a block and a half away from the Hotel Chelsea, to purchase what he needed tonight. Now, at a little past midnight, he made three trips up to Room 826. The first time he rode the elevator with a rectangular piece of plywood about an inch thick. The second time his arms were loaded with three two-by-fours. And the third time he carried a hammer and a package of steel bullethead nails. He propped the plywood against the door to Goro's old apartment and secured it to the frame with four nails. Then he began smacking in another dozen or so for good measure.

Three doors down a man stuck his head into the hallway and said, "What the hell do you think you're doing, Shane?" It was Quentin Eliot, a journalist, children's writer, and self-professed explorer. His thinning black hair was mussed, his thick eyebrows beetling over his eyes in annoyance.

"Get yourself to bed, Quent, I shan't be long." He hammered another nail home.

"But what in God's name are you doing?"

"What does it look like I'm doin', ye ape?"

"I see you're boarding up that room. But *why*? Do you know what time it is?"

Shane lined up one of the two-by-fours across the plywood at chest height and nailed it in place. Another door opened farther down the hallway, and an old hag with a face like a rotten apple stuck her head out. Shane recognized her but couldn't recall her name.

"What is going on out here?" she demanded in a German accent.

He nailed another two-by-four in place, this time at waist height.

"Isn't there enough noise here during the daytime with the construction workers, and you, young man, have to do this in the middle of the night? What *are* you doing anyway?"

"That's what I asked him," Quentin Eliot said.

Shane hammered in place the final two-by-four, then stepped back to examine his handywork.

Nobody, including me, is getting in there without a crowbar and waking the entire floor, he thought with satisfaction.

"Go on to bed now, Quent," he told the explorer again as he passed his room on the way to the stairs.

"The management will hear of this!"

"Outta the way," he told the hag a few steps later.

"I demand to know what you're doing!"

"Savin' my life," he mumbled under his breath.

CHAPTER 43

I have a bard too

Malcolm didn't dream or sleepwalk that night. In fact, he slept completely uninterrupted until waking at 4:30 a.m. Usually if he opened his eyes at this hour, it would only be for a moment or two before he fell back asleep. Now, however, he was wickedly alert and fixated on his horror novel. A hundred different thoughts seemed to be pressed up against the door between his subconscious and conscious, all of them clamoring to be let out and heard. Slipping quietly out of bed, he considered heading home, but he didn't want to sneak off on Jolene again. Equally so, he didn't want to waste precious time not transcribing his thoughts.

Navigating the small room by moonlight, he found a blue Bic pen on top of the set of drawers. When he couldn't find any paper, not even the paper Jolene used for her rubbings, he de-cided the Mary Higgins Clark novel on her minifridge would have to do.

Sitting down on the floor with his back to the wall, Mal-colm opened the novel to the title page and begin filling it with words.

◆ ◆ ◆

When Jolene woke two hours later and saw him on the floor scribbling in the paperback novel, she said, "That book's al-ready been completed, hon."

"Hey," he said, setting the book and pen aside. His right hand ached, and for good reason: he'd filled nearly every margin on every page with prose, often illegibly in his haste to get his thoughts down on paper. "Sorry about the book. I'll buy you a new copy today."

"Don't worry about that." Sitting up, she held the bedsheet against her chest. The burn marks along her forearms and biceps that he'd noticed for the first time the night before were visible in the morning light. She saw him looking and said, "I was in a fire when I was younger. I don't like talking about it."

"I wasn't going to ask," he said simply.

"You don't hate me because I'm disfigured?"

"Your stock's sunk a few points."

She threw a pillow at him. "So tell me what the devil you're doing down there?"

"I've started writing a novel recently. When I woke, I had a lot of the plot in my head. I wanted to get as much as I could onto paper before I forgot any of it."

"When did you start writing a novel?"

"The day after Harvey's dinner party."

"I hope not because of anything Shane said about—"

"No. Well, maybe. I don't know. I just found myself thinking about the novel I'd started and given up on, and I came up with an idea for a new one. It sounded like something I could write. It's a horror novel."

"Horror! What's it about?"

"This hotel."

"Ghosts?"

He nodded.

"*Our* ghosts?"

"No—it's completely fictional."

"And how's it coming so far?"

"I've already written the first hundred pages."

"Since Harvey's dinner party? One hundred pages in, what, *five* days?"

"I don't know what to say. The writing's been effortless." He checked his wristwatch. "Hate to run, but I have to be at the office in an hour."

"Wait, before you leave…" She was suddenly looking inexplicably troubled. "I think you should have a look under my bed."

Curious, Malcolm peered beneath the bed. "So this is where you keep all your paper! I could have used some two hours ago."

"Pull everything out."

Malcolm did so. Atop a two-inch-thick box of Pellon tracing paper—HVY DUTY WONDER-UNDER written on the side facing him—was a stack of Jolene's rubbings.

He flipped through them. "You have enough here to fill a gallery."

"I've been busier than a moth in a mitten this last week…"

He frowned. "This last week…?"

She nodded. "All those are of the hotel's old doors I told you about."

Some of the rubbings were done on plain white paper, some on butcher paper, others on rice or tracing paper. They were all extraordinary in their own way, each different than the next, a mélange of door numbers, colors, patterns, and textures.

"Could this productivity…yours, mine…be somehow connected to the sleepwalking…the ghosts?"

"If it isn't," Jolene said with a tight smile, "then I reckon it would be one mighty big coincidence, wouldn't you agree?"

CHAPTER 44

Hocus Pocus & The Good Boy Scouts

After showering and changing at home, Malcolm took a taxi to the *City Living* office on Sixth Avenue. Unlike traditional offices cluttered with disruptive cubicles, all the desks were organized in simple lines with no partitions. This saved on floor space, allowing for a lounge area (which included a table tennis table) where the staff could relax during breaks, several spacious meeting rooms, a large kitchenette, and several healthy-option vending machines.

Malcolm greeted his colleagues, dropped his laptop bag on his chair, and turned on his computer. He then went to Steven Perry's office. He saw through the window that the editor-in-chief was on the telephone and waited until his boss had ended the call before knocking on the door.

Perry waved him in. He was a middle-aged man, steely-eyed and bald except for a salt-and-pepper horseshoe of hair. He never wore suits, preferring to dress business-casual in polo shirts and khakis. As always, he smelled strongly of after-shave and stale cigarettes

"Morning, Malcolm," he said in his gruff smoker's voice before taking a gulp of coffee from a mug emblazoned with the words DO NOT DISTURB. "Enjoy the day off?"

"Always enjoy an extra day off." He passed Perry a USB drive. "The Hotel Chelsea copy."

"What did you think of the old place?"

"It's got some history, all right. About fifty long-term tenants are still living there, protected by rent stabilization laws.

Most aren't too happy with the construction."

"What are they like?"

"Friendly. Eccentric."

"Timeline?"

"Doesn't look like there's an end in sight right now."

"They should have just knocked the ugly fucking thing down if you ask me. I sent you an email outlining your next story. There's a chef in Midtown I want you to sit down with. He's into locally available produce and creating seasonally inspired recipes. Thought you might call the piece Farm to Table, but you might come up with something better. That's it, son. Get cracking."

◆ ◆ ◆

Back in front of his computer, Malcolm spent a good chunk of the morning transcribing his scribbles from the Mary Higgins Clark paperback novel into a Microsoft Word document. Once finished, he began researching the Midtown restaurant and chef, though he quickly lost interest. Instead he turned his attention to learning what he could about hauntings at the Hotel Chelsea. There had been many alleged ghost sightings at the hotel over the years, but two well-documented incidents kept popping up again and again.

The first involved the ghost of a young woman named Mary. After the *RMS Titanic* sank in 1912, many of the survivors were put up at the Hotel Chelsea. Mary was one of them, a widow whose husband died when the ship sank. By all accounts, she was an exceedingly vain woman who took great pains with her appearance, often seen in a hat with a plume, her hair swept up in a Gibson Girl bun. However, she was unable to move on from her husband's death, became deeply depressed, and ended up hanging herself in her room on the eighth floor. She was often reported to be seen on the eighth-floor west wing of the building where the entrance to her apartment had once been.

The second incident involved the ghost of another young woman named Nadia. According to a *New York Times* article from 1922, Nadia was a talented artist who created Japanese-style paintings on silk, which she cut from bolts of cloth that her father, a wealthy silk merchant, brought home from the warehouses. While still a teenager, Nadia married a roguish songwriter against her parents' wishes. In retaliation, they kicked her out of the lavish suite of rooms where they lived in the Hotel Chelsea and cut off her allowance. During her ostracization, she gave birth to two children. The songwriter supported them by selling his songs along Tin Pan Alley on 27th Street. When his career didn't take off as he'd believed it would, he turned more and more to the bottle, eventually becoming a penniless alcoholic. No longer able to feed her children, Nadia begged her parents to allow her family to move back into the Chelsea. They agreed, under the condition she take responsibility for all the domestic chores, including hand-washing her incontinent mother's underthings. The never-ending housework, combined with raising her two children, left her little time to work on her paintings. As the years passed, she became bitter and disillusioned. All the washing, cleaning, and needlework had calloused and knotted her hands. Her knuckles became stiff and sore, and she could no longer hold a paintbrush without pain. This took a heavy toll on her mental health, leading to a stint in a Long Island hospital. Finally one night she snapped. She'd been working on her latest painting, a scene of cranes cavorting in Central Park's Bethesda Fountain, but her inability to place brush-strokes where she wanted drove her into a rage. She sliced up the canvas with the pair of industrial shears she used to cut the silk fabric for her art. Then she placed her right wrist between the blades and leaned on the handle with all her weight, severing her hand. The pain was so excruciating she threw herself from the fifth-floor window onto West 23rd Street, screaming in agony as she fell five floors to her death. On moonless nights Nadia's ghost, some report, has been seen hovering outside the Hotel Chelsea's balconies, or floating up and down the fire escapes, in a futile attempt to get back inside the hotel that had once been her home.

Malcolm massaged his eyes with the heels of his hands. While these tales were interesting, they weren't exactly what he was looking for. Nevertheless, when another half hour passed, and he'd failed to dig up anything relating to people sleepwalking at the Hotel Chelsea, or people encountering the ghosts of the hotel's more famous residents, he turned to researching supernatural activity in general.

In a nutshell, it seemed that most professional ghost hunters and paranormal investigators believed in two distinct kinds of hauntings: residual and intelligent. Residual hauntings, they propose, are not so much hauntings but recordings of past energy. The argument is that when a person dies in a heightened emotional state, he or she can release a large amount of energy that can embed itself in the surrounding physical environment. This can manifest itself either as a kind of psychic tape recording of the past, allowing the living to hear the deceased's voice or footsteps or what-have-you, or as a psychic movie, allowing the living to see the deceased in one manifestation or another.

By contrast, intelligent hauntings involve conscious ghosts or spirits who interact with the living. Several theories exist to explain why a wraith-like being would elect to remain on the physical plane after death. Some spirits, for instance, simply do not realize their life has ended and so continue to behave as if they were still alive. Others remain behind to ensure the safety of a loved one, or to avenge a wrong committed against them, particularly if they had been a victim of a murder. And others have a particularly strong bond to a place, item, or person in this world that prevents them from moving on.

If Malcolm had to choose between these two theories to explain what he'd experienced in Room 100 at the Hotel Chelsea, the idea of an intelligent haunting initially seemed to make more sense. Sid Vicious, after all, had acknowledged his presence. He'd invited him to enter the room and to shoot up with him. Yet the more Malcolm thought about it, the more he wondered if perhaps he had in fact witnessed a recording of the past. From what he'd read, hauntings tended to ramp up when a structure was being renovated. Also, perhaps Sid hadn't been communicating to him, but to someone else who had been in his room in 1978? Someone who Malcolm had been unable to observe?

He decided he preferred this possibility. A psychic recording was less threatening than an intelligent entity. It was a mirage, ephemeral, harmless. Lacking intelligence, there could be no malicious intent.

He was ruminating on all of this when Steve Perry said from behind him, "Ghosts, huh?"

Malcolm started, and with a flush of embarrassment, realized his boss was referring to the webpage open in Malcolm's browser, the headline proclaiming: WHY WE SHOULD BELIEVE IN GHOSTS.

He cleared his throat and said, "Some of the tenants at the Chelsea told me they believed in them. Thought I'd look into it for kicks."

"Don't bother, Malcolm," the editor-in-chief said, clapping a hand on his shoulder. "Your copy is fantastic as it stands. Absolutely fantastic. I've made a few notes and suggestions, but you outdid yourself on this one." He returned Malcolm's USB drive to him. "Ever hear of The Good Boy Scouts?"

Malcolm shook his head. "I take it they have nothing to do with the youth development organization?"

"They're an up-and-coming rock band from Canada. They're kicking off a US tour with a show at Webster Hall tomorrow. They've got a press conference this afternoon at the Sheraton. I thought you could check it out."

"But Andy covers music...?"

"Can't hurt to expand your portfolio, right? Also, these guys are going to be the feature next month. But if you don't want it—"

"No, I want it." He'd never been given the feature before. "What about the chef story?"

Perry waved a hand dismissively. "I'll freelance it out," he said, then: "And Malcolm? I don't think I have to point out that this is a big opportunity for you. Don't fuck it up."

◆ ◆ ◆

Malcolm ate a hotdog for lunch while walking the dozen or so blocks to the Sheraton Hotel on Seventh Avenue north of Times Square. On the way he gave Jolene a call. When she didn't pick up, he felt inexplicably anxious, and he told himself to dial back the paranoia. She could be doing any one of a thousand innocuous things that had parted her with her phone.

CHAPTER 45

More questions than answers

T he Good Boy Scouts' press conference lasted for roughly forty-five minutes.

The band was composed of four good-looking young men. The singer and the drummer, both with long hair and visible tattoos, did most of the talking. The shaved-head bassist threw in an ad hominem attack on their critics every now and then, and the short, blond guitarist said next to nothing and appeared to want to be anywhere but where he was.

When the Q & A finished, Malcolm introduced himself to the band's manager, a polite, manicured man named Todd. As luck would have it, Todd invited him up to the band's suite on the twelfth floor.

The party had already started, with the four bandmates all drinking Coronas and passing around a huge joint. They didn't object to Malcolm interviewing them, even when he explained his questions would be more personal than those asked earlier.

"Bring it on," the singer said, returning from the kitchen with a full bottle of beer.

Given how standoffish the band had been downstairs in the conference room, Malcolm had expected more of the same attitude. Yet with no cameras on them (and their tongues lubricated by the beer and pot), they told a compelling story of four small-town friends from Kingston, Ontario, who met in high school, performed local gigs for several years with little success, and were thinking about disbanding the group when they were discovered by a record producer while performing at a wedding reception. That had been fourteen months ago. Since then they had released their debut album, been nominated for three Juno Awards, and were topping charts across Canada.

It was your typical rags-to-riches rock and roll tale, heard a hundred times before, but by the time Malcolm left the Sheraton two hours later, something great in the making was already brewing inside his head.

◆ ◆ ◆

Instead of returning to the office, Malcolm stopped in a café down the street from the Sheraton. He ordered a coffee, opened his laptop, and sketched out the bones of The Good Boy Scouts' feature. After about an hour and a half, he took a break to call Jolene.

Once again, she didn't pick up.

The agita Malcolm had felt earlier in the afternoon returned with a wallop. Why wasn't she answering her phone? Where could she be? He told himself not to overreact. She could very well be a person who didn't carry their phone around with them. She could have gone to the cinema to catch a matinee show. She could have gone to Bloomingdale's or Macy's for an afternoon of shopping.

She could have, but she didn't.

He had no way of knowing this for sure, but he felt it in his core.

And he wasn't being paranoid, he told himself, because shit was happening at the Hotel Chelsea, unexplained shit, terrifying shit—and who was to say it only happened at nighttime?

Packing up his computer, Malcolm left the café and headed south on Seventh Avenue, an urgency to his step.

CHAPTER 46

Thanks, Darnell

The Hotel Chelsea stood tall and unbowed against the pinkening evening sky, yet there was a sense of emptiness and despair about the once grand dame of New York City; a sense she stood because she had always stood, not because she had any real reason left to continue doing so. The construction netting that draped her face promised a rebirth, but in the fading light of dusk it seemed more than ever like a funeral shroud, masking her blind, boarded-up eyes, and carving thick shadows beneath them like swollen bags.

Malcolm pressed the buzzer next to the door and stepped into the uninviting lobby.

Darnell looked up from a magazine he was reading and said, "You're becoming a regular around here."

"I'm visiting Jolene. Have you seen her today?"

"Don't think I have. Why?"

"She hasn't been answering her phone."

"She doesn't know you're here to see her? If that's the case, buddy, I shouldn't be letting you past this desk." He showed his gap-toothed smile. "But I like you, Malcolm. You don't get under my skin like the whiny leftovers infesting this place like so many cockroaches, so go on up. I never saw you."

CHAPTER 47

Dancing in the pale moonlight

Malcolm knocked loudly on the door to Jolene's room.
"Jo?" he said. "It's Malcolm."

She didn't reply.

He took out his phone and dialed her number. After six unanswered rings he hung up.

He hadn't expected Jolene to answer; he was listening to hear if the phone would ring inside her room.

He had not heard it, which meant 1) she likely wasn't in the room, hiding out from him for whatever reason, and 2) she had the phone with her, wherever she was (which made him all the more concerned as to why she wouldn't answer or return his calls).

He backtracked down the main hallway and entered Room 105, Edie Sedgwick's old haunt. The interior was straight out of the 60s or 70s, only now showing more than forty years of wear and tear. The teal ceiling and gold walls were not only dated but grimy. The paint around the window had been stripped in places but the wood was never repainted. A film of dust covered the glossy white shelves in the bookcase built into one wall. A satin teal sheet in lieu of proper curtains hung limply in front of the window. A threadbare comforter no thicker than a tablecloth covered the single bed. Perched atop a chest of drawers was a cathode-ray TV and an old remote control. An armchair that very well could have been salvaged from a curbside trash heap was shoved into a corner next to a silver-painted radiator.

Charming, Malcolm thought, wondering how the hotel had ever found success renting out such atrocious rooms.

He poked his head into the small bathroom (which had a large hole in the white subway tiles), opened the closet where Edie Sedgwick had hid when the room went up in flames (I LOVE THE SMELL OF STALE URINE IN THE MORNING graffitied with a black Sharpie on the back wall), and even got on his knees to peer under the bed.

Disappointed (even though finding Jolene in Room 105 had been a longshot at best), he rode the elevator to the tenth floor and took the stairs up to the roof. The last of the red had bled from the sky, leaving it big and black and dominated by a pale gibbous moon. A cool wind blew, mussing Malcolm's hair as he hurried to Quinn's pyramid. He heard classical piano music and thought Quinn was making it at the baby grand she'd found in the hotel's basement. Through the window in the door, however, he saw the old woman—clad in a black leotard, white stockings, and pink ballerina slippers—gliding from one side of the room to the other in a flurry of pirouettes and leg lifts and leaps that defied her age.

Malcolm knocked on her door and took a few steps backward so it didn't appear he'd been spying through the window.

The music—a tape cassette or CD—stopped. Then Quinn's face appeared on the other side of the glass, her eyes bright and her cheeks flushed. She wore her usual over-the-top eye makeup but no wig. Her silver hair, shorn short and feathered, suited her better, Malcolm thought, than the blonde curls. She appeared regal rather than Vaudevillian.

Smiling, she opened the door. "Why, Mr. Clock, what do I owe ze honor of zis visit?"

"Hi, Quinn," he said. "I hope I'm not interrupting."

"Not at all. I was only dancing. Can you believe that? Who would have ever thought at seventy-two years of age, I would still be dancing? Would you like to come in? Jolene is not with you, I see?"

Malcolm followed Quinn inside and said, "Jolene's why I came to see you."

"Oh? Let me put on some tea." She went to the stove and turned the electric ignition. It clicked twice and a flame whooshed into existence beneath the kettle.

"Glad your gas is working again."

"You and me both." She retrieved two mugs from a cupboard and said, "Black? Green? I also have peppermint."

"Black's fine, thanks."

"Milk?"

"Yes, please."

She took a carton of full-cream milk from the fridge and set it on the counter. "I hope you and Jolene aren't in a lover's spat. You've only been together now for a couple of days!"

"No, it's not that at all. It's...well, this is going to sound a little silly, but she hasn't answered her phone all day."

"And?"

"That's it. I was wondering if you might have spoken to her...?"

"No, I have not."

"I called her around noon, then again around six. I knocked on her door before coming up here. There was no answer."

"I must say, Mr. Clock, Jolene is a grown woman. I don't find it unusual that she might be out all afternoon doing one thing or another, and I don't think you should either."

"Why wouldn't she answer my calls?"

"Perhaps the battery in her phone died?"

"If that were the case, the calls would go immediately to her voicemail. But her phone rings until I hang up."

The teapot began to whistle. Quinn filled the mugs with the hot water and added a dollop of milk to both. "Here you go," she said, handing Malcolm his. "Careful, it will be hot." She gestured him to follow her to the sitting area, where she settled down on the bird nest sofa. He took a seat on the zebra-striped chair with the ruby-red heels. "Is it possible Jolene simply might not want to talk to you today?"

"It's possible," he admitted. "But I can't see why."

"You think something's happened to her?"

"That's what I'm worried about."

"And you think this has something to do with the hotel itself."

After a beat, Malcolm said, "Yes, I do."

Quinn sipped her tea thoughtfully. "Tell me, Mr. Clock, what do you think has happened then? Do you believe the ghost of Edie Sedgwick has snatched her away from the world of the living?"

"No, I don't. But I do think whatever is happening here at the Chelsea has something to do with it."

"And what is happening here? You and Jolene have both been sleepwalking. You have both had dreams of former residents. This doesn't sound threatening to me. In fact, it doesn't even sound very exceptional."

"You told me you started dancing when you were a girl in Bucharest, Quinn. Have you been dancing ever since?"

"I stopped dancing professionally when I was somewhere around your age. Recreationally, a few years after that, which I do regret."

"Yet you were dancing tonight?"

"I've felt inspired lately."

"Lately as in the last week or so?"

Quinn's eyes narrowed. "What are you getting at, Mr. Clock?"

Malcolm set his untouched tea on a side table. "Ever since I first came to the Hotel Chelsea last week," he said, leaning forward, "I've been having incredible writing sessions. They occur only after I've visited the Chelsea. The longer I'm away from the hotel, the more difficult it becomes to write until I reach a complete impasse."

"You mean you are experiencing alternating bouts of creativity and writer's block? Name me a writer who hasn't! It is the nature of your craft."

"That's what I originally believed. But this morning Jolene

told me the same thing's been happening to her, only with those rubbings she does. She has a huge stack in her room of the old hotel doors being stored in the basement, all done in the last week or so."

"If I'm following you correctly, Mr. Clock, you're implying that the Hotel Chelsea is somehow...boosting...your creativity and productivity, and Jolene's too?" She smiled woefully. "I have to wonder if you are letting the hotel's legacy go to your head. Has it been a cauldron of creativity over the years? Absolutely. But has it been *responsible* for that creativity? Of course not. The residents of the hotel have. The Warhols and the Dylans and the Twains—they brought their creativity and genius here, they inspired others to create, who inspired others still. *That* is the magic of the Hotel Chelsea. The people who populated her walls, not the damned walls themselves!"

"So how would you explain—"

"You and Jolene have both been inspired, that seems clear. But by the hotel? No. I imagine you have inspired and energized *each other*. Romance can do strange things to the chemicals in one's brain."

Malcolm clenched his jaw. "And what about you, Quinn? Your inspiration to dance? Is romance playing with the chemicals in your brain too?"

It was a veiled barb, and he regretted the words as soon as they left his mouth. Quinn's smile tightened. "I'm sorry I can't help you any with Jolene's whereabouts, Mr. Clock. But I'm sure she will return home safely." She stood. "Now, if there isn't anything else I can help you with, I would like to resume my dancing."

CHAPTER 48

Not you again

Malcolm searched each floor of the hotel for Jolene, beginning on the tenth. He ran into several tenants coming or going. None of them had seen Jolene, and one middle-aged woman was openly hostile, demanding to know who he was and what he was doing in the building (she was only slightly mollified by his answers and berated Darnell for allowing "strange men" to wander the hallways).

While in the first floor's west wing, Malcolm heard guitar music coming from Shane's room, an admittedly impressive medley of fast fingerpicking and bluesy chords.

Back in front of Jolene's door, he knocked once again. When there was no answer, he thought about Lisa Brooks pale and unbreathing in his Brooklyn basement room, his inability to save her, the paramedics' inability to save her. He didn't believe Jolene had overdosed on anything. But if she'd been sleepwalking again, who knew what might have happened to her? She could have stumbled or fainted, smacking her head on the way down. She could have seen something that had scared her into a massive heart attack. Anything was possible.

Which meant he needed to get into her room.

For a moment he considered driving his foot into the door. Instead he went back down the corridor and climbed through the window onto the fire escape. The wind whistled past his ears. In the distance he heard cars honking and an ambulance siren wailing. Maneuvering around the steep stairs that led up to the second floor, he recalled hanging out there with Jolene the other night during the blackout, drinking Budweisers, Jolene telling him about how she used to live in cemeteries.

The band of anxiety around his chest tightened.

At her window, he cupped his hands against the glass but could only see darkness inside her room. He shoved the top of the sash. It slid easily upward, and he eased himself inside.

Picturing the layout of the room in his mind, he moved slowly and blindly to the wall where the light switch was located. When his foot nudged something solid, his stomach dropped. He slapped the wall until his hand hit the light switch.

It wasn't Jolene's body he'd toed; it was the box of tracing paper and rubbings he'd pulled out from beneath her bed that morning.

His relief lasted only a moment, however. The room was empty.

He still had no idea where Jolene was, or what had happened to her.

He turned off the light, crossed the room in the dark, and left through the window, pulling the sash down behind him. He had one leg through the fire escape window when he heard the nearby toilet flush.

The bathroom door opened and Shane appeared just as Malcolm swung his other leg inside.

"Hey," he said casually. "I was getting some air."

"Aye, right. Getting some air. On the fire escape."

"I'm waiting for Jolene. I'm early. Thought I'd get some air rather than stand around in the hallway."

"C'mere to me," Shane said, sauntering toward him. "Let's have a word, you and I." The Irishman was a far cry from the manicured rock star he'd presented at Harvey and Jeffrey's dinner party. His hair was flat and unwashed, his jaw scraggly with growth, his feet bare. His green Roots sweatpants had gaping holes in the knees, and his too-large flannel shirt was stained and unbuttoned to mid-chest.

He stopped two feet from Malcolm, reeking of whiskey.

"What do you want?" Malcolm asked.

"Got plans with Jo, do ye?" he said.

"Yeah, I do. Have you seen her around today?"

"I have not." His lips turned downward. "Why would it matter if I had?"

"It wouldn't."

"Then why did you ask?"

"She's a bit late."

His frown lines hardened. "Not a moment ago you confessed to be early. Now she's late? Tell me, lad, which is it?"

"When I arrived, I was early. But now I've been here for a while, making Jolene late."

"What are youse doin' tonight?"

"I don't think that's any of your business."

Shane's eyes smoldered, and Malcolm tensed in anticipation of a fist flying toward his face. But Shane only brushed past him and returned to his room. He closed his door loudly behind him.

Malcolm stared after the guy, wondering suddenly whether he might have had something to do with Jolene's disappearance. He'd seen Malcolm leaving her room in the middle of the night. Maybe he'd seen or heard Malcolm leaving her room this morning as well. Had this propelled him into a jealous rage? Had he confronted her? And when he didn't like what she told him, he what...? Beat her unconscious? Was she tied up in his room right now?

Shane clearly had anger management issues, so these possibilities weren't implausible. Yet what could Malcolm do? Bang on his door and demand to search his room? Call the police with zero evidence to support his accusation?

He went down the hallway and stopped out front Shane's room and dialed Jolene's number.

Her phone rang and rang and rang.

But no corresponding ringtone came from other side of Shane's door.

CHAPTER 49

Say it ain't so, Jo

Malcolm wandered outside until he found a bar around the block on West 22nd Street. It was a cave-like place accentuated with red lights and disco balls hanging from the ceiling. He got a booth to himself and discovered it was a gay bar when the waiter told him he was entitled to a free drink if he created a profile on an LGBT website. He demurred and ordered a gin on the rocks. Then he took his laptop from his bag. With Jolene's disappearance burning a hole in his mind, he didn't think he would be able to get into The Good Boy Scouts' feature, but he ended up bashing out a very solid first draft, only breaking once to use the restroom. Glancing at his wristwatch, he was surprised to find it was already ten thirty. He checked his phone.

No missed calls, no text messages.

Buzzing heavily—how many gins had he knocked back? Five? Six?—he called Jolene. She didn't pick up. He typed out a message but didn't send it. What was the point? If she were going to get back to him, she would have done so already.

Malcolm slumped back in the booth. The place had filled up with good-looking men as well as hetero couples and mature single women. The muscled, go-happy bartender was performing bottle tricks behind the bar, while raunchy drag queens performed on the stage to an enthusiastic crowd of onlookers, with some sitting on the pool table to score the best view.

While watching a touchy-feely lesbian couple in the booth across from his, a thought struck him.

What if Jolene's on a date right now?

The possibility floored him, and embarrassment burned when he realized what a fool he'd been if this were the case. He'd called her how many times today? Five? She'd likely rolled her eyes each time she saw his number, thinking he'd morphed into a lovesick Shane 2.0 who couldn't manage a day without talking to her.

He tipped his drink back, found only ice remaining, and shoved the glass away from him.

Could she really be on a date?

Why not? He'd known her for less than a week. Last night was the only time they'd been intimate. They were still a long way from the point of expecting fidelity from one another.

Which led him to wonder about the sex they'd had. He'd thought it had been good. But what did he know? He'd had little practice over the last several years.

So had Jolene, finding him inadequate, called up some other friend for a better time tonight?

The explanation, if true, ought to have offered some comfort. It meant she was safe. She was not being held against her will somewhere, or dead. And on some level, Malcolm did feel relieved. But on another, baser level, he felt slow-burning anger. She might not have an obligation to be faithful to him, but that shouldn't exclude her from being straightforward and honest. If she wasn't interested in him, then answer the phone and tell him as much. Ignoring his calls in the hope he simply went away was juvenile and disingenuous.

The smiling waiter appeared at his booth. "Another gin on the rocks?"

"Yes," Malcolm said. "Make it a double."

◆ ◆ ◆

Malcolm left the bar an hour later at eleven thirty. He walked up Eighth Avenue to West 23rd Street with the intention of catching a taxi home. But he ended up standing on the corner, reconsidering. Although he'd had a lot to drink, he wasn't smashed. Years of abusing alcohol had not only pickled his liver but had also given him the tolerance of a vodka-swilling Muscovite. Also, the brisk air was helping to clear his thoughts.

Jolene might have been ignoring his calls all day because he was shit in the sack and she no longer wanted anything to do with him. She might have been on a date tonight rolling her eyes at his barrage of phone calls.

But he didn't believe either of these scenarios.

He might not have known Jolene for long, but he'd already gotten a good sense of who she was. She wouldn't kick him to the curb without an explanation.

Not only that, but they'd stumbled onto something much bigger than the two of them.

The Hotel Chelsea is haunted. You believe that. You believe that Jolene believes that. So what the fuck are you doing even considering going home when her life could be in jeopardy. Maybe you're more drunk than you realize, Mac.

Malcolm went east toward the hotel, the neon signage suspended in the darkness welcoming him back.

CHAPTER 50

The jacks

S hane had been sober for two days now.

After barricading the door to Room 826, he slept un-interrupted until ten o'clock the next morning, waking not perched on an eighth-floor balcony but safe and warm in his bed. All that day he fought the urge to hit the bottle, and succeeded. Instead of drinking himself into a coma, he worked on his music, ate three square meals, and walked a lap around Central Park. In the evening he played guitar and watched two movies back to back. The following morning he woke at seven a.m. and filled his day with much of the same routine. He went to bed early and woke early.

Today he'd booked a recording session for later in the week at a studio on West 41st Street near the Lincoln Tunnel.

He felt good for the first time in recent memory, healthy, and optimistic about his future.

He still didn't know what had prompted his nocturnal death wish, but it seemed blocking access to Room 826 had stymied the demon puppeteer pursuing that goal, forcing it to retreat into whatever hole in his mind from which it had crawled.

Seated on the edge of the sofa now, the curved body of the Fender guitar resting on his thigh, Shane played his latest song, a bleak, spoken-word track about keeping the devil at bay, and while the devil could be a metaphor for a number of things, for him it was booze. The guitar was melodically unhinged, the lyrics a lonely monologue of a man questioning the choices he'd made in his life. After this he played another new song, something more surrealist and lighthearted, a kind of children's song for adults. Then he got up and went to the kitchen to fix himself a snack. He poured a glass of milk, dumped some crackers onto a plate, and sliced up what remained of a block of cheddar cheese.

While he nibbled, his mind went to Jolene, wondering what she would think of his new music. He was confident she would like it. She'd liked his old stuff, and the songs he'd created over the last week or two were all next level. He imagined himself playing not in half-empty bars but on proper stages in proper venues with proper, paying audiences. This wasn't a daydream. He had a real shot at landing a record deal with a major studio. His recent stuff, he believed, was that good.

The Siamese cat leapt up onto the counter, startling him.

"Sweet baby Jaysus," he grumbled, rubbing it between the ears while it sniffed a slice of cheese. It looked up at him and meowed. "Here then." He poured some of his milk onto a plate he withdrew from the drying rack over the sink.

The cat ignored it and pawed the cheese.

"Scat!" he said, pushing it away. "That's mine—"

The cat slashed his hand with its claws.

"Ow!"

It hissed at him.

"Fack aff!" He yanked open the window and shooed it outside.

Standing on the windowsill, the cat stared at him for an unnerving moment, hackles raised, before slinking off into the night.

Shane turned his attention to the cut. It was deep and bleeding profusely. He dabbed it with paper towel, which did nothing to stop the flow. He rummaged through his cupboards for the first-aid kit. Then he remembered he'd left it under the sink in the shared bathroom. A few months ago he'd spilled some boiling oil onto his bare foot, blistering much of the skin away, and forcing him to treat it with a topical burn ointment and non-adhesive dressing for close to two weeks.

Pressing more paper towels to the cut, he went down the hallway to the jacks. Light seeped from the crack between the bottom of the door and the floor.

"Jo?" he said, wishing he were wearing something nicer than a frayed sweat suit.

She didn't answer.

"Jo, is that you in there?"

No reply.

Figuring she'd forgotten to turn off the light after her last visit, he pushed open the door—and started in surprise.

Malcolm what's-his-name was sitting on the toilet, slack-faced, eyes open and showing mostly the whites. A string of drool dangled from his parted mouth.

A cold fear gripped Shane. The bastard looked dead, save for the fact he was sitting upright.

"Are you feelin' all right, lad?"

He didn't react.

Shane stepped closer and gripped his shoulder, to shake him from the stupor.

The bastard's hand locked around Shane's wrist in a sweaty, vice-like grip, squeezing hard.

CHAPTER 51

Old friends

Malcolm could scarcely believe he was about to shoot up with Sid Vicious and Dee Dee Ramone. They were crammed into the small bathroom with him, both freakishly skinny in their leather jackets and looking very punkish. Sid held a bottle cap he was going to use as a cooker, a paperclip bent around it to serve as a handle so he could hold it over the Sterno stove sitting on the sink. Dee Dee, however, had the hypodermic needle and was demanding he get the first fix.

"Fuck off, mate," Sid said, snarling. "It's my dope. I go first."

"Maybe I'll go find my own dope then," Dee Dee said in his outer-boroughs accent, his eyes manic beneath his Beatles-style haircut. "Good dope. That shit you got there looks like the stuff we used to cop on 10th and Avenue B in the late 70s. Has it been in your pocket all these years?"

"Greatest thing about being dead, mate, you can blow through all your dope one day, and the next morning, it's all right back there, like you've never touched it."

"I should have died with some dope in my pocket," Dee Dee said grouchily.

"I wish you had," Sid said, "because then you wouldn't be following me around all the time. Has it occurred to you that you have a pretty bad addiction, Dee Dee?"

"You think? Fuck it, let's let the new guy decide."

They both looked at Malcolm.

He said, "Maybe I should go first."

"*You*, mate?" Sid said, surprised. "I thought you didn't want to shoot up. He ran out of my room the other night," he told Dee Dee.

"That was then," Malcolm said. "I've been dealing with some heavy stuff today, and I'm pretty stressed. Getting high might help me out."

"Fine, you go first," Dee Dee said. "You are the new guy, after all."

"Then who goes second?" Sid asked.

"Me."

"Fuck that, Dee Dee! No fucking way. I'm going first." He stuck the bottle cap over the stove's flame to liquify the heroin, then twisted the chain he wore around his neck to tie off. "Right there, mate, in the big vein."

Grumbling, Dee Dee filled the syringe with heroin and jabbed the needle in Sid's neck and depressed the plunger.

"Ahhh," Sid said happily.

"You know that chain doesn't hide the track marks," Dee Dee said. "I don't know why you bother hiding them anyway. Everyone knows you're a junkie."

"I don't wear this chain to hide my tracks. I wear it because Nancy gave it to me."

"After she stole it from one of my old girlfriends—"

"Quiet!" Sid said suddenly. "Someone's on the other side of the door."

"Probably some junkie looking to steal our dope. This place is filled with lowlifes like that."

"He lays a finger on my shite, I'll smash in his face."

"He's opening the door. Get ready..."

PART 3

"Who is the third who always walks beside you? / When I count, there are only you and I together / But when I look ahead up the white road / There is always another one walking beside you."

—T.S. ELIOT, *THE WASTE LAND*

CHAPTER 52

A bad dream?

Malcolm woke stiff and cold and uncomfortable—and wondering why the hell he was in a bathtub.

Sitting up, he realized it was the bathtub in the bathroom that Jolene and Shane shared on the first floor of the Hotel Chelsea. He replayed the previous night. It took a few moments to clear the hangover fuzz before recalling the gay bar, coming back to the hotel, and slumping down outside Jolene's door. He'd been tired, struggling to keep his eyes open, but kept nodding off.

I sleepwalked again, he thought with a punch of dread. *Came in here and—*

Sid Vicious and Dee Dee Ramone.

They'd been in here with him. Arguing about who got to shoot up first. And Malcolm had wanted to shoot up too. He remembered that clearly. The hunger. Waiting with building anticipation for his turn to stick the needle in his arm.

Shrugging off his jacket, he pushed up his sleeves and checked for needle marks.

None.

Of course there aren't any, Mac, he thought. *Ghosts are phantoms, intangible, impalpable. They're not flesh and blood. They can't give you physical items.*

Besides, he'd never had the chance to shoot up, had he? Because someone had interrupted the session. Someone, another junkie, had come into the bathroom to steal their drugs.

After that...well, he didn't know what happened. That's

where his memory of events ended.

Grabbing his laptop bag, Malcolm got gingerly to his feet and waited for feeling to return to one of his numb legs that had succumbed to pins and needles. The overhead light was on, stinging his eyes. His mouth was cotton dry, his throat parched, and a small headache pulsed behind his temples.

And Jolene. Fuck, Jolene was missing. That wasn't a bad dream.
Was she back in her room now?

Malcolm stepped out of the tub and went to the sink. His intention was to turn on the tap and stick his mouth under the faucet, but he froze in surprise. Bright red blood smeared the white porcelain. Stepping backward in alarm, he noticed more blood on the floor, dried and darker than the blood on the porcelain.

Careful not to step in it, he returned to the sink and looked at himself in the mirror. No cuts, no bleeding nose or lips. He looked at his hands.

Clean.

Where the hell did the blood come from?

On shaky legs he left the bathroom and breathed deeply in the hallway. He went to Jolene's room and knocked. When she didn't reply, he thumped his fist against the door. Leaning against it, head dropped, eyes shut, he fought a fresh wave of fear and confusion and gloom.

Then, telling himself to get his shit together, he dug his phone from his pocket, and called the police.

CHAPTER 53

Keep your friends close &
your enemies closer

I n front of the door to his apartment was a large gift basket filled with colorful fruit: bananas, strawberries, grapes, oranges, apples, and pears. A card was tucked in between two McIntosh apples.

Malcolm carried the basket into his apartment and set it on the kitchen table next to the fire extinguisher and hunting knife. The card read:

Apology to my favorite neighbor. Nikki.

Malcolm contemplated going next door to thank her for the gesture, but he decided he wasn't in the mood to talk to anyone, especially Nikki. Kicking off his shoes, he went to the bedroom, drew the curtains closed, and got in bed beneath the covers. He hated doing nothing while Jolene was missing, but he didn't know what more he could do. The police officer he'd spoken to on the phone had been blunt in his assessment that Jolene's disappearance seemed neither dire nor concerning, and he'd told Malcolm to wait another twenty-four hours before filing an official missing person's report.

Furious, Malcolm walked three blocks to the NYPD 10th Precinct on West 20th Street and filed one anyway, though the officer he spoke to there didn't take Jolene's disappearance seriously either, especially when Malcolm couldn't provide her date of birth or a description of the clothing she had last been wearing (which had been nothing but a bedsheet).

As his brain shut down and his muscles relaxed, foreboding images of Jolene, wherever she was, played out in his exhausted mind, Jolene alone and afraid, caged by an unseen evil, wondering why he was doing nothing to save her.

These images followed Malcolm into a deep sleep plagued by dreams better left unremembered.

◆ ◆ ◆

The ringing of his mobile phone jolted him awake. He scrambled out of bed and dashed to the kitchen, believing it was Jolene calling to tell him she'd returned from Philadelphia or Providence or Boston, or some other city where she'd visited to do some new gravestone rubbings.

He snatched the phone off the counter where he'd left it.

When he saw Quinn's number, his heart dropped.

He cleared his throat and answered. "Hi, Quinn."

"Hello, Mr. Clock. I hope I'm not disturbing you at work?"

"I'm working from home today."

"I see. Well, I was going to ask if we could talk when you got off, but if you're home, perhaps we could get together sooner? It is rather urgent."

"What did you want to talk about?"

"I believe it would be best if we sat down in person."

Malcolm clamped his jaw. The last thing he wanted to do right then was play games. But Quinn was not one to beat around the bush for no reason. "I can be at the Chelsea in a half hour."

"It's a rather beautiful day, and I could do with getting out of the hotel. Why don't we meet in Union Square Park? That should only be a twenty minute or so walk for each of us."

"All right, Quinn," he said. "I'll see you there in twenty minutes."

◆ ◆ ◆

He was locking his door behind him when Nikki emerged from her apartment.

He swore silently to himself.

"Hi, Mac!" she said brightly. "Seems like you're a bit late for work today."

"What about you? Day off?"

She nodded. "I only work three days a week."

"Um, thanks for the gift basket. That was nice of you."

"I thought with your terrible diet, you could do with some more vitamins. And...it was my apology for how I acted the other day."

Malcolm wanted to tell her he didn't have time to talk about this right now, but he held his tongue and said, "That's all right. The knife in the door was sort of funny in retrospect. I'll bring it by later, but I need to get going."

"I'll walk with you."

"I'm—" He frowned, annoyed. "Where are you going?"

"Nowhere. Out for air. What's the big deal? I'll just walk to the train station with you."

"I'm not going to work. I'm meeting someone."

"Your Southern friend?" she said tightly.

"No, someone else," he said, walking to the stairs.

Nikki followed. "You have a lot of girlfriends these days."

"She's in her seventies."

"Oh."

Malcolm descended the stairs first, and they didn't speak again until they were outside heading west on East 9th Street.

"So who is she?" Nikki asked.

"Someone I met at the Hotel Chelsea."

"Ah, a source!"

"What?"

"For your article."

"Yeah," he said simply, wondering how he was going to shake Nikki. He didn't want to spend the next fifteen minutes with her.

"Are you walking *all* the way to Chelsea? That's right across town."

"No, we're meeting in a park."

"What park?"

"Union Square."

"Sounds very clandestine."

"What?"

"Park benches are where spies always meet to pass along classified documents."

"She wanted to meet outside because it's a nice day."

"It is nice out, isn't it? I like days like this. Brisk days. Fall's my favorite season."

He didn't say anything.

"Aren't you going to tell me yours?"

"My favorite season?" he said, wondering if Nikki had always been this irritating.

"I told you mine, so you're supposed to tell me yours. That's how small talk works."

"Winter."

"Winter! God, why?"

"I like sitting around inside."

Nikki laughed. "You're such a grump, Mac. What's wrong?"

They turned north on Fourth Avenue, which led straight to the park.

"Nothing."

"Something's up! You're acting weird."

Weird, huh? he thought. *My friend's been missing for twenty-four hours. I think something terrible has happened to her. Something involving the supernatural. So I have every right to be acting weird, you fucking psycho. Now leave me alone!*

He didn't say anything, however. Nikki didn't either, and they walked a full block without speaking.

"I love that place," she said, breaking the silence and pointing across the street to a seasonal Halloween store that sold masks, magic kits, toys, props, and just about every sort of costume imaginable. "I went in the other day to look for something to wear on Halloween. I think I might be a nun—a sexy one. What do you think?"

"Sounds good," he said.

"What are you going to be?"

"Haven't thought about it."

"What about a priest? I think you'd make a good priest. You'd just need a robe and collar. Easy. Then we could go somewhere together, priest and nun. What do you think?"

"I'm not interested in doing anything for Halloween."

"Jeez, Mac! Seriously, what's *wrong*? I'm trying to be nice here."

He stopped. "Look, I think I'd just like to be by myself right now, okay?"

Her eyes widened in surprise and maybe hurt, making him feel like shit.

"Sorry, Nikki. I have a lot on my mind. Maybe we can talk later?"

"Sure, Mac, later." She turned back the way they'd come. "Sorry for ruining your morning."

CHAPTER 54

The answer is in the amygdala

Malcolm entered Union Square from the south, passing an impressive equestrian statue of George Washington. The park was a green oasis in the middle of the steel-and-concrete city, filled with university students, tourists, and locals walking their dogs or pushing their bikes or playing chess. The grassy sections were roped off for reseeding, so most of the visitors had congregated in the paved area, including a street performer drawing a crowd of onlookers.

Malcolm spotted Quinn—wig, cape, and all—seated stiffly on a bench facing a fenced children's playground. He sat down next to her.

"I do enjoy zis park," she said without looking at him. "Zey hold farmer's markets here on ze weekends. I try to come once a month."

"I've never been to one," he said.

"The park's especially beautiful around Christmastime. It's filled with lights and festive music and vendors selling holiday food. I like to buy a hot chocolate and shortbread cookies and watch the carolers."

"What did you want to talk about, Quinn?"

She sighed, a tired, withered exhalation of air antithetical to her usual conviviality.

"I'm not sure where to begin, Mr. Clock, so I will start by telling you that I know the Hotel Chelsea is haunted. I have known this for a long time." She finally looked at him. "Only it's not haunted by the dead. It's haunted by the *living*."

◆ ◆ ◆

"What the hell are you talking about, Quinn?"

"I apologize for not being forthright with you previously. It was wrong of me. That is why I am here now—to correct that wrong. So please allow me to work my way through what I have to say. It is not easy to put into words what, on the surface, seems extraordinary."

"I'm listening," he said, his brow knitted in curiosity.

"Before visiting the Hotel Chelsea for the first time, had you ever felt an energy or a presence in a room with you, even though you knew you were by yourself? A feeling of not being alone, or of being watched?"

"I can't recall any particular incident off the top of my head. But I suppose I have had such a feeling. Hasn't everyone?"

"I believe most people have, yes. Psychologists refer to the phenomenon as a 'sensed presence.' Typically, it is a cognitive and neurological mechanism that becomes stimulated in a threatening or ambiguous environment. Say you are walking down a dark alley at night and you hear a noise. This prompts a threat-activated vigilance system inside you that creates the feeling of a malevolent presence, and you respond with a heightened sense of arousal and highly focused attention. It is a kind of survival instinct, you see, that has evolved to protect us from harm at the hands of a predator or enemy. Because if the noise turns out to be nothing but a gust of wind or a stray cat, you have lost nothing by overreacting. But if an actual threat exists, you will be much more prepared to either fight or run."

"Err on the side of caution."

"That's right. So why does a sensed presence feel like a sixth sense, or even a supernatural event? According to science, the human sense of self has two components, one on each side of the brain. The left hemisphere sense of self is the dominant one. It originates in childhood when we learn to think in words, when language becomes our main method of relating to others and the world. The right hemisphere sense of self develops over a longer period and is ultimately visual and intuitive rather than verbal and analytical."

"Left-side/right-side brain people. Lefties are better at math and logic. Righties tend to be more artistic and creative."

"Correct, Mr. Clock. However, even though the two sides of the brain are concerned with opposite cognitive functions, they are linked by bundles of nerve fibers and work together to complement one another. It doesn't matter if you are performing a logical or creative function, you receive input from both sides. The left brain deals with language, but the right brain helps you to understand context and tone. The left brain deals with mathematical equations, but the right brain helps you with comparisons and estimates. And although the two hemispheres almost always work together in unison to create a single sense of self, on occasion they may fall out of sync. When this happens, the subordinate self in the right hemisphere intrudes into the awareness of the dominant self, the linguistic self, in the left hemisphere. We perceive this intrusion as a separate, external presence."

"Such as a feeling of not being alone," Malcolm said, intrigued, "or of being watched."

Quinn nodded. "The sensed presence can manifest itself in many ways when the communication between the two senses of self is disturbed. Take, for instance, someone engrossed in a job...perhaps a magazine reporter writing an article who feels as though he is no longer writing the article himself. His words seem to be originating magically from somewhere outside of himself. In reality, the right-hemisphere self has taken over much of the job of writing the article and, due to some disturbance, has intruded into the left-hemisphere self. The reporter perceives it as an external presence. A muse, or a ghost, or perhaps a higher being? You would know better than I, wouldn't you, Mr. Clock?"

Malcolm thought about his recent writing sessions. The Hotel Chelsea article, the horror novel. The ease with which the words came. The sense they were not even his own. Sometimes not even remembering what he had written after writing it. Could Quinn's left-brain/right-brain analysis be the explanation to all of this?

"My home isn't exactly a threatening or ambiguous environment, Quinn," he said. "So if what you're saying is true, what could be causing the disturbances between the two hemispheres in my brain?"

"Something other than a perceived or real threat, clearly."

"Something at the Hotel Chelsea, I'm guessing?"

"I'm afraid so."

"Knocking my right-brain hemisphere out of balance with my left and contorting my sense of self?"

"While also gifting you with a creative boost."

"Do you, by chance, know what this 'something' may be?" he asked with a trace of asperity, disliking the cloak and dagger.

"I believe I do, Mr. Clock. But one step at a time. I don't want to get ahead of myself."

"I'm still listening."

"As I mentioned," she continued, "a sensed presence can manifest itself in many ways. I have provided you with two examples. They have both been subtle experiences that can be easily brushed aside as inconsequential when the left-hemisphere self regains dominance. But the manifestations can stretch over a vast spectrum of intensity. Psychologists refer to them collectively as 'visitor experiences.' In fact, they can become so intense it becomes difficult to distinguish them from reality itself."

Malcolm felt a strange, tingly feeling inside him. "Such as a conversation with a long-dead punk rocker?" he said.

"I'm not a scientist or neurologist, so forgive me if I outline what I am about to tell you in broad, layman terms. But know that it is based on years of...I don't know if you would call it research...but at least interest in the subject of visitor experiences."

"This 'something' at the Hotel Chelsea isn't a recent phenomenon, is it, Quinn?"

"No, it isn't, though its presence has always been much more muted than it has been in these last two weeks."

"Why? What's changed?"

"One step at a time, Mr. Clock," she told him again.

A mother emerged from the playground area with her young, crying daughter, who clearly hadn't wanted to leave. The mother threatened her with no lunch if she kept it up. The girl became ever more hysterical, plopping down on the spot and forcing the mother to scoop her up, squirming and screaming.

"First," Quinn said, "you need to understand that visitor experiences always begin in the amygdala on the right side of the brain."

"Amygdala?" he said.

"Humans have two of them, one on the left side of the brain and one on the right side. They are located deep within the temporal lobes and are the most sensitive and active structures of the brain, processing memory, decision-making, and most importantly, emotional responses. The amygdala on the left deals with self-affirming emotions such as happiness. The amygdala on the right deals with the opposite, such as anxiety and fear. So when you experience a threat, or a perceived threat, and your emotional response is fear, the amygdala on the right side of your brain is stimulated. If the event that caused the fear is mild, such as a noise in a dark alley, the neural activity in the amygdala will likely be mild as well, and the sensed presence will be equally so. A vague feeling of not being alone, or of being watched. If, on the other hand, the event that caused the fear is intense, the neural activity can become so excited it spills over into other structures of the brain. If it spills into the occipital lobe and the visual cortex, the visitor experience can become a vision of an entity of some kind or another—say a face in the mirror, or a man staring at a wall. A kind of hallucination if you will. If it spills into the olfactory cortex, the experience can involve specific smells. If it spills into the language centers of the temporal lobes, the experience can involve voices and sounds. If it spills into all of the above and other structures, the visitor experience can play out as an episodic vision—a fully extrapolated inner environment in which you believe you are interacting with a ghost, or an angel, or the spirit of a beloved dead friend or loved one, or sometimes even God or the Devil."

Malcolm thought all this through and said, "But how could I conjure up a hallucination of a man I've never met...?" The question died on his lips when he realized he already knew the answer. "There was a photograph of Roger James and a woman, most likely his wife, next to his bed. I saw it when I was in his apartment..."

Quinn said, "In it I presume he was wearing his trench coat and porkpie hat?"

Malcolm nodded slowly in agreement before shaking his head in puzzlement.

"Two things, Quinn," he said. "First, the blood in Roger James' apartment had been rather frightening. I understand how that could have caused my amygdala to go a little haywire. But aside from that, I haven't experienced anything else even remotely fearful at the Hotel Chelsea that would cause me to have the full-on sleepwalking hallucinations. And second, even if I *had*, why the hell would I be conjuring Sid Vicious of all people?"

"Fear is not stimulating your amygdala, Mr. Clock. As I told you, something else at the hotel is, which I will get to shortly. As to why you've conjured a vision of Sid Vicious...well, you were writing a story about the hotel. Sid Vicious is its most infamous figure. Perhaps he was on your mind more than you realized...or perhaps he represents something to you?"

"I don't see what he would represent. I'm not a punk. I'm not in a band. I—" Malcolm closed his mouth.

"Yes, Mr. Clock?" Quinn said, arching an eyebrow.

"I used to—well…" Before he could shy away from continuing, he said, "I used to have a drug habit." Since finding sobriety, he'd never talked to anyone outside of his support group about his addiction. "I was a heroin user," he added tersely and reluctantly. "It destroyed my life, and after one incident…" He dragged a hand over his jaw. "After my girlfriend overdosed, I was in a dark place. In the following days, I found myself thinking about overdosing almost nonstop."

Quinn's face had turned grave. "I'm terribly sorry to hear about your girlfriend, Mr. Clock, and your addiction. I never would have guessed, as you seem very…put-together. But we all have our own struggles, don't we? And the fact you have bounced back as well as you have from yours speaks, I think, to your character. Nevertheless, given the article you were writing about the hotel, combined with what you've told me about your past, I don't find it very surprising at all that you had an intense visitor experience involving Sid Vicious."

"What about the others though?" he asked, feeling ashamed by his confession but also heartened. Quinn had not reacted to his dark secret with disdain or repugnance or criticism as he'd always feared a non-addict would. "Why would Jolene conjure Edie Sedgwick?"

"That answer is quite simple really. Did Jolene tell you about the fire she caused when she was younger?"

"She *caused*? Shit, no. I've seen the burns on her arms. But she didn't want to talk about what happened."

"I'm not surprised. It was several years before she opened up to me." Quinn paused, as if considering how much to tell him. "Jolene set fire to her family house in Arkansas. It was an accident, a tragic accident. She had been out with friends one night. She came home late and put something on the stove. She fell asleep while waiting for it to cook and woke to find the entire first floor engulfed in flames. She escaped through the front door. Her sister survived by jumping from her second-story bedroom window. Her parents, unfortunately, suffocated in the smoke before the firefighters arrived. This was the same year Jolene and her sister moved to New York City, in fact. They wanted, needed, a new start. Poor girl. Poor, poor girl, to have to live with that sort of guilt." Quinn shook her head sadly. "In any event—Edie Sedgwick. She was a young, beautiful woman—one who nearly burned down the Hotel Chelsea in 1966. If Jolene were to conjure a former resident, I couldn't imagine anyone more relatable to her."

Malcolm's heart went out to Jolene. He knew all too well the emotional devastation of being responsible for someone else's death; he couldn't imagine the sorrow when the deaths involved your own parents. He said, "This is what I'm getting at, Quinn. Why is everyone conjuring a former resident? You think there would be more important people—deceased friends, loved ones—on their minds."

Quinn frowned. "What makes you believe everyone's conjured a former resident?"

"The only people aside from me that I know who have experienced a so-called visitor experience while sleepwalking are Jolene and Jeffrey—and they've both seen famous former residents."

"Whoever do you think Jeffrey has seen?"

"Dylan Thomas."

"Jeffrey told you that?"

"No, Harvey did."

Quinn chuffed. "Why am I not surprised? I take it Jeffrey wasn't present when Harvey told you that?"

"No..."

"A dear friend of Jeffrey's used to live in Dylan Thomas' room on the second floor," she explained. "He had a fatal stroke last year. Jeffrey was the one who found him lying on the middle of his floor, about four days after the man had died. It really shook Jeffrey up. And *that's* the man he conjured in Room 205 recently. His deceased friend. At least, that's who he told me he saw."

Now it was Malcolm's turn to frown. "Why would Harvey

say it was Dylan Thomas?"

"Because Harvey is Harvey! He tells stories. And the ghost of Dylan Thomas is much more sensational than the ghost of some old man you have never met. But I will tell you this. I've spoken with others in the hotel this last week, and of the few who admitted to having visitor experiences of varying intensities, both while sleepwalking or not, none mentioned a famous former resident. They told me only of deceased relatives or friends. And in one case, a deceased pet."

Another mother emerged from the playground, this one with three young boys in tow. Each boy had a yellow Tonka truck in hand and was alternatively flying them through the air and begging their mother to go to the ice cream store.

Malcolm rubbed his forehead, feeling a headache coming on.

"Why sleepwalking, Quinn?" he asked, befuddled. "Why is that when the most intense visitor experiences occur?"

"When we are asleep, and not dreaming, our brain activity all but ceases. If you hooked yourself up to an EEG in non-REM sleep, your brainwaves would appear small and uniform. Our sense of self, in both hemispheres, is not 'present' then. It is in this state, I believe, when our brains are largely free of electrical activity, that our amygdalae can be most easily stimulated and manipulated."

"By the 'something' at the Hotel Chelsea?"

"Exactly, Mr. Clock."

"Well, Quinn," he said with an forced smile, "don't you think it's about time to tell me what that something is?"

CHAPTER 55

Quinn comes clean

"To answer that question, I need to first tell you about my late husband." Quinn folded her gloved hands together on her lap, her fingers fidgeting. "His name was Bill Sherman. Yes, unlike me, he had two names. Bill died in 1993, or I believe he did. He was fifty-four years old at the time."

Malcolm frowned. "You *believe* he died? You don't know for certain?"

She nodded, her fingers still fidgeting. "We met at the Hotel Chelsea in the early 70s. I was a principal dancer in the New York City Ballet then. Bill was amongst a large group of Hotel Chelsea residents who came to my debut in a revival of *The Firebird*. We used to be like a big family at the hotel, a big, supportive family. If someone had their art showing in a gallery, or were performing on stage, you could count on forty or fifty of us from the hotel coming along to show support. That night the ballet was a success, the choreography was flawless, and we all ended up back at El Quijote. Bill had only been at the Hotel Chelsea for about a week then. He was a broad-shouldered African American man with the kindest smile, and I had absolutely no idea who he was when he offered to buy me a drink. Even so, I ended up spending all evening in his company. He was such an intelligent and fascinating gentleman."

"What did he do?"

"Bill was a Voodoo priest."

Malcolm blinked. "Oh..."

"I know what you're thinking, Mr. Clock. And, no, Voodoo isn't a cult. It doesn't involve black magic or devil worship. Practitioners are not witch doctors, sorcerers, or occultists. It has little to do with Voodoo dolls and zombies."

"It's been rather misrepresented then."

"Indeed it has. Voodoo was first practiced in America and the Caribbean by slaves of African descent who were not accepted as fully human. Consequently, their religion was dismissed as superstition, their god and spirits as evil. Throughout the 20th century, American pop culture propagated this misinformation. Books and movies portrayed Voodoo as a kind of sensationalized horror, as something that can hurt us. Because of this warped mythology, many Voodooists do not openly practice their religion for fear of being mocked or shunned, which, unfortunately, reinforces the suspicion that they practice in secret to conceal forbidden rituals. Secrecy breeds mystery, ignorance, and exaggeration. Fear begets fear."

"So your husband…?" Malcolm wasn't sure exactly what he wanted to ask. "What does a Voodoo priest do?"

"When I met Bill that night at El Quijote, he was still an attorney. He was born on the bayou in New Orleans into a poor family. His mother was a housekeeper, his father a chef in a small Cajun restaurant. But they prioritized his education so he could make something of himself, which he did, accepting a job offer in a New York City boutique law firm. After ten years of practicing law…well, Bill had made a lot of money by then, and he didn't see what more there was to gain from that career other than making more money. He'd always been a spiritual man with strong roots in the Voodoo community in which he'd grown up, and he decided to return to those roots. He traveled to Haiti to undergo a series of Voodoo initiation rituals, after which he was ordained a *houngan*, or priest. When he returned to New York, he became a spiritual leader for the largely invisible Voodoo sects in the city. At first he split his time in the slums of Harlem and the ghettos of Brooklyn and Queens, and all over the Upper West Side, providing teachings about what most black Americans simply called The Religion. He would also perform ceremonies at specific times of the year for his growing 'family,' or in special circumstances, such as an illness. These became more and more frequent. Before long he was conducting them on the rooftop of the Hotel Chelsea, almost weekly. He built a small *hounfour* —temple—to house them up there. It was quite impressive, I must say."

"What happened at the ceremonies?"

"I have told you what Voodoo is not, Mr. Clock. Now I must tell you what Voodoo *is*. It is a monotheistic religion. There is one Supreme God, which is the creator of the universe. The Supreme God created numerous sub-gods, called *loa*, to oversee mankind. Every person at birth is allocated a specific *loa*, who apportions health, happiness, and favor, helping the individual to live a full and productive life. They are guardian spirits, of sorts, which is essentially what 'Voodoo' translates into English as. Nevertheless, the identity of one's spirit can only be revealed by a priest during an initiation ceremony."

"Your husband helped people find their guardian spirits?"

"Connect with their guardian spirits, yes, when they needed assistance or guidance. Bill would put a devotee into a trance-like state and summon a *loa* into their body."

"Spirit possession?"

"Spirit possession in Voodoo has none of the negative connotations that it does in Christianity. It is accepted and in fact coveted. However, it's quite a scene, I can tell you that much. Drums pounding out arcane, primitive rhythms. Dancers twirling and juking in stooped positions. Acolytes chanting. Bill hopping from one leg to the other, shaking a rattle in one hand and a machete in the other as he called down the lesser gods. Then suddenly in the middle of it all, the devotee in the trance falls to the floor and shakes as though they're having a seizure. This signals that they've been possessed, that they've become their guardian spirit, or it has become them, temporarily ousting their soul. It's terrifying to witness. Absolutely terrifying. I've seen devotees under this spell contort their bodies in completely unnatural ways, speak in tongues, sometimes inflict self-harm. While all this is going on, the other participants offer fetishes or food such as bananas or coconuts, sometimes dried animal carcasses, as signs of respect to the *loa*. Almost always there are live animal sacrifices, sometimes chickens, sometimes rats or mice caught around the hotel. They chop off the animals' heads and douse the offerings with blood. They pour honey and palm oil over them. Bill always had a lit cigar and a bottle of rum, so he could blow smoke and spray rum from his mouth. Yes, it's quite a scene... After a dozen or so ceremonies, I stopped attending them. It simply became too much."

"Do you think the devotees were actually possessed by spirits, Quinn?"

"During one of the first few ceremonies on the Hotel Chelsea's roof, I offered myself as a medium." She chuckled at the memory. "I didn't think anything would happen to me. I wasn't a Voodooist. I didn't believe in their spirits or their religion. While the drums and dancing and chanting were filling the temple, and Bill was reading from his ancient grimoire, I remember thinking only about what I was going to say to him when the ritual didn't work—and that was the last thing I remembered. When I 'came out of it,' I could vaguely recall...not being in control of myself. And I'm rarely ever not in control."

"So you *do* believe in these possessions?"

"No, I don't, Mr. Clock," she replied. "I believe that while in a trance state, the medium *thinks* he or she is being possessed. In other words, I don't think anyone was faking the theatrics. I suppose the possessions are most akin to hypnosis. The drums and the chanting work like a hypnotist's repetitive and droning voice to lull one into a suggestive state. Bill, however, believed the possessions were authentic. I have no doubt about that. When word spread around the hotel about the ceremonies, a lot of the residents, including many of the more famous ones, asked to participate. Bill didn't seem to mind that, like me, they weren't Voodooists, and he began performing rituals in rooms throughout the hotel. The Chelsea being what it was in the 1970s, drugs and alcohol were often involved, psychotropic drugs. Well...it all got out of hand. It really did. I asked Bill to stop. He wouldn't. He had become convinced that the Hotel Chelsea was an especially religious place, and that he had been...specifically chosen...to be a high priest above all others whose work was too important to be impeded." Quinn's voice turned melancholic. "Throughout the 80s, the excessive drug and alcohol abuse began to take a toll on Bill's health. And the people he was associating with —well, some of them were downright frightening. I loved Bill with all my heart, and I feared he'd become blinded to his apostasy, so as a last resort I went to Stanley Bard. I told him what was going on. The drugs, the animal sacrifices, everything. In typical fashion, Stanley didn't want to hear any of it. He turned a blind eye to it like he did to all the other deviant behavior at the hotel. Until, that is, a ceremony Bill held on the first floor incited a riot. In the room next door to the one in which the ceremony was being performed, some bikers were throwing a party. They became irate at the razzmatazz Bill's group was making, and vice versa. One thing led to another and one of the bikers was stabbed in the neck. Well, all hell broke loose after that. It took fourteen police officers hours to restore the peace. The ruckus made the newspapers the next day. Stanley, ever protective of the hotel's image, loathed the bad publicity and banned Bill from performing any further ceremonies."

"Did your husband stop?"

"To my knowledge, he stopped performing ceremonies at the Hotel Chelsea. But did he stop them completely?" She shook her head. "He would disappear for hours on end, never telling me where he went, only that he was performing a ceremony for someone in need." She paused for a long moment. "Then one day he went to one of these rituals and never came home."

◆ ◆ ◆

"You never heard from him again?"

"Bill left no note, nothing. I remember his last words to me. 'I won't be too long. How about we go out for dinner tonight?'" Quinn wiped a tear from her cheek. "I held a candlelight vigil for him every night for a week, praying he would return the next morning with some perfectly fine explanation for where he'd been. He never returned, and I became heartbroken. He's been missing for just over twenty years now."

Malcolm was wondering if perhaps Quinn's husband had simply run off with another woman, when she seemed to read his mind.

"He wasn't having an affair," she stated testily. "Bill was not like that. We might not have always seen eye to eye, especially with regard to the initiation ceremonies and his deteriorating health, but he loved me as much as I loved him. We were happy. He would not leave me for another woman. And even if you don't believe that, believe that he would not leave the position of influence and respect he'd built in the Voodoo community for another woman."

"What do you think happened to him?"

"To this day, Mr. Clock, I have no idea."

Malcolm shifted his weight on the park bench, failing to understand where Quinn was going with all this. "You have my condolences, Quinn," he told her. "But I'm not sure if I'm following. What does your husband, or his disappearance and presumed death, have to do with what's been happening at the Hotel Chelsea recently?"

Quinn nodded knowingly, as if she'd been waiting for him to ask such a question. "A few weeks after Bill went missing, I began to sense his presence at the hotel. Sometimes I woke in the middle of the night, convinced he was laying by my side in bed. Sometimes I thought I glimpsed him from the cororner of my eye, or beyond one of my windows, out on the roof. Once in the elevator I was nearly overwhelmed by a feeling that Bill stood right behind me, though I never looked, I couldn't, knowing if I did, I would find myself alone."

Malcolm raised his eyebrows. "You were having visitor experiences?"

"I was, Mr. Clock. However, I didn't know that then. I had no idea what visitor experiences were then. At first I thought what I was experiencing was a natural byproduct of my bereavement. Yet even as my grief subsided, Bill's presence did not. Eventually I feared I might be going crazy, which prompted me to see a psychologist. She introduced me to the psychology of sensed presences and other visitor experiences. This knowledge was a mixed blessing. Naturally, I was relieved to learn I wasn't going crazy. On the other hand, I became severely depressed. Because although my initial reaction to Bill's presence, or what I'd believed to be his presence, had been fear, that lessened with time until I found myself looking forward to the encounters. Bill was no longer with me, but his spirit was. That had been comforting."

"Did the visitor experiences continue?"

"They lasted for roughly three months. Which, frankly, is unheard of. Typically a person may have a sensed presence or other visitor experience on a rare occasion. For someone to have the experiences continuously for an extended period... yes, it is unheard of. I often wondered why I was different. In the end I decided it wasn't me but the Hotel Chelsea—specifically, the religious energy Bill had been convinced permeated the hotel. He believed it was his Supreme God. For whatever reason, it had chosen to inhabit the hotel, which explained why he'd had so much success invoking the lesser gods during his initiation ceremonies."

"Whoa, hold on, Quinn," Malcolm said, alarmed at the direction the conversation was heading. "Let me get this straight. You believe what's been happening at the Hotel Chelsea involves *Voodoo*?"

"No, I don't believe that at all, Mr. Clock. This is what *Bill* believed. The reason I have told you about Bill, and his work as a Voodoo priest, is so you would understand why I came to conclude there was a 'something' at the hotel. Not a god, not a ghost—never being religious, I could not bring myself to accept either hypothesis—but an energy...perhaps a psychic energy? I will not bore you with the many different paths my investigation into this subject matter took me—I believe I have already stretched this talk far too long—except to say I ultimately learned of a scientific experiment that had employed electromagnetic fields to stimulate the right side of a subject's brain...producing, under laboratory conditions, the ghostly symptoms evident in visitor experiences: sensed presences, hallucinations, even intense episodic visions."

Malcolm was floored, and it took him a moment to gather his thoughts. "You're saying the 'something' at the hotel is electromagnetic energy?"

Quinn nodded. "An electromagnetic field, yes. It's what was responsible for stimulating the amygdala in my right-hemisphere brain, causing the visitor experiences after Bill's disappearance."

"But why just you, Quinn? Why, until recently, at least, have only you experienced this electromagnetic—"

"Just me!" she interjected sharply. "Come, Mr. Clock! The Hotel Chelsea has the reputation as being one of the most haunted buildings in America for a reason. Those who've lived there have been reporting visitor experiences for more than a hundred years now! Ask most long-term residents and they'll have their own ghost story to tell you. And all the poor souls who have committed suicide there over the years? Well, conjuring what they believed to be the ghost of a recently deceased friend or lover night after night might just be enough to drive them to leap from the tenth-floor landing, wouldn't you agree? And do not forget about all the great works of literature and art created at the hotel. Many of the writers and artists responsible for them had an abundance of natural talent, clearly, but I don't find it a stretch to extrapolate that the electromagnetic energy—which seems to predominantly stimulate the right-hemisphere brain, the side where one's creativity is housed, and thus disproportionately affecting those with a creative flair—has given them a little creative boost."

"Haunted not by the dead but by the living..." Malcolm said, slumping back against the bench as he tried to get his head around the enormity of everything he'd been told. "Shit, Quinn...this is a lot to take in."

"I understand that, Mr. Clock," she said, patting the top of his thigh in an affectionate, motherly way. "But you have taken it all very well, I must say. So let me end with this. After learning of the scientific experiment using electromagnetic fields to stimulate the right-side brain into producing visitor experiences, I purchased a Gauss meter, an instrument that measures the strength and direction of magnetic fields. Mine was rather basic, though much more sensitive ones are used to measure the magnetic signatures of things like large mineral deposits, shipwrecks, submarines, and buried archaeological sites."

"Did yours detect an electromagnetic field at the Hotel Chelsea?"

"Of course. It detected many. Any kitchen appliance or electrical device creates an electromagnetic field disturbance. But did it detect anything excessively *abnormal*? Not at first, no. Not until I made my way down to the basement of the hotel."

❖ ❖ ❖

"The basement?"

"Electromagnetism obeys what is called an inverse square law. This means the strength of an electromagnetic field diminishes rapidly at increasing distances. I discovered no real electromagnetic anomalies on the roof and upper floors of the hotel. But when I reached the lower floors, I began to detect an extremely high-frequency and powerful electromagnetic field disturbance, which peaked in the basement."

"What was causing it?"

"That I never learned, Mr. Clock. I searched every inch of the basement to no avail. I found nothing that might have been causing the strong readings I was receiving."

Malcolm was fascinated. Quinn's narrative was extraordinary, yet it explained everything he'd been experiencing. Moreover, an electromagnetic field messing with his brain activity was admittedly more digestible than an ephemeral ghost crossing over from the afterlife to give him a good scare in the middle of the night.

After thirty seconds or so of silence, he said, "I don't get it, Quinn. I mean, I get what you're saying. I believe what you're saying. I think. But if you knew of this electromagnetic field, why didn't you tell Jolene and me about it the other day when we told you about our sleepwalking episodes?"

Quinn's lips tightened into a thin line before she answered. "Because I was acting selfishly, Mr. Clock," she said. "I might not have known what was causing the electromagnetic field, but I knew it was responsible for my visitor experiences—both in the past and recently. Yes, I too have had episodic visions while sleepwalking. Four in the last two weeks."

"Involving your husband?"

She nodded. "They were so much more real than any of the previous visitor experiences. They filled me with sadness, but there was no fear, only love, so much love. The first occurred the day immediately following the stoppage in construction. It was my belief that the workers had inadvertently discovered or uncovered the source of the electromagnetic field in the basement. But when I dusted off my Gauss meter, and went to investigate, I found no physical indication this was the case. However, the readings I measured down there were through the roof, at least ten times the strength of those I'd detected years before. Whatever the reason for this, I believed some of the workers had likely been affected by the electromagnetic field as I had been. With each day that they didn't return to the hotel, I became more optimistic that they might never return. That whatever was causing the energy had scared off the developer. He'd finally leave us in peace! But then Jeffrey told me he had experienced a powerful vision while sleepwalking. Then others told me similar tales. Then you and Jolene... People, you see, were talking. Word was going to get out that the Hotel Chelsea was not only haunted but verifiably haunted. Anyone could come stay for a few days and likely have an intensely powerful visitor experience. This would attract ghosthunters and scientists alike. They would identify the electromagnetic field. The hotel would be torn down brick by brick to discover its source. And when this was found, it would be taken away somewhere to be studied. When that happened..."

"You would lose the visions of your husband."

"They may not be real, Mr. Clock, but they're all I have. I've never been as happy since I lost him as I've been these last two weeks. Can you understand that?"

"Why are you telling me all this, Quinn? Why now?"

"Last night you mentioned Jolene had been making rubbings of the hotel's old doors being stored in the basement. Well, I returned down there this morning in the hope of discovering what might have become of her."

Malcolm felt the first shine of hope all day—minced with gnawing fear. If Quinn had found Jolene cooped up in the basement engrossed in her rubbings, she would have come out and said so. He swallowed a hard lump in his throat. "She wasn't down there, was she?"

"No, she wasn't. But I did find her art supplies. They were on the floor of the room that contained the doors. It appeared... well, there was a stack of completed frottages...and one a work in progress."

Malcolm's thoughts spun as the implications of this revelation sank home. "She stopped in the middle of it...? Why would she do that...? Did she have a vision? Did something happen to her *during* the vision?"

"Prolongued exposure to electromagnetic fields can cause one to experience headaches, paranoia and, in some cases, violence and psychosis. If Jolene was down there for a substantial amount of time—"

Malcolm shot to his feet. "Fuck, Quinn! We've been sitting here for the last hour while Jolene could be in serious jeopardy!"

"What can we do, Mr. Clock? She's not in the basement. I searched every nook and—"

He left the park in a full sprint.

CHAPTER 56

The basement (2)

He arrived at the Hotel Chelsea, puffing for breath. He jabbed at the buzzer next to the door. Darnell, however, was not behind the desk.

"Shit," he said, pacing beneath the awning.

He waited restlessly for five minutes, but when no one entered or left the building, he hurried down the alley that ran between the hotel and the synagogue. At the back of the hotel he found a door kept open with a wedge of wood. Seeing a nearby wooden chair and an overflowing ashtray, he guessed this was where Darnell took his breaks.

Malcolm slipped inside and skipped down the building's stairs to the basement two at a time.

◆ ◆ ◆

Halfway to the bottom he slowed, as the basement was as dark as the crypt in Marble Cemetery. He took out his mobile phone and activated the flashlight. He located the light switches that controlled the overhead fluorescents and began methodically exploring each of the rooms he saw. The first few were overflowing with neglected cleaning supplies, sloppy paint cans, folded linen, all sorts of tools, and copious amounts of junk. Then he came to the room containing a hundred or more doors. Most were leaning up against the dirty and dilapidated brick walls, though a good number had been stacked atop one another in the middle of the room. Next to these were Jolene's art bag, chunks of wax and charcoal, and at least a dozen rubbings, including the unfinished one Quinn had mentioned.

Malcolm's chest tightened as questions of what might have caused Jolene to abandon it rushed through his mind. He searched the room to make sure Jolene was not hiding behind any of the leaning doors (why she might be doing that he didn't know and didn't care to speculate), but didn't find her—or any clue as to where she might have gone.

He searched the adjacent boiler room just as thoroughly before returning to the hallway and discovering the next circuit of fluorescents did not function.

Much as a priest might wield a crucifix in battle against an unseen demon, he held his phone before him to ward off the overwhelming darkness and continued deeper into the bowels of the basement.

◆ ◆ ◆

The cold light revealed a warren of rooms cluttered with junk, trash, and all sorts of miscellaneous supplies that would have been needed to keep the hotel operating while it had been open to guests. Malcolm felt increasingly uneasy the further he went. The darkness became more oppressive, and the feeling he was trespassing in sinister territory grew ever stronger, urging him to turn back.

He pressed on and came to a room that appeared lived-in. There was a bookcase, a bed, and some chairs and a desk, all arranged to make the most of the small space.

Was someone *living* down here? he wondered, his heart beating hollowly in his ears, his skin clammy and tight.

"Jolene...?" he said to the empty room.

The bed was neatly made with a threadbare cover and a lumpy pillow encased in white linen. He lowered himself to his knees and swept the light beneath it.

A pair of yellow eyes shone back.

A startled cry escaped his lips as he pushed back and fell onto his side. In the same instant the huge rat darted along the wall into the darkness.

"Christ," he said, getting to his feet, goosebumps breaking out all over his body.

He turned to leave the room—and sucked back air.

Someone stood in the doorway.

At least he thought someone had been standing in the doorway because nobody was there now.

Yet Malcolm remained in shock, unable to move, rooted in place.

The person had been garbed in a robe, a cowl masking his face, arms at his side, white hands clenched into fists.

I saw him. He was there. He was—

A sensed presence.

Malcolm's chest unlocked and he released his caught breath.

A sensed presence.

Like the face in the mirror.

Like the man facing the wall.

Like the ghost in the photo.

All in my mind.

"Hello?" he called, his voice sounding weak. "Hello?" he added with more bravado.

When he was greeted with silence, he returned to the hall-way, his footsteps on the cement floor the only sound in the still, cloying darkness.

As Malcolm made his way back to the stairs, he rechecked each room he passed, aiming the light from his phone behind rolls of carpet, stacks of boxes, foul-smelling garbage bins, and the other crap he came across. All he found were water stains, mold, rat droppings, and decades of dust.

Yet on several occasions, just beyond the reach of his light, was movement.

Phantom movement.

Because nothing was ever there when he illuminated the spot an instant later.

The menacing feeling of being watched, of not being alone, of being in danger, nagged at his heels until he'd returned to the refuge of the overhead fluorescent lights.

Quinn, he decided, was right about the basement being the source of the electromagnetic energy. He didn't need a Gauss meter to tell him. He could *feel* the overwhelming effect of it on his fear-sensitive right amygdala.

It was terror, immediate and raw, lying in wait.

"It's not real," he told himself, drawing a trembling hand over his damp forehead. "You're alone. You're fine."

He glanced behind him into the blackness from which he'd just emerged—and saw something move in the dark beyond the reach of the fluorescents.

"Jolene?"

No reply.

But did he hear something? A shoe scuffing cement?

He tilted his head.

"Jo...?"

No reply.

But something was there. He could see it—almost. An amorphous coalescing of shadows. And if he weren't breathing so damn loudly, he would likely be able to hear it as well.

"Jo...?"

No reply.

Briskly, Malcolm continued to the stairs.

In his rush to leave the dungeon-like basement, he almost

missed it.

A large section of the floor next to the staircase was a slightly different color than the surrounding cement. It was in the shape of a rectangle, long and wide enough to be—

"Holy shit," Malcolm said. *It's a staircase.*

Or *was* a staircase. It had been filled over long ago—so long ago, in fact, it was really only a shade lighter than the rest of the floor, which was why he hadn't noticed it when he'd first entered the basement.

But it was there; he wasn't imagining it.

Which meant a subbasement existed beneath the main one.

◆ ◆ ◆

Malcolm went to the nearby elevator, which had been hidden in the darkness. To his surprise, he found the twin panels propped open laterally with a wood chair.

He glanced down the shaft.

Protruding from it was the top of a ladder.

CHAPTER 57

Into the belly of the beast

Malcolm stepped over the chair and carefully mounted the ladder, the top of which was a good three feet below the floor level. The first few steps were the most hazardous as he had nothing to hold onto, but after a few more steps down he could grip the ladder's rails.

The ladder was aluminum and placed at an angle that was neither too steep nor shallow, making the descent relatively simple. Even so, when he was about halfway to the bottom his right foot slipped off a rung, causing his body to pendulum in that direction. He grunted in alarm. His mobile phone, which had been clamped between his lips, fell away. It struck the ground six or seven feet below him and the flashlight went dark.

"Shit!"

He continued down the ladder. At the bottom, he stepped off the last rung and crouched, feeling blindly on the hard-packed dirt for his phone. Above him, light from the main basement's overhead fluorescents filtered through the opening-closing elevator panels, but little reached the subbasement.

His hand brushed the phone. He snatched it up and felt spiderwebs in the glass display and a chunk of plastic missing from one corner. He depressed the power button, holding it for several long seconds, praying the display would come on.

It didn't.

◆ ◆ ◆

Malcolm moved from the elevator shaft into the subbasement, feeling his way forward with his feet, his arms held before him so he didn't run face-first into anything. The air was dry, musty, spoiled, leading him to believe there was little if any ventilation on this level.

"Jolene?" he called. "It's Malcolm."

No reply.

"Jolene?" he said again, wondering what he was doing. He should climb back up the ladder, leave the hotel, and buy a flashlight so he could see whatever the hell was down here.

Yet that would all take time, and a strong premonition told him time wasn't something he had in great supply. Jolene was here. He didn't know how he knew, but he did. She was here, and she needed his help.

"Jo!" he said urgently. "Where are you?"

The total blackness was not only distressing but disorientating, and soon Malcolm realized he was no longer sure which way the elevator shaft was. This kicked his fear response into an even higher gear, and with each sightless step he took, he became convinced someone shared the dark with him.

Someone other than Jolene.

The man in a cowl? The man who lives beneath the Hotel Chelsea? The man who had attacked Jolene and had brought her to the depths of the hotel for whatever vile reason?

The man who's sneaking up behind you right now...?

Malcolm spun around, swinging his hand in a knifehand chop, expecting it to strike flesh and bone.

His hand sliced unimpeded through the air.

He waited for an attack, a fist to his face, a shoulder to his gut.

Neither came.

"Stop it," he mumbled to himself between his hoarse breaths.

Malcolm resumed the direction he'd been moving in—or he thought he'd been moving in. He no longer had any clue which way was which.

Beads of cold sweat stung his eyes and traced an icy trail down his spine, causing his shirt to cling uncomfortably to his back.

Get out of here. Go get a flashlight. Get help.

His foot kicked something.

His pulse raced.

"Jo?" he said, crouching to feel before him, touching some sort of cloth, and beneath that, something solid, cylindrical, rigid. He could curl his hand around it.

Broken furniture? Part of a chair? A spindle? A table leg?

He continued touching, feeling. More cloth. Covering firm, oddly shaped objects.

Then something large and bulbous, a kind of cage with parallel—

"Jesus!" he said, shooting to his feet.

That's someone's ribcage—someone's skeleton!

In his haste to flee from the horror, he slammed into what felt like a heavy table. His probing hands knocked over what he believed were thick candles, several rolling off the plane and falling with soft thumps to the earthen ground. He also made out a glass bottle, a crusty bowl, an unidentifiable item covered in what might have been matted fur, and small, brittle sticks he realized belatedly were more bones, these belonging to a small animal.

"Fuck!" he cried, yanking his hands away and stumbling into the darkness, driven by repulsion and fright—

He tripped over something and landed hard on his elbows. His instinct was to scramble away from it—yet it had been heavier and softer than the skeleton.

He reached for it, touched it, squeezed it.

Flesh—warm, pliable.

A leg?

"Jolene?"

No reply.

He moved his hand up the leg, feeling clothing—shorts?—a round hip, a flat stomach, firm breasts beneath a bra and soft sweater. He could smell Jolene's soaps, her shampoo.

"Jo!"

He cupped her face in his hands. Her cheeks were warm. She was alive.

"Jo, can you hear me? Wake up! What's wrong?"

His hands brushed her forehead, her nose, her lips and chin, which were slick with drool. He wiped it away with his sleeve, placed two fingers on her neck.

Her pulse was strong, regular.

"Jo! Wake up!"

When she didn't respond, Malcolm decided he was going to have to carry her out of the subbasement. Before he attempted to lift her, however, he patted down her pockets and felt the ground around her, discovering her phone nearby. Yet his attempts to power it on failed; the battery was dead.

Sliding one arm beneath Jolene's back, the other beneath her legs, he stood.

"No..." Jolene breathed.

"What?" he whispered, encouraged by her voice.

"Stop..."

"We need to leave, Jo. You need help—"

"No... Edie..."

"Edie? Edie Sedgwick? *She's not here, Jo.* She's in your head. She's—"

Jolene screamed.

CHAPTER 58

Groovy, man

Jolene was at a fabulous party in one of the upper apartments in the Hotel Chelsea. It was spacious and strikingly colorful, like Harvey and Jeffrey's, with large windows overlooking 23rd Street. The ceiling was painted blue to resemble the sky, while unicorns, elves, dragons, and other fantasy creatures graced the walls. Beneath clouds of incense and pot, two dozen or so partygoers, most of whom were young and beautiful, packed the suite of rooms, some spilling into the hallway. Models with their spider lashes and boyish frames; hippies in bellbottoms and miniskirts; beatniks in black turtlenecks and black-and-white mime shirts; and a few folkies in torn jeans and checkered shirts. Free love was in the narcotic-soaked air, with people making out against the walls or in the overstuffed chairs, lips locking, bodies intertwining, hands exploring with serpentine caresses. On a small stage Bob Dylan, hidden beneath his snarled afro and behind dark sunglasses, was performing "Like a Rolling Stone." In another part of the room, Andy Warhol, wearing his usual striped shirt and dirty dungarees, held court with his entourage of lovely superstars. Indeed, everywhere Jolene looked was somebody famous: William Burroughs and Brion Gysin marketing their new invention (a machine to create a psychedelic experience for the user without the use of drugs) to a skeptical-looking Arthur Miller; Arthur C. Clark eliciting inspiration from Allen Ginsberg for the novelization of his latest film; Leonard Cohen, in a rakishly cocked beret, trying to woo a plastered Janis Joplin with his best poetry; the Irish poet Brendan Behan passed out drunk on the floor, a half-full mug of whiskey next to him.

It was a wild time, and Jolene, curled up on a sofa, couldn't be happier.

Edie Sedgwick—her hair cut in a blonde bob, her skin pearly white, her boudoir features pouty—sat next to her in a tee-shirt and black stockings. "Did you know this song is about me?" she said. "Yeah, nobody knows, but I'm seeing Bob. That's between us because, you know, he just married that girl."

"I won't say anything," Jolene promised.

"He likes me because I'm smart—and hates it when I appear dumb to fit in. He says I have Marilyn Monroe syndrome. He also says I look like a fool in Andy's films, and Andy's going to drop me when he tires of me."

"They're friends?" Jolene asked.

"No, Bob hates Andy," Edie said. "He thinks his art sucks too. I've tried to get Bob to come to the Factory. I think they should work together, Bob and Andy. They would make something really special." She shrugged. "Bob's right, by the way."

"About what?" Jolene asked.

"Andy dropping me," Edie said. "He thinks I'm getting too much attention. He doesn't like that. Also, he's furious I got rid of my silver hair. Says it no longer matches his 'look.' Probably because it no longer matches his wig."

"You don't need him," Jolene said. "You're beautiful. You're smart. You don't need to be someone else for him."

"You know who his new girl is? Nico. I don't know what he's thinking. She's so *gloomy*. But, whatever, I don't care."

Jolene smiled. She liked Edie. They had so much in common. They could sit around for hours and chat about silly stuff, like sisters, and that's just what they'd been doing for a long time now. Jolene enjoyed hearing about all the glamourous people Edie knew. She wasn't being pretentious. She wasn't name-dropping. She was simply recounting her life, and her life was filled with celebrities.

Jolene was about to ask Edie about the next movie she was going to star in when she suddenly felt invisible hands lifting her off the sofa. Startled, she reached for Edie Sedgwick's hand, but Edie was now up and dancing in the middle of the room, oblivious to her plight.

"No!" Jolene cried.

Someone replied to her, someone she could not see.

"Stop!"

The person was telling her she had to leave, she needed help.

"No!" she cried. "Edie!"

The person told her Edie Sedgwick didn't exist, and when Jolene looked around the room, she found Edie gone, all the revelers gone. It was empty save for her. Cold, empty, desolate.

She screamed.

CHAPTER 59

Out of the frying pan...

"Calm down!" Malcolm told Jolene. "It's okay! You're okay!"

She continued to scream, though it faltered in strength, the glassy fear waning to something broken and filled with despair.

"Shhh," he said gently, and kissed her on the forehead. "Shhh, it's okay."

Choked sobs became groans, and then she went quiet.

Malcolm turned in the blackness, seeing nothing. He wanted to get out of the hotel as quickly as possible. The energy down here had clearly done terrible harm to Jolene's mind, and he could already feel it working its malevolence on his own well-being. He felt hot, faint...not himself. His eyelids had become like weights, his thinking foggy and unmotivated.

Worse, he felt watched.

Eyes in the darkness watching him, waiting for him to lower his guard, to sink to the ground and close his eyes.

So the watchers could do what...?

Malcolm's head nodded forward. His eyes sprang open. He immediately stiffened.

"We need to go," he told Jolene, and started walking. He had no idea whether he was heading toward the elevator shaft or not. If he wasn't, he would follow the wall he came to in one direction. If the subbasement were one large room, he would eventually make his way back to the shaft. If, on the other hand, it was a maze of smaller rooms like those on the main basement level…well, he hoped he wouldn't have to deal with that.

After only a few wary steps he discovered his arms ached. Jolene wasn't a heavy woman, maybe 120 pounds. But 120 pounds was still 120 pounds. And the fact he couldn't see where he was going made her feel twice as heavy. He could very well be walking in the opposite direction he should be. Moreover, even if he reached the shaft before collapsing, how was he going to get her up the ladder? Flop her over his shoulder fireman-style? She'd likely start screaming, maybe kicking. He was going to have to try waking her up—

Malcolm's forward-stepping foot fell through air. His body followed, toppling forward. His instinct would have been to raise his arms to protect himself. Yet with Jolene cradled in them he instead rolled his shoulders, so he would land on his side or back, and not on top of her.

He struck the ground with jarring force. His chin drove into the crown of Jolene's skull. A jolt of pain seemed to flash-freeze his entire face. He tipped dangerously toward unconsciousness before the stars and disorientation subsided.

As he laid on his side, his head resting against something that was cold and hard, something that was not the ground, he realized his arms had gone slack. Jolene had slipped free from them. He wanted to check on her, to make sure she was okay. Yet he couldn't move. His mind was unplugged from his body, and it seemed like far too much effort to plug it back in.

He tried speaking, calling to her. His numb lips felt as large as sausages. Whatever words he managed were muffled gibberish. His eyes slid shut, and he sank into blissful rest.

◆ ◆ ◆

"Wake up, mate. You hear me? Snap out of it."
Malcolm opened his tired eyes.

He could see nothing but darkness.

"Ah! There you go. Knew you weren't dead."

Malcolm recognized the London accent immediately. "What do you want with me?" he said, tasting sludgy blood in his mouth.

"What do I want with you? What kind of question is that for your old friend, Sid? I'll tell you what I want, mate. I want you to stop being such a wanker and shoot up some dope with me. That's what I want."

Malcolm remembered falling into some kind of hole while carrying Jolene. He looked around—and of course couldn't see anything in the lightless subbasement. He worked his tongue a little. The tip was a needle-like bundle of nerves, and he wondered if he'd bitten it off. "Where's Jolene?" he asked.

"Right next to you."

"Is she okay?"

"Couldn't be better, mate. Just having a nap. Visions of sugar plums and all them nice stuff dancing in her head. Don't you worry about her, mate."

"I'm imagining you."

"Imagining *me*, are you?" Sid Vicious said. "I don't know if I like the sound of that. Because if you're imagining me, that means I'm not really here. How do you think that makes me feel?"

Malcolm raised an arm before him. The gesture felt slow, thick. He dropped his arm back onto his lap. "You're not there."

"Don't be daft, mate. Dee Dee, am I here?"

"Don't know where else you'd be," Dee Dee Ramone grumbled. He was somewhere to Malcolm's left. "Now, are we gonna sit around on our asses holding hands? Or are we gonna get high?"

"My rocks are already cooked up," Sid said. "Syringe is full. I think I'll just go ahead and take my fix first. You don't mind, do you, Dee Dee?"

"Get on with it so the rest of us can get go about getting

high too."

"Whose idea was it to wear these bloody robes? They make it a real pain in the arse to find a vein—"

"*Shhh!*" Dee Dee said. "Did you hear that?"

"Hear what?"

"Someone's coming."

Malcolm listened, and he did indeed hear someone. A voice. Smooth, authoritarian, familiar...far away at first, but getting closer, growing louder.

CHAPTER 60

Payback

S hane was aware of the fierce pain pulsing behind his eyes and the dryness in his mouth before he opened his eyes. He found he barely had enough saliva to swallow. A headache and a mouth like a fur boot were not unusual sensations for him to wake to, as hangovers had been a lifestyle recently.

But not within the last two days.

That's right. He'd been sober for two days now, so why did he feel like boiled shite…?

Jolene's new man.

Now Shane did open his eyes, finding himself lying flat out on the ground. Grimacing—his head still sleepy, his muscles weak—he pushed himself into a sitting position. The pain in his skull flared. It was no hangover headache either.

He touched a gash on the left side of his head, above his ear. His hair there was matted, gunky. He tweezed a lumpy patch of hair between his fingers until he felt some blood crumble free. He held his hand before him. The blood was plummy purple-red, dried and scabby.

He looked around the apartment. It wasn't his. It was the one across the hall. He'd stuck his head inside it not long after moving into the Hotel Chelsea when someone told him it was where Sid Vicious had stabbed Nancy Spungen.

That fucking Malcolm what's-his-name must have dragged me here.

He remembered going to the shared bathroom, finding it occupied, nobody answering. Opening the door. Malcolm on

313

the crapper, looking for all the world like a glassy-eyed, slack-faced addict who'd just shot up a John Belushi-sized speedball.

Shane had attempted to shake some sense into the man, but Malcolm grabbed his wrist and sprang to his feet—and the last thing Shane recalled was the arsehole gripping a fistful of his hair and driving his head into the sink.

Did he drag me all the way back here?

Wincing in discomfort, Shane got to his feet and crossed the hallway to his own apartment. He filled a bowl with warm water from the kitchen sink and cleaned the blood from his hair the best he could. He changed into some fresh clothes, then marched to Jolene's room and fisted her door.

"Jo? Open up. It's Shane." He pounded some more. "Jo? Don't be hidin' from me. Is yer man in there? Tis time we have more than words, him and I."

When neither Jolene nor Malcolm answered, Shane tried the handle.

The door swung open.

He stuck his head inside. "Jo?"

The room was empty. He glanced at his wristwatch: 10:10 a.m. Malcolm, he realized, had likely gone to work. But where was Jolene? She didn't work nine to five. She never went to the cemeteries until after dark. Out for breakfast? If so, she would return shortly.

He was about to leave when he spotted a stack of rubbings on the floor. On closer inspection, he realized they were of the doors in the basement of the hotel she'd told him about.

Shane headed back down the hallway toward the stairs.

CHAPTER 61

Darnell's haunted hotel tour

Malcolm recognized one of the two voices as belonging to the front desk clerk, Darnell, though he'd never heard the other, a female's, before.

The woman asked, "Why are you aiming that flashlight at your shoes?"

Darnell said, "Don't want to ruin the surprise."

"I can't see anything in this dark."

"That's the point, baby. I don't want you to see nothing till I've set the stage. Don't worry. There's a generator right here. When I power it on, you'll be able to see what I got to show you clear as day."

"I already know what you got to show me, Darnell."

"How the hell would you know that?"

"You think women don't talk? That's *all* we do, honey. I know you took Naomi down here Monday, and Kayla on Wednesday, and Aisha on Thursday. Mmm-huh. Don't say you didn't, Darnell."

"I didn't think you still spoke to those girls?"

"I know you didn't. Otherwise, you wouldn't be trying to get into all our pants in the same week."

"You think that's why I brought you down here? To get into your pants?"

"I know you, Darnell. Getting into a woman's pants is a full-time occupation of yours. And I'll tell you this. I'm not happy about being fourth in line. I know we ain't dating or nothing. But we've had some fun. I thought I was better than *fourth* on your list."

"You ain't fourth, baby. You're first. I'm saving the best for last. That makes you first, you know what I'm saying?"

"Mmm-huh. I know what you're saying, all right. Now are you going to turn on the damn lights or what? I heard this thing gives you radiation if you stand around it for too long."

"Who the hell told you that?"

"Kayla. She said it messed with her head, and she was feeling sick all day after seeing it."

"How're you feeling right now?"

"Fine."

"Then you're going to be fine. Me, I've never felt a thing. It affects people differently. Which is why it ain't giving off no radiation. Radiation affects all motherfuckers the same. So don't you worry about motherfucking radiation."

"How do you know it affects people differently? Maybe you just spent more time down here getting into Kayla's pants than Naomi's or Aisha's? Maybe that's why she got sick. She spent more time down here."

"You believe what you want, baby. But I know what I'm talking about. The construction workers who dug it up, there were about ten of them, seven were fine."

"What about the other three?"

"Nothing too bad. They started seeing things and stuff."

"'Seeing things and stuff' don't sound like anything good to me. And what were ten construction workers doing down here anyway?"

"Nobody knew a second basement existed. They found it when they were working on the new elevator. Plan always was to turn the first basement into a nightclub. When they found the second one, my boss figured why not make it a two-floor club? But this level, you'll see, it don't got much headroom. Low ceilings. He wanted to excavate the floor by another three feet so people don't feel like they're in a basement. That's when they dug up the spaceship."

"Spaceship, right. Kayla said it looked like one of those big

TV satellite dishes people had in their backyards in the 80s."

"What would a TV satellite dish be doing buried in the basement of some old hotel?"

"What would a *spaceship* be doing there? Now let's get this show on the road. I don't like sharing the dark with dead people."

"The girls told you about them too?"

"Of course they did! It ain't every day you get to see dead Satan worshipers. And to tell you the truth, *they're* what I'm here to see."

"The Satan worshipers? Jesus Christ. Okay, hold on. Okay, here's the pull cord. I'm about to turn on the generator. You ready?"

"As I'll ever be."

There was a surging sound like a lawnmower engine reaching full speed, followed by bright light that stung Malcolm's dark-adapted eyes.

"That's the altar over there!" Darnell said loudly above the rattling noise of the generator.

"Can we go closer?" the woman replied, equally loud. "I've never seen real skeletons before... Look, that one has a knife."

"My guess is he killed the others, then killed himself. Some sort of u suicide cult. Course, won't know till the coroner gets his hands on 'em."

"What were cultists doing in the basement of this hotel?"

"There used to be all sorts of crazies living in this place, baby. You don't know the half of it. Looks like these guys have been dead since the hotel's heyday. Probably figured this was as good a place as any to practice their black magic shit. See the bones on the altar? Rats. They were sacrificing rats. That's not exactly something you do in public."

"Why hasn't anyone removed their bodies? Or, for that matter, why hasn't this place been secured if there are dead bodies down here—and a spaceship to boot?"

"'Cause my boss didn't want to delay the construction project any longer since it's already so far behind schedule. From what I hear, he's given up the idea of building a club on this level. He's going to seal it up again and pretend he never found no bodies or spaceship."

"Like people aren't going to talk. Look at you, Darnell. You've already taken half your girlfriends on a tour! Now, let's go see this TV dish."

"I told you, baby, it ain't no motherfucking TV dish."

"Well, it ain't no UFO from outer space—" The woman stopped midsentence. Her voice jumped an octave. "Who are *they*?"

"Malcolm?" Darnell said. "What the hell are you doing down there, man? Is that Miss Hathcock with you? You two aren't allowed here, goddammit! You gotta... Malcolm...? Hey, bro—you okay, man?"

CHAPTER 62

Losing it

"What the fuck are you on, Malcolm?" Darnell said. He was standing up on the lip of the excavation, looking down, sleeves rolled up to his elbows. "Why's your mouth covered with blood?"

"Let's get out of here, Darnell," the woman said, her expression frightened. She was in her mid thirties, wearing bright lipstick and large gold hoop earrings, her long espresso-brown hair woven in crochet braids. "Look at his *eyes*."

"Miss Hathcock?" Darnell said. "Can you hear me? Shit, I gotta get her, baby, then we'll leave."

"I don't think that's a good idea—"

"I can't leave her!" Darnell glared at Malcolm. "You stay back, you hear, Malcolm? I'm just going to lift Miss Hathcock out of there."

Malcolm didn't reply. He felt apart from what was going on, as though he were a third-party spectator, an audience member watching actors perform a dramatic scene on stage.

Darnell climbed down into the excavation. The dug-out cavity in the ground was about the size of a large swimming pool. In the center of it protruded what did indeed appear to be an old TV satellite dish, maybe a dozen feet in diameter. Although not fully excavated, it was clear the dish was attached to some sort of spindly limbed platform, as well as a boom that featured a collection of sophisticated scientific instruments covered in thermal blanketing.

Darnell cast Malcolm a wary glance, then crouched before

Jolene, saying something to her, trying to wake her.

"He's gonna find our dope, mate."

Malcolm realized Sid Vicious stood to his right, shirtless, his pallid skin stretched taut over his thin frame. His white bass guitar hung from his shoulder, the strap emblazoned with SID.

"Why'd you hide it on that girl, dipshit?" Dee Dee Ramone said, standing to Malcolm's left. He wore a tight Lynyrd Skynyrd wifebeater and also had his beat-up bass guitar with him.

"Because I didn't want you copping any when I wasn't looking, you mangy thief. Besides, she looked like an honest sort."

"You gotta stop that fucker before he leaves with the dope, Malcolm."

"Me?" Malcolm said. "Why me?"

"That's the deal. You wanna get high with us, you gotta protect the dope."

"How am I supposed to stop him? That's Darnell. He's a big guy."

"Here," Sid said, passing him his bass guitar. "Give him a good whack with this. Don't worry about getting blood on it. That's why it's white. Blood shows up great in photos."

"Hurry up, for fuck's sake," Dee Dee said. "He's about to leave with the girl—and our dope."

Malcolm got to his feet and started toward Darnell, who was in the process of lifting Jolene into his arms. The woman standing on the edge of the cavity cried out.

Darnell twisted around just in time for the body of the guitar Malcolm was swinging to strike him in the face. Darnell dropped Jolene and staggered sideways, bumping into the spacecraft and sinking to his side. His out-of-place nose gushed blood. His eyes were wide open and exceptionally white. His lips were pulled back in a grimace, and he no longer had a space between his two front teeth because he was now missing both. He seemed to be trying to say something, but Malcolm couldn't hear what because the women with the crochet braids continued to scream hysterically.

He cocked the guitar like a baseball bat and hit another homerun with Darnell's face.

◆ ◆ ◆

He turned toward the woman. She was still screaming, but she was cursing too, calling him all sorts of names.

When he tried climbing out of the excavation, she stomped on his hands with her stacked heels.

Sid and Dee Dee were laughing at him, telling him he was getting bested by a five-foot-nothing girl.

Enraged, he grabbed the woman by her ankles and yanked hard. Shrieking, she dropped to her ample bottom. He tugged her down into the cavity, then fell on top of her, his hands locking around her throat.

CHAPTER 63

At daggers drawn

When Shane reached the bottom of the stairs that led to the Hotel Chelsea's basement, he found it to be pitch black except for incongruous white light emanating from within the elevator shaft. A ladder protruded from it, and he could hear the drone of an out-of-sight machine.

Was Jolene down there? Was that where the hotel doors were being stored? He never knew the hotel had a second basement.

"Jo?" he called. "That you?"

There was no reply.

"Jo?" he said louder in case she hadn't heard him above the machine.

Nothing.

"Dammit," he said, stepping over the chair and lowering himself to the ladder. He descended the rungs to the earthen ground below. Stepping out of the elevator shaft, he found himself in an exceptionally large, low-ceilinged, brick-walled room. A portable generator the size of a chest freezer powered several commercial-grade light towers that were all aimed at a giant hole in the middle of the room surrounded by piles of unearthed soil.

Off to his right, hidden in shadows, he made out four people in white clothing sprawled out on the ground like discarded dolls.

"Hello?" he said, his heart suddenly racing as he ventured

toward them.

He slowed when he realized they were not living people but skeletons. Brown, flaky skin stretched across their exposed skulls and hands, though most of their other body tissue had decomposed, leaving little beneath the white clothing but bony contours.

Nearby was a waist-high desk or altar on which stood half-melted pillar candles and the withered remains of what might have been rats or large mice.

Every instinct was telling Shane to return to the ladder, leave, contact the police...but he knew he couldn't do any of this until he checked the pit in the center of the room.

◆ ◆ ◆

He saw the partially exhumed spacecraft first, but what it was and why it was buried beneath the hotel left his mind in the next instant.

"Jo!" he said, leaping into the excavation and kneeling next to her. She was on her side, facing away from him. He rolled her over. "Jo?" he repeated, his stomach sinking. Her eyes were open, and they held the same glassy, faraway look Malcolm's had the night before.

The gobshite gave her drugs!

He looked over at Malcolm, who was sitting up and staring straight at him, his mouth and chin covered in blood. A black woman in hot-pink pants lay facedown on her stomach next to him. Darnell was a short distance away, slumped against the spacecraft, his face a bloody mess. On the ground before him was a blood-stained shovel.

Shane looked back at Malcolm.

Is he on crystal meth? PCP? Both?

Is Jolene?

He pressed his ear to Jolene's lips. She was breathing. Leaving her for the moment, he scuttled over to Darnell, trying not to look at the man's ruined face. He knew the poor fella was dead before he attempted and failed to find a pulse.

Shane picked up the shovel and faced Malcolm. "He's dead. Was it you who killed him?"

"He was going to make off with our dope," Malcolm replied in a flat tone.

"And yer one there?" he said, meaning the facedown woman. "Did you kill her too?"

"Had to stop her."

Shane grimaced, feeling empathy for Darnell and his friend, and dread that he and Jolene could be next if they didn't get out of there quickly.

Without taking his eyes off Malcolm, who was clearly still tripping out, Shane returned to Jolene.

"Don't touch her," Malcolm snarled, getting to his feet.

"Calm down, lad. She needs help."

"Sid wants his dope back first."

"Who's Sid?"

"Sid Vicious."

Shane stared at him. *Tripping out? He's lost his bleeding mind.*

"Give us the dope," Malcolm said, "and you can take her."

"Where is it?"

"In her pocket."

"There's nothing in her pocket."

"You didn't check!"

Shane checked. "Nothing," he said.

The glassy, faraway look in Malcolm's eyes vanished.

They burned with black menace.

CHAPTER 64

No-holds-barred

"Rush the lying thief," Sid Vicious said.

"He's got your guitar," Malcolm said.

"Be a man," Dee Dee Ramone said. "Suck it up."

Feeling as though he didn't have any alternative, Malcolm rushed Shane. The Irishman choked the guitar and swung it. He was going for Malcolm's head, but Malcolm threw up his left arm, deflecting the blow. He was hoping to drive his shoulder into Shane's gut and knock him to the ground, but the slippery fuck spun out of the way, a full one-eighty, and whacked the guitar across Malcolm's backside. This propelled him forward onto his hands and knees. He flipped over just as Shane sank his knees into his chest, one of them right on his solar plexus, winding him. At the same time, Shane drove a fist into Malcolm's jaw. Another fist in the same spot. White sunbursts danced across his vision. Fearing a third blow, he shoved his hands into Shane's face, his thumbs searching for the fucker's eye sockets.

CHAPTER 65

Now's not the best time, Goro...

Shane reared his head back just as Malcolm tried to burrow his thumbs into his eyeballs. He couldn't land another punch through Malcolm's arms, so he performed a hammer strike over them, though his fist bounced ineffectively off Malcolm's forehead.

Malcolm went for his eyes again, and Shane, scrapping any sort of *mano a mano* combat honor, planted his hand on Malcolm's face, pressing it sideways into the dirt. He drove his thumb between Malcolm's left eye socket and eyeball.

Malcolm wailed in pain.

Shane pressed his thumb deeper, the lubricated eyeball tearing up and retreating farther into the eye socket.

"Stop..." Malcolm grunted.

Feeling sick at what he'd done, Shane tugged his thumb free of the wet orifice and pushed backward off Malcolm, who was covering his face with his hands.

Shane decided this was his chance to get Jolene the hell out of there when Malcolm said, "I thought we were friends..."

Shane snorted. "Are you mad?"

Malcolm lowered his hands from his face—only it wasn't his face.

It was Goro Yazawa's.

Pudgy, affable, innocent.

Left eye blackish red and bleeding freely.

Shane shied back in confusion.

It wasn't Goro. It couldn't be. He was dreaming.

Only you're not. You've just been in a fight for your life, your heart's beating like a drum, and you've never been more awake than you are right now. Don't give me any of that 'you're dreaming' shite.

But how could he be seeing Goro?

Goro was dead.

"I know what you think," his old friend told him, reading his mind. "You think this not real. You think you dream. But you don't. I'm here. I'm real. And you tried poking out my eye! I can't see from it. I probably never see from it again. Friends don't do that to friends."

Shane glanced at Jolene. She was still herself...whatever that meant. He wasn't thinking clearly, he realized. The world seemed suddenly upside-down, his thoughts muddled, pulsing, somehow...not his.

Goro was laughing at him, though no sound came from his mouth. All Shane could hear was the clanking drone of the generator and the whumping of his pulse inside his head.

Leave. Now. Hurry up.

Sweat stinging his eyes, he scooped Jolene's limp body into his arms, stumbled to the edge of the excavation, and heaved her up onto the higher ground. He was searching for hand- and footholds to mount it himself when ringing pain exploded across the back of his skull. His legs noodled beneath him and he crashed onto his back.

The last thing he saw before blacking out was Malcolm towering above him, the blood-stained shovel clutched in his hands.

EPILOGUE

The Pentagon, Washington, DC

Sydney Hayden, the US Under Secretary of Defense for Intelligence, stood next to his desk in his office on the fifth floor of the Pentagon's C Ring. He was holding a framed photograph of his five-year-old granddaughter, looking at it without seeing it.

Hayden was the architect of a compartmentalized government initiative called the Advanced Aerospace Threat Identification Program (AATIP), a multi-agency effort to collect and evaluate information about unidentified aerial phenomena. Since the program launched in 2007, it had researched everything from sightings of unknown objects that moved at high velocities with no discernible signs of propulsion, to those that hovered with no visible means of lift, to unusual aerial systems interfering with American military aircraft. Yet any hard proof that these UAPs existed had proved frustratingly elusive. Which was why last year, in 2012, the Department of Defense cut off funding to the program.

Believing that the initiative was too important to the security of the nation to abandon, Hayden had continued working with select officials from other intelligence agencies for much of the last year. Yet with no money and internal opposition from some higher ups at the Pentagon, any real progress had all but stalled, prompting him to consider handing in his resignation to the Secretary of Defense in protest.

Thank God I didn't, Hayden thought now, as the Skype call he'd been eagerly awaiting came through on his computer.

He sat down behind his cluttered desk and joined the video conference. The faces of Dr. Julie Wong and Michael Polmar appeared on his flat-screen computer monitor. Dr. Wong was a veteran astrophysicist at M.I.T.; Polmar a former NASA space shuttle engineer and the author of over a dozen nonfiction books on spaceflight. While managing the AATIP over the last five years, Hayden had relied on them often, developing strong friendships in the process.

Hayden tilted the photograph he was still holding so they could see his granddaughter. "My daughter's daughter, Lisa," he said. "She wants to be an astronaut one day."

"She's adorable, Sydney," said Dr. Wong, her jet-black hair tied into a ponytail that cascaded over the front of her white sweater.

"In thirty years, most of us *will* be astronauts," said Polmar, an affable Texan with a craggy outdoorsman's face and gray in his sideburns.

"I imagine you might be right, Mike," Hayden said, setting aside the photo. He cleared his throat. "Thank you both for getting back to me earlier today and agreeing to this call. I'm aware of the highly classified nature of what you and others have been tasked with investigating at the Hotel Chelsea. I sat in on a briefing with Secretary Bowen this morning regarding the spacecraft. But since then…well, I've been more or less in the dark. Everybody's been extremely hush-hush around here. Nobody who should know something knows anything."

"You've always kept me in the loop, Sydney, classified information or not," Polmar said. "So I'm happy to return the favor. I just don't want to be outed as a 'source,' you hear?"

"Your confidentiality is assured," Hayden promised. "Yours too, Julie. You have my word. Now—where to begin? Do we know which Voyager it is?"

"Neither," Polmar said.

"*Neither?* What are you talking about, Mike?"

"Three Voyager spacecrafts were built for the 1977 missions," he explained. "A flight-test model called VGR77-1,

and two flight-ready models called VGR77-2 and VGR77-3."
He paused. "When the craft beneath the hotel was fully exca-
vated earlier this afternoon, it was identified as VGR77-4—
Voyager 3."

Hayden blinked. "Voyager 3? The United States never created a Voyager 3."

"I'm not aware of the details of your briefing, Sydney, but
the general consensus that has evolved over the course of the
day is that we're dealing with some form of interstellar time
travel."

"This much was assumed. How else could a probe the
United States launched into deep space end up buried beneath
a hotel that's stood for nearly a century before the probe was
ever built? But Voyager 3... Can someone help me out here?"

"According to the laws of quantum mechanics, Sydney," Dr.
Wong said, "a single atom can exist in two different places
at once. But scientists believe there is a limiting size beyond
which this quantum behavior is lost. In other words, larger
objects play by different rules. A single soccer ball cannot
score two goals at once. Similarly, if you or I were whisked
back in time, we could not exist simultaneously in both the
present and the past. It's either one timeline or the other. And
if you or I ceased to be in the present timeline, due to the temporal paradoxes of time travel itself, all evidence that either
of us had ever existed there would dissapear too. This, we believe, is what happened to Voyager 3."

"Erased from our timeline..." Hayden said thoughtfully.
"Yet this doesn't change anything, does it?" he added.
"Whether it's Voyager 1, 2, or 10 buried beneath that hotel, it's
still *our* spacecraft...and it's still our understanding that an
advanced extraterrestrial civilization discovered it and sent
it back to us? Am I correct?"

"That reasoning hasn't changed, correct."

Hayden ran a hand through his hair while exhaling a deep
breath. "Do either of you have any idea as to how far into the
future this civilization may be?"

"I'm not sure we'll ever know for certain, Sydney," Polmar said. "What I can tell you, however, is that the closest star to our solar system that might support a habitable exoplanet is thirteen lightyears away. To put that into perspective, if the Milky Way galaxy were the size of the United States, thirteen lightyears would be the equivalent of taking a stroll across New York City's Central Park. Voyager 1 is traveling at eleven miles per second. If we assume that was Voyager 3's velocity for the duration of its journey, it would have taken the probe hundreds of thousands of years to reach that star."

"But remember also, Sydney," Dr. Wong said, "thirteen lightyears is likely the *closest* scenario in which Voyager 3 could have encountered intelligent life. Space is a vast and empty place. Voyager 3 might have traveled hundreds of lightyears, thousands even, before it was intercepted. Which means its journey could have taken millions of years."

"So to answer your question," Polmar said, "the advanced alien civilization could be millions of years into the future. Which explains why they sent the Voyager 3 back in time. Because while Earth might still be here millions of years from now, it's likely humankind won't be. We will either have gone extinct or dispersed into other parts of the galaxy. Any alien civilization intelligent enough to have the technology to manipulate spacetime would certainly know this as well. So sending the spacecraft to Earth millions of years after we first sent it into space wouldn't make much sense."

"Nobody would be home to receive it..."

"The golden records located on the Voyager spacecrafts," Dr. Wong said, "were information-laden time capsules, containing songs, images, and sounds of Earth. Most importantly, a diagram emblazoned on the covers of the records displayed a cosmic map identifying the location of Earth in the galaxy. How familiar are you with pulsars, Sydney?"

"Give it to me in layman's terms."

"Simply put, to locate where the Sun, and thus Earth, is in the galaxy, you need a frame of reference. When scientists were considering how to represent this criterion, they ruled out depicting what our night sky looks like because stars move relative to one another, which would drastically alter how the sky looks even over timescales as short as thousands of years. They also ruled out mapping the brightest stars, located at vast distances from our solar system, because these could die in supernovas or collapse into black holes. In the end they went with pulsars. Basically, pulsars are rapidly spinning, ultra-dense leftovers of exploded stars. They beam radio waves in narrow cones, some of which periodically sweep across Earth like lighthouse beacons. Like all stars, pulsars change positions in the night sky as they orbit the Milky Way, but because their pulse frequencies remain stable for billions of years, they can be timed and measured to act as a sort of celestial Global Positioning System, identifying any object's position in space."

"The map on the golden records," Polmar said, "used fourteen pulsars to pinpoint the location of our solar system. And by measuring the pulse frequencies over time, any intelligent lifeform that discovered the map would not only be able to reconstruct where Voyager 3 was launched from, but *when* it was launched as well."

"So let's say for argument's sake," Hayden said, "this extraterrestrial civilization is a million years ahead of us, a million years in the future. They find Voyager 3 and decide to send it back to us. They decipher the map on the record, so they know where and when to send the spacecraft. Here's my question—why not send it back to us in September 1977, right after we launched it? Why send it back to us when humans were still living in caves?"

"Let me give you an analogy, Sydney," Polmar said, "and that's all I can offer, an analogy. Say this advanced civilization is thirteen lightyears away, getting the spacecraft back to us right after we sent it might have been like throwing a strike over home plate from the pitcher's mound. In other words, rather doable. But if you're a hundred lightyears away, or a thousand, it could be more akin to throwing a strike from second base, or from the outfield. Your accuracy is going to be a little off. The fact they landed Voyager 3 within a thousand miles from where it originally launched, and within a few thousand years from when it originally launched—well, to me, that's a pretty amazing feat, all things considered."

Hayden nodded and said, "I guess what I'm wondering is this. If the alien species went to all this trouble to send the probe back to us, I assume they might have wanted to send a message along with it? Have we found any evidence of this?"

"We haven't, unfortunately," Dr. Wong said. "However, the spacecraft is producing a high-frequency electromagnetic field that seems to interact with human brainwaves in very unusual ways."

"This wasn't in the briefing," Hayden said, concerned. "What do you mean by 'unusual'?"

"Some of my colleagues who were near the spacecraft today have experienced different degrees of sensory hallucinations. Could these be an attempt at communication? Will they lead us to some sort of hidden message? We simply don't know at this juncture."

"I was informed the civilians discovered next to the probe had likely been under the influence of powerful narcotics. The three who were alive, at any rate. They were reported to be completely debilitated. Could their conditions...?"

"Have a direct correlation to the spacecraft?" Dr. Wong nodded. "From what I've witnessed today, yes, I have little doubt about that. Of course, we won't know exactly what that correlation may be until they're thoroughly examined. And even then..."

◆ ◆ ◆

Some twenty minutes later Sydney Hayden ended the Skype call. Despite it being eight o'clock in the evening, he didn't leave his office for another hour as he contemplated the deeper, paradigm-altering implications of what he'd learned.

When he finally grabbed his jacket, locked up, and started down the concentric ring of corridors that spanned the largest office building in the world, he was grinning with boyish, wonderous delight.

Whoever would have imagined that the smoking gun to finally corroborate the existence of extraterrestrial or extradimensional life would come not from the skies but from beneath the ground?

Holiday Inn, Manhattan, New York

Quinn had been a nervous wreck the last forty-eight hours, from the moment the NYFD announced there was a "gas leak" in the basement of the Hotel Chelsea and evacuated everyone from their residences. The American Red Cross had put them up in the Holiday Inn on 6th Avenue, where they'd remained ever since.

Quinn, of course, knew the gas leak story was fiction.

Whatever was emitting the high-frequency electromagnetic field that had eluded her all these long years had finally been discovered by someone other than the developer's lackeys.

Who could this be?

That was a relatively easy question to answer given the timing of Malcolm's departure to the hotel's basement in search of Jolene, and the evacuation of the building the very next day.

Quinn, however, hadn't been able to contact either Malcolm or Jolene since. She'd spent hours on West 23rd Street, in front of the Hotel Chelsea, behind the police tape and pylons, badgering the police on the street. They repeated the gas leak lie and told her to go away. The people she shouted at who entered or left the hotel—government or military officials, she suspected, despite their unassuming appearances and civilian clothing—ignored her completely.

Last night, unable to sleep, Quinn had walked the three

blocks to the Hotel Chelsea sometime after midnight, only to find West 23rd Street between Seventh and Eighth Avenues cordoned off behind sawhorses. The Hotel Chelsea's iconic awning, the front doors, and the brickwork surrounding them had all been removed, the resulting orifice braced with metal support beams. Parked out front under the secrecy of darkness was an eighteen-wheel tractor-trailer with something the size of a large van strapped down on the flatbed, covered by a tarp. Surrounding this were a half dozen black government vehicles.

A soldier in military fatigues and armed with an assault rifle had appeared seemingly from nowhere and told her to move on, which she did. She'd been shaken. She'd finally glimpsed what had been hidden in the Hotel Chelsea basement, and despite not seeing any specifics, the size of it alone was beyond anything she'd imagined.

Now, the following morning, she was boiling water in the hotel room's plastic electric kettle to make tea when there was a knock at her door.

She froze, fearful of who it might be. She peered through the peephole and found two men in gray suits standing in the hallway, both freshly shaven with short, neat haircuts.

She opened the door. "Yes?"

"Mrs. Sherman?" the one on the left said. He had brown eyes and a dimple in his chin.

"Zat was my husband's surname, though I never took it. Can I help you?"

"I'm Agent Andrew Wray. This is Agent Christopher Gischler. We're with the CIA."

"The CIA?" Quinn said, wondering whether they'd been monitoring her visits to the Hotel Chelsea. Did they know of the one in the middle of the night? Did they know she saw what had been removed from the basement? Were they going to haul her off to wherever they were likely holding Malcolm and Jolene? "Is this about the gas leak at the Hotel Chelsea?" she asked innocently before adopting an indignant air. "It really has been an inconvenience, this whole fiasco. Are you here to tell me we're allowed to return to our homes?"

"Unfortunately not," Agent Gischler said. He had white hair, tawny skin, and hawkish eyes. "We'd like to ask you about your husband's disappearance in March 1993, if we could?"

Quinn frowned. "How do you know about my husband?"

"We've read the missing person report you filed. The court issued an order presuming him dead in 2000?"

"Yes, at my request. That was after many years of... Are you here to tell me what happened to him?"

"His body was recently discovered in the basement of the Hotel Chelsea."

Quinn nearly fainted. She gripped the doorframe until the hot flash subsided.

"Ma'am?" Agent Wray said. "Are you okay?"

"What are you talking about?" she asked angrily. "I've been to the basement of the Hotel Chelsea. I've searched and searched and..." She shook her head, not knowing what more to say.

"Have you been to the basement recently?" Agent Gischler asked.

Quinn was about to tell him yes, the other day, but something in his eyes changed her mind. "No—no, I haven't. Not for years. Where was my husband? Where was his...body?"

"Are you aware the Hotel Chelsea has two basement levels?"

"*Two* levels?" she said, her thoughts spinning. "No, I wasn't aware of that."

"The lowest level was closed, sealed off, a long time ago," Agent Wray said. "The firefighters investigating the gas leak discovered it at the bottom of the elevator shaft."

"The elevator shaft?" she said, staring at them.

"It seems your husband discovered it too, as that's where his body was found, in the lower basement."

"A lower basement..." Quinn said, wondering if she needed

to sit down. "What was Bill...what was my husband doing down there?"

"What did your husband do, ma'am?" Agent Gischler asked her.

"He was an attorney here in New York...that is, before he became a Voodoo priest."

The CIA agents exchanged glances.

"What?" she demanded.

"We're not judging your husband's profession," Agent Wray assured her. "What you've told us...well, the circumstances of his death now make a little more sense. Did you know him to perform religious rituals?

"Yes, he used to perform many..." Quinn said, comprehending what they were getting at. *After Stanley Bard banned you from performing ceremonies in the hotel, Bill, you merely moved them to the basement, the secret basement...*

This made her wonder if there was a connection between her husband's death and the object on the tractor-trailer flatbed.

"How did he die?" she asked carefully.

"We believe it was a suicide," Agent Gischler told her.

"*Suicide?* No, you're mistaken. Bill wouldn't have killed himself... He was...he wouldn't have done that..."

Only Quinn knew these men were not mistaken, they were not making up these horrible details. Performing ceremonies within such proximity to the object had warped Bill's mind, had made him...

"How...?" she asked quietly.

"It appears he used a knife. A machete."

"Oh my... Oh goodness me..."

"Three other bodies were discovered as well. It's not yet clear whether their deaths were suicides as well, or homicides."

"Homicides...?" The fog occluding her thoughts made it almost impossible to think straight. "You're saying Bill... Oh, no. No, this is too much. Bill would never do...*that.*"

"The New York County Medical Examiner's office will make that determination, ma'am. On that note, your husband was identified through his dental records. But it would help to have a next-of-kin confirmation."

"After all these years, you want me to...?" She shook her head, overwhelmed. "I'm sorry, gentlemen, I'm not feeling very well at all. I believe I need to lie down."

"Of course," Agent Gischler said. "Just one more question, if I may? Some of the residents of the Hotel Chelsea have reported feeling a little...off...the last two weeks. Bad dreams. Forgetfulness. Some claimed to have even been, well, seeing things."

"Hallucinations?"

"That's right."

"Whyever would they be hallucinating?"

"We believe the gas leak might have permeated much of the hotel. Residents might have been breathing toxic air without even knowing it. Have you experienced any unusual symptoms recently?"

"Me...? No, I've been fine," she said, straight-faced. "I live up on the roof, you see, in a pyramid, a pyramid built by Sarah Bernhardt... But no, I've experienced nothing odd at all. I'm sure all the fresh air up there would have dispersed any gas long before it reached me." *Stop blathering!* "I guess...I guess I should count myself rather lucky."

Agent Gischler gave her a long, hard stare. "Thank you for your time, ma'am. We're terribly sorry about your husband."

Nodding silently, Quinn closed the door and sank back against it, her entire body trembling.

Fort Hamilton, Brooklyn, New York

In the dream Shane was back in Ireland, at one of his parents' restaurants, seated with his mother and father in a green-leather booth. His mother—an austere woman with a pointed chin, square jaw, and aquiline nose—was fussing over the menu, complaining there was nothing Irish to eat, while his father—small, balding, with a rust-colored handlebar mustache and goatee that exuded 19th century upper-class sophistication with a hint of cowboy—was busy bringing up photographs of beautiful young women on his mobile phone. He showed each woman to Shane, extolling their good looks and personalities, eager to set him up so that he could get married, settle down, and take over the family business. Shane wasn't interested, explaining he had already met someone. She was waiting for him in the basement of the hotel in New York City. In fact, he shouldn't be in Ireland; he should be back in the US right now looking for her. He should—

The door at the front of the restaurant burst open. Blinding white light flooded through it...and in that light, Shane thought he could see Jolene, her arm outstretched, reaching for him. He wanted to go to her, he wanted to call to her, but he could neither move nor speak, and he was forced to watch in silent horror as she floated farther and farther away until she disappeared completely.

◆ ◆ ◆

Shane opened his eyes to find the blinding white light was real. He was in a brightly lit hospital room. To his confusion, he was hooked up to a life-support machine, with all sorts of tubes (including one stuffed down his windpipe) and colorful wires (most attached to his bare torso) going from it to him. He had no idea where he was or what had happened. His vision wouldn't focus, and his hearing was dampened, as though he were wearing a pair of earmuffs.

Before long, a man in a yellow hazmat suit appeared. He took Shane's hand in his and told him to squeeze. Shane squeezed. He told Shane to follow his finger as he moved it back and forth. Shane followed it with his eyes.

Despite all the questions on his mind, sleep seemed much preferable, and he slipped back into it.

◆ ◆ ◆

He woke later to a powerful, crawling hunger. He was able to push himself into a semi-sitting position without disturbing the electrode pads stuck to his chest, the intravenous drip in his arm, or the urinary catheter snaking beneath the white sheet that covered him from the waist down. The breathing tube, thankfully, had been removed.

Another person in a yellow hazmat suit appeared.

"Brought you something."

Although Shane couldn't see much behind the black face mask and respirator, he recognized the voice. It was the same man who'd visited him before.

He set a tray on Shane's lap that contained an open can of Coke with a straw and a small bag of pretzels. Shane finished both as quickly as he could despite his drugged clumsiness.

"How are you feeling, Shane?" the man asked.

"Where...am I?" he asked in a dry, scratchy voice.

"You're in a hospital."

"Why...? Why are you wearin' that?"

"It's just a precaution."

"Precaution...?" He frowned, not understanding.

"You've had a traumatic brain injury."

"What happened...?"

"I was hoping you could tell me that?"

Shane tried thinking back. "I—I don't remember anythin'."

"You don't remember being in an altercation?"

Did he? Vaguely. He remembered looking for Jolene and... No, before that. Going to the bathroom in the middle of the night. Finding Malcolm in there.

He raised a hand to his head. It was wrapped in bandages, but he didn't feel any pain.

"He pushed me..."

"Who pushed you?"

"Malcolm..."

"Malcolm Clock?"

Shane nodded. "Pushed my head against the sink. Dragged me to a room..." He frowned when he recalled waking up in Room 100. Had that been a dream? Because if he was just waking up now, in this hospital...?

"What room?"

"In the hotel. Where I live. The room across from mine."

"When was that?"

He didn't know. "Yesterday...?"

"You've been in a coma for the last week as a result of sepsis. You had a temperature of 105—gave us quite the scare."

"A week...?"

"Do you remember any other altercations?"

He shook his head.

"Malcolm Clock struck you across the back of your head with a shovel. The impact fractured your skull and likely caused the blood infection. The weekend front desk clerk at the Hotel Chelsea found you."

Shane touched his bandaged head again, this time the back of it. No pain there either.

How much morphine were they feeding him?

"Do you remember going to the basement of the hotel, Shane?"

The basement...? He remembered going to Jolene's room, looking for Malcolm. Neither of them had been there. Had that all been a dream too...?

Damn, he was high. Nothing was making sense.

"Why would I go to the basement?"

"I'd like you to tell me that."

"I can't remember."

"Were you drawn there?"

"Drawn there?"

"Compelled to go there? Perhaps in your sleep?"

Shane recalled his sleepwalking episodes, waking on Goro's balcony, boarding up the door to his room, the drinking. This all seemed like a lifetime ago, and he once again found him-

self questioning whether it had really happened or not. "I've...
been sleepwalkin'. I think. Not to the basement. To the eighth
floor..."

"Why the eighth floor?"

"My friend lived there. He killed himself. But I went there.
Because...I could still talk to him."

"You could talk to your deceased friend?"

"It wasn't real. It was in my head..."

"What was your friend's name?"

Shane blinked in surprise. Goro Yazawa—clad all in black,
including his trademark bandanna—stood behind the man in
the hazmat suit. Eyes wide, afraid, he was shaking his head, as
if to warn about saying anything.

Then he was gone.

"Why do you want his name?" Shane asked suspiciously.

"You've had a traumatic brain injury. I'm trying to—"

"Why are you wearin' that suit?"

"I told you. It's just a precaution."

"Precaution against what? Brain injuries aren't...conta-
gious." A moment of clarity cut through the fog of the morphine.

With vague panic, Shane looked around the hospital room
to see where Goro had gotten to—and spotted a CCTV camera
in the ceiling, the round lens pointed directly at him.

Something was not right. Something was definitely not
right.

"Are you a doctor?" he demanded.

"Yes, I'm a doctor, Shane," the man in the hazmat suit said.
"You know what? I think you need to rest. I'll be back to check
on you in a little while." He started to leave.

"Where's Jolene?"

The man stopped mid-step. "Jolene?"

"Jolene. You know her. I know you do." Although Shane
wasn't sure how he knew this, he was certain it was true—and
certain that it mattered.

"Jolene Hathcock was in the basement of the Hotel Chelsea with you, Shane. Why was she there? Why were you both there? Only you can tell me that."

Shane was shaking his head, frustrated and scared that he couldn't answer these questions, paranoid too because he didn't trust the man in the hazmat suit, didn't trust him one bit.

"Where am I?" he asked.

"You're in a hospital, Shane."

"What hospital?"

"You need to rest. We'll continue this talk later."

"What hospital am I in?"

The man didn't reply.

Shane heard a heavy door open and close.

And then he was alone once more.

Fort Hamilton, Brooklyn, New York

"What are you painting over there?" Jolene asked from the bed she was lying in.

Standing behind a wood easel supporting a large canvas with a paint-riddled palette in one hand and a fan-tipped brush in the other, Edie Sedgwick said, "A picture of home."

"Can I see it?"

"When it's done."

"You've been painting that for an awfully long time." Jolene looked around the hospital room. "How long have we been here anyway?"

"More than a week, I'd say."

"I wonder why no one's come by to see us yet. We're in a hospital, ain't we? Where are all the nurses and doctors?"

"They've been by."

"I ain't seen them."

"Because you're not really awake."

Jolene didn't know what her friend meant by this, but it was something she didn't want to talk about.

"I wonder if Vali Myers will be having another party soon. I

343

really enjoyed that last one."

"They're all the same after a while. Same people, same conversations."

"You know, I can't even remember how I got there."

"I invited you, of course," Edie said. "I called your name. Someone had left the elevator doors propped open, and it was just a quick climb down the ladder." She dabbed some more paint on the canvas. "I think I'm almost done."

"Will you show it to me now?"

Edie rolled the easel across the tiled floor toward the bed and swiveled it around. Jolene gasped. She'd never seen anything so beautiful before in her life. The colors were impossible to describe and unlike any on the visible spectrum. In fact, the entire painting was an impossibility beyond description, beyond comprehension.

"That's your home?" she asked in awe.

"We haven't had a home, in the sense that you mean, for a long time now. We've advanced beyond the natural world and the physics that govern it. But yes, for simplicity's sake, it is our 'home.'"

"Who are you, Edie?" Jolene asked. "Who are you really?"

"I'm a messenger," her friend replied, smiling benignly. "I was sent here to say congratulations...and welcome."

❖ ❖ ❖

"Look at the hemodynamic response in her limbic system," said Dr. Raymond Mansfield, a US Army neuroradiologist. Three black-and-white images of Jolene Hathcock's brain —axial, sagittal, and coronal—were displayed on the large monitor in the control room. He indicated the image of the top-down axial plane with his index finger. "Her amygdalae and hippocampi are lit up like a Christmas tree."

Dr. Joy Maxcey, a diagnostic radiologist, glanced through the viewing window at the gowned woman on the motorized bed, her helmeted head positioned inside the bore of the donut-shaped MRI scanner. She remained unmoving. "Must be having one hell of a dream."

"Dreaming is a function of normal sleep, Joy. This woman is comatose. She shouldn't be dreaming at all."

"Could her interaction with the spacecraft be causing the excessive neural activity?"

"More than a week after contact?"

"She was exposed to the electromagnetic radiation for much longer than any of the others. Could the effects be longer lasting than anyone believed possible?"

Dr. Mansfield remained focused on the data from the scan popping up on the monitor. "Given we're dealing with something that's allegedly been to the deepest realms of space and back again, Joy, I think it would be safe to say that anything at this point is possible."

Bellevue Hospital, Manhattan, New York

The common area of the psychiatric ward was chaos as usual. A dozen drugged patients loitered around the open space. Some were crying, some mumbling incomprehensibly, some performing acts of self-abuse such as slapping themselves or pulling their hair. Middle-aged Nolan Kenen, who believed himself to be over one thousand years old, sat in a chair and stared intently at his slippered feet without speaking. Wild-eyed Megan Rodriguez, who claimed to speak a half dozen languages except English, hocked lugie after lugie onto the same spot on the floor in front of her. Kyle Watts, who believed he was sexually abused by Elvis Presley, stood inside the telephone booth, as if waiting for an apology call from the King himself. And every so often frazzle-haired Larry Rainey, still in his red pajamas despite it being well after lunch, would appear from one of the other rooms to shout, "Happy Holidays!" at the top of his lungs.

Malcolm, sitting in a chair off on his own, repeated to himself that he shouldn't be there, that he wasn't like these other people, that he wasn't crazy. Yet it was getting harder and harder to believe the longer he was locked up inside the madhouse.

It was the drugs, he knew. They were fucking up his mind. *Stealing* his mind. He had refused to take them at first, arguing that nobody could force him to take medication without a court order. During this time, he befriended a female patient named Sherice Teehee. Sherice had a long Mohawk and tattoos and used to be a mixed martial artist before becoming addicted to cocaine. After she attempted suicide, her mother checked her into Bellevue against her will, and now she was stuck there, unable to check herself out. Malcolm had little in common with Sherice (save for the fact he had once been an addict), but she was the only other patient in the ward capable of rational discourse, so they ended up hanging out in the afternoons and evenings. Malcolm didn't tell her about the spaceship in the basement of the Hotel Chelsea, or Sid Vicious and Dee Dee Ramone (both of whom he was still seeing on a regular basis), or his nearly three-week quarantine in Fort Hamilton, or the daily interrogations that accompanied this stay. He knew it would only make him sound as crazy as everybody else in the place. So they talked of other stuff, inconsequential things, to pass the time and help block out the maelstrom of madness surrounding them.

The nursing staff hated that they spent so much time together.

Perhaps it was because Malcolm and Sherice were acting like normal human beings and not tormented lunatics. Whatever their reasoning, the staff were constantly breaking them apart, eventually banning them from conversing together in the common areas. Because they were not allowed in one another's rooms, the only place they could socialize were the hallways—standing or leaning against the walls, as they weren't permitted to sit on the floor.

On Malcolm's fourth day in the psychiatric ward, he and Sherice had been doing just this, chatting in the hallway outside his room, when a passing orderly called Sherice, who was Native American, a gas-huffing Injun. Malcolm and Sherice told him off—only for him to return shortly with three staff members who wrestled them to the floor and stuck needles in their arms. Malcolm woke on the cot in his room, too drugged to get up let alone refuse the powerful cocktail of drugs the nurse all but shoved down his throat. And from that point on —how many days, he had no idea—he had been on one long, uninterrupted high that was, yes…slowly stealing his mind.

Malcolm suspected Sherice had been put on the same "treatment," for whenever he saw her now she appeared just as out of it as he felt.

When three-hundred pound Chapelle Musgraves, who often wandered the common areas in various stages of undress, entered the so-called music room and started singing along to the rap music playing on the stereo (it was always rap, all day, every day, because that's what the nursing staff preferred), a beefy, dreadlocked orderly named Tyrone hurried into the room after her and switched the station to one playing jazz.

Sadistic asshole, Malcolm was thinking as he began to nod off contently in the chair.

"Mr. Clock? Wake up. Someone is here to see you."

"Huh?" he said, recognizing the woman speaking to him as Dr. Foster, the ward's attending psychiatrist.

"How are you feeling today?" she asked. "Are you able to stand? There's someone here to see you."

Malcolm followed her down the hallway, moving in a slow shuffle so he didn't fall over. She stopped at the doorway to the dining room. When he entered, a person in a dark blue suit at one of the tables stood and said, "Mac?" To Dr. Foster, he added, "What the hell do you have him on? He can barely stand up!"

"A nurse mixed up his night and day meds this morning. We're terribly sorry about that. I'll be back with the discharge papers shortly."

The man came over to him, and it took Malcolm a moment

to recognize his brother.

"George?"

"Yeah, yeah, it's me, bud. I'm getting you outta here."

◆ ◆ ◆

By the time they were climbing the six flights of stairs in Malcolm's building, Malcolm was feeling a little more clear-headed and surefooted, though George followed directly behind him so he didn't lose his balance and fall backward.

George dug a key from his pocket and unlocked the door to Malcolm's apartment. He stepped inside first and flicked on the light. "Your landlord gave me a spare key," he said. "I've paid your rent for this month, so don't worry about that. Come on, come sit down."

He led Malcolm to the sofa. Malcolm sat, finding it very odd to be back in his apartment. "What time is it?" he asked.

"Time?" George checked his gold wristwatch. "Six thirty. What? You got plans?" He chuckled.

"I missed my meds," Malcolm said, feeling a niggle of panic in his gut.

"Meds? They were tranquilizing you, for God's sake! You don't need that shit."

"I won't be able to sleep without them," he said, the niggle growing.

George sat next to him and cupped a beefy hand over his shoulder. "Do you remember what happened to you, Mac?"

Malcolm didn't say anything.

"There was a gas leak at the Hotel Chelsea. It made some of the air toxic. You and a coupla others suffered hypoxia—not enough oxygen to your organs. You were taken to Fort Hamilton in Brooklyn because the doctors there deal with hypoxia with Air Force pilots."

Malcolm remembered his time at Fort Hamilton perfectly, and the people there had most definitely not been treating him for hypoxia.

"When you got mostly better," George continued, "they sent you to Bellevue Hospital to finish recovering."

Finish recovering, right. They put me in a psychiatric ward to make sure I would never be taken seriously if I started talking about aliens.

Malcolm asked, "Do you have them with you?"

George frowned. "Do I have what with me?"

"My meds."

"Shit, Mac! You have a history with addiction. The last thing you need right now is to get hooked on—"

"I'm not hooked. But I need them tonight. Just tonight. Can you go back to the hospital...?" He was almost pleading, and he hated himself for this.

George scowled. "I'll take you to a doctor tomorrow. He might have something he can prescribe for the time being." He stood decisively. "Just relax for now, take it easy. You're home."

"Where's Bitcoin?" Malcolm asked, trying to fake a normalness he didn't feel. He really needed his fucking meds.

"He's fine. I picked him up last month when I learned what happened to you. You want me to bring him by tomorrow? You can watch him for me again until you're back on your feet. Might be some good company?" He produced a black cell phone from the inside pocket of his jacket and gave it to Malcolm. "My number's in there. You need anything, you call me."

"I need my meds," he snapped.

"I gotta run, Mac. I bought some groceries for you. Make something to eat, then relax, get some rest."

"I was at Fort Hamilton for twenty-one days. You never visited me."

"They didn't let me. I tried, but they didn't let me. Some bullshit about it being a military fort."

"Twenty-one days seems like overkill to treat hypoxia."

"They told me..." He seemed to weigh his words. "They told me you suffered some minor...very minor...brain damage. Nothing to get worried about. They said it was causing you some cognitive difficulties..."

"Hallucinations?"

"They mentioned hallucinations. You're not still having them, are you?"

"No."

"That's good," George said. "See? You're going to be fine. You don't need any fucking medication. I'm going to file a lawsuit against those assholes at Bellevue on your behalf. Now get some rest. Tomorrow will be here before you know it."

◆ ◆ ◆

A little later Malcolm found the energy to get up and make some food. He hadn't eaten since lunch and realized he had a sudden craving for spaghetti Bolognese and was glad to find that George had purchased all the necessary ingredients. While the pasta boiled, he fried some onions in a skillet, then added the ground beef. When the meat had cooked through, he emptied a jar of tomato sauce over it. He was in the process of straining the pasta in a colander when he sensed somebody was behind him. He set the colander in the sink and turned around.

The apartment was empty. He looked toward the bathroom.

"Sid?" he said quietly. "Dee Dee? You guys in there?"

Neither answered him.

"You can come out."

They didn't appear.

He was about to turn back to the pasta when a knock at the door made him start.

"Mac? That you?" The voice was female. "I can smell your cooking!"

"Who are you?"

"*Who am I?* Holy shit, Mac. Have you forgotten what I sound like? It's Nikki!"

He went to the door, hesitated, then pulled it open.

Holding a large brown paper bag in her arms, filled presumably with groceries, Nikki was dressed like a colorblind toddler in orange jeans, a yellow top, and an asparagus-colored denim jacket. She looked just as Malcolm remembered, except her tangles of crimped blonde hair had been lopped off at the shoulders. She beamed a smile at him. "Hey, Mac! Long time."

"You cut your hair."

"You like? I was getting tired of dealing with it. What are you cooking?"

"Spaghetti."

"Got enough for two? You owe me dinner. Remember that great one I made you? And look what I just picked up from the store." She tugged a bottle of red wine from the paper bag. She walked past him to the kitchen. "Oh, yeah, you have plenty. Which cupboard are the glasses in again?"

Malcolm set two on the counter.

Nikki filled them with wine and hoisted hers. "Cheers!"

He raised his as well.

"You feeling okay, Mac? You seem a bit slow."

"I'm okay."

"Got anything to nibble on?" She opened the fridge. "Holy smokes! What is *this*? I thought you didn't grocery shop. How about…some cheese?" She withdrew a small wheel of cheddar covered in a black rind. "Grab a cutting board and a knife, and we're all set."

◆ ◆ ◆

Seated cross-legged on the red leather sofa, Nikki bit into her slice of cheese. "This is fun, Mac. Sorta like old times. Oh, hey, wanna see what just arrived for me?" She pulled a bubble-padded envelope from her black handbag. "Guess what it is."

"I don't know."

"Here." She tossed the envelope to him. It struck him in the chest and fell to his lap. "Nice reflexes. Go ahead, open it."

Setting aside his glass of wine, he opened the package and

withdrew a pair of skimpy underwear.

"They're from that club I'm in. That's my November pair. What do you think?"

"They seem pretty small."

"They fit—do you want to see them on me?" She shook her head. "Sorry, Mac. I'm kidding. No more weird Nikki, I promise. So where've you been hiding out? I haven't seen you around here for more than a month. Have you been with that Southern bi—girl?"

Malcolm frowned. He'd been wondering a lot about Jolene lately, where she was now and how she was doing. The people at Fort Hamilton had told him she was fine and in quarantine like him. They said they would release her after three weeks. Had they sent her to a psychiatric ward too? Was she locked up in one now, or had her sister gotten her out already? Was she back at the Hotel Chelsea? *With the spaceship still in the basement?* No, the government would have likely taken that away. There was probably nothing in the basement but a big hole—

"Hey, hello?" Nikki said, waving her hand. "You still here, Mac? What have you been smoking? And do you have any more of it?"

Malcolm was surprised—yet happy—to see Sid Vicious sitting next to Nikki on the sofa. He had his motorcycle boots up on the coffee table and his leather-clad arm stretching behind Nikki's head.

"Tell her, mate," Sid said. "Spill the beans. You're gonna have to tell someone sooner or later, so why not her? She's got a few screws loose, so she might just believe you."

"Mac...?" Nikki said.

"Did you hear about the gas leak at the Hotel Chelsea?" he asked her.

"One or two people died, didn't they? Did you mention that in the article you were writing? Speaking of which, why haven't I received a copy?"

"There was no gas leak," Malcolm said. "It was a cover-up."

"Cover-up? What are you talking about?"

"There's something buried in the basement of the hotel. Or at least there used to be. They've probably taken it away by now."

"They? Who's they?"

"The military, the CIA, I don't know."

"Taken what?"

"A spaceship."

"What!"

"The USA built it and sent it into outer space. An alien civilization found it millions of years from now and sent it back to us through time."

Nikki was staring at Malcolm with huge eyes and an upward curl to her lips. "Seriously, Mac, I want whatever you're on."

"They sent a message with the spaceship. It communicates with whomever gets close to the ship, and it gets stronger the closer you get. It's not in their language. We can't understand that. It communicates using our own language by making us talk to ourselves through visions, hallucinations, those kinds of things. It manipulates the right side of our brain to do this, the creative side, which is why it affects creative people much more than others."

"How does it 'affect' them?"

"The visions and hallucinations are meant to be lowkey and harmless, but because they force you to look within yourself, to look deep within yourself, they can bring out your dark side."

"Your dark side? Like in *Star Wars*?"

"Like in Carl Jung, though he called it the 'shadow.' Everybody has a shadow side. It contains all your negative personality aspects that you can't or won't acknowledge. Some people are aquainted with their shadow side. Some, unfortunately, are not, and their imaginations, when provoked, manifest the worst parts of themselves."

"Have the aliens communicated with you. Mac?"

"Yes."

"Have you faced your shadow side?"

"Yes."

"How did that turn out for you?"

"Not good."

Sid Vicious grinned as he listened on.

Dee Dee Ramone appeared behind Sid and Nikki and said, "You're wasting your time, Malcolm. She's never gonna believe you. Nobody's ever gonna believe you."

"Mac?" Nikki snapped her fingers. "Yoo-hoo, I'm over here. Mac?"

Malcolm looked at her.

"This is all fucking crazy," she said. "Lunatic-asylum fucking crazy. But I'm going to bite. What did this alien civilization from the future, in its message, want to say to us?"

"Hello."

"Hello? That's it? They went to all the trouble of sending our spaceship back to us through space and time just so they could say hello?"

"I don't think we matter very much to them. Sending the spaceship back was a courtesy, that's all."

"Can we wrap this up, guys?" Dee Dee said. "I'd much rather be getting high than talking to this blonde ditz."

"I don't got my Chinese rocks with me, mate," Sid said. "And Malcolm doesn't have his meds. So how the fuck are we gonna get high?"

Nikki was refilling her glass of wine from the bottle on the coffee table. "You're blowing my mind, Mac," she said, grinning. "And you're doing it with a straight face. If you don't tell me what you're on, I'm going to have to go get some of my stuff so I can join the party. But first, I have to pee. Can I use your bathroom?"

"Sure," Malcolm said.

Nikki took a long gulp of wine, got up, and went to the bathroom, humming an upbeat song. She closed the door behind her.

"That's one fucked-up chick," Dee Dee said, coming around the sofa to sit next to Sid. "And I've seen my fair share of fucked-up chicks."

"I wonder what she meant by 'my stuff,'" Sid said, a calculating look in his eyes. "She seems like an LSD bird to me."

"Forget it," Malcolm said. "I'm not doing LSD with her. Dee Dee's right. She's nuts."

"What do you wanna do instead? Sit around here scratching our balls?"

"I'm with Malcolm, Sid," Dee Dee said. "No way I'm popping acid with a fucking murderer. That's right. She's probably a murderer. Think about it. She can't get her story straight about where she grew up. Why's that? I'm betting it's because she whacked her parents when she was younger and has made up alternative childhoods. That's probably why she has all their furniture in her place too. Got it in the inheritance."

"You might be onto something, Dee Dee," Sid said. "She did try to drug Malcolm, after all. So why don't we just whack *her*? Will serve the bitch right. Plus, we'll have all her LSD to ourselves."

"You want me to kill her?" Malcolm said.

"You've got a perfectly fine weapon right there," Sid said, pointing to the knife on the cutting board. "All you gotta do is shove it in her chest. Piece of cake. If she's anything like Nancy, she won't even scream. Just give you a strange look before dying and leaving a lot of blood on the bathroom floor."

"And the best thing is," Dee Dee said, "they'll likely send you back to Bellevue, where we'll have all the meds we want. No more hustling, no more bullshit."

Malcolm considered this in silence until he heard the toilet flush.

"Better hurry up and decide, mate," Sid said.

"Don't pussy out," Dee Dee said.

Malcolm picked up the knife and went to the bathroom.

AFTERWORD

Thank you for taking the time to read the book! If you enjoyed it, a brief review would be hugely appreciated. You can click straight to the review page here:

Hotel Chelsea - Amazon Review Page

Best,

Jeremy

BOOKS IN THIS SERIES

World's Scariest Places

Suicide Forest

Just outside of Tokyo lies Aokigahara, a vast forest and one of the most beautiful wilderness areas in Japan...and also the most infamous spot to commit suicide in the world. Legend has it that the spirits of those many suicides are still roaming, haunting deep in the ancient woods.

When bad weather prevents a group of friends from climbing neighboring Mt. Fuji, they decide to spend the night camping in Aokigahara. But they get more than they bargained for when one of them is found hanged in the morning—and they realize there might be some truth to the legends after all.

The Catacombs

Paris, France, is known as the City of Lights, a metropolis renowned for romance and beauty. Beneath the bustling streets and cafés, however, exists The Catacombs, a labyrinth of crumbling tunnels filled with six million dead.

When a video camera containing mysterious footage is discovered deep within their depths, a group of friends venture into the tunnels to investigate. But what starts out as a light-hearted adventure takes a turn for the worse when they reach their destination—and stumble upon the evil lurking there.

Helltown

Since the 1980s there have been numerous reports of occult activity and other possibly supernatural phenomenon within certain villages and townships of Summit County, Ohio—an area collectively known as Helltown.

When a group of out-out-town friends investigating the legends are driven off the road by a mysterious hearse, their night of cheap thrills turns to chills as they begin to die one by one.

Island Of The Dolls

Deep within an ancient Aztec canal system on the outskirts of Mexico City lies Isla de las Munecas...a reportedly haunted island infested with thousands of decrepit dolls.

While there to film a television documentary, several friends discover a brutal murder. Soon fear and paranoia turn them against one another—even as the unknown killer stalks them throughout the longest night of their lives.

Mountain Of The Dead

The greatest unsolved mystery of the 20th century—until now.

Fact: During the night of February 1, 1959, in the remote reaches of Siberia, nine Russian hikers slash open their tent from the inside and flee into a blizzard in subpolar temperatures.

Fact: By morning all are dead, several having suffered gruesome, violent deaths. What happened to them has baffled investigators and researchers to this day.

It has become known as the Dyatlov Pass Incident.

Now, an American true-crime writer seeking answers to the enduring mystery sets out to retrace the hikers' steps on their fateful expedition—though nothing can prepare him for what he is about to discover...

ABOUT THE AUTHOR

Jeremy Bates

USA TODAY and #1 AMAZON bestselling author Jeremy Bates has published more than twenty novels and novellas, which have been translated into several languages, optioned for film and TV, and downloaded more than one million times. Midwest Book Review compares his work to "Stephen King, Joe Lansdale, and other masters of the art." He has won both an Australian Shadows Award and a Canadian Arthur Ellis Award. He was also a finalist in the Goodreads Choice Awards, the only major book awards decided by readers. The novels in the "World's Scariest Places" series are set in real locations and include Suicide Forest in Japan, The Catacombs in Paris, Helltown in Ohio, Island of the Dolls in Mexico, and Mountain of the Dead in Russia. The novels in the "World's Scariest Legends" series are based on real legends and include Mosquito Man and The Sleep Experiment. You can check out any of these places or legends on the web. Also, visit JEREMYBATESBOOKS.COM to receive Black Canyon, WINNER of The Lou Allin Memorial Award.

9 781988 091495